/ 25

WRITTEN ON THE WIND

BY ROBERT WILDER

WRITTEN ON THE WIND

A Novel by

ROBERT WILDER

G. P. PUTNAM'S SONS

NEW YORK

Third Impression

MANUFACTURED IN THE UNITED STATES OF AMERICA

To
George Hirliman
Compadre!

This book is fiction. No character in it is drawn from or relates to any living person.

WRITTEN ON THE WIND

What a man tells a woman and a woman tells a man should be written on the wind.

I

A LATTICED MOON, caught in the slender line of trees straggling across the ridge, tossed a wavering stencil on the wall; a pattern of curiously humped shapes that danced nervously when the wind tugged at the branches, darting back and forth in a torment of nervous indecision. With arms twisted uncomfortably beneath his head, Reese stared at the fluttering design until his eyes ached. Then he closed them again and listened.

The house was talking to itself in the night. It spoke incoherently, mumbling fitfully as do the very old. It groaned and muttered in the complaining accents of parting joints and ancient beams. Sometimes it squealed with a high note of protest as though its weathered bones were being twisted in dry sockets. Now and then the whole structure seemed to shudder as the foundation tried to settle deeper into the Carolina soil; crouching away from a world in which it had become alien.

A soft, moist wind drifted through the windows near the bed; plucking at starched white curtains and bringing with it the sweet odor of grass, still warm from the long day's sun, and the sharp scent of wet piney woods and bleached earth. Feeling the dampness on his face, Reese almost smiled. It was odd, he thought, how heavily memory leaned upon such things. There could be a sudden turn in a road, the fluting notes of a familiar whistle, or this fleeting, earthy perfume; small in themselves but bearing a procreative magic, and the years turned back or were for an instant reborn. Carried on the night were strangely unrelated moments: the hot smell of fatwood burning at dusk; the fast, hard beat of rising birds; the ecstatic yelp of an eager puppy at sunrise; the enveloping loneliness of a solitary deer stand; the way a woman had once smiled or laughed; the taste of water in a tin dipper. They had no connection and yet they came together, solitary wanderers at a chance meeting on the highroad. They came together and peopled the room, each waiting to be recognized. Reese opened his eyes again and the shades scrambled into the tangled reflection on the wall and were gone. Still, the house whispered and murmured, lamenting tiredly against the days and what they had brought.

It was an uncompromisingly ugly house, standing astride the only elevation for miles around Winton. From the base of the slope the countryside flattened away in loose and scraggly disorder, dotted with pine, turkey oak, and scattered clumps of tough, wiry grass. The town lay in an irregular rectangle, one corner cut by the river. Beyond it were small farms, the graying, slatternly houses of Negroes, and barren stretches of flats, sterile and unyielding.

The house looked down upon Winton or, perhaps, Winton looked up to the house and in acknowledgment of fealty, the townspeople, by long custom, rarely referred to the Whitfields, who lived there, by name. Instead, the house and its family were spoken of as "The Hill." No one thought this odd and no one misunderstood. "The Hill" was going to do this or that. "The Hill" is away for the summer. "The Hill's" kids were in trouble again; drunk in Raleigh, arrested for speeding, giving another party, or off to college.

The Hill was a rambling monstrosity; homely bastard of an era, with broad, rounded porches, bay windows, intricate, lacy scrollwork fanning out from the veranda's thin square pillars to join the second story. Its color was the brown of cured tobacco, the tobacco that had built it and Winton, also. The leaf that had nourished the Whitfields after being predigested in millions of jaws, pipes, and cigarettes. Old Andrew Whitfield hadn't wanted an ugly house, and when The Hill was finished he hadn't found it so.

"I want the biggest, by God house in North Carolina," he told the architect.

As the excavations and foundations spread and the walls rose to shape the rooms and long, narrow halls, Andrew had walked restlessly over the rise. With hands clasped behind his back, shoulders bent slightly under the shiny black alpaca coat he liked so well, his sharp eyes grew foxily bright with pleasure as he watched The Hill take form. When the house was finished, the ground graded and planted, Old Andrew had populated his acres with a bewildering assortment of iron and stone animals. Flocks of sheep waited stolidly in the lush grass. Dogs and antlered bucks peeped from the shrubbery. Squirrels, three feet high, rested on their haunches, holding metal acorns in their front paws, staring with melancholy intensity in the direction of Winton.

A couple of hundred feet down the slope from the front porch Andrew had ordered a red granite mausoleum built in the center of the lawn. A huge door of bronze, on which had been worked a wrinkled pattern of tobacco leaves, guarded the entrance, and inside there was room for only one casket. When his wife and visiting relatives protested against the glaringly inappropriate site for a tomb and his selfishness in having it designed for a single interment, Old Andrew had chuckled with a brittle, waspish sound of delight.

"I figure on gettin' in there alone an' sleepin' that way, a habit I might have took up a long time ago. The rest of you can find your own holes. This here is mine an' I'm puttin' it right there so's them that come after me can walk out on the porch an' say, Thank you Andrew. If it wasn't for you we'd be in the fields this very minute instead of settin' on our fat behinds in these fine wicker chairs."

And so, for these many years, the remains of Andrew Whitfield had moldered in the crypt. His wife was buried in Winton's cemetery, and his family, to the second and third generations, had progressed from twittering, self-conscious apologies for the shocking spectacle of a tomb in the front yard to complacency and, ultimately, something not far removed from aggressive pride in the eccentricity of the old man and what he stood for. Who else, their attitude implied, but a Whitfield would dare choose such a burial place?

Old Andrew was more than a legend. Dead half of a century, he was still most of the county, much of the state, and part of the nation. More than anything else, though, Andrew was tobacco, and where men grew or bid for the leaf the name of Whitfield was never far away.

Only a few years removed from the soil and his own small tobacco barn, Andrew Whitfield had not followed his destiny. Instead he went out to grapple with it and in a furious battle threw it for a breathless fall. Andrew looked beyond the raising and selling of tobacco to the finished product and saw where the money lay. He began to grind his own leaf and then the crops of others. It was Andrew Whitfield who first refused to accept the manipulations of northern banking interests and monopolies which kept the small grower on the eternal brink of poverty with uncontrolled prices. Scheming quietly or openly cursing and shouting defiance, Andrew gathered the planters into a loose association and forced them to hold their leaf until the market came begging for it. As the co-operative gathered strength, prices rose to a gratifying level and for the first time, after the auctions and the annual settlement of debts, the farmer had a few dollars of his own to rub together. In a tiny office cluttered with old almanacs, fading calendars,

5

yellowing stacks of financial reports and eastern newspapers, Andrew began to eye the forming tobacco trusts with bright intelligence. It was Old Andrew who first realized the possibilities of a dude fad, the cigarette. The Whitfield name went around the world; first on a little cotton sack holding the tobacco for handmade cigarettes, and later on the gaily colored packages that came spilling from flashing machines.

From the Texas plains where cattlemen sifted his fine golden flakes from a sack into a creased oblong of rice paper, to the streets of London, San Francisco, Manila, Shanghai, and Cairo where the famous "Carolina Brights" could be purchased in every hotel and shop, the name of Whitfield became a familiar and welcome trade-mark. When Wall Street sniffed hungrily at the profitable blue smoke curling from billions of cigarettes as they passed from a novelty to an international necessity, Andrew Whitfield talked business. When he had finished and a newborn industry was having the breath of life spanked into it, Andrew both held the infant and wielded the hand. Small units were absorbed or clubbed to death in the formation of a gigantic trust that had no duplicate in the world, and Old Andrew's fortune billowed to incredible proportions.

Winton grew from a backwoods village with a single, rutted, red clay main street, to a brisk city of broad avenues, fine hotels, gracious homes, and a business district with more banks for its population than any other section of the state. Winton had little time for the gentle traditions of the Old South. It was new, vital, and electric from its fine modern schools to the great stemmeries over which the sweet odor of the tonka bean clung in an almost visible cloud.

Andrew Whitfield was no shaggy philanthropist. When his money poured into Winton, it did so with Andrew carefully tilting the horn of plenty. Each dollar he spent on the water front, the hotels, public utilities, business buildings, and residential subdivisions came back with half a dollar profit clinging to it. By the time he was ready to be laid away in his granite cell the Whitfield fortune was so vast that a large and complex organization had been formed to manage it. Andrew left everything, save for a few indifferent offerings to distant relatives, to his two sons Cassius and Joseph. He made his will with loud snorts of skepticism and ribald croakings at the inadequacy of his offspring, proclaiming in public that neither of the boys had sense enough to change their pants after they wet in them and could see a dollar only when it had been placed in their hands. On the night of his death he sat moodily in the empty dining room, finished a full quart

6

of red whisky, and went to sleep in his chair. The servants found him there in the morning.

Cassius, the elder, never quite recovered from being the possessor of so much money. He was a quiet, almost humble, and timidly apprehensive man, who felt that there was something unmoral in the magnitude of his weath. It frightened and bewildered him. He married a simple girl of a good family in Roanoke with little thought of the day when he must bear the responsibility of a portion of the Whitfield millions. When they were thrust upon him after his father's death, he blinked perplexedly at his young wife, shrugged helplessly, and silently pleaded with acquaintances and friends alike not to blame him for what he could not help. Though there was little need for his presence, he went determinedly each day to sit in the paneled offices of the Carolina Trust & Investment Corporation. There he made small decisions, gazed abstractedly at the ceiling, and drummed nervously with his fingers on his neatly rounded, dovelike paunch. He fretted constantly over his fortune, secretly believing that no one man or family should hold so much, and fearful of the consequences. He strove continually to be a plain man. He joined all of the civic associations and attended their luncheons, wearing a celluloid lapel button urging everyone to: "Call Me Cass." It was proof of his futility that no one ever did.

On The Hill he and his wife Laura tried to gather a circle of friends but never found the warm companionship they strove for so eagerly. They did their best to entertain, but the gatherings were stiffly sedate. No one ever laughed suddenly or out of sheer exuberance. Dinner on The Hill was a somber ritual that left everyone exhausted. Laura bore two children: Ann-Charlotte, a mysteriously intense girl, alarming in her beauty and willfulness, and a son, Cary, who grew into a defiantly nervous boy of uncertain temper whose fits of rage were as unpredictable as were his periods of tender gentleness. Cassius and Laura found them both equally disturbing and inexplicable.

Cassius tried desperately to spend the Whitfield fortune. He poured millions into a university; underwrote charities and research laboratories; gave thousands upon thousands to Winton for parks, playgrounds, community centers, and improvements. He built libraries, churches, and financed archeological expeditions without causing a ripple in the constant stream of unwanted dividends. Sometimes, as he contemplated the apparently inexhaustible storehouses Old Andrew had erected, he felt something close to terror

If the younger son, Joseph, ever experienced any of his brother's misgivings or uncomfortable moral twinges, he was remarkably successful in keeping them secret. On his broad shoulders the weight of the Whitfield name and what went with it were balanced with an airy grace. The bronze doors had no more than closed on Andrew's casket before Joe was playing with the taps of the many financial reservoirs. He returned from two highly unproductive years at the University of Virginia to attend his father's funeral and announced that the halls of learning would no longer echo to his reluctant footsteps.

For years he disported himself with innumerable fancy ladies from Buenos Aires to the Riviera. He fought a duel at Carlsbad over an Austrian duchess who was no better than she should have been; which was exactly the way Joe liked her. He was shot and nearly killed in Turkey by the paid assassins of a minor official who was outraged over the ease with which the American had led his wife to bed. He traveled grandly over the Continent in private trains, always accompanied by two or three enchantingly beautiful women, and dismissed them with a tender and regretful caress together with imposing cash settlements as a more practical form of heart balm. His escapades provided certain unfamiliar jobs for the Whitfield lawyers, but Joe always felt they had little enough to do anyhow.

With cheerful indifference Joseph shrugged off any claim he might have had to The Hill and told Cassius that for all of him he and Laura and their brats could haunt each other there. He was bound, though, by sentimental ties and boyhood memories, to Winton and had a fancy for returning there in the fall. He built a place of his own just outside the town limits and retired to it each autumn, refreshed and soothed by his rowdy pilgrimages. The winters he spent shooting over his fine setters or sitting before the huge stone fireplace, warming his insides with brandy and waiting for spring. The idea that there was a Whitfield tradition and The Hill its symbol never entered his head. Cassius, he admitted, fitted The Hill better, and if he and his small family ever felt the need of company, there were enough relatives scattered over the state to fill his home. Joseph neither admired nor disliked his brother, although he was ready to admit that Ann-Charlotte and Cary were hell's own bastards who would probably slit their parents' throats before they emerged from puberty. It was inevitable that the brothers should meet in a town as small as Winton, and when they did their manner was gravely courteous, nothing more. Joseph secretly pitied

8

Cassius without exactly knowing why and described him once as having been "old in the womb."

Winton eventually erected a statue to Cassius in Confederate Park; a bust which, aside from its dubious artistic value, was remarkable for the fact that it had been paid for out of funds not contributed by a Whitfield. Joseph achieved an immortality of his own which was not reflected in bronze but in the unconfessed admiration of the county and state where his adventures on both shores of the Atlantic were followed with thigh-cracking delight. When a New York newspaper devoted two pages to Joe's amorous European adventures, Radkin County was barely able to control itself, as something of Joe's wicked glamour touched everyone. As a young man, and later in middle age, Joseph fitted the popular notion of a splendid rakehell who dressed in a glittering fashion, drank champagne and ate lamb chops and creamed potatoes with parsley on them for breakfast; had a roving and compelling eye for the ladies, and roared back and forth between Winton, Fayetteville, and Raleigh in the largest, fastest automobile the state had ever seen. Joe was, also, an easy man to find when any of his friends were really in trouble. That Joseph in his later years, when some of the fires had been dampened if not quenched, could go quail or deer shooting with Tom Purdy, who ran a barber shop, or sit on the curb before Hancey's drugstore yarning earnestly with a lean and anxious share-cropper, was accepted as additional testimony to his magnificence.

Winton respected Cassius, but a large section of the state's population loved and admired Joe Whitfield and so he never felt slighted when no one suggested erecting a statue of him to stand in gloomy unconcern in Confederate Park.

While Joe's home rambled with careless design on the riverbank, absorbing mellowness with the years and its owner, The Hill stubbornly refused to achieve a grace. Despite its discomforts Cassius and Laura clung to the place long after they had built an elaborate gray stone lodge near Asheville in the mountains. There were times when Laura and her husband felt the oppressive weight of loneliness and wished vaguely they could escape from themselves and The Hill. Sometimes they would both stop in the middle of a conversation and stare at each other down the length of the massive dining room table, silently asking why they had been unable so much as to touch the seemingly wonderful, shining thing so many other persons found in life. They tried desperately to escape. Dutifully they went to the mountains in the summer. In the fall they moved to Hot Springs. Each

9

winter, for a month, they occupied a suite at the Plaza in New York and went determinedly to theaters and concerts, but the trips were without gaiety and they hurried back to The Hill, perplexed and weary without knowing why.

Although Cary and Ann-Charlotte would have hooted with scorn if anyone had been ninny enough to suggest that they felt an affection for and sense of security in The Hill, they never suggested it be abandoned. It was home as were the hot pine flats, the small-town friendliness of Winton, the scrub-scattered countryside, and the warehouses heavy with tobacco in September. The Hill represented something; a solid value in a world their portion of which, at least, was seemingly forever pitched on the brink of hysteria. "The Rock of Ages," Cary called it scornfully; but without realizing it, he and Ann-Charlotte reached their arms out to it. As they and The Hill grew older, they took a defiant pleasure in its ugliness. Old Andrew's sheep, deer, and squirrels remained where he had placed them. No carpenters violated the narrow windows and doors. The only concessions made were in the modernizing of the bathrooms and the kitchen, and the commissioning of a landscape architect to bring some order out of the tangled grounds.

A lake behind The Hill was dredged and widened and a combination boathouse and pavilion built along its shores. Cassius and Laura felt that this was an almost breath-taking novelty, and it added a touch of excitement to their well-ordered lives. When the building was finished, they held elaborate picnic suppers on the rail-enclosed roof. Japanese lanterns nodded jerkily overhead, and beneath them a select few from Winton exclaimed delightedly over the innovation, sipped iced tea, and experimented daintily with unfamiliar delicacies shipped by special express from New York. On the lake their youngsters streaked back and forth in the noisy two-cylinder speedboat Cassius had daringly purchased, and shouted with unintelligible enthusiasm to their parents on the roof who were following their antics with alarmed pride.

In later years, when Ann-Charlotte and Cary took over the burden of entertaining, both guests and hosts provided stiff competition to the uproar created by a newer, faster, and noisier boat. Instead of rocking quietly on the boathouse roof, their mouths filled with *pâté de fois gras* and gossip, they guzzled enormous quantities of gin and corn whisky. Shrieks of laughter echoed over The Hill as guests tumbled from the landing dock into the lake and were hauled out, dripping and unabashed, to fortify themselves against a sudden chill by additional potions of corn and coca-cola.

Old Andrew's house had been badly used and acquired the transient atmosphere of an inn. Perhaps that is why it complained in the night, for it wasn't at all what Andrew had intended.

Lying on the bed, thinking of the house and the Whitfields, Reese Benton wondered what Andrew would do or say if he could stride from his tomb out there in the yard and have a few mortal moments again. If he could talk with his grandson Cary; Cary's wife, Lillith, or Ann-Charlotte, what would Andrew have to tell them?

Over the small noises, flitting like invisible rats through the house, Reese heard the sharp snap of a latch as a door down the hall was closed. Footsteps gently padding in the corridor halted before his room, and after a moment the doorknob was turned softly.

Lillith Whitfield stood framed in the narrow opening. The hall light, catching at her loose, black hair as it fell around her shoulders, touched one side of her face, blocking in the high cheekbone and accenting an elliptical line from chin to forehead.

"Are you awake, Reese?" The question was whispered.

"I'm awake."

Reese didn't move, but with his head half-turned in the crook of his arm he watched her and wondered at the curious trick of lighting which suddenly accentuated the indefinably Oriental characteristics of her features. In the full light, without these odd, geometrical shadows, Lillith Whitfield was possessed of a vivid and at the same time subtly shaded, dusky beauty. Now, though, she seemed inscrutably foreign.

"Cary went to sleep, but...," she hesitated over the words, "he cried again."

"I heard him." Reese shifted his eyes and stared at the ceiling.

"May I come in?" She waited on the threshold.

"Sure, why not?" Reese didn't turn.

"It's pretty awful to watch a grown man cry, Reese." She crossed the room silently and stood beside the bed, looking down at him.

"It's only liquor." He deliberately infused the statement with impatience. "You shouldn't let him drink so much."

Lillith sank slowly to a corner of the bed and leaned against the end post. She watched Reese for a moment and then fumbled at a breast pocket of her pajama coat. She lit a cigarette quickly, cupping the match's brief flame in her two hands.

"He never drank this way before."

Reese laughed shortly and without humor. "He always did, only you never noticed it so much before you were married."

Lillith allowed the smoke to curl out from between her half-parted lips and studied him with serious concentration.

"It's not the same," she finally said. "It isn't the same and you know it. He cries now as though he were haunted and someone or something was speaking for him. I—I don't know any longer what he is trying to say, Reese."

Her voice was tense and he could sense the tightness gathering within her. He wanted to reach out, to say something gentle, but neither the action nor the words would come.

"He'll be all right in the morning."

She just stared at him. "You don't care, do you, Reese?"

"Of course I do." He shut his eyes and then opened them again quickly, searching her face in the semidarkness.

"No you don't." There was faint surprise in her tone and she repeated the words in the manner of someone suddenly discovering something. "No you don't, and I wonder why. Why don't you care about him, Reese?"

"Oh, go to bed!" He twisted his face away with a gesture of irritation.

"What were you thinking about, Reese?" She persisted. "What were you thinking about, lying here alone when you know you can always talk to him when he gets this way?"

"God damn it!" The words were explosive and violent, although he didn't move as he spoke them. "I'm not a male nurse."

"But . . . you're Cary's friend, Reese. That isn't the same thing." She held her cigarette straight out between thumb and forefinger and wrapped both hands together, leaning forward slightly in an attitude of expectancy.

Reese tightened his fingers about the base of his neck and began counting the figures on the wall. He didn't want to talk. After a moment Lillith rose, stubbed her cigarette out in a tray on the bed table.

"Want something to eat?" The invitation was friendly and casual, nothing more.

Reese grunted and shook his head.

"Stubborn?" She was mocking, treating him as an elder with a petulant child, and he grinned for the first time.

"No, just not hungry."

12

Lillith stood in the center of the room, waiting. "Well, come down and have a drink while I make myself a sandwich."

"Uh-uh."

"Not hungry and not thirsty, is that it?" Her nose wrinkled and Reese grunted again. "And not very well-mannered either, are you?"

"Go to hell," he said pleasantly.

She walked to the door. "No, I'll go to the kitchen and eat some cold chicken."

"Shut the door when you go out."

He heard her sandaled feet whisper along the hall carpet and then reached for a cigarette. The smoke bit harshly at his throat as he inhaled deeply. The moon had lifted above treetop level and the shadows on the wall were growing shorter. He listened intently. The house was without sound again, retiring within itself when people moved and spoke. The breeze over the ridge was quickening and felt heavier as it carried rain. Reese rose, closed the window, and went back to the bed, stretching out again without bothering to take off his clothing. Lying once more in the darkness he smoked without pleasure as Lillith's question returned to nag spitefully at him.

"Why don't you care, Reese? Why don't you?"

The query pounded with the monotonous beat of a child's senseless goading. Why? Why? Why? Why don't you? Why can't I know? The line of his mouth grew fixed, hard and chiseled.

"You're Cary's friend, Reese."

With what confidence people said such a thing and so casually laid responsibility and obligation on another. Even Lillith, who took little for granted; who was an outspoken and sometimes fierce champion of individual privacy, could utter the phrase so effortlessly. Why was he Cary's friend: because they had lived, eaten, laughed, fought, and grown up together? You became someone's friend and because of that you did certain things. Like Siamese twins you were bound together forever. It was as simple as that.

Reese swung his feet over the edge of the bed and stood up. He jammed the cigarette into the tray and watched the tiny coals die quickly like scattered powder grains. Once he too had spoken those words, cried them out in bewildered and frustrated anguish and no one had understood. He could almost hear himself again as he called in the desolation of a young boy suddenly knowing himself to be alone. He could remember, also, that a man had once kicked him, and he marveled, as always, that the memory could be so sharp after almost

13

twenty years. All of his life, he thought, he would carry the imprint of that kick, for the man who had so savagely booted his lean buttocks had done so with contempt and not anger.

He turned abruptly and walked quickly across the room and along the hall, trotting down the broad staircase and through the silent library and living room and to where a small penciling of light was drawn along the bottom of the kitchen door.

II

Lillith looked up at him across a half-gnawed chicken leg. She was seated on the corner of a heavy chopping table, one foot swinging idly. A full glass of milk and a platter of sliced and jointed chicken were within easy reach. Without taking the drumstick from her mouth she nodded, looking absurdly childish and wide-eyed as though she had been caught out after hours.

"There's grease on your nose," Reese said.

She set her teeth into the plump meat and stripped a long sliver from the bone, chewing stolidly. Then she licked quickly at her upper lip, a fast, semicircular flicking of her tongue.

"You always get grease on your nose when you eat chicken this way. Some people even get it in their ears and on their chins."

"But you only get it on your nose?"

"That's right." She watched him, waiting; and when he only stood and looked, reached for her milk. "Want something to eat or a drink?"

"A drink, I guess."

She ate her chicken with unemotional concentration, watching him out of the corner of one eye as he brought in whisky, took ice and soda from the refrigerator, and made a long highball. Then he swung a chair around, sitting on it facing the back and resting his glass on the top crosspiece, while he looked up at her.

"Why did you change your mind, about coming down, I mean?"

Reese pressed his nose against the cold, damp rim of the glass.

"Something you said," he answered slowly. "I said it myself, a long time ago, to Cary but he didn't hear me and so I've never said it again, not to anyone."

He tilted the glass without raising it and allowed the drink to dribble into his mouth. It was sharp and icy in his throat and he closed his eyes like a cat at a saucer of milk.

"Yes?"

He shook his head. It seemed so long, long ago. He and Cary were both ten years old that summer. Their birthdays were only a week apart, and in some mysterious fashion this seemed to bind them in a

15

kinship which survived the fact that Cary was "The Hill" and he Lance Benton's son.

Against Laura's gentle suggestion that the children be sent to a private school Cassius had stood firm. Winton had a day academy for the youngsters of the town's upper middle class who could afford a small tuition, but Cassius insisted on the public school.

"It'll be good for them. I don't want them to grow up thinking they are different."

"But," Laura Whitfield could never quite understand her husband's obsession, "how are you going to help it? Everywhere they turn they know that they are the Whitfield children. How is public school going to change it? Anyhow, I don't think they learn anything in their classes."

"I don't want them to grow up into nasty little snobs. That's all they turn out at Miss Roger's school. Brats."

"Stuff." That was about as vehement as Laura Whitfield ever allowed herself to become. "Stuff!"

"It's true." Cassius shook his head stubbornly. "I've listened to them and their parents, too. I want Ann-Charlotte and Cary to go to the public school and that is all there is to it."

Laura bent her head to her embroidery, then raised it quickly. "You're being a snob about not being a snob, Cassius Whitfield," she said abruptly and rose, hurrying from the room before he had a chance to reply.

Nevertheless Cary and Ann-Charlotte went down into Winton each morning to line up outside the new public school with the sons and daughters of the milkmen, bus drivers, farmers, and cigarette factory employees, all of whom owed their existence in Winton to Andrew Whitfield. Cassius saw nothing incongruous in the fact that they were taken and called for by his colored chauffeur.

"Lopsided democracy," Laura teased him and was surprised when he took her words seriously.

"I guess you're right," he admitted sheepishly. "After this they can get to school on their bicycles or walk."

"Make them take off their shoes, too, why don't you? They can hang them around their necks by the laces and put them on when they get ready to go in."

"Damn foolishness," Cassius snorted irritably.

"Damn consistent"—Laura pressed one hand against her mouth in

16

astonishment and looked so startled at her own words that Cassius had to laugh.

Whether they went to public school or Miss Roger's Academy seemed equally unimportant to Cary and his sister since they disliked the idea of both with equal vigor. But, because it was obvious that it was one or the other, they secretly preferred the rowdy intimacy of the former.

Through the grades, where they made uninspiring progress, Cary and Reese wove those tenuous bonds of youth, strands which hold so surprisingly well at times only to part and dissolve without apparent reason. At the beginning of each term they were early at school to pick out adjoining desks from where they could whisper or furtively pass notes of dark import back and forth. They shared their lessons, plotted ways to escape with a minimum of work, and raced from the yard with the echoes of the three-o'clock bell to spend the long, smoky afternoons of fall and winter along the river or in the woods surrounding Reese's home.

Cary found the weathered and sagging cabin where Reese and his widowed father lived mysteriously exciting. It was little better than one of the Negro huts, save for the fact that it boasted a limply uneven porch. There was one large room and a kitchen, or "cooking room" as Reese called it, tacked on at the back as sort of an afterthought, but Lance Benton and his son kept their place clean, and since they used the house only for eating and sleeping it served them well enough. In the tall, hard, and soft-spoken Lance, young Cary felt sure, reposed all of the world's most desirable virtues. Reese's father could knock a fast-winging quail out of the air with a rifle, knew where the wild turkeys roosted. He had shot a huge black bear once, skinned it himself, and cured the pelt to make a rug for the cabin. He could whittle a graceful boat out of a block of white pine with the careless air of a man peeling a potato, and he knew a thousand and one stories of the mountain fastnesses and secret places in the Great Smokies. He built rabbit and animal snares with cunning and could hold a fist-sized quid of tobacco in one cheek while he related shivering tales of feuds and Negro witchcraft. By comparison Cary saw his own father as a pallid and uninteresting man of authority who did nothing more spectacular than sit in an office all day and for one reason or another seemed too occupied to pay more than passing attention to his son. He was vaguely aware that his father had a lot of money. The knowledge was inescapable, but money above a dollar had small meaning and seemed

17

a poor thing to balance against the wisdom and lore possessed by Lance Benton. Afternoons Cary would bring Reese to The Hill and they would play around the lake, over the boathouse, or crouch in tremulous anticipation behind Old Andrew's tomb in the hope of hearing a ghost. Later they would have milk and cake in the big kitchen, a room larger than Reese's entire house. Frequently Reese was invited to dinner, a meal he endured in silent torment, confused by the many forks and the sparkling sheen of linen and crystal.

"He's such a strange boy," Laura remarked to Cassius one evening on the porch. "He just looks at you with those grave eyes and never says anything. I wonder what he and Cary talk about? It doesn't seem as though they have anything in common."

With the candor of youth Reese and Cary exchanged opinions concerning the relative merits of their homes and parents and decided that if Lance Benton and Cassius Whitfield could each give a little of what they possessed, one completely satisfactory household could be put together, and they wondered audibly at the general mismanagement of adults. It was only a question of adding a little here and taking away a little there and the result would be a perfect world. Funny that grownups couldn't understand something so simple and easy.

With the aggressive resentment of the poor, Lance told Reese that he didn't want him running up to The Hill all the time; but the fact that his boy could go and come there almost as he pleased filled him with an unspoken pride. These hard-baked acres were good enough for them now but Reese was growing up and it was fine for a boy to have friends, such friends as the Whitfields. Lance expressed his approval by elaborating on his best stories and retracing his footsteps along mountain trails and the road that first brought him from Kentucky to North Carolina when he and Reese's mother were young. The shining-eyed, breathless attention they gave him was a stimulating reward. He took them fishing on the river, and once, during Christmas vacation, they spent four days of wonder on a camping trip, rising at dawn, cooking their meals over small hot fires, and lying in their blankets at night staring with silent fascination into the fire, weary and contented.

That summer, Reese remembered now, was the hottest anyone could recall. The heat lay in heavy layers along Winton's streets and the river. The Whitfields were going to the mountains, and Reese wondered dismally how he was to spend the long months until September. He and Cary sat in the shade on the riverbank and talked about it.

"I don't see why you don't come to Asheville with us," Cary suggested.

Reese bit through a long-pine needle. "No one asked me," he said matter of factly.

"Well," Cary was unimpressed, "I'll ask my father to ask your father."

Reese shook his head. "No," he objected quietly, "that's somethin' your folks would want to think of first."

Cary kicked a small hole in the dry earth with the heel of his shoe. "If you want somethin' you gotta ask for it," he said.

"Not somethin' like that." Reese was firm.

Cary stared out at the dull surface of the river; then his eyes brightened.

"Let's go down to Staples'," he suggested.

"What for?"

"You know what for." Cary rose and beat at the seat of his knickerbockers with both palms. "Come on, let's have some fun."

Staples' was a bottling works at the end of Clover Street near the railroad tracks. There, moving on a circular belt, rows of bottles of various shapes passed beneath spigots from which spurted ginger, root beer, cream orange, strawberry, and coca-cola syrups. The bottles clanked and rattled, each with its measured amount of flavoring, past a second spout which filled them with carbonated water, and finally under a capping machine where a small metal disc was clamped to each bottle's mouth. From that point they slid off into the hands of a waiting Negro boy who sorted the drinks into their proper cases for delivery to the drugstores, pool halls, lunchrooms, and such private homes as could afford the luxury of soft drinks in case lots.

Staples' was a dim and moistly cool retreat of heady odors. Furthermore, Staples' was an establishment of exchange, for Staples himself would pay half a cent for all empty bottles returned. Winton's boys, combing through waste cans, trash barrels, or searching along the depot platform, could gather as many as a dozen bottles in a morning and turn them in to Staples for pennies.

The bottling works had been Cary's idea in the beginning, and when he had explained it, Reese had stared in slack-mouthed astonishment at the genius of its remarkable simplicity.

They had hooked a ride on the tail end of a wagon as is creaked along Clover Street. The driver knew they were there but they thought he didn't, and so the otherwise uneventful and tedious trip had a fillip of adventure. They lay back, feeling the warmth of the boards through their shirts and squinting up at the great, blue vacancy of the sky. As the wheels banged against the railroad tracks, they sat up and jumped to the ground. If they waited, maybe a freight train would come along and they could swing to the iron ladders on the box cars for a brief ride as far as Yadkin Street before the engine gathered too much speed.

Standing in the middle of the tracks, they looked far down the rails, wondering at the mysterious way the lines of bright steel ended in a point. Once they had discussed this phenomenon heatedly, arguing as to what happened when the train reached the spot where the rails joined.

"I guess that's Georgia," Reese had said.

It seemed to be a reasonable enough explanation, and so they had allowed the world to end somewhere in Georgia.

"Want to make some money?" Cary picked up a heavy clinker from between the ties and hurled it at a telegraph pole.

"How?"

"Over at Staples'." Cary ran a few dancing steps along a rail before he lost his balance and had to step off.

"You got any bottles?" Reese was gratifyingly curious.

Cary shook his head. "No, but old man Staples has."

Reese was puzzled and Cary giggled, hugging his secret to himself.

"Come on," he said, "I'll show you. I figured it all out by myself last night."

With elaborate and unnecessary caution they skirted Staples' plant and ducked through a hedge separating it from an adjoining yard. With ominous gestures Cary crept on his belly through the grass, followed by Reese who, in the novelty of these maneuvers, had forgotten their ultimate goal. In the rear of the yard Cary halted and carefully parted the thinning hedge with his hands. He thrust his head through the opening like an apprehensive gopher. Then he wriggled through, and when Reese joined him they stood breathless and flushed in the lot behind the plant. Stacked about them were a hundred or more cases of empty bottles and piles of loose ones were scattered in every corner.

"Take some," Cary began snatching at the empty bottles, filling the cradle of one arm.

Reese grabbed three in each hand, as many as his fingers could hold, and they bounded back through the hedge to comparative safety. Cary was panting, Reese could see his heart beat against his chest.

"Come on now," Cary strolled up the yard and then across the sidewalk. "I guess we got enough for one trip."

Together they sauntered down to Staples' and inside, rattling their bottles on the counter. Staples looked up, nodded, and came over.

"Six, eight, ten, twelve, fourteen." He drew seven cents from the wooden cash drawer. "Who gets the odd one?" he said pleasantly.

"You take it, Cary." Reese pushed the extra copper to one side. After all, he thought, anyone who could conceive and execute such a wonderful swindle as this was entitled to the larger share.

Outside again, breathing the sweet air of freedom, they raced each other down the street to Goldman's candy store, spending the proceeds of the venture on long and delicious whips of licorice and a dozen sour-balls, made doubly good because they were slightly flavored with dishonesty.

"How did you ever think of that?" Reese sank his teeth into the licorice.

"I don't know"; Cary was suddenly importantly cocky. "I just got to wondering about it the other night."

It never occurred to either that an actual amount of seven cents was involved, a few pennies Cary could have had for the asking at home. They climbed into a mulberry tree, perching on a large branch like a couple of raccoons while they finished the candy.

"I'll bet your pa would give you hell if he found out. Mine would." Reese chewed thoughtfully. "He'd give you sure enough hell for stealin', specially when he's got all that money."

Cary nodded agreeably. "I'll bet your pa would fan your tail for sure if he knew."

Reese dangled the remnant of the stringy licorice between his legs and his face drew into a puzzled frown. Finally he shook his head.

"No," he said, "Pa would just be ashamed. It'd be different with him somehow. He wouldn't beat me for that."

They coddled the secret of their trove, whispering about it to each other, and worked up enough courage to tap the inexhaustible lode once a week. Even with this caution Staples began to display an uncomfortable curiosity.

"Where the hell you boys gittin' all them bottles?" He asked the question sharply one day, peering through lowered lids. Reese could feel his face grow hot, and he watched Cary. Maybe they ought to run. Cary only stared back at Staples.

"We find them," he answered, "we find them every place, an'

21

besides my father's got a lot of bottles in the cellar, bottles he never sent back."

"By God, I never seen two boys find so many empties before, that's a sure enough fact." Staples was not entirely convinced.

They had stayed away from the plant after that, shunning it as a pesthouse and spending Cary's allowance without enthusiasm.

"Well," Cary tossed a pine cone at a log floating in the river, "what do you say? Want to go to Staples' again?"

"All right." Reese got up reluctantly. It would be better, he thought, just to lie here in the shade. They'd just work up an awful sweat crawling into Staples' back yard.

They walked back along Decatur Street and then cut down Clover, bounding into the empty lot next to Staples' and throwing themselves flat in the grass.

"I'm gettin' kind of tired of bottles," Reese whispered as they inched up to the hedge.

"Me too." Cary was a little hoarse from excitement. "But we came this far. No sense in goin' back now without some."

"We'll do it just one more time." Reese pulled himself forward on his stomach.

They were hunched over a pile of bottles when Staples' outraged roar froze them. They were too frightened to run or drop what they held and turned to face the furious old man, guilt wrapped tightly in their fingers.

"By God, I knew you wasn't gittin' them bottles honest. There ain't that many empties lyin' around town an' you know it." He glared menacingly and advanced slowly, trapping them in a corner of the yard. "I ought to beat the livin' hell out of both you."

"Don't you touch me," Cary screamed in shrill terror, "you—you," he stammered, unable to enunciate, "if you touch me I'll tell my father, that's what I'll do." He backed away, his face drawn with fear and helpless mortification.

"You ought to be ashamed of yourself, Cary Whitfield"—Staples was shaking, he was so enraged—"stealin' pennies from an honest man when you an' The Hill's got all the money in the world."

"We weren't stealin'." A little confidence crept into Cary's tone. "We, we were just stackin' some bottles up for you. That's all we were doin', wasn't it, Reese?"

Slowly Reese allowed the bottles to drop from his hands and they

22

fell to the sand with soft thuds, each thump pounding on the weight of guilt.

"No," he said, "I guess we were stealin' 'em all right, Mr. Staples."

"I know damn well you bin stealin' 'em." Staples refused to be mollified. "Even a fool, what I ain't, could see you were a-stealin' 'em. I'm goin' to git me a switch an' tan your bottoms, that's what I'm a-goin' to do, an' after that I'm a-goin' to the marshal an' your folks, too."

He strode determinedly toward them and suddenly Cary cried out, yelping in hysterical fright. He bent low and darted around and away from Staples' outstretched arm, racing down the areaway and out into Clover Street. Staples watched him disappear and turned to Reese.

"Get out of here," he snarled with trembling fury. "This is what The Hill gits for lettin' its kids play with trash like you." His hand whipped forward and fastened on the frayed collar of Reese's shirt. With a powerful tug he wheeled the boy around. "Git out of here, you little bastard," he spoke quietly and kicked Reese viciously with the flat of his foot.

The blow pitched the boy forward on his face and his half-opened mouth dug into the dirt. He pulled himself up in a crouch and saw Staples walking away toward the rear entrance of the plant. The man never even glanced back at him, and suddenly Reese began to vomit.

After a moment, when he could control the retching tearing at his insides, he rose and walked unsteadily down the alley. Automatically he turned up Clover Street, his bare feet making a soft, rasping sound on the pavement. His eyes were hot and feverish, but what tears there were to spill remained locked within him. As he walked he kept his head bent, counting his steps by the steady flicking of a soiled bit of rag wound about one of his big toes where he had cut it. The little tassle of dirty cloth appeared and vanished before his fixed stare. It darted forward and then back out of sight with the motion of his foot. He began to wait for its appearance with interest. It was like a rabbit hitting the brush, he thought. Going in so fast that the only thing you could see was the white nubbin on its rear end. He raised his head and his eyes followed the sweep of the road as it spread out to join Memorial Avenue with its big double lane, divided by a row of trees.

I ought to be cryin' this minute, he thought proudly. I ought to be sittin' right out there on the curb an' bawlin' my head off. No one but Lance had ever struck him before, and you had to expect that now and then from your pa, he reasoned. He wondered why he wasn't crying, and then he knew why the tears wouldn't come. It was because of the way Staples had booted him. Just like a chicken-stealin' hound; he curled a little inside at the thought. That was the way a mutt would get kicked, and the man wouldn't look at him twice or pay him much mind because a stealin' dog was made to be a thief and there wasn't much to do about it unless the man wanted to kill him. If he wasn't goin' to kill him, then a man would just boot him out of the way and watch him run. If he hadn't just walked away after he kicked me, Reese thought, then maybe I'd think it was important, big enough to cry about an' I'd feel better.

Cary was waiting near the corner of Memorial Avenue, staring intently at a blue jay in the top branches of one of the tall elm trees. Reese started to walk past.

Cary allowed him to pass and then he called out hurriedly. "Hey! Aren't you goin' to wait for me?"

Reese halted and then turned slowly. Cary was flushed and uncertain. "You didn't wait for me," Reese muttered. He bent down, poking at the loose end of the rag, tucking it in while the tears were hot now in his eyes.

"Well, I thought you were runnin', too." Cary wasn't convincing and he knew it. "I didn't figure you were fool enough to stand there an' take it." He tried to laugh.

"You ran away an' left me there." Reese was having trouble forming the words. "You just lit out and left me behind an' all the time you knew Staples wouldn't lay a finger on you an' he sure couldn't do anything to me unless he did it to you."

Cary's eyes darted around and over Reese's head, trying to find something on which he could focus his attention and escape that accusing stare.

"Well, how'd I know?" He mumbled and tried a different tack, simulating the excitement of a fellow conspirator and offender. "Did he tan you? Did he lay it on like he said he would? Did he?"

Suddenly Reese was crying and his skinny arms flailing as he charged into Cary. He could feel the sharp bones of his fist crack as they landed on the boy's surprised face and beat about his head.

"You were my friend." He wailed with a lonely cry. "You were my friend. God damn you." He was blubbering. "He just kicked me, do you hear. He just kicked me an' walked away."

They were in a screaming, sobbing tangle on the grass. Reese felt Cary's shirt rip in his hand and saw blood smearing his knuckles.

Cary gave up trying to fight back and tried only to protect himself by crossing his arms over his head and attempting to twist away and from beneath Reese. Then, without warning, Reese felt two strong hands beneath his armpits and he was swung up and off the ground.

"It ain't," a soft voice chided while a steady grip held him, "that I object to your killing him, only I don't think you ought to do it way out here on Memorial Avenue where so few people will see you."

With the weight of Reese's body off of him, Cary uncovered his face and looked up, then shouted with relief.

"Uncle Joe."

He scrambled to his feet and posed aggressively now that danger was past and help at hand.

"He was tryin' to beat my head in, Uncle Joe." Cary was indignant and accusing. "You saw him. You saw him doin' it."

Reese felt the pressure on his shoulders relax and turned to stare at Joseph Whitfield.

"If I was fixin' to beat his head in, Mr. Whitfield," he said slowly, "I'd take a rock."

Joe Whitfield, who for reasons best known to himself had decided to stay at home that summer, nodded imperturbably. He stood straight, unruffled and immaculate as usual in a suit of cream-colored pongee, one of the suits Winton insisted he changed every hour or as soon as a wrinkle appeared. There was a faint tracing of a smile around his mouth.

"I've always said a good rock was easier on the hands," he said agreeably.

"You saw what he was doin' "—Cary didn't like the composure with which his uncle had witnessed his near-annihilation. "We were just standin' here, talkin', when he jumped me." He stared hopefully at his uncle.

Joseph Whitfield rubbed thoughtfully at his chin. "I guess you were just born under some kind of an unlucky sign, Cary," he mused. "It must be a real hard luck sign, otherwise people wouldn't be jumping you for nothing the way you always say. Yes, sir, I expect you're a real, marked boy if I ever saw one." He grinned and winked companionably at Reese. "Right now you are, anyhow." He regretfully took a handkerchief from his breast pocket and tossed it to his nephew. "Here. Wipe that bloody snot from your nose."

Cary daubed his face, sniffling into the linen and darting a wary glance out of the corner of his eye at Joe Whitfield. He was disappointed that the incident had been dismissed in such a casual fashion. With studied carelessness Reese slapped an accumulation of twigs and dirt from his knickerbockers. Looking up suddenly he was surprised to discover that the man was regarding him with a half-grin of understanding as though they had shared a particularly amusing experience. Reese smiled shyly, feeling warm and for some reason no longer alone.

Joe scorned the handkerchief when Cary timidly thrust it at him. "You ain't home yet. Maybe it'll come in handy."

Marshaling the boys on either side of him, Joe led them to the curb where his car, a bright yellow Renault with red leather upholstery, waited. The car was custom built and he had brought it back from Paris together with a French chauffeur who long ago had resigned himself to both his employer and a barbaric country; a land inhabited by savages whose delight in life was, apparently, only exceeded by their capacity to pay for it.

When they were settled in the rear seat, Joe turned abruptly to Reese.

"You're Lance Benton's boy?"

"Yes, sir." Reese turned and looked up, wondering what was coming.

Joe Whitfield nodded with satisfaction. "Look some like him." They rode in silence for half a block. "Best damn shot in North Carolina," he said for no apparent reason. He blew a whistling note through his front teeth, seemingly deep in thought. "Probably the best damn shot this side of the Potomac."

"Yes, sir." Reese fought to keep pride out of his voice.

The car rolled silently down Memorial Avenue, through the deep shade cast by the arching trees. Cary, hunched into a corner of the seat, pressed his face against the window and stared with frowning concentration at the opposite side of the street. Reese, glancing down at the heavy gray carpeting on the floor, saw his grimy bare feet and the twist of dirty rag on his toe and tried to tuck the offending member out of sight.

"What the hell were you fightin' about?"

Reese wriggled uncomfortably. Cary ignored the question.

"Guess you don't need a reason." Joe Whitfield rolled the thought over, examining it with detached interest. "Don't recollect I ever did when I was your age."

"Yes, sir." Reese nodded solemnly. "That's it. We were just fightin', I guess. More like for the hell of it."

"That's the best kind of fightin'." The man looked straight ahead,

26

past the shoulders of the chauffeur and down the length of the broad avenue as though he were watching a small and shadowy figure in the distance.

Cary turned and shot a glance past his uncle at Reese. "It wasn't anything, Uncle Joe." The words hurried each other. "We were just cuttin' the fool and then an argument started. That's about all it was."

Joe Whitfield leaned forward, opened a small compartment in the back of the front seat and drew out a slender glass tube containing a fat and richly brown cigar from a narrow cedar box. He broke the container open and applied a match to the cigar. When the tip was glowing roundly, he looked down at his nephew.

"I'd say there was more to it," he suggested gently, "otherwise you wouldn't be in such a hurry to cover it up. I also suspect that if there was trouble you were at the bottom of it." He drew musingly on the cigar, and the rich aroma filled the compartment. "I can't say," he added without rancor, "that I ever counted you among the noblest of my acquaintances, son."

"Yes, sir." The tone had a subduing effect upon Cary although he wasn't quite certain what the words meant. "Yes, sir, I guess you're right."

At Division Street, Joe called the car in to the curb, and as the boys crawled awkwardly out he twisted a hand down into his trousers pocket and pulled out a crumpled wad of bills, one of which he handed to Cary after a moment's hesitation.

"Go in an' buy yourselves a soda or two. Maybe that'll cool you off." He smiled almost happily. "An' if I catch you fightin' again I hope I find you on top, Reese. There ought to be someone in Winton to kick the hell out of a Whitfield now an' then. It's got to be somethin' of a lost art hereabouts." The driver was about to swing the door closed when Joe stopped it with a hand. "Come down an' see me, Lance Benton's boy," he called, and then, catching sight of the complete desolation on his nephew's face, he relented. "You too, Cary. Belle of Gray Glen's just had a litter of pups. I'll let you see 'em."

Cary and Reese stood on the edge of the pavement until the car was out of sight. Reese scraped the calloused ball of his foot against the cement and the sound was that of emery paper being rubbed on a board. He looked over the rooftops across the street, wrinkling his brow with the effort of profound meditation. Cary attempted a jaunty whistle, but the sound trailed off on a ragged note.

"Want a soda?" Cary tossed the suggestion indifferently.

27

"Nope." Reese stared down the street.

"Uncle Joe said." Cary waited.

"I don't feel like a soda." Reese felt his throat go dry as the lie scorched it.

"How could you feel like a soda?" Cary was aloofly superior. "What does a soda feel like?"

"I'm goin' home." His feet moved reluctantly as Reese forced them to obey. It could be a pineapple soda with two scoops of cream and at the bottom of the glass a little golden mound of fruit to be dug out with a spoon. It could be a strawberry soda with big, frothy bubbles breaking around your nose when you leaned over. "I don't feel like a soda."

"Are you mad?" Without seeming to follow Cary scuffed a few paces behind.

"Nope." Reese bent his head to count the squares in the pavement.

"See you tomorrow?"

"I guess so."

"Well, so long."

"So long."

Reese walked slowly, conscious that he was alone. He kept his eyes averted, raising his head only when he came to an intersection. Methodically he kept track of the cross lines in the sidewalk until he reached Market Street and the railroad tracks. Beyond was a twisting dirt road and his feet, released from the mild torment of gritty stone, slapped into the soft clay powder. Then he began to run, and as he ran, small but terrible sobs tore at his chest and the face he lifted to the tops of the slender pines was streaked with tears.

LILLITH slid from the table, carried her empty glass to the sink and rinsed it with a quick spurt of water from the tap. With his chin sunk into the backs of his interlaced fingers Reese watched her, and his eyes were steady when she turned to face him.

"Want another drink?" She nodded at the empty glass on the floor beside his chair.

"Not now."

She lit a cigarette and then tossed the package across to him.

"You came down to tell me something and then you changed your mind. Why?"

Reese shook his head. "I came down for a drink." He stretched his long legs before him, straddling the chair. "You were the one who wanted to talk." He smiled up at her. "I'll bet you were a nasty little brat when you were a child, always asking 'Why?' "

Twin shafts of light sliced across the room from a window as a car swung through the driveway, its tires squealing against the gravel. There was a moment of silence and then the heavy slamming of a door and the quick tapping of heels on the back porch. Lillith walked over and opened the screen.

"I saw the light. Having a party? God, I'm tired." Ann-Charlotte closed the door behind her and leaned against it with a sigh of half comic resignation. "Take my advice and don't stay out after dark with a polo player. They've got the idea that the whole world is something to ride." She glanced brightly from Reese to Lillith. "Hi! Lil. What are you two peasants doing in the kitchen?"

"Hi! Ann-Charlotte." Reese watched her with almost sleepy indifference.

"Well, hi! yourself, Reese." The greeting was infused with mock surprise. "I thought you weren't speaking to me."

"That's only when you are a bitch."

The girl moved toward him with an exaggerated slink, her slender body twisting sinuously and her scarlet mouth writhing in a shockingly dissolute leer. With a caressing hand she pushed suggestively at the strap of her gown until it slid from her shoulder, baring the upper part of her breast.

"Sort of puts a limit on our conversation, doesn't it, *compadre?*"

"Where did you go?" Lillith smiled companionably at her sister-in-law.

"Oh, the usual places." Without bothering to rearrange her dress Ann-Charlotte went to the pantry and took down a bottle of bourbon. "We went to the club after dinner at the Warren place. Galen puked all over the bar and passed out. That's when I met this polo player, he's on his way up to visit Bob North in Aiken. God, what a chukker!" She poured a large straight drink into Lillith's glass on the sink shelf and tossed it down. "Where's Cary?"

"He's asleep." Lillith's tone was level.

"Drunk again, huh? Give me a cigarette, Reese."

He lobbed the package and a tab of matches into her waiting hands. "Thanks."

She rolled the cigarette between her fingers, leaning back against the shelf. The movement tightened the white sheath of her gown into sculptured lines.

"Do you suppose anyone will ever want to marry me?" She asked the question of Lillith with wide-eyed innocence. "Not that I give a damn, but a girl just wonders sometimes." She flicked a thread of tobacco from her tongue with a fingernail. "Reese would have married me once. Wouldn't you have, Reese?" She turned to Lillith. "But now he hates our guts. Did you know that Reese hates us, Lil?"

"You're tight again." Reese rose from the chair and pushed it in under the table. "I'm going to bed."

"He thinks we stink." Ann-Charlotte sighed perplexedly. "Oh, to hell with it." She put her glass down, looked speculatively at the bottle and then shoved it away. "Let's all go someplace. I'm sick of Winton. Maybe we should go to Asheville, or how about Maine? We could wear dungarees, get all covered with fish smells and be hardy as the devil. What do you say?"

Lillith linked her arm through Ann-Charlotte's. They made a striking picture. The subtle, shadowed beauty of Cary Whitfield's wife and the clear, hard brilliance of Ann-Charlotte played against each other. Ann-Charlotte, Reese thought as he studied them, was like a Fourth of July sparkler the kids played with; electric, metallic brilliance that concealed a searingly hot core. It always surprised him that the two got on so well together.

"Maybe," Lillith kept her eyes on Reese, "maybe Cary might like Maine. He said something about going to the lodge in Asheville, though."

"If he's going to be potted all of the time, I don't see that it makes any difference whether it is Asheville or the Cape." There was no bitterness in Ann-Charlotte's words. She uttered them as simple facts.

"Well, let's talk about it in the morning." Lillith moved to the door and stood waiting as Reese and Ann-Charlotte filed past. She snapped the wall switch and followed them.

Reese stood in the hall before his room. At the other end Lillith opened her door gently, then turned and whispered good night to Ann-Charlotte.

"Reese?" Ann-Charlotte called to him. "Do you want to come and sleep with me?"

He could hear her laughing softly as she entered her room and then her head was suddenly thrust out.

"I may be an old bag, Reese, but I've got eight or ten million dollars, too."

The catch on her lock snapped with the sharp sound of a breaking twig. Reese closed the door behind him and began undressing slowly. The old house was silent again. He slid the windows up full and stood staring out at the night. The moon was down and the darkness was without form or substance. He turned away and crawled into bed.

In the large corner room she and Cary occupied, Lillith stood looking down at her husband. His head was twisted in an uncomfortable position on a crumpled mound of pillows, and his legs sprawled beneath the sheet like the blades of an opened pair of scissors. His breathing was heavy and irregular. Lillith reached over and touched his hot cheek with the backs of her fingers.

"What is it, darling?" The words were gentle, almost maternal. "What is this thing that rides you so?"

She sat on the edge of her own bed, bending over and watching him as a mother might lean toward a crib. Cary's dark hair, damp with perspiration, curled lightly over his beaded forehead. In sleep there was a slackness about his features. The fine cut of his chin and mouth seemed to dissolve, leaving a face of childlike, almost pitiful weakness. There was no hint of gaiety or charm and the lazy, drawling vitality Lillith had once found irresistible. She felt an impulse to gather him in her arms, cradling his head against her breast. Smiling a little at the fancy, she reached up and drew the chain on the bed lamp.

In the darkness she stretched out on her bed, not bothering to pull back the counterpane, and listened to Cary's labored breathing. She wondered, as she had many times before during the past three years, where along the lonely road Old Andrew Whitfield had stepped aside, taking away the strength that should have sustained his grandchildren.

Too much money and too little to do. The explanation was pat, coming readily to glib and envious tongues. That was only part of the story. The sap was thinning out, and what was left was not sufficient to nourish the branches. Like an old but not completely stricken oak the line had food enough only for the glistening bunches of mistletoe decorating the tree while robbing it of life.

Joseph Whitfield knew this. He told her so, bluntly and without preamble, when Cary had brought her to Winton as his bride.

"You ought to have a baby quick. There's blood in you that hasn't run to water. The Whitfields need a transfusion damn bad."

They were standing in a dark recess of the porch while music, laughter, and the excited chatter of people bent on having fun spilled around them. Inside the house the lower floors were filled with eager and friendly guests who had come to meet Cary Whitfield's wife. It was a big party even by The Hill's standards. The grounds were dotted with shimmering clusters of colored lights, and beneath them strolled the young men and women Cary and Ann-Charlotte had known at school, met during the summer months in the mountains or on West Indian cruises. Their softly accented voices, the easy, attentive assurance of the men and the studied, fragile gestures and movements of the girls brought an almost theatrical elegance to the scene. Lillith felt, somehow, that it wasn't real. Under the trees long tables had been set and they shimmered icily in their white cloths, decked with frosting buckets of champagne and a bewildering variety of food. Colored men, darkly perspiring, padded back and forth under huge silver trays of plates and glasses while an orchestra, brought down from New York, beat out its muted rhythms.

"Any minute now," Lillith couldn't resist the temptation, "I expect to see the young Confederate cavalry officer ride up and call: 'Ahm ouf to th' wahs, mah honey. Them damn Yankees are a-comin'. Jeff Davis is a-callin' foah volunteahs!'"

"You're more likely to see the flower of the South strip off its clothes an' go runnin' to the lake for a buck-naked swim. Things have changed a little." Joe Whitfield smiled down at her.

32

She linked her arm in his and they strolled the length of the porch, halting at the far end. Lillith breathed deeply of the night.

"It's true, after all, isn't it?" She spoke more to herself than to Joe. "I mean the people down here, they're nicer somehow. There is something inherently gentle about them, isn't there? Maybe it's the climate."

"The climate produces its share of sons of bitches here the same as anyplace else." Joe lit a match and applied it to his cigar. Lillith studied his face in the brief glow. Cary had made a legend of his uncle, and she sensed that her husband had never recovered from a boyhood awe of this fabulous relative.

"I'm glad you're here," Joe continued, "although I've got a feelin' that you're too smart to stay. I've always wondered what sort of a girl would marry Cary. I'm kinda surprised."

"Is that good or bad?" She looked up at him.

"Better for Cary than he had a right to expect. I've been wonderin' some whether it's goin' to be good for you. Are you plannin' to have any children, or is this one of those modern marriages with a gin bottle at one end and a pessary at the other?"

"I imagine," Lillith controlled her surprise, "that is supposed to shock me."

"No-o-o." Joe Whitfield examined the ash on the end of his cigar carefully. "I gave up tryin' to shock people after my twenty-first birthday."

"Well," she felt a quick surge of anger, "then you're being impertinent."

Joe shook his head. "It's almost impossible to be impertinent at my age. After forty a man can only be a damn fool." He ducked his head in a quick, shy grin and Lillith couldn't resist smiling back. "I think we'll get along, Mrs. Whitfield." He took her small, cool hand in his.

"I hope so, Mr. Whitfield." Lillith met the pressure of the long, hard fingers.

Cary came then, flushed and a little unsteady, and took her away to meet some more people. She looked back once and saw Joseph Whitfield leaning against the porch railing, staring down at the tomb of Old Andrew.

Lying on her bed now Lillith thought about Joe Whitfield. What sort of a marriage is this going to be? Well, what sort of a marriage was it? There had been no children. After the first year she had gone to a doctor. Following an examination, humiliating almost beyond endurance although she could never explain to herself why, the physician had shaken his head.

"There's nothing wrong with you, Mrs. Whitfield." He had hesitated for a moment. "Maybe, maybe Cary ought to come and see me."

She never told Cary of the visit. He never brought up the subject of children. It was almost as though the possibility of conception didn't exist.

A movement on Cary's bed caused her to turn her head. He muttered and pushed petulantly against the light sheet she had drawn over him. He shoved it down and away and dropped back, his arms outspread as a man in surrender. Lillith rose and turned on the electric fan at the other side of the room. The night was growing sultry.

Back in bed she waited for the fitful snatch of breeze as the fan swung in its arc, lulled into a half-sleep by its steady, hypnotic hum.

"Cary," she spoke softly and waited. There was no reply. She hadn't expected one.

Ann-Charlotte stabbed a cigarette viciously into the tray on her dressing table, indifferent to the small eruption of sparks flying up to sting her fingers. Turning impatiently from the mirror, she rose and paced the length of the room; kicking off her mules as she walked and experiencing a childish satisfaction as they slapped against the wall. As always, she had only succeeded in making herself cheaply ludicrous by attempting to probe beneath Reese's studied contempt.

No, she thought, contempt isn't the word. That has feeling behind it and would be easier to understand than this passive unconcern.

She halted before the long mirror occupying an entire panel of the wall and studied herself. Her body was slim, hard and virginal. Dropping the sheer negligee from her sloping shoulders, she turned slowly before the glass, admiring the sharp profile of her small breasts and the faintly curving line of her hips.

I'm not a slut, she argued fiercely.

Her body was a delicate instrument of pleasure and she had played upon it as such. That men's hands could tune it to a shrill pitch of ecstasy was a phenomenon she accepted without question or reservation. Men had never taken her and she had frequently sensed their bafflement and smoldering resentment when they realized that they had been the hunted and not the hunter. She smiled at her reflection, recalling a furiously puzzled man she had met one winter in Nassau.

He stood beside their bed, staring down at her.

"Christ," he muttered, "why don't you pay me twenty dollars and get rid of me?"

Without a word she had walked to the chair where her clothing was piled, opened her purse and held out a bill. He slapped her full in the face and her mocking laughter had followed him out of the room, down the hall, and, perhaps, farther than she could ever know.

Reese infuriated her at times not because she particularly wanted him as a man; although that was there, also, and she was too honest to deny it completely. Her puzzled anger was born of his attitude. It defied analysis. Sometimes, she thought, he looks at me the way a keeper in a zoo might notice the antics of an amorous monkey.

Who the hell does he think he is? No. That wouldn't do. She had tried to dismiss him before with an assumed superiority, snarling the question to herself. Somehow she had never dared voice it to him directly. The trouble was that Reese knew who he was. He walked with complete confidence and, the notion never ceased to plague her, with a purpose. Where was he going and why? Who was he taking with him?

She dropped wearily into a chaise longue, digging her crimsoned toes into the thick pile of the beige carpet where they burned like scattered drops of blood.

She was afraid of Reese. There was the truth. He frightened her because she was unable to understand him, and yet he had been a part of their lives for almost as long as she could remember. He and Cary had been about twelve and she nine when she first became conscious of him as a person. At recess time she had stood in the forefront of an envious and silently admiring group of younger children while the older boys played ball, swung briskly over each other's backs in leapfrog games, or wrestled with terrific grunts and heavings. Always there had been Reese, moving with a quiet determination, his features drawn into a serious mask. Then, sometimes, he would laugh and the sound left her tingling and she couldn't take her eyes away from him. He was poor. She wondered now how or why she should have considered that. Many of the children, most of them in fact, came from cropper families who lived miserably from planting to harvest, eternally in debt and with desperation crouching on the hearthstone. From nine o'clock in the morning until three in the afternoon, though, such distinctions were lost in a common playground and classroom. Only Reese wore his poverty as a badge, displayed it with successful defiance until, when he came to school in the winter not wearing

35

shoes, the more fortunate children scuffed unhappily in their heavy footgear and looked enviously at his brown and unfettered toes.

Ann-Charlotte used to watch in abject melancholy as Cary and Reese raced from the schoolyard with the echoes of the three-o'clock bell, envying her brother a freedom denied to her but more than anything else the mysteriously exciting pleasure of being near Reese Benton. She would wait with unabashed eagerness for Saturday because Reese usually came to The Hill. At such times the boys accepted her as a playmate and together they would roam through Old Andrew's carefully tended acres, swim from a float in the shallow water of the lake near the boathouse, and sometimes have a picnic supper on the shore with a fire of their own. Reese had seemed so effortlessly wise upon such occasions. He could build a fire quickly, a fire that would blaze instantly, instead of the smoking, smoldering things that Cary so clumsily kindled. They would hunch together just within the circle of light while the shadows darkened about them and whisper of the story that Andrew Whitfield left his crypt at midnight to walk in silence through the house. Usually, on Saturday, Reese would spend the night. If there was no picnic and Cassius and Laura weren't having guests, they all had dinner together in the big dining room. It was accepted by now that Reese had his place at the table, sitting next to Ann-Charlotte and across from Cary. For the most part the meals were silent affairs. Cassius made painful efforts to talk with the children, but his conversation was principally in the form of questions which could be answered with a simple yes or no, followed by depressing intervals of silence. Laura was flutteringly solicitous; eat your potatoes, Cary, drink your milk, Ann-Charlotte, Reese, you haven't touched your salad, don't you like it? Her concern only succeeded in embarrassing them. Somehow, though, Ann-Charlotte sensed that her father liked Reese. It even seemed to go beyond to the point of being grateful that Lance Benton's boy was a friend of his children.

Sprawled in the chair now Ann-Charlotte smiled a little wistfully. Funny, she thought, that I should remember these things after all the years. They had been at the table and her father, with the unconsciously patronizing tone adults sometimes adopt with children, turned to Reese.

"What are you going to be when you grow up, Reese?"

Reese stared thoughtfully at his plate for a moment and then said gravely:

"Just Reese, I reckon, Mr. Whitfield."

For some reason both she and Cary had thought this excruciatingly funny. They howled with laughter, doubling up over the table while Reese regarded them solemnly. For months afterward they both called him "Just Reese." In the schoolyard Cary would yell, "Throw it to me, Just Reese," or "I'll race you to the corner, Just Reese." Without quite understanding what it was all about the other children took up the name, and for the balance of the term he was Just Reese. With summer vacation the nickname was lost. Now and then, though, Cary and Ann-Charlotte would remember and use it, but only when the three of them were together and then with affection.

Dropping her head back against the cushions, Ann-Charlotte closed her eyes. So many memories crowded and jostled each other. There was that Saturday night when Reese stayed at The Hill. He and Cary slept together in the enormous double room that had once been Old Andrew's. When she was certain Cassius and Laura were no longer awake, she had crept down the corridor and into Cary's room. Hiking her trailing nightgown to her knees, she crawled in between the boys, indifferent to Cary's whispered vehemence. Once in bed she lay shivering with excitement, fearful that Cary would make her leave. When he didn't she touched her cheek against Reese's shoulder, lightly at first and then with more confidence, listening with silent gratitude while he and Cary made hushed plans of the things they would do when they were grown, conspiring to great deeds and fabulous adventures in which, obviously, she was to have no part.

Where along the way had they, the three of them, lost each other? The separation was there, a gap no longer to be bridged, although it was not apparent away from The Hill. Did Reese really hate them? Ann-Charlotte's eyes flew open.

"I believe he does," she said aloud.

She rose and went to the table for a cigarette. The notion frightened her for a moment before she could throw it off, and her hand trembled lightly as she reached for a match. Suppose he does? she thought.

She laughed nervously and dropped the unsmoked cigarette into a tray.

IV

THERE was a year when fall came early to the Piedmont, came in looping gusts of swirling rain and wind, snatched from the restless storms prowling the distant seaboard from Cape May, in New Jersey, to the West Indian cays. It came, also, in bright, crisp mornings with dustings of silvery frost on the ground and clear, metallic evenings when smoke from scattered cabins in the fields rose straight into a gun-metal sky. The land lay bare, stripped of the wealth so carefully husbanded through the summer. There was the peace of exhaustion upon it while it gathered strength as it always must.

It had been a rich year, and men looking at their bulging cribs where yellowed ears of corn were stacked knew the relief that comes with a full harvest. In the pack barns the tobacco waited; broad of leaf, firm, and silken-textured. Hogs in their pens were wallowingly fat, and when the weather turned colder, hot fires would be kindled beneath soot-blackened iron kettles in preparation for the slaughter that would transform them into heavy-linked sausage, moist and glistening hams hanging darkly in the curling gray warmth of hickory smoke, and shimmering slabs of side meat bedded down in salt.

As always, though, men wondered what the tobacco would bring, for upon its price rested their economic structure. Somewhere other men who had never knelt to press a young plant into its mound of earth or crumble soil between sensitive fingers would say: So much a pound for your labor, that and no more. The words would have the terrible finality of God's thunder from which there was no appeal. If the word was good, then accounts at stores from Winton to crossroad hamlets would be settled in full. Bolts of cloth and shapeless dresses would be lifted from shelves and hangers to be draped across eager shoulders. New shoes, on feet that had known only the touch of warm loam for months, would creak and scuff heavily on unfamiliar pavements. Money could be laid by for fertilizer, a new axe or oil stove purchased. A man would be able to lift his head, take the children into town and stand gossiping with his peers, gravely advancing opinions while the youngsters and women with fluttering gestures and rapt expressions went from store to store excitedly making small purchases. Often, though, the word was bad, and then the men could only wait in dumb silence on the warehouse floors while their crop was hammered down to less than what it cost to produce. They would stare at the heavy bundles, tossed so carelessly on the boards, and remember the long days of torture, the weeks and months of anxiety and care. They would recall the planting and the transplanting, the fierce beat of midsummer sun, the hours when they fed the flues in the curing barns, and remember the endless torment of staring into unpredictable skies. Their backs would ache again in memory of what man must do to force the earth to yield its substance. These were the things in their eyes as they silently cursed God and the distant men and shuffled away. Maybe, there would be work in the mills or factories. The older children wouldn't be able to go to school this year. Throughout the winter months gaunt-faced women would plod about their tasks in drafty cabins and the mail order catalogues would be resolutely thrust out of sight. The barren season lay at hand, and then spring and another time for planting and hope.

The price of tobacco, though, was high this year. Money jingled in the pockets of stiff new overalls. Small wads of bills, lovingly counted and recounted, were thrust into hundreds of jars, chipped vases, or tin cans and tucked out of sight on closet shelves. Merchants looked up from their ledgers and smiled, knowing that they would not have to steel themselves against shamefaced, half defiant pleas for more credit. Here and there new Fords stood in shining magnificence beneath trees in front yards, their acquisition so unexpected that the still incredulous owners hadn't thought to prepare better shelter. Women hummed softly at their work, children played shrilly at their games, and men sat comfortably on the weathered boards of their porches reveling in the luxury of not giving a damn whether it rained or hailed or grew too dry or wet.

Good crops and prices shot a new vitality across the land, and it passed quickly from the smallest patch through the heavy doors of banks and factories. It was felt in the oil-lit homes of the backwoods and on Winton's broad streets. Only on The Hill was the current unnoticed, for The Hill and what it represented was too far removed now from field and warehouse. It drew its incalculable strength from a thousand sources. If one dried up temporarily, there were freshets in the others. That which Old Andrew had built through greed, cunning, and a sheer delight in competition maintained its own calendar and wrote its own balance sheets seemingly without human effort.

The Whitfields came back from Asheville and, as always, found the homecoming charged with excitement and an anticipation difficult to explain. It was almost as though with the equinox some great change was, also, brewing in their lives. Always they felt this way and always they were just a little disappointed after the novelty of resettling themselves in the old house had worn off.

During the first week Cassius went early to the office, cherishing the wistful idea that during his absence unexpected problems had developed which he alone could cope with. There were hands to be shaken, questions to be asked or answered, families to be inquired after. Then one day he would be seated in his office, staring at a row of push buttons or riffling through unimportant mail, and he would bend a little unhappily beneath the knowledge that there was actually nothing for him to do. He could have stayed away a year or ten and it wouldn't have made the slightest difference in the smoothly efficient operation of the complex machine created by Old Andrew.

For her part Laura, also, must play at being necessary. Back from the mountains, relieved of the tedious necessity of endless dinners, parties, fetes for obscure charities, week-end guests, she tried to spend her pent-up energy on the house. Returning to Winton, she forced herself to believe that while they were away the place had fallen into a state of disreputable confusion. With Aunt Harriet, a Negress of ferocious mien who ruled the lesser servants with invective and dark prophecies of mayhem in this world and Hell's own fire in the next, Laura would make a determined inspection of the house from attic to cellar in the hope of discovering that it was in imminent danger of falling about their heads. She would poke here and there while Harriet waddled behind mumbling dire threats and witchlike mumbo jumbo against this invasion. Brought up on some trivial disorder, Harriet would regard her mistress with the open pity one might display in the presence of a maundering idiot until Laura, weary and defeated, retired to her room. To suggestions that she see to this or that, old Harriet had one answer, a reply that had served her well during her lifetime.

"Ef Ah live, Miz Laura. Hit'll git done, ef Ah live."

Old Harriet lived, although no one could imagine what her years numbered. She ran The Hill with lugubrious perfection, brooking no interference, jealous of her position and long service, and descending with terrible wrath on minor delinquencies. She spared neither the staff nor the Whitfields when she felt that her authority or prestige was menaced. Laura finally gave up, as she always did, facing with a wry smile the fact that she was a guest in her own home.

For Cary and Ann-Charlotte the homecoming was an event to be translated into a bubbling enthusiasm over everyone and everything. School had already been in session two weeks when they came back from Asheville, and this, they felt, gave their return a touch of the dramatic.

Also, by sulking, screaming petulance and fawning obsequiousness Cary had persuaded Cassius to buy him a car of his own.

"I'm seventeen years old," he had yelled hysterically when a more casual approach had failed; "what do you want to do, keep me a baby all of my life?"

"But Cary," Laura had done her best to mediate, "why do you need a car? You can use mine or your father's and Josh can drive you whenever you want to go someplace."

"I don't want your old cars. What are you going to do, bury all that stinkin' money? Part of it's mine, mine and Ann-Charlotte's. I know that. I know what Grandfather's will says. You're trying to steal it, that's what you're doing."

"You can go to your room now, Cary." Cassius, trembling visibly, made an attempt to assert himself.

"I won't go to my room and you can't make me and if you do I'll set fire to the whole place. You're stinkin' mean, that's what you are, just stinkin' mean."

Shaking with fury Cassius had made an ineffectual lunge at his son, not really knowing what he would do if he managed to collar him. Cary had fled with tearful screams. For two days he remained in his room, his eyes and cheeks burning with fever. He moaned and wept, tore sheets into strips or lay with his face turned toward the ceiling, his features cast into a waxen mold. When she could stand it no longer, Laura had called in a physician, hovering anxiously just inside the door while he examined Cary. Cassius slipped apologetically into the room. Maybe the boy really was sick. He waited apprehensively.

Muttering incoherently, Cary had turned his head on the pillow, opened his eyes and stared at his father. Suddenly a gentle smile

41

touched his lips and he made a weak gesture of reaching out his hand. Cassius walked quickly to the bed and took it.

"What is it, Son?"

"I'm sorry, Father," Cary's voice was reedlike in its delicacy.

Cassius snuffled and wiped at his eyes quickly with the back of his hand.

"That's all right, Son. Forget it and just get well."

"I'll try, Father." His eyelids fluttered and closed.

Dr. Murcherson straightened up from his position beside the bed. "What is it, Doctor?" Cassius strove to keep his tone normal.

Murcherson smiled a little grimly. "Nothing that a hell of a hiding wouldn't cure."

Cary's eyes flew open. "You're a damned old quack," he yelled. "Just a damned old quack. Don't you believe him, Father. I've been real sick, just real sick." He turned a piteous expression in the direction of his mother.

Laura was uncertain. She liked and trusted Murcherson. They had always called him when anyone needed attention at the lodge.

"Are you sure, Doctor?" She hesitated. "He, he did feel feverish to me."

Murcherson shrugged and picked up his small bag. "Self-induced," he said shortly, "or just the general cussedness coming out. Anyhow," he turned and regarded Cassius and Laura shrewdly, "I suppose you can cure it by giving him whatever it is he wants."

Later in the afternoon Cary had tottered feebly to the front porch where his father was sitting. Cassius forced himself to keep his eyes on the newspaper in his hands. In his heart he knew that Murcherson had been right, and as always he experienced a numbing inadequacy when dealing with his children or, for that matter, life itself.

"Father," Cary's voice quavered, "I want to apologize."

Cassius dropped the paper to his lap, experiencing sudden nausea. Somehow, he felt, he would have been happier if the boy had continued to yell and rant for what he wanted, humiliating as the experience had been.

"You can have the car," he said wearily. "I would probably have let you have it anyhow if you had given me time to think it over."

"But," Cary felt his way cautiously, "don't you want to talk about it?"

Cassius smiled sadly and shook out his paper.

"No," he said slowly, "I don't and I'm certain you'd never understand why."

The trouble hadn't ended there. Ann-Charlotte didn't cry.

"If Cary is going to have a car, then I want one of my own, too."
She had made the announcement at the breakfast table, speaking
as casually as though she were noting a minor deficiency in her
wardrobe.

"But you're only a child, dear." Laura shook her head, smiling with
gentle wisdom. "No other girl your age has a car."

Ann-Charlotte didn't raise her voice. "No other girl my age has as
much money as I have or will have. Anyhow, I'm almost fourteen
and twice as smart as Cary." She glared at her brother who regarded
her with smug superiority. "If he can have a car, then I can. When
may I get it?"

Cassius displayed an unexpected firmness in the face of a brewing
rebellion. He placed his napkin deliberately beside his plate and rested
the tips of his fingers on the table's edge.

"You are not going to have a car," he announced slowly. "When
you're eighteen, perhaps."

There was a little of Old Andrew and something of Joe Whitfield
in Ann-Charlotte's scornful laughter.

"When I'm eighteen, Father," her voice was unemotional, "I'll do
as I damn please. If I can't have a car now, I'll steal Cary's, and if I
can't steal Cary's, then I'll find a boy who has a car."

"Ann-Charlotte!" Laura couldn't keep the anguished bewilderment
from the cry.

Cassius rose abruptly from the table, and for a brief moment he
approached dignity as he considered his daughter. His words were
measured but implacable.

"You'll go to your room now, Ann-Charlotte."

"Certainly, Father." She slipped out of her chair and hesitated a
moment as though to gauge his temper. "It's silly, you know."

Watching her as she walked deliberately from the room, Cassius
knew she was right. That was the easy way out and accomplished
nothing. Ann-Charlotte would go to her room and eventually he would
be forced to relax the punishment and nothing would have been
achieved save, perhaps, a further sapping of authority. He looked
helplessly at Laura, who sat staring at her plate, and felt only contempt
for himself.

"I'm going for a walk," he muttered and was conscious of the veiled amusement, if it wasn't actual scorn, on Cary's face as he digested the scene and stored it away for future use.

He didn't find an answer to the problem along the laurel-shielded path or on the high ledge back of the house from where he could look out over the broad valley. In torment he wrestled with his conscience. People liked him, friends and acquaintances respected him. Or, did they? Was the attitude of his children only a reflection of what others felt? He didn't want the answer and he knew it. He tried to imagine what Old Andrew would have done under similar circumstances, but that was no good. Old Andrew would never have permitted such a situation to evolve. Why, he wondered, was one man denied authority when it flowed so easily from another?

"I love my children," he spoke aloud. "By God," he continued after a moment. "I wonder if I do. I really wonder?"

He knew that he and Laura had somehow failed the children and themselves. Youngsters, he thought, didn't grow into selfish, inconsiderate little bastards by themselves. They had to be helped along the way.

To the limit of his ability Cassius had tried to conduct himself with wisdom and simplicity. Their lives were without ostentation. Looking over his shoulder at the lodge back of the ridge, he knew that it was no larger than many of the summer places in the mountains. He and Laura entertained a great deal during the hot months, drawing friends and business acquaintances from half a dozen states, but that was part of his obligation. If he had wanted to, he could have built an estate that would have occupied the valley. He could have created an entire village of his own, laying it out with the magnificence of a motion picture set. He hadn't done that. The place was roomy and comfortable, with a swimming pool, stables, and gardens. He and Laura had been happy in their plans, feeling somehow that they had broken away from The Hill. This was their own. Old Andrew didn't haunt it.

"Damn it," he said, "do I have to live in a cave to keep my kids decent?"

Both here and in Winton he attempted to rear Cary and Ann-Charlotte in normal channels. He gave them only a little more and frequently less than other youngsters of their age had, yet they were growing up without any values of their own. At seventeen Cary was slyly conscious of the fact that he was a Whitfield. There was arrogance in his manner when he spoke to the tradespeople in the village. He no longer asked for something but demanded it as his right. He had few friends although he was constantly being invited to parties and picnics and the small entertainments other summer people gave for their children. He was asked because there was magic in the name of Whitfield. Perhaps Cary himself knew that, understood why he was invited, and he either accepted or declined with churlish scorn. Ann-Charlotte, on the other hand, had the cool friendliness of a well-bred Scottie bitch. She gave little and asked less, preserving an alert but not particularly interested attitude toward what was going on. It was, Cassius thought, almost as though she were saying: "Listen, let's not have any nonsense. I know very well who I am and so do you. If you like me and I like you, all right. If I don't like you, you'll know it, and if you don't care for me, well, to hell with you."

Recalling the scene at the breakfast table, Cassius winced. Cary would have cried, been tearfully emotional or hysterically enraged at being sent from the table to his room. Cary would have made everyone a little ashamed and anxious to pay whatever price he demanded just to avoid a scene and its inevitable aftermath. Ann-Charlotte had succeeded in making him look and feel a little foolish. She displayed the poise of an adult, an almost icy detachment. Thinking of her, Cassius realized suddenly that his daughter not only behaved as a young woman but looked like one. The transition from a gawky girl to what she was had been so smoothly effected that he hadn't realized what was happening. Her carriage, her physical development, her mental processes were those of a girl of twenty. There was something almost indecent, he felt, in such precocity.

Old Andrew, Cassius thought unhappily, or even his brother Joe would have known how to handle Cary and Ann-Charlotte. What exactly, though, he asked himself, would they have done? You can't, he argued, beat children into submission and respect for authority. Cassius Whitfield couldn't make his children live in a hovel, work in the fields or sell newspapers on the street corners of Winton just to teach them that life is real, life is earnest. Must they all be penalized simply because of Old Andrew? Where had he failed? When were the twigs so bent?

To Cassius' surprise and secretly confessed relief Ann-Charlotte made no attempt to renew her demand for a car. Seemingly she had dismissed the matter as unimportant. Laura, however, did not share her husband's complacency. She and Ann-Charlotte were driving back from a morning's shopping in Asheville.

45

"I'm glad, dear," she said gently, "that you gave up the idea of a car. It worried your father. You know he doesn't like to deny you anything. After all, you are awfully young." She reached over and patted her daughter's hand. "There'll be plenty of time for all of those things, grown-up clothes, cars and everything."

Curled up in a corner of the seat, Ann-Charlotte lifted her eyes to meet her mother's approving glance. Then she smiled as though she were coddling a special secret.

"But I haven't forgotten, Mother. I've just stopped talking about it."

When they returned to Winton a salesman delivered a blue La Salle roadster to The Hill. He was no more than out of the seat when Cary was in his place and with a screaming of tires and the shriek of second gear out of sight down the driveway. Cassius and Laura watched apprehensively from the porch.

"Oh! I do hope he will be careful." Laura strained on tiptoes to catch a sight of the flashing car.

The salesman shook his head. "That's a little too much to ask, Mrs. Whitfield, but maybe he'll be lucky."

Cary returned later and tossed an invitation to Ann-Charlotte.

"Come on, I'll take you for a ride."

To his surprise Ann-Charlotte stepped into the car, examining the upholstery and many-dialed dashboard critically.

"Don't think you're fooling me," she said later as Cary drove down Memorial Avenue, "I know why you asked me and it's not because you're nice. You're a stinker, that's why."

With elaborate nonchalance Cary dodged in and out of traffic, draping one arm out over the door and lolling back on his spine as he shot around slower vehicles and jumped traffic lights.

"I hope you get arrested," Ann-Charlotte remarked without rancor. "I hope you run over someone and kill him and then you'll go to jail for manslaughter or whatever it is."

It took three trips up and down Memorial Avenue before Cary felt that he had exhausted that thoroughfare as a medium of public display.

"Let's go out and see Reese," he suggested.

"Reese won't care." Ann-Charlotte was maddeningly casual. "Reese won't care if you have a car."

"I don't care whether Reese cares." Cary was defensively angry.

"Oh, yes you do!" Ann-Charlotte laughed with a throaty bubble.

46

"You care because you are a stinker. Maybe if you weren't a stinker you wouldn't care, but a stinker like you just couldn't help caring. That's why a stinker is a stinker." She patted her skirt out around her knees and eyed her brother with bright satisfaction.

Reese was sitting cross-legged on the narrow porch cleaning an old single-barreled shotgun. He looked up at the insistent pounding of a horn as Cary raced down the rutted road, slewing recklessly from side to side and skidding to a halt in front of the cabin.

"Hi! Reese." Cary affected a casual greeting.

Reese put the gun down, dropped a greasy rag on the stock and rose.

"Hi! Cary. How you, Ann-Charlotte?"

He walked toward them, tall and rangy, a faded pair of blue jeans his only garment. Ann-Charlotte watched him and felt something catch at her. He had grown during the summer and there were small ridges of muscles cording his arms and chest. The sun had turned his skin to satiny brown.

"Where did you get the car?" Reese put his hand on the door and looked down the length of the hood.

"It's mine," Cary didn't try to keep the jubilant pride from his voice. "The old man," he was just a little patronizing, "bought it for me."

Reese grinned. "My old man," he suggested quietly, "would kick the hell out of me if he ever heard me calling him the old man."

"Come on"—Cary felt that he was being made to sound foolish— "come on, we'll go for a ride. It goes like a bat out of hell. Eight cylinders."

Reese nodded. He trotted back to the porch, put the gun and cleaning rags inside the door, and then came back to push in alongside of Ann-Charlotte.

"You're getting to be a big girl," he said.

They drove out along the river road, all of them feeling strange and uncomfortable as though the summer had left a vacuum they didn't know how to fill.

"You look awfully old, Reese." Ann-Charlotte glanced up at him, suddenly feeling awkward and exasperatingly shy. "I don't mean old old," she added hastily, "just that you're sort of different."

"How's school?" Cary allowed the speed to drop.

" 'Bout the same. They're going to have a football team this year. Got a coach, fella from Duke." Reese chuckled. "He says he was hot stuff there. He'll have to be, teachin' these rabbits here in Winton to get the lead out of their pants. You coming back?"

"Sure." Cary nodded. "Ann-Charlotte's a freshman this year, too. What'd you do all summer?"

"Worked for your Uncle Joe." Reese dropped his head back on the seat and stared at the sky.

"What for?" Cary was openly curious.

"For money."

"Well, I'll be damned." Cary looked with undisguised astonishment at his friend. "Didn't Uncle Joe go away at all this year?"

Reese straightened up and dropped an arm casually across the seat, his fingertips touching Ann-Charlotte's shoulder.

"No," Reese blew softly at Ann-Charlotte's hair, "he said he didn't want to go to Europe until they had more time to get over the war. Said all that killing stunk up the place and he might as well stay home."

"Well," Ann-Charlotte turned her body slightly in the crook of his arm, "what did you do for him, working, I mean?"

"Not much," Reese admitted, "went fishing mostly. Now and then I drove a truck hauling manure for his flower beds. But mostly we fished and talked. You're Uncle Joe is a great man for talking."

"He never talks to me." Cary was unconvinced.

"That's because you're a stinker," Ann-Charlotte crowed triumphantly.

"You say that again and I'll—I'll slap you good!" Cary's face was crimson and he drew his mouth into a thin, hard line as he twisted viciously at the wheel, turning the car across the road. He slammed the gears into reverse and then straightened out on the way back. "I only brought you along to be nice and this is the thanks I get."

"You only brought me along to show off and to make me jealous." Ann-Charlotte giggled demurely. "That's a stinker's trick and I'll say it again."

Reese left them at the crossroad near his house. "I'll walk on down from here," he said. "Thanks for the ride, Cary. It's a beauty, all right. Coming to school tomorrow?"

"Sure, anyhow, I guess so." Cary hesitated. "We'll go someplace afterwards if you want. Just cut the fool around."

"Can I come?" Ann-Charlotte whined a mocking plea and Reese knew that she was laughing silently to herself.

"You can go to the devil."

"Ooo! What you said!"

48

Reese couldn't help grinning although he knew that it would only infuriate Cary.

"I'll see you in the morning, then?"

"Sure, I'll, I'll come down and get you if you want and drive you to school." Cary waited, almost hopefully.

Reese shook his head. "No sense in that. I'll walk. Tell your ma and pa hello for me." He started to move away.

"Reese," Ann-Charlotte regarded him pensively, "did you make enough money working for Uncle Joe to buy a car?"

"Not hardly."

"That's too bad." Ann-Charlotte was thoughtful. "Anyhow," she added, "don't worry about it. We'll get one. When·are you coming to The Hill?"

Reese kicked at the powdery, red clay dust. "I don't know," he said slowly; "now that I've been sort of a Whitfield hired hand, maybe it wouldn't be the same."

"You're talking crazy." Cary was genuinely concerned. "You know nobody would feel that way. Why, why you're my best friend."

"Sure," Reese nodded, "I guess you're right. Anyhow, I'll see you tomorrow."

He stood in the middle of the road watching the car until it disappeared in an enveloping cloud of pinkish haze and then walked slowly across a stubbled field on the way home.

V

WITH straining fingers that clawed almost desperately at the sides of the bed Cary waited in tense and unreasoning terror for the first shock of awakening to pass. It was always this way. Consciousness returned, not in gentle waves as it should, but with a crashing roar. The world exploded. The sleep holding him drained away with a swirling rush as though somewhere within his brain a hidden plug had been jerked out and the flood spilled saltily over nerves scraped raw and bloody. His heart pounded fiercely as he fought off panic, and after a moment the taut muscles relaxed. His hands fell open and dropped lifelessly. He listened then with senses abnormally acute, turning slowly on the bed to look across at Lillith. She was sleeping on her back; one arm thrown up and crooked about her head, breathing quietly.

With agonizing movements he drew his body into a sitting position and then thrust out his legs. The soft, blue night light in the bathroom was a fixed and distant star. He walked toward it with jerky, mechanical steps. Closing the door behind him, he leaned against the washbasin and after a moment reached out for the light switch. He held the little nub between his fingers for a long time before he flicked it upward and flooded the room with light. Then he stared at himself in the mirror and began cursing in a terrible monotone. The words spilled out, filthy and toneless, and Cary snarled at his reflection. It was a form of self-abasement, and he reveled in it with the unblinking zeal of a flagellant for the scourge.

In the cabinet above the bowl a large square bottle marked "Mouthwash" occupied an end of a shelf. It wasn't mouthwash and fooled no one, not even the skinny little colored maid. Lillith knew it contained whisky and Cary knew she knew it, but for some strangely perverse reason he clung to the pretense. He lifted it out now and poured a large drink. He could feel the liquor run in a hot rivulet to his stomach.

"You dirty, drunken bastard." He whispered the words at the mirror but they were without passion,

He washed then; scrubbing roughly at his face, deliberately allowing his mouth to droop slackly and almost relishing the sickening taste of soap, then he shaved. His hand was steady, the stroke of the razor sure.

Outside, the dawn was throwing up rumpled clouds of purple and he could see the movement of the early morning wind as it drifted through the damp pines. If the day would only stay this way, he thought, hanging suspended and with an expectant hush over the ridge. Standing before the window, he drew full breaths of the morning and watched two small gray squirrels as they hunted with nervous intensity through the trees. They were alert, filled with suspicion and fear as they raced from branch to branch, halting in sudden alarm for the things they could not see. Cary turned slowly from the window and to his reflection in the mirror, running a finger down a thin, white scar that curved along the line of his jawbone. It lay white and sickly-looking against the flushed skin. Whenever he drank the way he had been drinking during the past three days the mark appeared almost, he thought sometimes, as a warning. He had been drunk that night, also, and the knife that had carved the wavering gash had been meant for his throat and would have found it if Reese hadn't knocked it away.

Turning out the lights, he went back through the bedroom, walking now with stealthy assurance. It's funny, he thought, but I never seem to remember that one drink is enough and two too many. He picked up a light dressing gown from the foot of his bed. Lillith was still asleep. Sometimes, he knew, she only pretended not to hear and he could feel her eyes following him from behind their tightly drawn lids. He waited for a moment and then tiptoed out, allowing the doorknob to turn slowly in his fingers until the lock was settled without a snap.

In the kitchen two of the colored girls were hunched over a table. They had thrown protecting arms about their plates as though they momentarily expected to have them snatched away. They ate with stolid contentment, whispering to each other the way Negroes sometimes do when they are alone, although there was no need for such secrecy. At the sight of Cary they pushed back their chairs, bobbing their heads and making small, throaty sounds of embarrassment at his unexpected appearance.

"Lord, Mistuh Cary," Gracie, one of Aunt Harriet's innumerable nieces, daughters, or granddaughters, he could never keep them straight, almost choked on a piece of ham, "you scairt me."

"What the hell do you get up so early for?" Cary was genuinely puzzled.

The girls laughed softly, pleased at what they took to be a tribute to an industry they never felt, and then waited expectantly. White people were always saying funny things.

Cary looked about the room. The coffee smelled good. "Get me some coffee, Gracie."

"Want I should fix you some aigs an' toas', Mistuh Cary?"

"No, just bring me out some coffee." The drink was wearing off, leaving him irritable and jumpy.

He walked aimlessly through the silent lower floor, pausing for a moment at the heavily carved sideboard in the dining room. He knew that if he opened one of the doors he would find a temporary anodyne in the bourbon there, and wondered, as he moved away, why he should fight against it. Gracie brought coffee to him and he drank it black, propped up in a corner of a narrow seat curving around one of the bay windows. The sun was just touching the sloping lawn, lighting the dew-heavy grass and flashing across one corner of Old Andrew's tomb.

It was difficult to imagine what Old Andrew could look like in there after all these years, probably nothing but bones and with the silly grin skulls always seemed to wear. Cary smiled as he remembered how he, Ann-Charlotte, and Reese used to skulk around the mausoleum, pressing their ears to the cold granite, listening for they knew not what, and how Ann-Charlotte, one night, had crept to the bronze doors while he and Reese stood in fearful anticipation on the porch. With trembling defiance Ann-Charlotte pounded her small fist against the metal and called in a quavering, piping note:

"Come out, come out wherever you are!"

Shrieking with laughter she had scuttled back to join them and they waited for Old Andrew to split the tomb and emerge in wrath and thunder.

He reached over and poured more coffee from the slender pot on a tray beside the seat. The cup's edge rattled against his teeth as he tried to drink and he was finally forced to hold it in both hands to keep it steady.

Suddenly he felt old and lonely and a little abused that he was sitting alone. He put the cup on the window ledge and lit a cigarette. It burned with the taste of damp straw. Upstairs Reese, Lillith, and Ann-Charlotte were asleep and it was damn funny that they couldn't get up in the morning to have breakfast with him. He could have awakened Lillith and she would have come downstairs willingly, but Ann-Charlotte and Reese would only have grunted sleepily and told him to go to hell.

He lifted his fingers to his chin, tracing the thin welt. Reese always told him to go to hell. He had shouted it the night Duke Reid had made that scar and repeated it the following day.

It was a Saturday night and he had been cruising up and down Memorial Avenue in the La Salle looking for a girl, any girl. They walked in pairs, bright-eyed and eager in their fresh and ruffled cotton dresses, drawn tightly around full breasts and hips. He knew that they turned to watch the passage of his car and said: "That's Cary Whitfield." Then they would giggle, duck their heads together, and whisper. What they said to each other he could only guess, but he thought he knew. He had to be careful with the local girls who worked in the factories or mill. They were to be met secretly on dark corners where no one would see them get into the car. There were others, though, girls whose families had migrated from the north and who didn't give a damn. They came from the gutters of New York, Pittsburgh, and Chicago in a scattering of Poles, Italians, and Jews and huddled together in a section of Winton, clinging to the common bond of their outland origin. They found work in the cigarette factories but rarely in the fields, for they had been too long away from the soil to find comfort in it. They were products of the streets and pavements, looking with awe upon open stretches of the country. Winton, with tolerant indifference, referred to them generically as "factory," according them a niche in the social scale just above the Negro. Privately, most of the county was of the opinion that the order ought to be reversed, but after all these foreigners did have light skins, so what the hell could anyone do about it?

Cary had made one or two excursions with girls from the mills, but they had been uncomfortable experiences. Their curious accents fell harshly upon his ears, but what actually disconcerted him was their brassy indifference to the amenities of furtive assignation. When he tried to skirt the town, avoiding the principal and brightly lighted streets, they complained.

"What the hell's the matter, Joe? Are you ashamed to be seen with me? For Christ's sake, if that's the way you feel, let me out. Who do you think you are?"

How, without making them sore, could he explain that Cary

Whitfield couldn't sit with them in the car in front of Tanner's drugstore, waiting for curb service, or go out to one of the speakeasies on Yadkin Road? The little tarts ought to understand without having to be told. They ought to be satisfied to ride around in a new blue La Salle and not make any fuss when it was time to pull off the road and into the bushes.

He watched a couple of the girls as he waited for a traffic light. They walked slowly, turning to look at him and then waited for him to call or blow the horn. Instead he drove away, pulling up in front of the Rexall store to get cigarettes. Two girls that way were no good. They just kidded and talked about it but never did anything when they were together.

Reese was standing at the soda fountain drinking a coke and talking with Les Odum about baseball.

He waved a hand as Cary walked to the counter and whistled in appreciation of his spotless white flannels.

"What're you doin', just sportin' around?"

Cary came back, shaking out a cigarette. He smoked openly despite the fact that the high school principal had offered a halfhearted objection and suggested to Cassius that Cary was setting a bad example for the other boys.

"Come on," he said to Reese, "we'll ride around some."

They walked out to the car together, not entirely unappreciative of the fact that two or three men were staring at the La Salle with speculative envy. The sidewalks were crowded with Saturday night shoppers. Loosely jointed men in overalls loitered along, followed by their wives and children. They stopped to look in the store windows, the youngsters pressing their noses flat against the glass, and then moved on, silently happy. Negro women, in pairs, carrying heavy marketing bags, hurried along, keeping well over to the right and out of the traffic. The Winton people sat around small tables in the drugstores, eating sundaes, stood on the corners in gossiping knots, or debated the problem of a movie.

Reese and Cary sat in the car idly watching the constantly shifting picture.

"I'll swear," Reese wrinkled his brow, "but you could put a man down anywhere and he'd know that it was Saturday night just by the way people walk and talk. They sound different."

"Maybe its because they had a bath. What are you doin' up town?" Cary leaned comfortably back in the seat.

"Pa went over to Hendersonville so I just got tired of hangin' around the house. I was thinkin' some about a date, but it was too much trouble."

"There a lot of factory pigs out on the street tonight. We could pick up a couple." Cary tossed the suggestion off with airy worldliness, but Reese only laughed.

"You'll get all burned up with that stuff," he said. "I've heard those Hunky girls even sleep with their brothers and fathers."

A bright yellow convertible roadster with the top up slid past and dissolved into the traffic. Reese followed it with his eyes and then turned a puzzled glance toward Cary.

"If I didn't know better," he said, "I'd swear that was Ann-Charlotte in Duke Reid's car."

"You're crazy." Cary snapped a cigarette butt into the street. "What would she be doing in Duke's car?"

"I guess you're right." Reese hesitated. "What would she be doing out with a fella as old as Duke Reid?" He waited a moment. "Is she home?"

"I guess so. What's the matter with you, anyhow?"

"Nothing." Reese settled back. "I just would have sworn it was Ann-Charlotte, but she's only a kid so I guess it's crazy and anyhow she wouldn't know Duke Reid, would she?"

Cary bent forward, flipped on the ignition. "Let's ride around some."

They drove without purpose, loafing through the cross streets, around the monument circle and down past the business section.

"We could go out to Porter's place on Yadkin and drink some beer," Cary suggested.

"If you really want to drink we can get some of pa's corn at home. That beer of Porter's just gives you a gut ache."

"Let's go out anyhow. Maybe we can pick up something."

Vance Porter's speakeasy was one of half a dozen places scattered out along Yadkin Road on Winton's outskirts. It was part cottage, part barbecue drive-in, and an easy place for a quick bed if Vance knew you well enough. The back room, with a separate entrance on the side of the frame building, was airless and heavily curtained, lined with shallow booths dimly lighted by small bulbs in sleazy crepe shades. Vance sold a yeasty and powerful home brew for forty cents a bottle and good white corn for seventy-five cents a drink.

Ordinarily Vance didn't care who his customers were or what they did if they were quiet. He knew most of them, called them by their first names, and now and then sat down and bought a round of drinks on the house. The place was strictly a local institution and Vance didn't have much trouble, maybe a drunken argument once in a while and now and then a threat of a raid, but he paid off and kept his mouth shut. Tonight, though, he was sore. He stood with Duke Reid while Duke fed quarters into a slot machine.

"You're crazy, Duke, to be with that kid from The Hill. If the old man ever found out, he'd have you sent so far away that it would take ten years for a telegram to reach you."

Duke pulled the machine's handle, watching indifferently as the bands whirled and the combination dropped into place with sharp clicks.

"You gonna let me have a room," he repeated quietly, "or keep stallin'?"

"I ain't got a room, Duke, honest."

"Then get one." Duke dropped another coin in the machine.

"What do you want to make a fool of yourself for, Duke?" Vance was almost pleading. "That Whitfield kid ain't much more than fourteen or fifteen years old."

"If they're old enough to want to they're old enough to do it." Reid allowed the handle to fly back with a crash and regarded Vance coldly.

"I ain't got a room." Porter shifted uneasily.

"You wouldn't like to have this place of yours catch on fire some night, would you?" Duke asked the question with lazy insolence, and Vance flushed.

"You can't threaten me like that." Porter tried to make himself sound convincing.

"The hell I can't." Duke grinned pleasantly. "The hell I can't." He turned away from the machine. "Send us over another drink and then get me that room if you have to throw somebody else out. I can't keep that little fireball on ice much longer." He turned and walked away.

Ann-Charlotte watched him as he came toward their booth. She had finished two drinks of corn in tall glasses with ice and coca-cola and the liquor had left her with a warm, pleasantly detached feeling. This was the third time she had slipped away to meet Duke. Tonight she was supposed to be at the movies, but Duke had been waiting at the corner of Carter Street, the long yellow car pulled in close beneath a tree and away from the lights. He was as slickly handsome as black patent leather, and when she stepped into the low seat he had taken her and kissed her, his hands traveling with gentle persistency over her body. That was why she liked Duke. He was probably no good; a bootlegger and, maybe, a gangster, as people said, but he treated her as though she were a woman. He didn't fumble and paw or kiss her with a hard, tightly pursed mouth. She shivered and felt a strange constriction in her throat, finding it difficult to breathe.

"Miss me, baby?" He slid in beside her, his hand dropping over her knees and pulling them beneath his own until they were tightly locked.

"No," Ann-Charlotte leaned against him, "I didn't miss you. I knew you'd come back."

Duke turned halfway around and regarded her with an oddly puzzled expression. "You're really somethin', aren't you?" He couldn't understand this kid. She acted sometimes as though she could spit in his face, but when he touched her she was all over him, not like a kid either. "You aren't afraid, are you?" There was something close to wonder in his voice.

"No, aren't you?"

Duke really laughed then. His hand dropped away and he leaned against the back of the seat, shaking. Ann-Charlotte picked up her glass and swirled the remaining ice around in the bottom.

"Listen, baby"—Duke still thought it was funny but he stopped laughing—"what have I got to worry about? If you get caught with me, nothin' is gonna happen. Your old man wouldn't have any trouble. He might even try and make me marry you, but that wouldn't be too hard to take. I'd like sittin' on The Hill and some of that Whitfield dough." He linked his arm in hers and pulled her close.

"Marry me?" Ann-Charlotte put the glass on the table and pulled away. "Marry me?" She was incredulous and then she laughed and Duke found the sound unpleasant. "Why," Ann-Charlotte looked at him as though he was something in a zoo, "why you couldn't marry me if, if I had a three-headed baby."

Duke felt anger boil within him, but surprise held him quiet. She really meant it. No one had ever said anything like that to him before.

"Well, I'll be a bastard," he said, and there was baffled amazement in his voice. "Well, I'll just be a bastard."

"That's what I had in mind." Ann-Charlotte gathered her small purse from the table. "I want to go now." She made the statement a command.

"Why, you little bitch." Duke was deadly furious. "Do you think I'm gonna let you run out on me like this? I'm not good enough for you. Why, if it wasn't for all that Whitfield dough, you'd be a Saturday night tramp on Dexter Street."

Ann-Charlotte half rose. Her expression was quietly contemptuous. "We don't have to argue, Duke. What I said doesn't have anything to do with," she groped for a word, "well, with, you know what I mean." Suddenly she felt a little helpless, not frightened but inexperienced.

"The hell it doesn't." Duke pushed her roughly back in the seat. "I'm good enough to lay you, maybe, but that's all; like a man whore. That's what you said."

Hands grabbed roughly at Duke's coat and before he could balance himself against the unexpected assault he was swung halfway around in the seat and he looked up into the strange and hysterically violent face of Cary Whitfield.

"What are you doing here with my sister?" Cary almost screamed the question and heads popped up along the line of booths while curious eyes turned questioningly toward him.

With a slashing movement Duke struck Cary's hands away.

"Get out of here, kid. Beat it before you get hurt. Nobody's bothering your sister. Ask her. Go ahead, ask her."

"Cary." There was no alarm or excitement in Ann-Charlotte's exclamation. "Cary, don't make trouble. I'll go."

"You'll go when I'm ready to take you." Duke spoke over his shoulder, keeping one eye on Cary.

Vance came pushing through the gathering crowd, elbowing Reese who stood silently behind Cary.

"God damn it, Duke," he said. "I told you there wasn't nothin' but trouble comin' out of this." He turned to Cary. "Everything is goin' to be all right, Cary. Just don't make a fuss. I don't want any trouble here."

"Let me out, Duke." Ann-Charlotte pushed against him. "I'm coming, Cary."

Duke took her wrist in one hand. "I'll take you home like I said I would. You're not playing with kids in a sandbox."

Cary's scream was on a high note of frenzy. "Take your dirty hands off of her. Do you hear me? I said let go of her, you filthy pimp."

Duke swung the back of his hand full across Cary's livid face and with an insane cry Cary threw himself at the man, clawing strips of skin from his cheeks. Vance leaped in to pull the maddened boy away, and as he did Cary snatched up a coca-cola bottle and swung wildly. The bottle caught Duke a glancing blow on the side of the head, staggering him, and then as Vance dragged Cary back Duke hunched his shoulders and came out of the booth with the crazed snarl of an animal. A long-bladed clasp knife snicked open in his hand.

"I'm gonna cut you to pieces for that, you crazy son of a bitch."

Women in the booths screamed and there was a crash of overturning chairs as they fought their way out in panic, stampeding in unreasoning terror, clinging to the men with them, and yelling in shrill, fluting bursts of hysteria. The knife in Duke's hand snaked out. He was past caring now what he did, seeing only the wild-eyed boy struggling in Vance's arms. As he lunged toward Cary, Reese ducked beneath his arm and hit him solidly with both fists. Duke crashed against the table, falling half across it and scattering the glasses. The knife went spinning out of his hand. Reese snatched at Ann-Charlotte's arm, dragging her out and almost hurling her to one side. Cary was sobbing, half blinded by tears. There was a long narrow gash curving around his chin and the blood streamed over his collar.

Reese pushed Ann-Charlotte toward the front of the room.

"He ain't cut bad." Vance swung Cary about. "Just a nick on the chin."

"Get out of here, you and Ann-Charlotte." Reese whirled Cary away from Porter.

"I goin' to kill him. Let me kill him!" Cary cried frantically.

"Get out of here and go to hell for all I care." Reese spun him about and then at a shout of warning dropped flat on the floor.

Duke, missing his leap, sprawled across Reese's body, knocking the wind out of him. Reese gasped and felt himself choking, then as he twisted away he saw a flying chair catch Vance Porter on the side of the head. In a furious haze he glimpsed Cary and Ann-Charlotte run from the side door and then it seemed as though the entire room boiled over. Men, taking sides, not knowing why, slugged and cursed. Bottles, flung wildly, seemed to float lazily through the air and disappear with a crash as they smashed into windows. A stoop-shouldered man in bleached overalls bent over Duke and caught his shoulders in tough, work-hardened hands. He lifted Reid, seemingly without effort, and freeing one hand smashed a brutally deliberate fist into his face. Reese pulled himself to his knees, and as he did he saw two policemen crash through the door, guns in their hands.

Ordinarily, Joe Tatum and his partner Ralph Moody, who patrolled the Yadkin section in a squad car, wouldn't have stopped for a minor brawl. Those things usually settled themselves, or Vance Porter could be depended on to halt them before they got bad. What they heard from the outside, though, sounded like a full riot, and they had rushed into it not knowing what to expect. Their appearance brought a sudden quiet to the room. Several couples tried to duck back into their booths. Others looked uneasily around or sought to pretend that they were victims of unhappy circumstances.

"What the hell is goin' on here?" Tatum put his gun away and walked the length of the room to where Vance stood.

"Nothin', Joe. Just a little trouble." Porter shuffled groggily. He didn't want any trouble, particularly trouble that included The Hill's kids. "It's all right now," he suggested lamely.

"You're God damn right it's all right now." Tatum walked over and looked down at Duke. "Jesus," he murmured, "who hit him?" He glanced around the room. "All right," he shouted, anger and impatience in his voice, "who started all of this? What the hell is goin' on? Who jumped who? By God, I'll run you all in if somebody don't say somethin'."

An excited ripple of voices followed this announcement as several persons tried to talk at once. Reese straightened up, looked around the room and then faced Tatum.

"Guess I started it," he said. "Duke and I got into sort of an argument, that's all."

The patrolman stared at him. "I suppose you hit him, too?"

"That's right." Reese waited.

On the floor Duke groaned and pulled himself up into a sitting position. He looked about dazedly, his eyes traveling from Tatum and Reese to Vance. Tatum walked over and pulled him to his feet.

"What happened, Duke?"

"I said I hit him." Reese's words were sharp.

"I know what you said." Tatum steadied Duke. "I'm askin' Duke here."

"We got into an argument and I hit him. That's all there was to it. It was just a fight." Reese hurried the statement.

"God damn it, kid!" Tatum was getting mad. "I know what you said, but you ain't big enough to hit that hard, and if you did do it I want to know why."

60

"He's right, Joe." Duke spoke with difficulty. His mouth was swelling rapidly. "It was just a fight."

Tatum dropped Reid's arm and allowed his eyes to travel around the room. They met only blank stares.

"All right," he said, disgustedly, "if that's the way you want it." He turned to Reid. "You want to make a charge, Duke?"

"No, to hell with it. Get me a drink, Vance."

Tension in the room dissolved in a soft, shuffling sound as people moved back to their tables. Tatum looked at Reese.

"How old are you, kid?"

"Eighteen."

"Who did you come here with?"

"By myself." Reese waited.

"You're a God-damned liar." Tatum watched him carefully.

Reese managed a quick grin. "That's right," he said cheerfully.

Tatum sighed wearily. "O.K. If that's the way it's goin' to be. Come on, Ralph. You too, kid. You better get out of here. Got a car?"

"No."

"All right. We'll drop you off someplace up town." He shook his head wonderingly. "Christ, but we certainly hand out the service."

Cary came down to the Benton place early the next morning, appearing oddly lopsided with a bandage on one side of his face.

"They took three stitches in it," he explained with pride.

"What did you tell your folks?" Reese stood by the car door, one foot on the runningboard.

"I said I slipped and smacked my jaw on the curb. My mother fainted, right out cold." He assumed a cocky air. "I was a sure-enough mess, blood all over the car and Ann-Charlotte."

Reese stared in amazement. Didn't the fool know what almost happened to him, that he just missed having his throat cut? Cary was talking as though he had scratched his hand on a pin and that Ann-Charlotte being out with Duke Reid was something to laugh about today. Maybe, though—and the idea sent a quick surge of anger through him—Cary just took it for granted that the world was filled with Reese Bentons to keep him out of trouble.

"You're crazy," he said finally, "just as crazy as a cooter. If I was your pa, I'd flail the hell out of you." He turned his back on the car and walked slowly through the sandy yard to the house.

"Hey!" There was astonishment in Cary's voice. "Where you going? Don't you want to go for a ride?"

Reese turned. "No, I sure enough don't want to go for a ride and for all of me you can go to hell."

He mounted the steps and disappeared into the cottage. Cary sat in the car, a hurt and bewildered expression on his face. That was a funny way for Reese to act.

VI

CARY replaced his cup on the window sill. The coffee had become as bitter as the memory he was forcing himself to swallow with it.

What the three of them had lost that night at Vance Porter's seemed so unimportant at the time that they hadn't bothered to look for it. So, a little of their pride in each other, respect and an easy friendliness, was gone. Ann-Charlotte tossed her share away with scornful defiance. Reese grew older and wiser, taking a place where he could stand alone and apart and watching Cary and his sister with an almost impersonal curiosity.

Ann-Charlotte never learned that Cassius was told of the incident. Vance Porter went to him in fear and from purely selfish motives, telling only what had happened and leaving Cassius to measure the implications. When he finished, he stared apprehensively at the graying face of the man and then ducked hurriedly out of the office.

Reese and his father had eaten an early supper. Their few dishes were washed and drying in a rack and they sat on the porch in the still cool of late afternoon when Cassius Whitfield drove up. There was heaviness on the man's features and in his walk as he left the car and came toward them. Lance Benton didn't move. Pipe in hand, he leaned against a slim upright, his long legs stretched out over the steps. Reese hunched himself over his knees and waited.

"Hello, Lance. Hello, Reese." Cassius' voice was without life or color. He hesitated at the edge of the porch.

"How you, Mr. Whitfield." Lance swung his legs around. "Come an' sit." He displayed no surprise at the visit.

"Hello, Mr. Whitfield." Reese felt sudden pity for the man standing so humbly before them. "Want a chair?"

"No thanks, Reese." Cassius settled himself on the bottom step. The hat brim he was holding slid between his fingers, and he looked, not at Lance Benton nor at Reese, but across the fields as though seeking some distant strength. When he spoke again his words were spaced, deliberate, and thoughtful.

"I suppose," he said to Lance, "Reese told you what happened at Vance Porter's the other night?"

Reese didn't turn toward his father, but he heard the soft slap of cob against skin as the man knocked out the pipe in his broad palm.

"No," Lance was grave, "Reese don't usually tell me things unless he thinks I got some business knowin'. I trust him an' we get along pretty well with that arrangement."

Reese turned a face filled with shining gratitude and pride toward his father, but Lance wasn't looking at him.

"My children got into trouble there." Cassius forced the statement, and Reese noticed how his hands trembled.

"That's a good place for it." Lance examined the blackened bowl of his pipe and scratched with a fingernail at the flaking cake.

"Reese helped them get out, I understand." Cassius tried to keep his voice normal. "There was a fight of some kind." He turned, looking up, and his eyes were haunted. "What am I going to do, Reese? What am I going to do? You know Cary and Ann-Charlotte better, better than I do. You're their friend. I—I never have been."

Reese flushed. It embarrassed him to have a grown man, especially a man like Mr. Whitfield, talk to him this way. Tears stung his eyes and he blinked rapidly to hide them. There were tears in Cassius Whitfield's eyes, also, and the sight of them made him more uncomfortable. He twisted awkwardly, wishing his father would say something.

"It wasn't real bad, I guess, Mr. Whitfield." Somehow he managed the words. "Cary, Cary was just trying to take care of Ann-Charlotte."

"But why," the words were wrung from Cassius Whitfield by some inner torture, "why should he have to take care of Ann-Charlotte in a place like Vance Porter's? Why was she there and with, with a man, a man like Duke Reid? What in God's name was she doing there, Reese? She's only a child."

Cassius Whitfield wanted to believe that. On the rack he clung to this hope, and he stared pleadingly at Reese for confirmation.

"I reckon Ann-Charlotte is about the only person who could answer such a question, Mr. Whitfield." Lance cuddled the pipe bowl in both hands, staring out over his visitor's head. Reese knew then that his father had known all along of the trouble at Porter's.

"But she wouldn't tell me, don't you understand, Lance?" Cassius was pitifully defeated. "She doesn't know that I know. I didn't say anything to Cary either. I only have to guess. For God's sake, don't you understand what I'm thinking?"

"I reckon I can guess, Mr. Whitfield." Lance turned the pipe over in his fingers, peering down at it as though he was seeing it for the first time. "It ain't pretty, neither." He hesitated. "Why don't you shoot the son of a bitch?"

Cassius crushed the hat in his hands until the knuckles whitened. "I thought of that," he said hollowly, "but it wouldn't do any good. Don't you see," his voice cracked, "I've, I've got to know what is inside of Ann-Charlotte, what she thinks. Killing a man wouldn't tell me, would it?"

With arms wrapped tightly around his knees and his head bent toward the ground Reese heard the man's desperate question and its echo within himself. He knew what Ann-Charlotte's father was thinking; what he had to think because he, also, had been harried and tormented by the same thought. What other reason would a man as old as Duke Reid have for taking her out? She must have done it, otherwise she couldn't have been so sure of herself that night as she stood at the table while Cary went for Duke. She knew she could handle Duke, or, at least, she thought she could. That was the reason she hadn't been scared. Do you suppose he just took her in the car the way the girls from the factory went at it? The idea made him cringe.

"Well," the sound of his father's voice interrupted his thoughts, "I'd sure God do somethin'."

There was a long moment of silence. Reese watched the streaming progress of an army of ants as it wove rapidly between its hill and the half-consumed shell of a beetle near the steps. As the little creatures passed each other they seemed to pause and duck in greeting, or, maybe, they just touched each other to see that everything was all right. That was what Mr. Whitfield was trying to do, he thought, just trying to touch something or someone.

"Duke Reid is getting out of town and Vance Porter's place is closed." There was a harsh edge on Cassius Whitfield's voice, but then it disappeared and something of the old, soft futility took its place. "That was all I could do. There couldn't be a scandal that Ann-Charlotte would have to live with for the rest of her life. You can see how it is, can't you, Lance?"

Reese wondered then why Cassius had come to see them. He stiffened a little. Maybe he was going to ask if he and Ann-Charlotte—

65

No, a man, not even a man as upset as he was would want to hear anything like that right out.

"Yep, I guess, maybe, it wouldn't do to make a thing like that public." There was an almost regretful note in Lance Benton's voice.

Reese tried to concentrate on the struggling ants beneath his eyes. He wished that Mr. Whitfield would go home. All of this talk about something that had happened and was over. It made him a little sick at his stomach. God damn Cary, anyhow. He ought to have taken better care of Ann-Charlotte. Even as he said the words to himself, Reese knew it wasn't really Cary's fault. Ann-Charlotte did things her own way. Jesus, though, she didn't have to act like a little mongrel bitch in heat. Thinking back now, he could remember so much; the way Ann-Charlotte sometimes looked at him, from beneath eyes drawn into slits. How she curled against him in Cary's car although there was plenty of room in the seat, the times when they all had been swimming in the lake and Ann-Charlotte had dragged herself over him on the float when she could just as easily have come out of the water on the other side. She used to do those things when she was little more than a baby and he never thought much about them, but she wasn't a baby any longer. He was startled by the thought that, maybe, Ann-Charlotte would have done the same things with any other boy. Reese felt a hot, hard lump form within his chest. He didn't want to believe that. He, Cary, and Ann-Charlotte had kept something special between them. They used to sit in the big mulberry tree down by the lake and talk of what they would do when they were grown. Ann-Charlotte would listen and then turn solemnly, her lips smeared with purple juice from the fruit.

"You'll take me with you, Just Reese, won't you?"

He and Cary would laugh until tears sprang into Ann-Charlotte's eyes. Their schemes had no place for a girl, but Ann-Charlotte was resolute.

"You'll see, Just Reese. You'll take me with you."

Ann-Charlotte, he realized now, was smarter than either he or Cary realized. Little by little she insinuated herself between them, never taking too much for granted but never letting go of what she had. The time came when they walked as three with Ann-Charlotte skipping along in the middle. If they went swimming or fishing on the lake, daylight camping in the woods behind The Hill, or just walking and buying nickel candy in Winton, Ann-Charlotte was along. Reese used to watch her, feeling immensely proud and tender. It was almost as though she was his sister and yet better, somehow, that she wasn't.

"I wanted to come down here today and thank Reese."

Cassius spoke diffidently and the words jolted Reese. He lifted his head and looked at the man.

"I'm glad that you are a friend of Cary's and Ann-Charlotte's, too, Reese, and I wish you'd come up to The Hill oftener. They, we," he hesitated, groping for what he wanted to say, "we all like you and I think, maybe, you are good for us to have around. Cary's going to college next year, we, Mrs. Whitfield and I, we thought, maybe, you ..." Cassius halted miserably. "I wanted to talk to your father, some other time will do."

Reese was trembling, possessed by a sudden and unreasoning anger. He rose to his feet, steadying his back against the porch post. He could feel the tears in his eyes and didn't care. All he could think of was how Ann-Charlotte had looked as she stood beside Duke Reid in Vance Porter's.

"I hate every one of you," he choked on the words. "I hate the whole God damn lot of the Whitfields except, except Uncle Joe Whitfield." He realized as he spoke how foolish he sounded, but he wouldn't stop. "I don't care if I never see any of you again."

He whirled away and darted inside the house to throw himself face down on the narrow cot, burying his sobs in an old patchwork quilt.

For several moments Cassius Whitfield sat in silent anguish on the steps. He didn't dare look at Lance Benton. Finally he rose.

"I'll be getting along now, Lance," he said.

Lance Benton straightened up and together the two men walked out to the car.

"Tell Reese I'm sorry." Cassius opened the door and stepped heavily inside.

"I reckon he didn't mean what he said, Mr. Whitfield. A boy like Reese would be some cut up about what happened. He," Lance paused, "he's always been sort of proud of Cary an' Ann-Charlotte, an' I guess a boy takes things harder most of the time than older folks think."

"I'd like to come down and talk to you about Reese if you'll let me." Cassius bent over the ignition key almost as though he didn't dare face Lance Benton. "I mean," he added slowly, "about his future and what you'd like to do for him."

Lance waited until the engine was started. His hands rested on the door. When Cassius straightened up their eyes met.

"Reese," Lance spoke simply, "would have to be mighty sure why folks, folks like the Whitfields were takin' an interest in him. He never was a boy for just takin' a ride to be company. He'd have to know where he was goin' an' why, Mr. Whitfield, an' even then maybe he wouldn't want to go. God knows I'd like it for him, but he'd have to decide for himself."

Cassius nodded. "We can talk about it, Lance." He put out his hand. "In the meantime, maybe, you'd tell him again that we miss him on The Hill."

A light step in the hall caused Cary to turn from the window. Lillith stood in the doorway. A disreputable old bathrobe hung limply from her small shoulders and dragged about her ankles. She held a tall glass of orange juice in both hands with the air of bearing a devotional offering. Despite the moodiness clinging to him Cary laughed, and Lillith smiled with surprised pleasure.

"In the name of God," he said, "why do you wear that tattered piece of sackcloth?"

"Because it smells like you." She walked over, curling up in a chair, sipping from the glass with the serious concentration of a child who has been told to eat its breakfast.

"It ought to," Cary replied, "I've had it long enough. I don't know why it's never been thrown out."

"I hide it," Lillith explained simply. She put the glass down. "Come for a swim with me?"

He shook his head and reached for a cigarette. "It's too much trouble."

"You can stand on the dock and I'll push you off." She tossed the words lightly, but her eyes were somber. "Please, Cary."

"You know I don't like to be rugged in the morning." He experienced a wave of irritation. If people would only let him alone.

"What do you like to do in the morning, Cary?" She bent her head, pretending a minute examination of a frayed tassle on the dressing-gown cord.

"One of the things I don't like," he answered sharply, "is to be argued with." Even as he spoke he knew that he was being unnecessarily unpleasant and wondered why.

Lillith raised her eyes, studying him thoughtfully. "I wasn't arguing, Cary."

"I'm sorry, Lil." The regret was sincere.

He rose and went to her chair, standing beside it and looking down

68

at the top of her head, bent as though under the weight of a rebuke. After a moment he touched his fingers to the nape of her neck and she turned her head lazily under their pressure.

"We always seem to get off to a bad start in the mornings, don't we?" She leaned back in the chair in an effort to look at him.

"Maybe you shouldn't get up until noon." He scratched gently at the short hairs. "My disposition improves after eleven o'clock."

She sighed contentedly. "Sort of a case of the early bird getting the wormwood, isn't it?" With a startled yelp she leaped from her seat and stood, clasping a hand over her mouth. "My God, but that was terrible, wasn't it? Please come swimming with me. It'll be a baptism. I need to be saved."

"No. You go ahead. I'll have breakfast with you when you come back." He dropped into the chair, stretching his legs comfortably before him.

Lillith waited for a moment and then nodded. "No drinking, Cary, please?" She spoke almost fearfully.

His mouth twisted with a savage snarl. "For God's sake don't nag at me. I'll drink all I want whenever I want it. I'll bathe in it and put it in my hair for tonic. Stop trying to take care of me, will you."

"I'm not trying to take care of you. I want you to do that." She was angry now. "I'm sick and tired of seeing you dull-eyed, half alive. I want what I married. What's wrong, Cary?"

He sat, hands clasped beneath his chin, staring at the carpet, his lips compressed and unrelenting. After a few seconds she turned and hurried from the room.

Outside, the morning enveloped her with the bright freshness of an icy shower. The Hill sparkled as though it had been recently scrubbed and laid out to dry. Halfway down the path to the lake she turned and looked back at the house. Cary, she knew, would be sitting as she had left him, silently furious, steeping himself in the bitter tea of self-pity.

"I'm just a damn fool," she said aloud, kicking at the graveled walk and sending a shower of pebbles into the grass on either side.

One of the yard boys was working on the low hedge around the boathouse. He straightened up at her approach, pulling at a ragged straw hat.

"Morning, Josh." The sound of her voice almost startled her. It seemed unnecessarily loud.

"Mornin', Miz Whitfield."

As she walked out on the dock she knew that the boy's eyes followed, and she giggled to herself thinking of the picture she must make, swathed in a faded robe several sizes too large for her, flapping along like a sprightly scarecrow on the loose. Josh's sense of the proprieties was being outraged. This was no way for the gentry to appear. She dropped the robe from her shoulders, allowing it to fall in a resigned heap on the dock. For a moment she stood, slender, deeply tanned and vibrant, and then with an easy spring arched over and into the water.

She swam furiously toward the float, beating out the sharp chill of the water, feeling her body begin to glow. This was the time of day she liked best, only it was always better when she could get Cary to come along. She was sorry now that she had left him alone there in the house. A little more tact, a measure of patience and Cary could have been laughed out of himself. They could at least have started the day right. Now it would take most of the afternoon and several drinks to maneuver him into a good humor.

Dragging herself to the float, she stretched out on her back, breathing with full-chested regularity from the exertion of the churning swim. The sun carried only a breath of warmth as yet, but she lifted her face toward it gratefully. Under its soothing touch she could feel the tension gripping her relax. The stately wooden pile on The Hill seemed peacefully distant.

A little more tact, a little more patience, she thought. God in Heaven, must I eternally have to reassure and soothe, chasing ghosts for Cary?

"I get so damn tired." She spoke the words aloud and her lips moved almost prayerfully over them.

Opening her eyes she squinted against the glare and stared up into the sky. It was a ballooning canopy of opalescent silk, stretched neatly and without a wrinkle. On the shore she knew that the boy Josh had gone back to work on the hedge. She could hear the steady click-clack of the pruning shears. It was the only sound in the world at the moment, a comfortable, homey noise. It made her think of suburban streets and commuters hurrying for the 8:15. It was a sound belonging to small gardens and plots of lawn; to houses cut from a pattern, filled with middle-class people like herself, people who were so busy trying to keep up with the butcher, baker, Consolidated Edison Company, and automobile finance corporations that they didn't have time to develop a neurosis. At any rate if they did, they couldn't afford one. The poor, she mused, only go nuts.

Swinging herself up into a sitting position, she inched across the boards to the edge of the float.

70

"Lil," she spoke to her toes, "it's time for you to visit Uncle Joe. Whenever you begin thinking with the profundity of the heroine in a housemaid's delight, it's time for Uncle Joe. What do you say, should we go?"

Back on the dock she thrust her feet into the slippers, slung the robe over one arm. At least, she thought, I can spare Josh a second sight of that. She sprinted up the path, took half of the front porch steps in a flying leap and then halted. Gravely she turned and bowed in the direction of the granite tomb.

"Good morning, Grandfather Andrew."

Holding her head high with affected elegance, she crossed the porch and walked sedately to her room.

VII

As he turned the page on his sixtieth birthday, Joseph Whitfield made a friendly pact with God; at least, he offered his hand and took it for granted that an agreement had been reached.

Lord, he said confidentially, if you'll do your best to spare me the company of fools and help a little in keepin' a deservin' Democrat in the White House, an' you know there ain't hardly any other kind, I'll hold up my end here in North Carolina. I'll keep this place of mine as sort of an oasis of decency an' gentle manners so's whenever you can't stand things any longer you can come down an' always find good bourbon to drink an' fine dogs to shoot over. There ain't goin' to be many places like that in this world, Lord. You know I'm speakin' the truth, so it looks like you an' I better get together.

Joe was willing to let the matter rest there, confident that the Lord would appreciate the wisdom of such a suggestion. If, now and then, there were minor breaches in the covenant, he didn't hold them against Heaven. I guess, he said generously, the Lord is doin' the best he can.

The house beside the river mellowed with its owner. Its bluestone base, erected with rough slabs as they came from the quarry, acquired the oily, smoky sheen of pewter while the ax-hewn timbers, cedar sheathings, and redwood shingles became as softly lustrous as the coats of his Gordon setters.

Set back in a grove of oak and flanked by scattered pines, the house was a graceful compliment to its creator, carrying its years with dignity and charm. Joe accepted the miracle of effortless management as a matter of course. His servants had been with him for so long that both he and they found it almost impossible to recall any other way of life. The children and even the grandchildren of old Stokes and Hattie-Mae were in the house, kitchen, and yards, and they seemed to find their proper places and duties without instruction from their employer. Through consideration and a sense of the fitness of things Joe Whitfield had created a feudal state, eminently satisfactory to all concerned.

He was having breakfast on the shaded side of a flagged terrace overlooking the river as Lillith drove through the twisting dirt road from the main highway. He listened to the eager yapping of the dogs in the kennels, hearing in their cries a note of welcome. Knowing that the visitor was no stranger, he went calmly about the elaborate ceremony of eating. A few moments later a car ground to a halt at the side entrance. Only then did he condescend to raise his head.

Standing in the open car, Lillith waved, and then, leaping out, ran lightly up the steps. She halted on the terrace, looking at him with almost mischievous excitement. Joe rose with a grave courtliness, standing erect for all his years. He bowed with a gallantry which, somehow, didn't seem exaggerated.

"I ran away," Lillith called and walked toward him with both hands outstretched.

"It's all right," Joe led her to a chair, "I have sort of an arrangement with God about such people as you. Had breakfast?"

"No, and I'm starving. I went swimming alone and then decided I wanted to come down here and talk."

"Well," Joe reseated himself, regarding her with approval, "I have plenty of food and conversation. The food is always good and the conversation is sort of like the water in a finger bowl. It's there, but you don't have to use it."

They sat back, eying each other with warm affection while a boy brought additional service for Lillith. She spooned up some bright yellow peaches swimming in a delicate amber sauce, and her eyes widened in a tribute to the flavor.

Joe smiled contentedly. "That's just a minor example of how Nature can be improved upon," he explained. "Sliced peaches with a touch of Cointreau an' Jamaica rum justify, in a measure, the creation of man. If you'll try some of that Camembert with them you can face the future unafraid."

"It's wonderful." Lillith sighed ecstatically. "Do I have to talk now or may I eat first?"

"You can eat and you don't have to talk at all, unless that's what you really came down for."

They finished breakfast in silence and then dragged their chairs to the stone railing surmounting the terrace, propping their feet on the ledge and smoking contentedly. The morning was quietly drowsy, seeming to hum tranquilly. A kingfisher hunted up and down the river with silent purpose, and the small things of the brush talked with muted excitement.

"Why don't we have this on The Hill, Uncle Joe?" Lillith raised her voice barely above a whisper, half afraid that her words would intrude upon the spell. "This is an honest quiet. On The Hill it is something musty, the silence of a long-unopened attic." She laughed a little nervously. "It's silly, but sometimes I feel about The Hill the way I did about the first dynamo I looked at in a plant. It just squatted there, ugly and powerful, without sound, and yet I was terrified by the idea that a careless touch would tear it apart in a blinding flash."

Joe nodded, not surprised at the fancy. "Houses an' people get that way."

"It frightens me sometimes." She made the admission without affectation.

Joe drew on his cigar and then, taking it from his mouth, examined the gathering corona of silvery ash carefully.

"I was afraid you might find it so. The first night I saw you I wanted to say that The Hill wasn't the place for you, but I just kept my mouth shut an' hoped for the best, which don't usually happen."

Lillith pushed her chair around to face him. "That doesn't answer my question," she said.

"You didn't expect an answer, did you? Suppose," he hesitated, "suppose you tell me why you married Cary?"

"Because I loved him." Her reply was prompt and decisive.

"You know," Joe leaned back, looking out over the river, "I'm not always sure that's a good reason, despite all the textbooks. It might have been better if you'd married Cary for the Whitfield money. At least you'd have what you went after."

"I didn't need money, you know that. I was successful, on my way to being a star. I know that sounds a little slick-paperish, but it's true. Another season, the right show, and I could have had anything I wanted. There were plenty of other men with money and I could have married it."

Joe grunted an assent. "I checked into that, not because I really cared a damn but it gave me a better line on you. A lot of girls did want to marry Cary for his money. I guess you were probably the only one who didn't. Well," he continued soberly, "how do you feel about him now?"

Lillith smiled understandingly. "You're not even warm, Uncle Joe. Maybe I don't always understand him or what he wants, but I try. Sometimes I stumble a little—" She flashed him a shy grin. "I guess that's what I'm doing right now, stumbling a little."

Joe nodded, as though satisfied. "Are you happy here, Lil?" The question was gentle.

Lillith's eyes grew sober. "No," she said after a pause, "I'm not happy."

"You ought to be. At least that's what the books say. You're young, your husband is handsome. God only knows how large his income is. I stopped tryin' to spend my end of it years ago. There isn't anything you can think of that you can't do. What the hell's the matter with you, anyhow?"

"You don't believe any of that," she said crisply.

Joe half closed his eyes and a fluttering smile touched his mouth. He settled his shoulders against the back of the chair.

"No," he mused, "I guess I don't. Just wondered if it made any sense to you."

"That's what's wrong, it ought to." Lillith frowned. "But I don't know what to do with myself"; she was puzzled. "I have sort of a peasant energy that's been put under pressure. I need something to do and," she gazed helplessly at Joe, "so does Cary."

"You might try tenant farmin' for a couple of years."

"It isn't a joke," she said quietly.

Joe scratched thoughtfully at the back of his head. "Now look." He measured his words. "Winton's a fine town filled with all kinds of people, an' in it you're Mrs. Cary Whitfield. That's at the top of the heap. You could be somethin' of a community influence. There's the Women's Club, as fine a group of big-busted women as I ever looked upon, the Civic Improvement Center, the Winton Little Theater Organization, the Garden Club. Did you ever think of joinin' any of them?"

"Yes." Lillith sat straight in her chair and glared at him. "Yes, I did."

Joe dropped his feet from the ledge and his eyes were wide with astonishment.

"The hell you did," he muttered incredulously. "Well, I'll just be damned."

"I did and I only felt silly." There was a note of exasperation in her voice. "I even read a paper at the Garden Club—of course, I copied most of it out of an encyclopedia. I offered to haul props, play an extra, or paint scenery at the Little Theater, but they thought I was only trying to show off and be sarcastically humble. I wanted to be part of Winton, part of The Hill, but I'm not the clubwoman type, I guess."

"So," Joe was grave, "you're still a little unsatisfied?"

"Naturally." Her reply was emphatic.

"Well," he smiled, "there ought to be a sight of things for Mrs. Cary Whitfield to do in Winton. There could be Mrs. Whitfield's Society for the Improvement of Factory Workers. You could start a day nursery for workers' children, if you can catch 'em. You could organize a Christmas basket fund and deliver hampers filled with jars of caviar, *pâté de fois gras,* smoked turkey, an' Huntley & Palmer biscuits to the share-croppers. You might," his voice dropped to a whisper, "even try raisin' a family."

"I wondered when you would get to that." The words were a whip.

"Well?" Joe refused to be disturbed.

Lillith flushed. "It isn't my fault," she said quietly.

"No?" The question was a goad.

"No!" She was angry and made no attempt to conceal the fact. "No, it isn't."

Joe reached out and took her hand. "I'm sorry, then." He said. "Sorry I even mentioned it. How was I to know?" His speech was gentle.

She relaxed perceptibly. "That's all right. I suppose you've wondered. You and I can't be angry with each other. You see, if I can't talk things over with you, then there isn't anyone. Cary doesn't understand. I wake up every morning and say: Dear God, find me something to do today. He never does. When I try and explain to Cary how I feel, he just laughs and orders something from Cartier's or decides that we ought to have a party or take a trip. Usually we have a party. The house fills up with people who drink too much and crawl in and out of each other's beds like white mice that have taken an aphrodisiac. The whole business is so pointless."

"That depends," Joe laughed silently, "on whether you're a white mouse."

Lillith rose and stood looking down at him. She was icily furious.

"You don't give a damn, do you?" She demanded.

Joe motioned her back to the chair. "Of course I do," he said calmly, "only it won't help to tear our shirts off. What about Cary?"

Lillith sank back into her seat. "I think," she said slowly, "Cary is the unhappiest man in the world. Not because of me or our marriage," she added quickly. "He's stumbling through some terrible mental

76

swamp. He's a lost child, Uncle Joe, wailing in a treetop. Then, sometimes, he's insufferably arrogant. It's a defense he puts up against something we can't see. He tries to fight his own particular shades by getting drunk, but that doesn't help and he knows it. When the liquor begins to wear off he cries, not the tears of a man but the maudlin weeping of woman. He swears he has ruined my life; threatens to kill himself, wallowing in self-pity."

"If I were you," Joe said tonelessly, "I'd run like hell."

"No you wouldn't." She sat, staring down at her clasped hands. "Neither will I, but sometimes I want to scream. He needs to be interested in something. I've thought, maybe, that if we had a place of our own, if we could get away from The Hill, things might be different."

Joe shook his head. "I don't think so. Have you talked it over with him?"

"I've tried, but the only time he will listen is when he is drunk. He, he doesn't think much of my judgment. He doesn't trust himself or anyone, anyone except—" She broke the sentence off abruptly.

Joe looked up, his glance keen and probing. "Except Reese. Is that what you were goin' to say?"

"Yes," she murmured, "except Reese."

"Except Reese." Joe's words were an echo, and something about it caused Lillith to start.

"Tell me about Reese Benton, Uncle Joe." She leaned slightly forward.

"I don't know that there is anything to tell." Joe was not particularly interested. "He and Cary have been friends all of their lives."

"Have they? Is Reese Benton Cary's friend?" She shot the questions deliberately and watched for their effect.

Joe was undisturbed. He drew placidly on his cigar. "Why," he suggested after a moment, "why don't you ask Cary?"

"You know better than that. I'm asking you and you're trying to evade me or something. Why?"

"No particular reason except," Joe meditated, "except, maybe, I don't know the answer."

"You ought to, after all of these years." Lillith prodded him.

Joe only smiled. "You're witch hunting," he said calmly.

"No I'm not." She lit a cigarette and slumped back in the chair, her eyes never leaving Joe's face. "I want to know about Reese Benton; about Cary, Reese, Ann-Charlotte." She waited.

"Your curiosity's a little delayed, ain't it?" There was a touch of amusement in the question.

"Maybe." Lillith was honestly puzzled. "But I never knew before how much Cary depends upon Reese. Lately, when he's been drinking, Reese is the only one who can quiet him. They'll talk for hours, reminiscing over the things they did when they were boys. At least, Reese talks and Cary listens with a pitiful eagerness, prompting Reese as a child will a parent who is telling a well-worn story. He'll stop Reese and say: 'No, you're leaving out something. Remember, we did this first.' Then Reese will go back and fill in the details and Cary is satisfied. Sometimes," her eyes clouded, "Reese almost acts as a father would with a not too bright youngster." She stared imploringly at Joe. "It breaks my heart, Uncle Joe. I want to scream out: Stop it. I don't, because Cary wouldn't understand. He's proud of Reese."

"That doesn't sound very disturbing." Joe rose and stood looking down at her.

"No," Lillith was unsure of herself, "no, I suppose it isn't. Unless you've heard them it wouldn't mean anything. It upsets me, I guess, because Cary seems to be reaching back for something, as though the present frightened him. He likes to recall the hunting trips he and Reese went on, the little things that happened to them as boys; their first dates at college, the two summers they spent in Europe when Cary's mother was alive." She smiled almost tenderly. "Cary even likes to have Reese talk about the first time the three of us met in New York. I suppose I should be grateful to be included at all. What terrifies me, though, Uncle Joe, is the way he seems to come alive beneath Reese's hands. I've never been able to get that close to him. They pull away into a small world of their own."

"That's strictly a male characteristic." Joe put his cigar in a tray on the table. "Women never understand or quite forgive it."

Lillith watched him with quiet intensity. There was something disturbing in his manner. He was too casual, too disinterested. It was a false front.

"Last night," she said slowly, "Cary told me I should have married Reese. He cried, kneeling beside my bed and clinging to my hand. He said to me," she injected a note of defiance into her voice, "he said he was sterile, said he had known it for a long time. He told me to go to Reese. He said it would be all right, that we would all go on as before, that it wouldn't make any difference and if I had a child only the three of us would know." She waited breathlessly for some reply.

78

Joe held his hand out toward her. "Let's take a walk," was all he said.

Lillith hesitated, feeling defeated and, somehow, exhausted. What she had just told Joe Whitfield seemed so critically important to her, to all of them, and Joe was shrugging it off. She stared in wonder at him, searching his impassive face for some sign that he had heard and understood what she had been saying. Finally, she laughed nervously.

"Maybe you're right," she admitted, rising. "Maybe I am witch hunting, frightening myself by saying Boo! in the dark. Perhaps Cary didn't mean or know what he was saying." Her voice was creeping to an unnaturally high note and Joe looked sharply at her. "Or," she was forcing herself to speak, "or if he did know, it's all right. There's nothing unusual in a husband telling his wife to go to another man's bed. Is that what you want me to believe?" She was trembling violently.

Joe took her shoulders in his big hands and felt the tremor of her body. He shook her gently.

"Stop it," he commanded quietly. Her eyes were wide and staring, almost without comprehension. "Do you hear? Stop it."

She relaxed suddenly, sagging for a moment in Joe's grasp, then she lifted one hand and touched the side of her cheek with a fluttering gesture of self-protection.

"Of course," she said tiredly, "I'm being very foolish."

Joe tucked her hand beneath his arm, pressing it reassuringly against his side. She clung to him briefly and then he felt her straighten.

"No," he said, "you're not foolish. Maybe, just an edge on the hysterical side."

"I'm not the hysterical type," she said proudly.

"That's good." He spoke with gentle persuasion. "I never know what to do with a hysterical woman."

They walked arm in arm across the terrace and down the broad stone steps to the yard and along a flower-bordered path leading to the back of the house.

"Are you getting rid of me?" Lillith inquired with mock plaintiveness.

"Nope. I always walk after breakfast. Not far, only enough to satisfy my conscience, which is grateful for a few scraps of attention now and then."

Their way led along a narrow trail, hemmed in by pine saplings, standing straight and making an almost solid wall. The ground was

79

dusted with a brown carpeting of needles from the boughs and the scent of pine was fresh and exhilarating. Lillith sighed contentedly.

"This is a beautiful path." She looked happily up at him.

Joe was pleased. "It's sort of my widow's walk," he explained with wry amusement. "I pace it, looking out at the horizon for my lost youth. I guess," he chuckled, "I'd be scared to hell an' gone if I ever caught sight of it."

The path broke abruptly into the clear and they stood for a moment in the scattered sunshine as it was filtered to them through the oaks. The ground was the bright, tawny color of a leopard and the world was standing still.

"What were you like?" Lillith gazed up at him. "What was young Joseph Whitfield like?"

Joe shook his head. "Only a fool would try an' answer such a question, an' only an impertinent trollop like you would dare ask it."

Lillith met his eyes. They were laughing, sparkling in their depths with a contagious pleasure. She had an irresistible desire to touch him, and her hands reached out for his arm. There was something solid, comfortable, and reassuring in his strength.

"Do you know," she said, and the words were thoughtfully tender, "I love you very, very much, Joe Whitfield."

"Hell," Joe snorted impatiently, "I'd be some surprised if you didn't. Stop pawin' me." He made no move to pull away. "Come on now," he ordered gruffly, "I'll take you to your car. If there's anything I can't stand it's a simperin', over-sexed woman. I guess," he scratched meditatively at his chin and then grinned quickly, "come to think about it I guess, maybe, it's only the simperin' part I never liked."

They walked back along hedge-bordered walks and past an artfully contrived grotto from which water spilled and drummed into a pool where goldfish played in darting thrusts of color. At the kennels they halted while the dogs yammered with delighted frenzy, throwing themselves against the heavy wire netting in paroxysms of excitement.

"Shut up there. You, Bell, Don. Stop that fuss." Joe made a half-hearted attempt to still the uproar. "Don't think," he admonished Lillith, "that they are showing off for you. They'd do the same for the grocery boy."

"I know." Lillith was gravely respectful. "I wasn't going to take advantage of it."

He put her in the car and closed the door. "You'll come an' see me whenever you feel like it." He made a command of what might have been a question.

Lillith nodded. "Thank you, Uncle Joe. I won't forget."

"Maybe we ought to have a party, barbecue or somethin'. Get all of you off The Hill for a night. Must be gettin' sick of the movies." He seemed reluctant to allow her to leave.

"I'd like that," Lillith said, "and I think Cary would."

"Well, I'll study it over."

Lillith swung the car around the circular driveway and sent it toward the highway, turning once and raising a hand in a salute to the solitary figure, half hidden in the trees. Once on the concrete strip leading into Winton, she settled deeply into the seat, sliding down so far that she could barely see over the top of the steering wheel. She felt a strange sense of release, an almost airy detachment. The car took the long, sweeping curves with a silent rush, needing only her fingertip to guide it. The fog which had oppressed her all morning had been magically lifted, as though a clean, fresh draft had swept through a smoky room.

On Winton's outskirts she allowed the car to run at a normal speed. Straightening up, she lifted her face, the wind snatching at her hair, and laughed suddenly out of sheer happiness. Swooping past a lumbering truck she half turned.

"Hi! Charley!" She yelled the greeting out of exuberance and watched in the mirror as the driver lifted a hand in lazy greeting.

Winton was getting about the day's business as she threaded her way through the traffic. Cars were beginning to pack the parking places along the streets. Clerks were mounting the steps to banks and offices. Doors were being opened, shoppers were hurrying along, alert for early morning bargains. At the opposite end of town she knew that the factories and mills were humming their steady song of production.

"I belong to this," she said aloud. "I want to be a part of it. This is my home, mine and Cary's."

Turning off Memorial Avenue she took a short cut through side streets. By lifting herself slightly in the seat she could look ahead and catch glimpses of the open, broken country through the ordered ranks of trees. Beyond was The Hill, dark guardian and sentinel over Winton. At least, that was what it should have been.

Driving slowly, Lillith tried to imagine what Old Andrew must have felt as he walked across his acres and looked down and over the town drawn from his strength. Winton was his. He had shared with it a purpose and a plan. His home, The Hill, had been created, not built. In the mortar of its foundation the sweat, toil, hopes, and gnawing fears of the men and women whose loins had brought forth a community were mixed with his own. Now, though, The Hill had withdrawn itself and Winton long ago stopped looking to it for guidance and help. The seasons came and went. The years were good or bad. The Hill was unmoved, standing as a great brown citadel around which the currents swirled at a safe distance. There was something tragically impersonal in the isolation. Andrew's force, she thought, had been allowed to waste itself. At this moment, she knew, there were thousands of men and women in Winton who, if they looked at all toward The Hill, saw in it only a huge and ugly house. It was a house where some people named Whitfield lived, people who had a lot of money and who had once been vaguely connected with Winton and tobacco. Now, they didn't seem to have much to do with anything. They lived on The Hill for a few months out of the year and then disappeared, their arrival and departure duly noted in the newspapers.

"That wasn't how you planned things, was it, Old Andrew?" Lillith threw her question at The Hill in the distance.

VIII

Dropping lightly, two steps at a time, Reese loped down the broad staircase to the lower floor. He was freshly shaved and showered and wore only sneakers, an old pair of flannel slacks with sweatshirt. Once he had caught up with it, his sleep had been dreamless. Now he was hungry. Walking to the dining room on his way to the kitchen, he found Clarissa laying places for four at the long table.

"Mornin', Mistuh Reese."

"Mornin', Lissa." He glanced around the gloomy room with its heavy furniture and sniffed impatiently at the faintly musty odor which no amount of airing ever seemed to dissipate entirely.

"It's too nice a morning to eat in here, Lissa." He snapped off a stem of fat, purple grapes from the mound in a bowl on the table. "Let's have it out on the porch."

The girl looked up and hesitated, holding a fork an inch or so above the table, unable to make up her mind whether to put it down or whisk it out of sight.

"Mistuh Cary said . . ." She gazed unhappily at him.

"I want some steak, sliced tomatoes." Reese popped a grape into his mouth and crushed it against his palate.

"Yessuh, Mistuh Reese."

He walked from the table, turning at the doorway as though with an afterthought.

"On the porch, Lissa," he said softly.

"Yessuh."

Clarissa sidled hastily away as if fearful of being caught at or near the table in disfavor. Reese tossed a grape high in the air and with dancing steps maneuvered his head beneath its flight, catching it in his open mouth as it dropped. Then he walked slowly down the corridor and out on the porch.

Cary was lounging in a wicker chair, feet thrust out on the railing. At the sound of the opening door he turned quickly, almost guiltily. Seeing Reese, he smiled with wan resignation, indicating that the day was one not to be borne.

"Hi, Reese," he called.

"Hi, Cary." Reese strolled down, looking out across the sloping lawn. In front of Cary he perched himself on the railing and finished the few remaining grapes, tossing the bare stem over his shoulder.

"I feel like hell." Cary wasn't complaining. He made a statement as though in reply to a direct question.

Reese shrugged off the invitation to discuss the cumulative effect of liquor on the human system. He knew that Cary wanted to be told that he was drinking too much. For some unfathomed reason he seemed to derive a curious satisfaction out of being reminded of the fact that he had been drunk the night before. He waited now for Reese to pick up the cue, and when it was ignored he sank back in the chair with a petulant frown.

"You're up early," was all Reese said.

"I couldn't sleep." Cary wasn't interested.

"Lil upstairs?"

"No, she went swimming and then high-tailed it out in her car without saying where she was going." He paused. "Was I bad last night?"

Reese shook his head. "You're never bad, Cary. You know that." He grinned companionably. "Sometimes you talk too much, but hell, a lot of people do that when they're sober."

Clarissa and a second girl brought out a table, putting it down a few feet from Cary's chair. They spread a cloth and then hurried back into the house for silver and dishes. Cary watched as they returned.

"Are we having breakfast out here, Lissa?"

The girl looked up from her labors, startled and uncertain.

"Yessuh, Mistuh Cary, I—"

"I told her to bring it out here. The dining room was too stuffy." Reese put an end to the girl's embarrassment.

"Oh, sure." Cary was satisfied. He chewed at his lower lip for a moment and then his face brightened. "Say," he said, "how would it be, Reese, if we knocked out one side of that room and put a big picture window or French doors there. We could have a terrace with, maybe, a pool or a fountain."

Reese laughed softly. "Old Andrew'd come marchin' right out of that tomb and snatch you by the seat of the pants if you touched a board of The Hill and you know it."

Cary didn't smile with the joke as might have been expected. Instead, he nodded soberly.

"I guess it would look sort of funny. The Hill wasn't built to be changed, was it?"

"Not all at once." Reese swung his feet, drumming against the railing slats with his heels. "I'm hungry," he said irrelevantly.

"Hey!"

They both looked up at the call. Ann-Charlotte was standing in the doorway. She stepped out, walking the length of the porch with a lazy, free stride. Watching her, Reese could appreciate the perfection she represented. She wore a loose, knee-length coat of shimmering white material, drawn neatly at the waist by a braided, deep blue cord ending in thin gold tassels. No one knew better than Ann-Charlotte, he thought, that it was a costume designed to display the flawless symmetry of her beautiful bare legs. I'll bet, he said to himself, there isn't a damn stitch on her beneath it. Pausing, Ann-Charlotte regarded the recently laid table with open curiosity and then tapped one of its legs with the tip of a blue sandal.

"What's all this fresh air? Somebody been reading a Boy Scout manual?"

Cary snickered, burying his chin in his shirt front. "Reese," he said, "Reese the Robust."

"Do we eat here or just admire the idea?" Ann-Charlotte hoisted herself to a place on the rail beside Reese.

"We'll eat as soon as Lissa recovers from her surprise." Reese allowed his glance to travel slowly over her. "Suit you?"

"Sure. God," she sighed, "I'm hungry. I'm always hungry." She made the admission with an air of surprise. "It's got something to do with my sex life, I think."

"A substitute?" Reese asked mildly.

"No, my sweet," she patted him comfortingly on the knee, "an adjunct. Give me a cigarette."

Reese handed her one and lit a match without comment. Ann-Charlotte took the light, looking over the flame into his eyes and then, without changing her attitude, blew upon it with an extinguishing spurt of air.

"Thanks, my man. My good man, I should say. Where's Lil?"

The question was answered by Lillith herself as she trotted up the steps, her arms loaded with freshly cut flowers.

"Hey, you," she called, "La Violetera."

She covered the distance separating them with quick steps of excitement. Her face was radiant, flushed with the joy of being alive on

85

such a morning. She threw her head back to toss a strand of hair away from her eye, making the gesture seem impudently carefree.

"Sprig of lavender, mum?" She spun a rose into Ann-Charlotte's lap. "Bit of rosemary for you, sir," a second flower arched its way to Reese, "and a posey for behind your Spanish ear, M' Lord." She bent quickly and kissed Cary on his forehead. "And how," she inquired respectfully, "are all you representatives of the degenerate rich this morning?"

"Hungry," Ann-Charlotte said practically. "Look," she nodded toward the table, "what Strong Boy Benton is going in for."

Lillith surveyed the table and made a sound of approval. "Mmmm. I wondered when someone would realize we didn't have to eat breakfast in that embalming room. Thank you, Reese, for your courage." She jerked her head toward the mausoleum. "Is it O.K. with Andy?"

"He hasn't said a word." Reese smiled at her.

Clarissa trundled out a heavily laden tea wagon. Reese slid down from the railing and walked toward the table.

"We'll serve ourselves, Lissa. Come on, Ann-Charlotte, Cary, Lillith?"

Lillith transferred the flowers to Clarissa's arms. "I've already had breakfast," she said.

Cary, dragging his chair across the porch, looked up, surprised.

"You have?" he asked. "Where?"

"With a man." Lillith perched on the corner of a chair and lit a cigarette. "Go ahead," she said, "I'll sit here and talk."

When they were settled at the table, Cary repeated his question. "Where did you have breakfast?"

"You'll never guess." She was cockily pleased with her secret.

"And you," Ann-Charlotte peeked under a cover at Reese's steak and then regarded her own thin strips of bacon with disfavor, "you'll forgive me if I don't try. Why the hell didn't I think of steak? Give me some, Reese."

"All right, then," Lillith retorted, "if you are going to gorge yourselves on the fat of the land with no thought of what goes on in the world, I'll tell you." She paused dramatically. "I had breakfast with Uncle Joe."

The three at the table turned as one and stared at her in disbelief. Lillith sat erect with a pleased and smugly prim expression on her face.

"The hell you did," Ann-Charlotte said finally and speared a piece of steak from Reese's plate before he could catch her hand. "What do you know about that?"

"He never comes to The Hill to see us, so this morning I decided to go down to Bluestone to see him. And," she added, as though reciting a lesson, "he was very happy to see me."

"Why?" Cary turned to his coffee.

"Because," Lillith wrinkled her nose at him, "he likes me and thinks the rest of you are bastards."

"Did he say that?" Reese's eyes were laughing.

"He didn't have to. I can always tell when someone thinks someone else is a bastard. Can't you?"

"Not always." Reese chewed stolidly but continued to watch her.

"Also," Lillith pretended to be enjoying a major triumph, "he said he wanted us all to come down some night. He's going to have a barbecue."

Cary deliberately dropped his fork. "Did he say he wanted us to come down?"

Lillith thought for a moment. "No," she confessed, "he didn't exactly say he wanted us. He said he'd have us down. I guess there's a difference, isn't there?"

Cary, Ann-Charlotte, and Reese grunted in unison, turning their attention to breakfast. Lillith slid into a more comfortable position in the chair and looked at them. Why, she thought, couldn't all of their mornings be like this one. They captured these moments of unconscious intimacy so rarely. Sometimes Cary was morose, badly shaken with a hangover, or torn by the hidden fox gnawing at his vitals. Ann-Charlotte was frequently sulky, or stridently stormy. Reese, though, she thought quickly, never seemed to change. He might even be following some mental blueprint of life. Without making him feel her glance she watched him as he ate. He wasn't handsome, and there was nothing of Cary's electric magnetism about him. At least Cary once had the quality to draw and hold her, but it was being spent, trickling away through obscure channels. Reese, though, concealed something hard and relentless. He seemed so completely sure of himself. No wonder, she mused, Cary draws upon him in his uncertainty. Repellently charming, she thought, were the words for Reese; but even as she spoke them to herself, she knew they were dishonest. If there was something about him which spoke gently and alarmed her at the same time it was because she, herself, created the fancy. No one else, apparently, shared it. Everyone seemed to like Reese. He was popular with everyone they knew; an entertaining companion, possessed of a slow and, sometimes, bitter humor. He never seemed to commit the lapses most men displayed an affinity for. He never became too drunk to drive a car, never argued with waiters, doormen, or taxi drivers. He never pawed with a pretense of brotherly affection, and you could sit next to him at a table without being worked over with foot and knee. Women, she knew, liked him better than they should if they expected any return beyond the bedroom door.

Everyone likes Reese. She repeated the statement to herself. Everyone? She felt something gather and tighten within her. Everyone? What did Joe Whitfield see that she could only feel and no one else seemed to be aware of? She allowed her mind to race over the morning. Joe Whitfield had said nothing, had he?

Reese looked up from his plate, slowly as though compelled to the act. He caught her glance and for a moment he seemed puzzled by what he saw. Lillith fought herself back to the moment and ventured a quick smile.

"Coffee?" He asked, motioning toward the silver thermos jug.

"No, thanks. Uncle Joe did right well by me."

Ann-Charlotte leaned back, tilting her chair on two legs.

"Now what?" She yawned and stretched with the easy motion of a well-fed cat. "What can we do that isn't too dirty? For the morning, I mean," she added quickly.

Lillith leaned forward, resting her arms on her knees. "Do you know," she said, "I had a long talk with myself and Old Andrew this morning."

"I told you to stay out of that tomb, Lillith." Cary spoke with mock severity.

"Oh! I didn't go in, only whispered at the door. He doesn't like things the way they are."

Reese turned his chair from the table. "That's a common complaint of the dead."

"He didn't complain," Lillith corrected him. "He was mad. He said he had made a town, almost hacked it out of the brush by hand and his children's children didn't want anything to do with it. He said that instead of being a part of Winton the Whitfields passed through it like tourists."

Ann-Charlotte blew softly on her fingernails and gave them a quick, burnishing flip against her palms. "You and Old Andrew ought to buy yourselves a covered wagon," she said coolly.

88

"I know I'm not making out a very good case." Lillith was serious. "Old Andrew said it much better. He said that Winton, tobacco, the land itself shouldn't be in the hands of strangers." She broke open a fresh cigarette and spread the fine strands of bright leaf in her hand. "I haven't the slightest idea where this comes from." She rolled the tobacco between her fingertips. "What's worse, neither Cary nor Ann-Charlotte knows any more about it than I do."

"Well, now," Ann-Charlotte professed an eager alertness, "if you think it will help things, I'll get out my calico Mother Hubbard and drill a few plants before sundown. Maybe we ought to have an old 'baccy barn down the hill to fire up in the morning. That'd keep us in touch with LIFE."

Lillith smiled. "It sounds silly, doesn't it," she confessed, "yet, somehow, Old Andrew made sense this morning. He seemed to think that The Hill represented something and a responsibility went with it."

Ann-Charlotte whistled derisively. "Old Andrew," she said, "sounds like a God-damned Red to me."

Lillith turned to Reese with a small, helpless gesture. "You know what I mean, don't you?"

"Uh-huh. Only, you're wrong, of course. When Andrew Whitfield began clubbing his way up, it had to be a personal affair and it probably wasn't pretty to watch. He didn't build Winton out of any personal affection for the share-croppers and tenant farmers whose crops he bought, and he bought them for what he wanted to pay and not for what they were worth. He built Winton as a by-product, the material was handy. Finally the Whitfield stranglehold was so tight that the Government stepped in with an antitrust suit and loosened a few fingers. By that time Andrew Whitfield didn't have to care. He was secure."

"I don't believe it." Lillith was defending an emotion. "I think, maybe, he was proud of himself, of his family, and of Winton and hoped that all of you would feel the same way."

Cary shook his head wonderingly. "I suppose," he suggested, "that what you're trying to say is that I ought to have a shoulder to the wheel."

"I think you'd be happier if you had something to do."

"Well," Cary attempted to inject a humorous note into his voice, "I'm on the board of a dozen corporations."

"Did you ever attend a meeting?"

89

"Why should I?" He was becoming a little angry. "We have a law firm to take care of that."

"But don't you care, Cary?" Lillith was surprised. "Don't you want to know how you get your money, where it comes from, or anything about the people who make it for you?"

"That sounds a little on the soapbox side to me." Cary was impatient. "Thousands of people all over the country have jobs, homes, and security because of Andrew Whitfield. I get damn sick and tired of being patronized because of him. My father always worried about money, he had an idea, also, that he ought to do something to earn it. In the name of God why? It's there and I'm not going to make a clown of myself by pretending I'm a busy beaver while chasing my tail."

"Methinks," Ann-Charlotte spoke with a dreamy inflection, "I hear the creaking of the tumbril. Where's my knitting?"

Lillith laughed, and something of Cary's annoyance evaporated. She tilted her hand over a saucer and allowed the little mound of loose tobacco to spill out.

"All right," she said, "I still believe you are dodging something, but I can't think what it is."

Ann-Charlotte rose. "Summer is a-comin'," she reminded them. "Where are you going?"

"I don't know." Cary looked across at Reese. "How about the lodge?"

"I think I'll call the French Line," Ann-Charlotte made no attempt to stifle a yawn, "and see if I can get something on the *Ile*." She turned indifferently to Reese. "Come with me?"

Reese shook his head. "I don't think so. The mountains would suit me better."

"Sure," Cary was eager, "let's all go to the lodge. We had fun last summer.

Ann-Charlotte shook her head. "You're all getting too rugged. Paris for a couple of weeks and then the Riviera."

"I'll take my libido to the Lido." Reese hummed softly, looking innocently down the length of the porch.

"My," Ann-Charlotte's voice was breathless with admiration, "but you are getting to be a clever boy, Reese." She sighed regretfully. "I wish Oscar Wilde had said that." She turned to Lillith. "What about you, Joan of Arc who hears the voices?"

"Anything that Cary would like." She grinned. "You see, if you all had jobs you wouldn't have to worry about what to do during the summer."

"That's right." Ann-Charlotte was in immediate agreement. "Cary could come home all stinking of sweat and horse manure and you could wash his overalls between babies. You make it sound so attractive."

Reese scraped his chair back and stood up. "It's been nice meeting you all," he said.

"Early date?" Ann-Charlotte asked.

Reese shook his head. "No, just something I want to do."

"Take me with you?" Ann-Charlotte waited.

Reese looked at her solemnly for a moment. "All right," he finally said, "get some clothes on. I'll wait."

"You see," she turned to Lillith, "that's what fascinates me about Reese. He fairly pants at the thought of being alone with me."

Cary slumped back in his chair, a sulky expression clouding his face. Watching him, Lillith experienced a sharp stab of pity. She reached over and covered his hand with her own.

"Do you really want to go to the mountains, darling?"

"Sure. I don't care. Whatever you say." He almost pouted, she thought. "Where you going, Reese? Right now, I mean."

Reese smiled patiently. "Just down to Winton, and then," he paused, "I want to run out to Pa's place."

"Well, couldn't we all go? Just for the ride? What do you want to go out there for, anyhow?" There was something querulous in the questions. He spoke with the accent of a small boy being left at home.

Lillith rose quickly from her chair. This strange, unhealthy dependence almost nauseated her.

"No." Reese didn't attempt to ease the refusal. "I'm just going to run out for a few minutes. The family that has been renting it wants to buy. That's all. I'll see you later." He called over his shoulder to Ann-Charlotte, "I'll meet you around back in the car."

"Well, all right." Cary was defiant. "To hell with you then."

Lillith watched Reese as he vaulted over the railing and dropped lightly to the yard. Did he do these things purposely, she wondered, or was it just because he and Cary knew each other so well that Reese was sure Cary would never misunderstand anything he did?

Cary huddled himself in the chair, staring without interest straight ahead. After a moment Lillith turned and walked away. Cary didn't lift his head or speak.

91

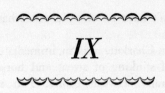

IX

On both sides of the road the fields lay richly dark and warm, stirring beneath the persistent touch of May's gentle sun. From weathered fence to fence the long, furrowed mounds stretched in even rows and above them were bent men, women, and their children resetting the plants but recently taken from the seedling beds. They, the planters, crouched in attitudes of almost devotional attention as they gave into the earth's care the precious green shoots. They worked carefully, for once out of their hands the tobacco would have to withstand the merciless caprices of sun and rain, drought and unseasonal frost. Throughout the summer men would search the sky, staring impotently at that burnished dome as though to force their will upon high heaven. If the rain they needed came, would it be too much? How could a man know when the gods had heard or if they listened and, listening, understood? By August the land would have erupted with plants of cascading green. Then the harvest and the curing, with each barn a private hell, the fires tended by sweating, red-eyed and anxious men. Now, though, they could only plant and pray, each after his own fashion.

Reese drove slowly and Ann-Charlotte, curled in a corner of the seat, one foot tucked beneath her, watched him without staring. They hadn't spoken after leaving The Hill, but the silence wasn't born of any sullenness on his part, and she had been content to ride without forcing small talk. Once Reese pulled the car to the side of the road, running through the knee-deep weeds and halting at the edge of a fence where a man was working.

"Hi! Carter," he called.

The man straightened up from a hill, squinting without recognition at the car and its occupants, and then walked slowly over to where they waited. He tugged off a ragged-brimmed straw hat and nodded to Ann-Charlotte without speaking, and then he identified Reese.

"Well, how you, Reese," he said with obvious surprise.

"Fine, Carter. How you?"

The man wiped his dripping forehead with the back of a dirt-smeared arm and then leaned gratefully against the fence, resting his hands on the top rail. He was a tall, sun-toughened man, and the overalls he wore were sweat-stained, patched, and bleached from many washings. His feet were bare and heavily caked with earth.

"It's sure enough makin' up for a hot day," Carter breathed gustily. "It's been a spell since I seen you around here, Reese. Ain't plantin', are you?" His eyes swept over Ann-Charlotte and the expensive car, and then he grinned in appreciation of his own joke.

"How's the soil?" Reese ignored the jest.

"Good," Carter said dryly. He bent down, picked up a small clod and tossed it across the fence. Reese caught it and it crumbled between his fingers.

"Feels right," was all he said.

Carter smiled briefly. "Didn't figure you'd remember."

Ann-Charlotte thought that she detected a quick flush on Reese's face, but she couldn't be sure. He was staring out over the half-planted field, and she realized with a shock that there was something almost hungrily wistful in his eyes.

"You don't forget things like that," he said absently.

Carter laughed shortly. "I'd sure God like to take a try at it sometime."

Reese nodded. "I suppose every grower feels that way now and then." He seemed to be on the point of saying more, and then his fingers sought and found the gear shift lever and clicked it into place. The car inched forward through the clinging tangle of weeds. "Well, so long, Carter." They pulled slowly away from the solitary figure.

"So long, Reese." There was unmistakable mystification on the man's face. He was wondering, as was Ann-Charlotte, what had prompted Reese to stop. When the car reached the road again, she turned and looked back. Carter was standing as they had left him. On an impulse she tossed a friendly wave and he lifted his hat in return.

Reese drove hard, swinging tightly around the inside of the curves, racing away from something. His face was set and his eyes never shifted from the road ahead. Not until they had run a fast mile did Ann-Charlotte speak.

"Why did you stop there, Reese?" She asked the question softly.

Reese's foot came up off the accelerator and he leaned back in the seat.

"That's what Carter wondered. Didn't you notice?"

"Of course." She wasn't prying. She knew now that Reese had been reaching out for something, a kinship with that lonely figure bent to the soil. "He'd have to wonder after all of these years, Reese."

"I just wanted to say hello." The explanation was as hollow as it was futile. "There's no reason why I shouldn't. Carter was an old friend of mine. He went to high school for a year with me, us."

Ann-Charlotte settled into a tight little knot in the corner. She knew she shouldn't speak, yet the words forced themselves to her lips.

"I never knew before that you were lonely." There was a muted tenderness in her voice. "I never knew, Just Reese."

His laughter was short and a little horrible in its harshness. "That's funny," he said, "you've been so damn sure of everything else."

He swung the car off the highway and into a narrow, crooked dirt road leading to the cottage. With his consent the Josephs, who tenant-farmed the small place, had added a room. The wing stood out, yellowly naked from the aging gray of the original building. Rusting tin cans cluttered the unkempt yard, and the skeletal remains of a blackened oil stove lay near the steps. From a limb of a mulberry tree a worn tire sagged on a length of rope, providing a swing for the Josephs' children. A couple of scrawny chickens hunted disconsolately for nonexistent worms in the baked earth, and they fled in cackling terror from the car's wheels. In the shade of the porch a scabby hound lifted its muzzle and barked dutifully once, then dropped its head with an indifferent thump to the space of boards between its paws. Reese drove under the overhanging branches of the mulberry tree and cut the motor. In the field across a narrow ditch they could see the Josephs intent upon their planting. Reese lifted a palm to the horn button on the wheel and then abruptly changed his mind.

"I'll walk over," he said for no apparent reason.

Instead of getting out of the car he relaxed and lit a cigarette while his glance wandered around the unkempt ground and over the sagging cottage as though he was mentally reshaping it as it once had been.

"It used to be kept neat and clean," he spoke to himself.

Ann-Charlotte turned to face him. Her hands were clasped limply in her lap.

"You never heard from your father, did you, Reese?"

"No." The word was clipped, short and ugly. "I never heard from him."

"Didn't you ever wonder?"

He turned and stared at her then. Hadn't he ever wondered? Wouldn't a youngster have wondered, cried out in the desperate loneliness of youth? He and Lance had stood beneath this tree, the man's jaws working nervously on a twist of tobacco as he tried to avoid the staring, pain-shot eyes of the boy before him.

"I've got to go away, Reese. I may be gone quite a spell. Mr. Whitfield wants you to come to The Hill an' live with them." Lance shifted uneasily beneath the accusing gaze.

"I don't want to go to The Hill, Pa. I just want to be with you like we always have. I wouldn't have any fun without you, not fun like we have together. You know how we've always been. I just wouldn't know what to do without you." Reese had seemed so pitifully small at that moment. Lance reached out and laid a hard, corded hand on his trembling shoulder.

"You always did like I said before, Reese. You been a good boy. I guess a man ain't never had a boy like you before. We been friends, Reese. Seems like there was never nothin' we couldn't talk over together. That ain't a common thing, Reese, between a man an' his son. Don't ever think I haven't knowed it."

Reese turned a stricken face upward, trying to fathom the man's unhappiness. "Then Pa," he said, "wherever you're goin' I ought to be there. You know you wouldn't like to get along without me."

Lance had kicked with methodical stubbornness at the ground, pretending great concentration on the small mound of earth raised by the toe of his heavy boot. He had been fighting against this moment ever since Cassius Whitfield sent for him.

Cassius had been humbly eager as they faced each other across the heavy mahogany desk.

"I wanted to talk with you about Reese." Cassius spoke with a little flutter of nervousness, uneasily conscious of the steady question in Lance's eyes. "He, he's a fine boy. Both Mrs. Whitfield and I are very fond of him. The children, Cary and Ann-Charlotte, look upon him almost as a brother."

"I knowed they see a lot of each other." Lance waited.

"They, Reese and Cary, graduate from high school this year. Cary's going to college. At least, I hope he is." Cassius' shoulders drooped in a gesture of helplessness. "I, we, Mrs. Whitfield and I would like, well, we'd be grateful if you'd let us see Reese through school, also."

Lance nodded, but his eyes never left Cassius Whitfield's face.

"That'd be a fine thing for Reese, I reckon," he said slowly. "I don't suspect he ever figured on goin' to a college."

"I'd like," Cassius clutched at the hope, "I'd like to do for Reese what I want to do for Cary, Lance. Maybe," there was a tinge of desperation in his voice, "maybe we can help each other. Cary needs Reese. His values are twisted, distorted. I think, maybe, if they are together Cary would be different. Reese is sound."

Lance rose from the chair and walked to the window, staring down into the busy street below. He turned finally and spoke with thoughtful deliberateness.

"Maybe," he said, "we've got to look at this some from Reese's end." He paused. "I don't think much of Cary, Mr. Whitfield, an' I might as well say it right out."

Cassius flushed and then dropped his eyes unhappily to the desk.

"We got to wonder a little what goin' away to school would do to my boy."

"He'd have the best." Cassius knew that wasn't what Lance meant.

"I was just wonderin'," Lance said gently, "if that kind of best is goin' to be good enough for Reese. It ain't helped Cary none."

"I know," Cassius slumped in his chair and stared blankly at the opposite side of the room.

"Maybe," Lance felt his way, "maybe he'll grow out of it, but if he didn't, what about Reese? Then there's another thing. I'd sure like to have Reese get the best, any father would. We're mighty close to each other, livin' alone like we have, but I'm wonderin' some how Reese is goin' to feel comin' back to a cabin on a tobacco acre after he's been away to college. Reese'll change, there ain't no use in shuttin' our eyes to that, Mr. Whitfield. I swear to God I wouldn't want to bring him discontent."

Silence dropped like a heavy curtain between them. Lance waited, holding back what he knew he would have to say. Finally, when he could endure the torment no longer, he sighed, wrenching the sound from deep within him.

"If it's the best thing to do, Mr. Whitfield, an' I guess it is, Reese ain't no sliver to be bent out of shape, I'd have to go the whole way an' that's a mighty lot. I'd want him to have it right, all the way through, not only the college but the home an' the friends an' the bringin'-up. It just wouldn't do for him to have the education an' the fine things half a year an' then come back to set with me on the patch the other half."

Cassius half rose from the chair and then sank back with a small, helpless sound. He watched the tall man by the window, sharing with him the moment of truth.

"I'd be goin' over to Tennessee or," Lance fumbled with the words, "or, maybe, someplace else where I got things to do."

Cassius played with a pen on the desk. "I wouldn't want to take a man's boy from him, Lance Benton."

Lance smiled for the first time. "I don't reckon anyone could do that, Mr. Whitfield, 'less'n I give him leave."

Cassius nodded. "He could have everything, it would be as though he was one of the family." His eyes grew troubled. "Do you think Reese would want to come with us?"

Lance twisted at his hands, staring down at them with unwavering intensity. "Reese is a good boy," he spoke in a whisper, "he's always trusted me. If I say it's the right thing, he'll understand." He raised his eyes and looked squarely at Cassius. "I wouldn't want to make no mistake about this, you understand, Mr. Whitfield. I'd never want to hear that things didn't turn out the way they ought an' Reese wasn't treated right."

Cassius stood up. "You can trust me, Lance. I've tried to be a good man and a father. I'll try twice as hard now."

They had shaken hands silently then, and Lance walked slowly to the door, turning there.

"Reese an' I'll be talkin' this over some, Mr. Whitfield, but I reckon it's the right thing I'm doin'." He paused. "That place of mine is free an' clear. I'd like to know it is there just in case Reese would want it. There'll be some small taxes an' things."

"You bring or send the deed and transfer to me, Lance. I'll see that the taxes are kept up for Reese. I'll do more. I'll see that Reese won't ever be dependent upon anyone, even after I'm gone. You can trust me."

Lance smiled. "I guess I can, Mr. Whitfield. I'd sure God better."

He was thinking of these things as he avoided the broken and accusing stare in Reese's eyes.

"You're right, boy." He spoke with an effort. "I ain't goin' to like gettin' along without you, but sometimes a man has got to do what he thinks best. I ain't never goin' to be so far away that you can't reach out for me. Besides, you're 'most a man growed now. You're eighteen. In a few more years you'd get the feelin' for a place of your own. You'd marry some little girl an' set up on a cabin an' things couldn't never be between us like they was before. You'd do that, an' without a proper education you'd be a cropper or somebody's tenant. This way you won't never have to take off your hat to no man." He smiled quickly, hopefully. "I ain't never done it, an' maybe that's why I ain't got no further."

"But Pa," Reese's voice broke and he was unashamed of the tears in his eyes, "goin' an' all. You don't have to do that. When summer comes I'll be back from school and we can be together."

Lance shook his head stubbornly. "It wouldn't be right for either one of us. A man sort of expects his son to look up to him. You wouldn't be feelin' much pride after a couple of years away at school. I want you to go to The Hill and live among the people in the right way."

"God damn The Hill," Reese cursed the sky, lifting his pale face and staring accusingly upward, "God damn The Hill and all of its money. They just can't take people and shake them around like they were dice in a cup. If I lose you because of them I'll hate 'em all for the rest of my life. I won't ever give up hatin'."

Lance took his boy's arms in his two hands. "You only think so now," he said quietly. "It'll be different an' you'll know later it was the very best we could have done. I'll write you a letter now an' then, an' the world ain't so big, like I say, Reese, that we couldn't find each other."

In such a fashion had Lance Benton walked away, and a longing hunger tore at Reese as he watched him go. He clung to the cabin, locking its shaky door against the importunings of Cassius and later Cary and Ann-Charlotte. He went about the small chores with dull-eyed determination, taking what little money he needed from a thin roll of dirty bills and a small mound of change in a broken china cat above the fireplace. At night when he sat down to his supper, he always put out an extra place and left the door open in case Lance should pass that way.

It was Laura Whitfield who finally broke through his protective wall of self-imposed isolation. She came to the cottage alone, leaving the colored chauffeur in the car on the highway and walking down the road by herself. Reese was in the yard, raking over the patches of tough, brown grass with as much care as he would have given to a well-planted lawn. He looked up as she approached and for a moment seemed to be on the point of dropping his rake and walking out to meet her. Instead, he waited, hands clasped tightly around the handle's end.

"Hello, Reese." Laura wasn't effusive.

"Hello, Mrs. Whitfield."

They stood, regarding each other in silence for a moment, and then she smiled faintly.

"May I sit down, Reese?"

He dropped the rake then, his face crimsoning with shame, and hurried toward her.

"You shouldn't have walked out here through the dirt, Mrs. Whitfield." He gazed with unhappy reproach at her dusty shoes.

"You wouldn't come and see me, so I had to come, Reese."

"I'll get you a chair."

Laura held to his arm. "No, I'll sit on the steps with you."

She settled herself on the bare stoop, and after a moment Reese took a place lower down. He didn't face her but kept his eyes turned resolutely to the fields.

"We've missed you, Reese." Laura spoke with compassion. "All of us have."

"Pa didn't have a cause to up and leave the way he did." He blurted the words out, holding tightly to the knees drawn up under his chin.

Laura's hand touched briefly at the top of his head. Reese didn't move beneath her fingers.

"You mustn't think that your father left because he didn't love you, Reese. Maybe, it's because he loved you so much that he went away. Cassius, Mr. Whitfield, has been brokenhearted because you wouldn't see him. He blames himself, but what he wanted to do, Reese, would be a good thing."

"How could it be good if it caused Pa to leave me? We've been together always."

"I know, Reese." Laura hesitated. "But you're growing up. It wouldn't be long before you would move out to make a life of your own. Don't you see how much better it can be this way?"

"I only know Pa left when he didn't have to." The words were bitter.

Laura reached down and drew his shoulders back until they rested against her knees. He resisted for a moment and then slowly, timidly, he leaned against her and she could feel a quiver of relief run through him.

"Come up to The Hill with us, Reese." Laura bent forward to breathe the words. "You'll be happy. There is all summer before us, and things don't have to be decided today. When summer is over and it is time to think about college, we can talk. If you still don't want to go, I'll find your father for you. That's a promise. You trust me, don't you?"

"Yes, Mrs. Whitfield." The voice was small.

"Will you come with me now?"

Reese rose then, turning to face her. "I'll come later," he spoke with difficulty. His eyes indicated the cabin. "I'd sort of like to clean things up good and leave the place right, just in case Pa decided to come back. He never could stand a mess." His eyes glistened but he made no move to brush at them with a hand.

Laura nodded. "Do you want to walk with me to the highway?"

Reese shook his head in immediate protest. "You wait here, I'll chase down and call your car." Before she could stop him he was flying down the road, his bare feet tossing up small puffs of red dust. When he returned, clinging to the car's door and standing on the runningboard, his face was shining. She walked out to meet him and he dropped off at her side.

"Do you want me to send the car for you later, Reese?"

He laughed for the first time. "No'm," he said with a shy eagerness, "I just guess that would make me feel so foolish I couldn't stand it. I'll walk up or hitch a ride on a wagon or a truck."

"We'll be waiting for you, Reese." Laura smiled with affectionate understanding.

He stood in the road watching the black car until it turned at the highway's intersection and disappeared, then he wheeled and walked slowly and with bent head to the cottage. Inside he looked around for a moment and then gravely began closing the windows, locking them with infinite care.

"Do you suppose he's still alive, Reese?" Ann-Charlotte's question snapped him back to the moment.

"I don't know." A faint smile of remembrance touched at the corner of his mouth and was gone. "It's been a long time. I never heard from him." He fumbled for a cigarette. When he had lit it, he drew the smoke deeply into his lungs and exhaled slowly. "I guess he must have been all right, though," he said thoughtfully. "Pa could always take care of himself, after his own fashion. But, we'd never known if he needed anything. He wouldn't have written for that."

"Are you going to sell this place, Reese?" Ann-Charlotte was watching him.

"No." The reply was emphatic. "I don't think I'd ever want to sell it. It isn't really mine, and maybe Pa would take it into his head to come back. He'd sure enough raise hell if he found strangers living here. I'm going to let the Josephs stay for as long as they want. They can rent it for a dollar a year, and sometimes they aren't even going to have the dollar." He opened the car's door and stepped out. "I'll walk over and talk to them now."

Ann-Charlotte slid along the seat and beneath the wheel. "Let me go with you?"

He turned and looked at her. "You keep this up," he said, "and I'll have to wear you around my neck in a locket. Come on."

Halfway out of the car Ann-Charlotte pulled up shortly and then drew back into the seat.

"Never mind," she said abruptly, "I'll wait here. I've a sudden touch of the vapors, induced, doubtlessly, by your overwhelming gracious-ness. Also, you can go to hell."

"Nope." Reese, she knew, was laughing at her. "I'll just hop across the branch here and have a talk with the Josephs. By the way," he added carelessly, "aren't you being a little sensitive for a Whitfield?"

Thumbing her nose languidly at him she sprawled back against the cushion as he moved away.

"The ol' marstah," she chanted, "visit he teants. Tote dat bar'l! Lif' dat bale!"

Reese ignored the gibe. She watched as he jumped lightly across the ditch and strode toward the open field. Squinting against the sun's glare, her eyes followed him as he walked carefully between the newly planted rows. She knew instinctively that Reese hadn't driven out here today simply for the doubtful pleasure of playing at being a landlord, and she experienced a momentary twinge of regret at the shallow derision of her mockery. Apparently, though, it had made no impres-sion.

Tapping reflectively against the rim of the steering wheel with the tips of her fingernails, she couldn't help but wonder why he had made the trip. If it was only to tell Joseph that the place wasn't for sale, then it was foolish, since he could have done that through the bank. Something more than a wish to say yes or no had impelled him to the visit. It was the unconscious action of a man wanting to stand again on land of his own. Why, she wondered, why should Reese feel so strongly about such a thing? What knitted him to the soil when neither she nor Cary, who had better reasons for such an emotion, could admit to it with any honesty? Lillith, also, had fumbled vaguely with the desire to be part of something. Talking that morning at the breakfast table she had tried to put into words her rebellion against their indifference. Lillith and Reese, she thought with a start, were uncommonly alike. Lillith's emotions, however, had yet to crystallize. A native energy and a shadowy conception of *noblesse oblige* confused her. Reese's ideas were as clearly defined as rock crystal.

She peered at him over the top of the wheel. Joseph had risen and was standing in earnest conversation. His wife and two children remained on their knees but they no longer worked. Their hands were idle as they stared at the two men. After a moment she saw Reese laugh and with a brief clap on Joseph's shoulder turn and retrace his steps. Whatever it was he had wanted to say had been said and well received. Joseph bent again to his planting.

Watching Reese as he came across the field, Ann-Charlotte realized that she was seeing not the man but the boy. His walk hadn't changed. It was the same easy gait, just short of a swagger. There was confidence in it. Reese had walked that way as he came to The Hill late in the afternoon following Laura Whitfield's visit to this cabin. Laura had told them she had seen Reese, that he was coming to stay, and warned against displaying surprise or curiosity.

"He didn't want to come," she explained, "and you must be careful not to allow him to think it is unusual or any different today than it has ever been. Now mind," she said severely, "what I am saying. Just go about whatever you are doing and don't let him think you have been waiting for a visitor."

Ann-Charlotte closed her eyes, tilting her head back against the leather. It all seemed so long ago, and yet it could have been yesterday. She remembered how she had hidden herself behind the full, floor-length lace curtains in the living room and waited. Reese hadn't spoken to her since that night at Vance Porter's, although they had passed each other in the school yard and in the halls. He and Cary were friends again, at least they seemed to have picked up where they had dropped things, only now Reese avoided her. From where she stood she could look down the long, circling driveway, and whenever anyone came into the room she pressed her body tightly against the wall. This vigil, she knew, was without dignity, but she wanted to see Reese first. When she did glimpse him, he was walking as she knew he was walking now in the field; indifferently and with an unstudied air of assurance.

X

REESE went to The Hill that day pulled by emotions he didn't understand and couldn't explain. The very act of trudging up the long-familiar driveway seemed new, something he had never done before. The trees and shrubs were strange, and even the house on the ridge was different; somehow, it had shrunk. Maybe, he thought, it is because I am going to live in it.

Behind the studied, expressionless mask he had forced himself to wear from the moment he walked from his father's land there was a sense of excitement and anticipation. How would he act there on The Hill? Would the Whitfields expect him to go and come as he pleased? If he was hungry, was he to go to the kitchen and ask for something to eat or tell one of the maids to bring it to him? If he didn't like this or that, would they want him to say so? Suppose he felt like using a car, should he go to the garage and take one? If he wanted to ride around the lake in the launch or invite a girl or some of the boys to go with him, could he just walk down to the boathouse or would they expect him to wait until Cary or Ann-Charlotte suggested things?

These and other uncertainties plagued him, and deep inside he could feel a small, hard core of resentment and defiance. As a gesture he had left the few clothes he owned neatly packed away in a cardboard box in the cabin. One pair of trousers, his best; a shirt with collar attached, and his new brown shoes, these things he had worn. Now he was confused. That had been a silly thing to do. The Whitfields, especially Mrs. Whitfield, would expect him to bring what he had. I don't care, he thought. If they don't like it, I'll leave and go look for Pa. He knew, though, that he wouldn't leave. For better or worse he was being tied to the Whitfields.

He climbed the last few yards to The Hill slowly, then his shoulders straightened. He had the feeling that unseen eyes were staring, peeking at him from the many windows; the fantastic notion that all of the Whitfields and all of their servants had taken up hiding places throughout the house and were at that moment gazing coldly at him. Then he was startled by the appearance of Laura Whitfield. She walked leisurely from behind the hedged gardens at one side of the house. A basket filled with flowers hung loosely on one arm and in her hand she carried a pair of shears.

"Oh! Hello, Reese." She called. Her voice was casual, friendly. It was devoid of any welcoming challenge. He moved toward her.

"Hello, Mrs. Whitfield," he said and waited.

Laura bent down and tapped at a plant with her shears, pretending great interest in what she saw.

"You know," she remarked, "the bugs in this garden get worse every year, worse and bigger."

"Yes'm." He experienced a quiet sense of relief. "It's been damp. That's what brings them out."

"If you're going into the house, will you take these for me?" She slipped the basket from her arm and passed it to him.

Somehow Reese knew she was acting. He was certain she had been waiting, planning this meeting in order that he might feel less strange. Until now he hadn't been sure how he should approach the house. He had been undecided whether to ring the bell and wait, or just walk in and hope someone would be around. Now it was easy and there was unmistakable gratitude in his eyes. Laura recognized it and smiled. Together they strolled toward the steps.

"You musn't feel awkward," she whispered confidentially, "you've been in the house a hundred times, Reese, and this is just another time."

"No'm," he said, "I won't." He swung the basket carelessly, almost happily. "I felt like I was going into some sort of an orphan asylum," he confessed abruptly.

"You musn't." Laura Whitfield didn't protest. She shrugged his statement away. "You ought to be happy here. I think," she said honestly, "we all ought to be happier. You and Cary have always been such good friends, now you can be as close as brothers." She smiled again with bright appreciation. "I know brothers, Reese. I had three of them. They don't always get along together, and so you musn't think you have to accept him any way he wants to be just because you live here now. A good," she hesitated and then continued with an air of a conspirator, "a good punch on the nose solves more things sometimes than mere bloodletting. Of course," she giggled, and Reese laughed with her, "of course, officially, I would have to protest, but you musn't think you have to take anything.

That," she added shrewdly, "goes for Cary, also, so don't bring your battered features to me, either one of you."

"No'm." Reese's eyes were twinkling. He never realized before that Mrs. Whitfield could be funny. "No'm. Neither of us will come a-running."

He held the door and then followed her down the long hall.

"I forgot to ask or, maybe, we didn't have time. Do you want a room of your own or would you rather share Cary's?"

"I guess I'd like to be in with Cary." There was the suggestion of a grin around his mouth. "Anyhow, we can start that way."

"That's fine." Laura nodded briskly. "He wanted you and made room for your things." She stopped shortly, and Reese knew she was embarrassed, realizing for the first time that he had come empty-handed to The Hill. She thought, probably, he had nothing to bring.

Ann-Charlotte appeared then. She had watched Reese from the moment he turned into the driveway below and began mounting the slope. She had seen her mother greet him and waited with a tingling sense of excitement as they came up the steps and crossed the porch. Somehow, this was a new Reese. Having him living here would be like having a strange man in the house. The idea possessed her but she strove to be casual.

" 'Lo, Reese." She looked around the hall, pretending a minute examination of the walls, searching for something. If he didn't speak, if he continued to ignore her as he had been doing, how would she act?

"Hi, Ann-Charlotte." There was no enthusiasm in his reply, but the moment had been saved. She smiled her gratitude.

"Cary," she said, "is down at the boathouse. Want to go?"

There was a moment of silence. "Sure," he said finally.

Laura Whitfield took the basket of flowers. If she had noticed anything odd or strained in their meeting, she ignored it.

"I'll take the flowers, Reese. Thank you for helping me." She walked away down the hall, leaving them alone.

Ann-Charlotte looked up at him, searching his face. Reese, she thought, just couldn't act this way all of the time.

"Will you walk down with me, Reese?" She asked the question with unusual softness and waited.

"Sure, Ann-Charlotte." He dropped his eyes to hers. "Sure, I'll go."

Without hesitation her hand slipped into his. She knew what she was doing now even if Reese didn't. The meeting had been planned, even to her knee-length pleated skirt of white flannel and the soft blue cashmere sweater molding her hard little breasts and slender waist. He had to look at her and, looking, would know that at fourteen she wasn't any longer just Cary's kid sister. Her hand in his wasn't a child's hand with a hard, impersonal touch. Her fingers snaked through his with clinging warmth. They moved toward the front door and in the gloomy foyer she turned, darting a quick glance down the length of the hall, and then, pressing against him, lifted her face.

"Kiss me, Just Reese," she whispered and there was an almost savage, husky note in her voice.

She felt his hand tighten uncontrollably and then he pulled away. His laugh was edgy, nervous.

"You're crazy," he said. "What do I want to kiss you for? Come on if you want to go to the boathouse. Stop trying to act like something in the movies."

He pushed out of the door ahead of her and Ann-Charlotte smiled to herself as she followed. He didn't look at her as they walked along the path to the lake, and she allowed her hands to hang carelessly at her sides. Now and then, though, her knuckles brushed his or their arms touched as they swung with the motion of their bodies. Reese gazed straight ahead.

They found Cary lounging in the grass in the shade of the boathouse. A canoe had been upended on two sawhorses, and scattered about were cans of varnish and green paint. Tod, one of the Whitfield's colored boys, was rubbing doggedly at the canoe's bottom with a piece of sandpaper wrapped around a wooden block. He darted a hopeful glance at Reese and Ann-Charlotte. Cary rolled over on his stomach and looked at them.

"How you, Reese," he said happily. "Took you long enough to get here. I'm fixin' up one of the canoes. Pa said it would be all right if we went down to Bingham's and got an outboard motor."

"You'll have to square off one of the ends," Reese said practically. "Does he know you're goin' to do that, too?"

"That's all right." Cary sat up, his interest aroused. "Soon's I get it varnished and painted, we'll take it down to the boat works."

"Soon's you git hit fixed, Cahry," Tod's features were creased in a scornful frown, "soon's you git hit painted ain' goin' to be soon enough." He grunted. "Heah ah am, supposin' to be cahrin foah

Miz Whitfield's gahdun an' ah'm scrapin' ol' boat instid. Youah mamma goin' to give me hell foah 'is."

Cary leaped to his feet. "I'll give you hell if you don't finish that bottom, and stop calling me Cary!"

"Yessuh, Mistuh Cahry Whitfiel', yessuh, boss, suh." Tod made an elaborate bow. His voice and words were dripping sarcasm and then he shouted with laughter, doubling up over the canoe and rocking back and forth, indifferent to the smearing of the varnish.

Cary advanced doubtfully a couple of steps. His face was white.

"I'll beat the hell out of you," he muttered strangely.

Tod's face sobered. He and Cary were of the same age. They had played together from the time they were children until a couple of years ago. Tod had been born on The Hill. Cary's sudden airs struck him as being ludicrous, but he wasn't smiling now. Instead, he dropped the block on the unfinished bottom and wiped his hands on the seat of his pants.

"Ef youah mamma evah heah you talkin' to me thataway, she'll fram you good an' no fooling. Ah don' caah how ol' you gittin' noah how biggity, neithah. Pain' youah ol' damn boat youahse'f." He wheeled and walked away with quiet dignity.

Cary looked after him. "You better come back here, Tod," he yelled, outraged and furious. The boy paid no attention and Cary turned, kicking out savagely at the legs of the sawhorses. "I'll kill that nigger," he snarled.

Reese grinned slowly. "You're talkin' a mighty lot like a Yankee," he said. "I never heard you call Tod or anyone a nigger before."

Ann-Charlotte snickered and Cary spun about. "All right, take up for him, both of you. Just wait until I'm twenty-one. You'll see."

"I can wait, sure enough." Reese straightened the canoe. "Come on," he added soothingly, "I'll help you with it. Ought to be scraped first," he suggested.

Ann-Charlotte waited. She was hoping that Cary would stay mad, then maybe Reese would remain with her. Cary, though, sulked for a moment and then halfheartedly picked up a putty knife, sliding it along the old paint as a scraper. Reese took the sandpaper and followed behind him. They worked in silence for a few minutes and then Cary straightened, turning to Reese. He smiled a little self-consciously.

"I guess it did sound crazy," he admitted with a rare flash of candor, "talking to Tod that way." He grew reflectively serious. "I

107

get sick and tired of people treating me like I was a kid. Anyhow," he added virtuously, "Tod oughtn't to call me Cary any longer."

"Why not?" Ann-Charlotte had seated herself cross-legged on the lawn. She chewed ruminatively on a grass stem. "Why," she asked innocently, "shouldn't Tod call you Cary? He always has."

Cary glared at her. "Because," he was being superior, "I'm almost a grown man now. That's why."

Ann-Charlotte rested her hands on her bare knees. "When you're really grown-up," she said with an infuriatingly quiet wisdom, "Tod'll know it and stop calling you Cary."

Cary grunted impatiently and then, unable to frame a truly crushing reply, bent again to his work. Reese glanced quizzically across the canoe at Ann-Charlotte, wondering at her knowledge. Sometimes she seemed agelessly wise. He rubbed at the splotched canvas surface. Cary, he mused, wasn't as bad as he sounded. They'd had a lot of fun together. Sometimes, though, he was hard to understand. He said things without meaning them. Besides, he thought, Cary was spoiled. It wasn't his fault.

"I'm going to stay in your room," Reese spoke without interrupting the steady rhythm of his sanding. "Your mother asked me what I wanted and I said that."

Cary looked up. He was surprised. "Why," he said wonderingly, "I never thought you'd want it any other way. I cleaned half the place out just for you." He hesitated. "I'm glad you're going to stay, Reese." He spoke hurriedly but there was sincerity in his voice. He almost seemed troubled at the thought of Reese taking any other room.

"Oh! Poof!" Ann-Charlotte didn't like being ignored. "You talk like a couple of biddies fixing up a nest." She rose and brushed at her skirt. "If you're not going to do anything but paint this old canoe, I'm going back to the house." She moved irresolutely toward the path. When no one attempted to stay her, she called plaintively to Cary. "Couldn't we take a ride or do something?"

Cary was grateful for the suggestion. Scraping a canoe wasn't half as much fun as watching Tod do it. He laid the knife down.

"What do you say, Reese? Want to go? We'll drive down an' get a dope. We can ask about that outboard motor at Bingham's, too." The diversion appealed to him.

Reese brushed his hands. "I guess Tod was right," he said. "As soon as we get this painted ain't goin' to be soon enough."

They walked to the garage together and crowded into the front seat. Cary backed the car out and then turned to Ann-Charlotte.

"I don't know why I'm taking you," he grumbled.

"Because I thought of something to get you out of work," she said modestly. "That's why."

They drove down to Winton, stopped at the drugstore for curb service and sucked heavily iced coca-colas through straws. Sitting in the car, Reese experienced a curious feeling of security. It wasn't just sitting in the car with Cary and Ann-Charlotte. They had done this many times before. Now, though, it was different. He sort of belonged to them and they to him. He dropped one arm across the back of the seat and allowed his hand to flop affectionately on Cary's shoulder. He had a desire to touch something. To be close and to be wanted. He knew, now, he had been desperately lonely. His father had never expected him to stay in the cottage after he left. Now, he couldn't explain why he had fought against The Hill.

Feeling the weight of Reese's hand, Cary turned. He smiled suddenly and there was warmth and affection in his glance.

"Think you're smart enough to go to college?" He asked the question chaffingly.

Reese tossed back his head and laughed, not because what Cary had said struck him as being particularly funny but simply because something within him had suddenly been released. These were his friends; his brother and sister, Mrs. Whitfield had said, and he was no longer alone.

"If they'll let you in a college," he said after a moment, "then I'm sure smart enough to go."

After the boy from the fountain had taken their empty glasses, they drove aimlessly around; killing time, idling up and down familiar streets and out past the cigarette factories and mills. Reese had the puzzling feeling that he was seeing Winton for the first time. It seemed different, somehow, today. He looked at it through the eyes of a Whitfield, experiencing something close to proprietorship. He could explain Cary to himself better now. It was easy to take things for granted on The Hill.

"I wonder what it was like," he said aloud, the words were out before he was conscious of having spoken, "I wonder?"

"What?" Ann-Charlotte turned her shoulder and looked at him.

"Winton." He was embarrassed. "Winton when your grandfather first came here."

"Oh!" Her interest waned. "Little and dirty, I guess."

Reese shook his head. That wasn't what he had meant. He was trying to imagine what Winton had looked like to Andrew. He must have seen more than a small, backwoods town, otherwise he wouldn't have built The Hill from where he could keep an eye on it.

"No," he said slowly, "I guess it was kind of exciting, too. I mean, making something with your own hands and brain the way he did."

Ann-Charlotte giggled. "He made more than that. I heard Uncle Joe say once that half the bright Negrahs in the county could claim Whitfield kin if they were a mind to."

Reese stared in amazement at her. "Where do you learn such talk, Ann-Charlotte? I'll swear, I never heard anything like it."

"You will," she answered, "when you grow up."

That evening, while he and Cary were dressing for supper, he thought again about what she had said.

"Where do you suppose Ann-Charlotte learns all that stuff?" he asked.

"What stuff?" Cary dug at one ear with the corner of a towel.

"About colored bastards an' all. She says the damnedest things for a kid."

Cary was uninterested. He came out of the bathroom and began pawing through a bureau drawer for a clean shirt. Watching him, Reese remembered that he hadn't even brought a coat. Leaving his things behind didn't seem so smart now.

"Say," he attempted an offhanded manner, "can I borrow a shirt and, maybe, a coat or something to wear at the table?"

Cary straightened up from his hunting. He was surprised by the request.

"Why, sure," he said. "Take whatever you want." He flipped open another drawer. "Anything you see."

He was frankly puzzled and Reese knew it. He even imagined that there was a note of condescension in Cary's invitation, as though he had been asked for charity. Impatiently he brushed the notion aside. It was crazy, he thought. Cary hadn't meant anything. He had been asked a question and answered it. What else could he have said?

"Thanks." Reese nodded and inspected the drawer's contents. "It's a good thing we are about the same size," he added with a forced lightness.

For reasons which none of them could explain, the evening meal was studded with moments of awkwardness. It was as though they all realized that an important decision, one which must affect all of their lives, had been made. There was an air of constraint around the table, made doubly apparent by the general effort to pretend it didn't exist.

Reese was physically uncomfortable in a coat of Cary's that was drawn too snugly across his broader shoulders. He twisted and squirmed in it, expecting to hear a seam rip every time he lifted an arm. Laura caught his guarded movements and sent a smile of understanding winging down the table. He grinned then and felt better.

"You and Cary," she spoke directly to Reese, "had better go down to Belcher and Wingate's tomorrow and pick up whatever you are going to need for the summer."

She made the suggestion so matter-of-factly that the purchase of clothing for Reese seemed part of the normal procedure. Her words passed unnoticed by the others, but Reese understood and was grateful.

Dessert came as a relief and they finished it as quickly as possible, each secretly hoping that once away from the table they could re-establish the old, familiar accord.

"I suppose you children are going to the movies?" Laura made the suggestion as they walked from the dining room. "Cass, would you like to go?"

"Maybe." He took a cigar from his pocket and bit at the end.

"Well, anyhow, I'll get ready." She moved toward the hall. "Come along, Ann-Charlotte. Cary, you take your car, Father and I will decide later."

The maneuver was so deftly executed that not until he and Cassius were standing on the front porch did Reese realize they were alone.

"Sit down, Reese." Cassius tried not to be clumsily casual. Reese took a chair beside him. "I know there are probably a lot of things on your mind," Cassius spoke thoughtfully, "but most of them are in your mind and so," he smiled in the semidarkness, "maybe, we ought not to try and take them up until they come out."

"Yes, sir." Reese hoped that was the right answer.

"The Hill is your home. We're your family, if you want us, only, I guess, no one can make it so except yourself. There will be little problems only you can answer. You can visit on The Hill for the rest of your life or be a part of it. I sort of hope you'll be a part of it. I," he hesitated, "I promised your father you would be, and," Reese knew he was grinning, "I've got a notion that Lance Benton would be a tough man to break a promise to and I have given him mine."

"Yes, sir." Reese was serious. "It's a little hard to get used to, like tonight at the table. It seemed different, somhow."

Cassius nodded. "That'll wear off when you decide not to be a visitor any longer."

"I still don't know how my father could have walked off the way he did." Reese made no attempt to conceal the hurt.

"He didn't do that, Reese, any more than you would have been leaving him if you had gone away to school. It's all part of growing up. You, Cary, Ann-Charlotte will make your own lives, and all parents can do is to stay around as long as they are needed."

"Yes, sir," Reese made the admission doubtfully, "I guess, maybe, that's right."

"There'll be small things, Reese," Cassius spoke with deliberate thoughtfulness, "you'll want to talk with me about. I wish you would. I want to be a friend." He was troubled and something of his concern communicated itself to Reese. "I'd like to be Cary's friend, also, only I can't get close to him. Maybe," he added hopefully, "I will be able to through you."

They could hear voices as Laura and Ann-Charlotte approached the door, and a moment later the headlights of Cary's car cut around the driveway. Cassius rose and Reese followed. At the sight of his wife and daughter Cassius turned and faced Reese squarely.

"Take care of Ann-Charlotte, too. Will you, Reese?" He walked away, as though ashamed of what he had felt compelled to say.

Cary shouted impatiently from the car, and when Reese and Ann-Charlotte were in he shot down the driveway. Out on the avenue he allowed the car to creep along.

"What were you and Pa talking about?" He made an attempt to sound only indifferently interested.

"Nothing." Reese leaned back, feeling the fresh breeze on his face and wondering exactly what he and Mr. Whitfield had said.

"Nothing?" Cary scoffed at the idea. "It took a mighty long time to say nothing."

"Well," Reese smiled to himself, "he wanted to know if I was satisfied with the plumbing on The Hill, if I liked cold chicken for supper, and," he added the last with elaborate disinterest, "if I would like a convertible Cadillac or, maybe, a green Packard."

"Now I know you're lying." Cary stepped on the accelerator. He seemed satisfied that what Cassius had said to Reese was unimportant. "What movie do you want to see?"

"I don't care." Reese slid comfortably down in the seat. "What about you, Ann-Charlotte?"

"I don't care either." She sighed with exaggerated ecstasy, snuggling down against Reese and pretending not to notice when he tried to draw away. "Why don't you go and get yourself a date and we'll just ride around someplace."

"I'll take you back home," Cary spoke without too much hope, "and Reese and I'll double-date something."

Ann-Charlotte's hand slipped into Reese's lap and found his fingers. He didn't pull the hand away and she looked at him with quick surprise.

"Reese," she said with quiet determination, "has a date, and if he hasn't then you'll both be sorry when I'm a little older and fascinatingly glamorous and, maybe, the toast of a couple of continents, whatever that means. I'll ignore both of you then."

"You're nuts." Cary spoke without emotion. "Just plain nuts and crazy to boot. We'd better go to a movie."

Ann-Charlotte leaned her head against Reese's shoulder, making the gesture seem confiding and helpless. Looking down at her cheek, he could remember nothing but how she had looked that night in Vance Porter's with Duke Reid. Even that didn't have much reality at the moment. It could have been part of a bad dream. He thought grimly of Cassius Whitfield's final words on the porch. Taking care of Ann-Charlotte was bad enough now. What was going to happen to her in four or five years?

"What are you thinking about, Just Reese?" She tilted her face in order to look up at him.

"Nothing."

"Well," she said dreamily, "you had better begin. Next month we are going up to Asheville. You'll like it there. It isn't like anything you can imagine. There are miles and miles of woods and mountains with roads running right up into the sky. We'll have all of the days together and maybe you'll get to like me again the way you used to. You'd better tell Father you want that Cadillac convertible after all and we won't have to depend on Stinker here. You can take me places and this year I'll go to the dances at the club and it will be a wonderful summer, Just Reese."

"Ann-Charlotte"—Cary was furious, her calm assumption of Reese and the tone she used in referring to him were maddening—"you talk," he almost shouted the words, "you talk like—like a whore!"

There was a moment of electric silence and then Ann-Charlotte broke it. She wasn't angry. Reese half expected her to hit Cary. She didn't change her position in the slightest.

"Uh-huh," she agreed amiably. "That's just what I was thinking."

XI

REESE halted at the ditch separating field from house and studied the slender rill of sluggish brown water at the bottom. The years played tricks with men and their memories. Once, he recalled, this narrow cut had seemed a chasm of terrifying proportions, a canyon to be spanned in a breathlessly heroic leap after many false, running starts from a point near the overhanging mulberry tree where Ann-Charlotte waited now in the car.

Standing on the crumbling bank, he could remember how Lance had laid a sagging board across the trench to make the crossing easier for him. He was supposed to walk over instead of clambering in and out of the slender moat. The board, of course, was never used. With flailing arms and driving legs Reese would throw himself at the ditch. Sometimes he soared across, rising triumphantly from a tangled heap on the other side. More often, though, he fell short and was forced to creep out in ignominy; wet and covered with the slime and clay. Lance deliberately avoided taking any notice of these failures and appeared unaware that the makeshift bridge bore no traffic. Thinking back, now, Reese seemed to hear the man's drawling comment when he glanced indifferently at his son after one of the more spectacular miscarriages of judgment. The morning had been damply cool and Lance went early to the field to top the thrusting plants. Reese stood near by, watching silently. His arms, legs, and face were smeared with the clinging ooze, but his attitude was serenely confident. Lance looked up and then turned again to his labor.

"That there board across the ditch is gettin' mighty dirty, ain't it, son? I reckon we'll have to put a clean one up." His jaws worked convulsively on a quid of tobacco in an effort to hide a laugh.

Strange, Reese thought, how Lance Benton's presence clung to this place. He rarely thought of his father. Months, years went by and he had difficulty in remembered what Lance Benton had looked like. Then, he could stand as he was now and the man was drawn sharply into focus. Time, for a moment, would step aside and he was able to look back. He wondered what Lance would think if they might pause here for a moment again; wondered what he would think of Reese Benton, Ann-Charlotte in the car there, even the car itself and what it represented.

"Pa," he said aloud, "it might scare the hell out of you."

He crossed the ditch with an effortless jump. Ann-Charlotte looked as though she were asleep. Walking toward the parked car, he frowned a little wearily, recalling Joseph's words of a few minutes ago. For the past five years he had been growing tobacco on the small Benton tract. More than half the time he was in debt, torn and tormented by the never-ending struggle to scratch a living from the earth. Tobacco was no easy crop. It tormented a man, scrabbled his soul and broke his back. Joseph and his wife would have been much better off if they had gone to work in the factory or one of the mills. He clung to the soil, though, with a dogged faith, scoffing at the free and easy ways of the mill people with their pay envelopes in their pockets on Saturday night. He even wanted to own the land that beat and abused him, although he knew in secret he couldn't raise the money for a down payment if his unsatisfied longing ever passed beyond the talking stage. When Reese told him he could stay on as long as he wanted and put the rent at a dollar a year, Joseph had felt defeated. He was still a tenant and there was a hopeless stare in his eyes, a look of accusation as though Reese was denying him his birthright. So stark was the man's frustration that for a moment Reese had been tempted to tell him they could make a deal on the spot. The words, though, stuck in his throat and wouldn't be forced out.

"I'd like mighty well to buy, Reese." Joseph looked helplessly around, and Reese was conscious that his wife had turned her face upward and was listening. "A fella gets took with a place, sometimes, an' that's what's happened to me. I'd sure enough like to step out in the mornin' an' push my feet in land of my own. It ain't," he added, almost reproachfully, "like you needed or used it for yourself."

For a moment Reese was angry. He was tempted to snatch Joseph by his lean shoulders and tell him to look around; to see his children as they were, dirty, almost ragged, the sap of youth turning into hard resin through improper feeding and neglect. Look at yourself, that woman on her knees and those youngsters, he wanted to shout, and then get the hell out of here and find a decent, steady job and take care of them. Can't you understand there is no place for you on the land any longer? None of those things would make any sense to Joseph, and so he didn't speak as he knew he should.

"I'll tell you what," he injected a hopeful note into his voice, "you stay on here and get your crop in and to market. Come and see me then and we'll work out something. If you can't make it this year, maybe, next year. I won't let anyone else have the place."

Joseph's gratitude was immediate and went no further than the moment. Perhaps in his heart he knew he would never have enough surplus cash to make a first payment, but that was an obstacle to be surmounted in some mistily vague future. Here in the field, though, he held hope in his hand. All a man had to do was work a little harder, bend a little quicker and he could stand on his own. The pleasure, so apparent on his features, almost made Reese feel ashamed of himself. He'd only given the man a haunting voice to call after, the laughter of an idiot to chase.

"That's mighty fine of you, Reese." Joseph's lips trembled. "I take it as mighty fine an' we'll be comin' to talk to you in September."

For a moment Reese almost believed with him that they had worked some magic there between the furrows. He laid his hand on Joseph's shoulder, tightening his fingers with a feeling of comradeship.

"You do that," he said. "In the meantime I'd sort of like to make a few repairs to the house, so if you don't mind I'll have a couple of carpenters down to look it over."

"Well, you do that, Reese," Joseph replied absently. He looked across the field. His mind wasn't on a house, a man could always raise a roof. What he was looking at had the eternal strength of God. He saw only the land. "You just do that an' we'll figure it out when the time comes to make the deal."

As Reese neared the car, Ann-Charlotte raised her head. "Next time I go riding with you," she said, "I'll bring a horse."

"Next time you go riding with me," the words were pleasantly confidential, "you'll wait until you are invited."

He stood by the car, his hands on the door, looking up into the massed green of the tree. How many pecks of the purple berries, worms, bugs, and all, had he stripped from those branches and crammed into his mouth?

"You know," he said for no particular reason, "I used to climb up there and get my lunch; supper, too, sometimes."

"You know," Ann-Charlotte mimicked, "I've known you almost as long as you have known yourself, so don't try and impress me with your rustic flavor."

He smiled; quickly, warmly, reaching over to take her hand. Ann-

Charlotte made no attempt to hide her surprise. Her fingers closed evenly over his.

"I forget, sometimes," was all he said. He drew back to open the door. "Any place in particular you want to go now?"

"Uh-uh." She watched him with a sleepy, indolent air.

"Home?"

"Not unless we have to." She paused. "How about out to the club and a drink? Maybe we could manage to stay away for lunch."

He nodded and leaned forward to turn the ignition key. "Whatever you say."

She straightened up with a jerk, eying him skeptically. "Say," she said wonderingly, "I'm in favor of this back to the old manse. It sort of uncurdles you. I'd even come out and live with you if that's what the sight of a cabin does for your disposition."

Reese swung the car around and headed it down the uneven road. They didn't speak again until they were out on the highway and streaking silently along in the direction of the club.

"Somehow," Reese kept his features expressionless, "I can't reconcile you with a cabin, sitting on the steps in the twilight chewing snuff or smoking a corncob pipe."

"Is that how they get all of those children?" Ann-Charlotte was wide-eyed, breathless. "Tell me some more, Daddy Reese."

"That's all there is to it."

"Well, what do you know." Ann-Charlotte was lost in admiration. "Just a ten-cent can of Whitfield's Unexcelled Snuff or a corncob pipe. I tell you, Reese, there's no end to the wonders of this world."

"It doesn't even have to be Whitfield's snuff."

She made a deprecatory sound. "I'm sure any other kind would produce decidedly inferior babies."

He smiled, cutting past a rattling farm wagon drawn by a sleepy, disillusioned mule drooping between the spindling shafts.

"Light a cigarette for me, will you?" he asked.

She lit two and passed one to him, smiling contentedly when he didn't comment, as she had expected, on the lipstick smear ringing the tip.

"This has been sort of nice, Reese," she said after a moment. "Why can't we always be this way, easy and friendly without everyone trying to bitch everyone else?"

"Sounds dull to me."

"Don't humor me, Reese. I'm grown. I know what's in your mind and, maybe, a little of what's in your heart. You can quit trying to beat ghosts out of the bush. It would be sort of wonderful if you'd stop."

At the sight of his mouth, drawn suddenly hard and thoughtful, she sighed unhappily. The sparkle within her died quickly and she leaned back wearily.

"That's what I mean," she continued. "You snap shut, swallow yourself like a wonk and no one can get near you."

Reese turned briefly. "You're only talking to hear the sound of words, Ann-Charlotte."

"I'm not." She skirted anger. "All of your stubbornness isn't going to change people. That missionary frock doesn't become you."

"I'm willing to take you as you are, only you aren't satisfied to leave it that way."

She moved her head with a gesture of defeat. "Reese, Reese," she murmured, "stop trying to devour yourself. Don't talk to me that way. Remember," her eyes searched his face, "remember I was your girl once?"

"Were you? When?"

"Don't you want to leave me any pride at all, Reese?"

His laugh was short, hard and scornful. "I didn't know the quality interested you."

"How," she asked with a lightning change of mood, "would you like a good poke in the nose?"

He smiled then and nodded understandingly. The tension between them evaporated.

"I'd prefer that to your drooling," he said.

Ann-Charlotte snapped her cigarette away and settled into a more comfortable position.

"Do you know, Reese," there was no malice in her tone, "I think you're a no-good bastard."

"It's the company I've been exposed to," he said. "Now, suppose we share a few minutes of silence until we get to the club and you have to open your mouth for a drink."

Not until they had turned into the club's driveway did Ann-Charlotte speak. Several times on the way out she looked at Reese, seemingly on the point of picking up the conversation, but changed her mind.

"I want more than a drink," she said as they drew up before the entrance. "I'm bored. Let's have a hell of a party, gather up all the rum pots and take them back to The Hill."

"Is that what you really want?"

"No," she said with disarming honesty, "it isn't at all what I want, but it seems like a good idea."

"Well, let's don't bother with it, then." Without waiting for a reply he started the car and swung back out. Ann-Charlotte didn't protest.

Cary and Lillith were sprawled comfortably in canvas beach chairs when they returned to The Hill. Between them was a low table bearing rum, limes, sugar, a siphon and a thermos ice jug. With several drinks resting easily, Cary was feeling better, and he greeted Ann-Charlotte and Reese with animation, pulling his chair about to face them. Watching the change, Lillith experienced a twinge of compassion. He was so pathetically anxious to have people around him, a group fed some gnawing loneliness within him which she could no longer reach. The morning had been pleasant, almost a relief. She had smiled several times to herself thinking of the domestic picture they unconsciously created; Cary with an iced drink in his hand and a book in his lap, she with her knitting. Ma in her kerchief, she thought amusedly, and Pa in his cap. They had talked in a desultory fashion, making plans for the summer, settling on the people they would ask to the lodge. Cary seemed more than eager that everything meet with her approval.

"We don't have to ask anyone up if you don't want to," he suggested. "Maybe, it might be a good thing if we had some time to ourselves."

"And Reese?" she asked.

"Of course, Reese will be here. I was thinking of people who usually come up." His surprise was an afterthought, and he glanced at her as though the import of her words startled him. "What made you say that?" He put his drink on the table, leaning toward her.

"No reason." She kept her eyes on her knitting.

Cary wasn't satisfied. "But you said it in such a funny way, as if you didn't want him."

"Why shouldn't I want Reese? He's your best friend, isn't he?"

Cary lounged back in his chair, satisfied. "Of course he is."

When Ann-Charlotte and Reese came across the lawn toward them, Lillith put aside her knitting and covertly watched Cary's expression, looking for she knew not what.

"The rich have all the pleasure." Ann-Charlotte poured herself a straight tot of rum and drank it without a chaser. "Is this what you've been doing all morning?"

"Uh-huh." Lillith held out her glass. "Do for me, will you? Have fun?"

"Not much." Ann-Charlotte put fresh ice into the glass. "I tried to drag Mr. Benton out into the bushes but he screamed."

Lillith laughed. She knew that what Ann-Charlotte had said was no less, probably, than half truth. She was fond of her sister-in-law. Her frankly amoral attitude amused and sometimes even fascinated her. Ann-Charlotte, she thought, probably had the morals of a guinea pig and yet she, apparently, remained unsullied.

Reese stretched out on the grass with his back against a tree. "Make me a drink, Charl."

Ann-Charlotte turned. "You know I loathe anyone who calls me that."

"Like Chotty better?" Reese looked up innocently.

"I spit in the eyes of people who call me Chotty."

"She does, too," Cary said. "I saw her do it once."

Lillith rose. "Let's take a swim before lunch?" She thrust the small patch of knitting into a bag. "Afterwards we can figure out something to do. Cary? Reese?"

"I still want my drink," Reese said plaintively.

"Fix it yourself." Ann-Charlotte linked her arm through Lillith's. "My God," she exclaimed with surprise, "did you hear that sound? It was a worm turning and biting itself. What do you know?"

"We'll be along in a minute," Cary called as they strolled away. He watched them for a moment and then turned to Reese. "Why don't you marry Ann-Charlotte?" he asked simply.

"Do you know," Reese said without humor, "I sometimes wonder about that myself. It would serve her right." He closed his eyes, tilting his head against the tree's trunk and scratching his scalp gently against the bark.

"Want to go for a swim with them?" Cary waited.

"Might as well." Reese didn't move.

The morning was heavily drowsy with summer. It made him sleepy. Through half-closed eyes he watched Cary, sitting on the leg rest of the chair, leaning forward on arms doubled into his lap.

"Reese?" Cary's voice seemed far away. "Reese, tell me about Lil. Do you think she's happy?" He glanced up hopefully, waiting to be reassured.

The damn fool, Reese thought irritably. Do I have to go through this again?

"Why shouldn't she be happy?" He brushed the question aside.

"I don't know. It's just that she seems restless, as though she wanted, needed something to do."

"Well," Reese rose, went to the table and mixed a drink for himself, "what do other women do?"

Cary brightened, nodding sagely. "Sure, what do other women do?" He repeated the question, savoring some small satisfaction in it.

"Some of them," Reese took the chair left empty by Lillith, "some of them scrub floors, wash pots and diapers, work in factories or follow a plow. I don't think any of those things would appeal to Lil."

"I guess not; probably just my imagination, but you know the way she talked this morning after she came back from Uncle Joe's."

Reese grinned reflectively. "Sounded to me as though she was going to make you go out and look for a job."

Cary yawned. "Maybe," he suggested, "we ought to have a party." That had become his solution to anything he couldn't understand. Have a party, broadcast invitations, fill the house with people and turn them loose on The Hill.

"Sure, why not." Reese glanced sharply at him, wondering if he could possibly be serious. "Lil," he added after a moment, "will like that." He buried a smile in his drink.

"We could take them all up to the lodge with us when we go." The idea was beginning to appeal to him, and what had started out to be a party was developing into a summer excursion.

"This time," Reese was solemn, "let's only take the ones who are conscious. The others get to be a lot of trouble after a while."

Cary laughed reminiscently. "I was thinking, sitting out here with Lil before you and Ann-Charlotte came back, about the summers when we were kids. That was a lot of fun, Reese."

"Was it?"

Something harsh, unrelenting in the question caused Cary to look up quickly. "Why, sure," he said slowly, "don't you remember?"

Reese felt a smoldering anger within him take fire. It burned with a fierce but blanketed heat. Didn't he remember? He stared at Cary and saw only astonishment over what must be written on his own face. Had any of them forgotten? He wondered, fixing his gaze on his hands as he thrust a bumping thumb across the knuckles.

"Sure, I remember. We had a hell of a time, didn't we?"

Remembering wasn't difficult. Without half trying he could trace every step of that first summer when he came to The Hill. He hadn't been very smart then, just a lonely kid who was willing to give so much more than anyone intended he should. How could he have been expected to know that? Laura Whitfield did, she even tried to warn him.

"You mustn't let anyone hurt you, Reese," she said gently. "Keep something of yourself to yourself."

He hadn't had any idea of what she was trying to tell him and she sensed it, sighing regretfully and touching him quickly on the arm with her hand.

They were getting ready to open the lodge and at her instructions he and Cary had gone down into Winton to Belcher and Wingate's. Embarrassed, he had stood to one side while Cary grandly ordered white flannels, sports jackets, shirts, socks, tan and white shoes until the pile on the counter grew so high that the clerk had to come around front in order to check the final purchases. It looked like a waste of money to Reese, since he had already seen Cary's packed bureau drawers and clothes closet and it didn't seem possible that anyone could need so much. Cary sauntered back from the rear of the store, clutching a fistful of neckties.

He dropped them on the rest of the order. "I guess that's all," he said to the salesman and then turned to Reese. "Get everything you want?"

Reese almost laughed. He knew why they had gone to the store but he hadn't been able to summon courage enough to pick out anything. He couldn't help but think that Cary ought to have tried to help him. Even now, when the way was made open, he couldn't force himself to order anything.

"Sure," he said awkwardly, realizing that the clerk was eying him with undisguised curiosity, "I guess so."

Laura came to their room that evening. Cary had spread everything out on the bed and was examining it all without enthusiasm. She touched a few of the purchases and nodded, satisfied.

"And Reese," she said, "where are your things?"

He flushed, could feel the color creeping up from his neck. "Well," he mumbled helplessly, "I didn't figure I'd need anything much."

Laura made no attempt to hide her surprise. "Do you mean to tell me, Cary Whitfield, you only bought things for yourself?"

Cary didn't know what to say. Somehow, he was being accused of doing something he shouldn't have done. "Why sure," he said, "Reese said he had everything. Didn't you, Reese?" He turned wonderingly.

"I see." Laura nodded. She flipped over a few of the new ties and then walked from the room.

After she left, Cary looked at Reese. "Now, what do you suppose got into her?"

Reese could have told him, but he didn't.

The next morning Laura made a point of mentioning at the breakfast table that she had to go down to Winton, and later, finding Reese alone, called to him.

"Reese, would you mind riding down with me? I'll need some help with a few things." She made it sound very brisk and businesslike.

In the car, driving from The Hill, she turned to him. "Why didn't you get what you needed yesterday?"

He twisted uncomfortably, trying to avoid her eyes. "I don't know, I guess I—" The words wouldn't form themselves.

"Were you ashamed? Did it seem like charity to you?"

He looked up helplessly, almost pleading with her not to force an answer.

"But don't you see, Reese," she continued with a gentle insistence, "this won't work out at all if you don't help. Cary isn't selfish, at least I hope he isn't. He's thoughtless, that's all. It never occurred to him someone might want, might need something and not ask for it."

Reese wanted to cry and he turned his head almost rudely for fear she should see this weakness. No one had ever talked to him this way. Even Lance Benton, who was kind, could never be tender. The words twisted at his heart, and he bit at the inside of his lips to still their trembling.

"You see, Reese," the words were softly persuasive, "we want you. I mean that for all of us, and so you'll have to share some of the responsibility. Will you try?"

He nodded dumbly but kept his face turned toward the window.

Downtown, Laura took his fingers in a quick, friendly grasp. He looked at her, unabashed now.

"Do you think," she said laughingly, "you can go into Belcher and Wingate's and order what you want, or should I go with you and buy things for a little boy?"

He had to grin a reply to her smile. "No'm," he said huskily, "I guess I can do it this time by myself."

"Everything. From the skin out?"

He blushed, realizing it made him look foolish. "Yes'm."

"I want to see twice as much as Cary brought home yesterday. Tell them to have it ready and I'll stop back for you in the car when I finish down at Meecham's."

Somehow, he had expected Cary to display some surprise when he came up to the room later and saw both beds covered with neat stacks of underwear, shirts, sweaters, flannels, and the other things he had bought. Cary only looked, commented favorably on a couple of the more brilliant ties, and then turned to him.

"Well," he said, "why didn't you do this yesterday? You had plenty of time. Let's go swimming. Ruth Stevens, Johnny Clark, and Ann-Charlotte are down on the float waiting."

XII

NONE of them could know that tragedy, wearing an innocently lazy smile and speaking softly, would be waiting for them that summer when they went to the mountains as a family. It stood there, though, not bothering to conceal itself; confident and unhurried, certain of the meeting.

Reese learned many things during those months, acquiring small, social graces and a new ease as he moved among people who, without question, accepted so much of the world's bounty as their proper heritage. He discovered a bright, mellowing comradeship in young men and girls of his own age, and found, somewhat to his surprise, that people seemed instinctively to like him. Not the least of the surprises, though, lay in the certain knowledge that Cassius Whitfield feared and hated The Hill. It took him some time to understand why.

From the moment they drove from the big, brown house the man underwent a curious transformation. As the miles accumulated, piling distance between the car and Winton, he became a different person. The load of apprehension under which he was perpetually bent seemed to slip from his shoulders. He laughed as a man might upon release from a prison and made small, though not always funny, jokes with the family and the chauffer. He talked eagerly of the lodge as if it represented a distant but not unattainable heaven, and discussed plans for picnics and excursions. Reese, caught up in the excitement and novelty of being away from Winton for the first time in his life, was only vaguely conscious of the overtones in his voice in the beginning, but as the morning lengthened he caught himself wondering, puzzled by this unnatural gaiety. Cassius seemed to have left some oppressive burden back there on The Hill. For the first time Reese understood that Cassius was a troubled and unhappy man.

The knowledge bothered him, and he thought of something Joseph Whitfield had said one day when they were fishing while he was supposed to be working for him at Bluestone.

"Don't ever develop scruples, Reese." Joe made a short cast from the rowboat and watched the bright, red top of his float with critical interest. "You won't always be popular, because it offends people, somehow, to see a naked man, but you'll be a damn sight more comfortable."

Reese was puzzled by the statement, it seemed to have no connection with fishing, but then Joe Whitfield frequently said odd things which were seemingly without point.

"That," he continued reflectively, "is what is wrong with my brother. He's made a spade of his conscience and digs his grave with it."

Listening to Cassius, Reese recalled the words. What, he pondered, bothered him? He allowed his imagination to take momentary flight. What was the dark thing plucking at Cassius Whitfield's conscience? Why was he so glad to get away from The Hill? Maybe, the fancy caused him to shiver, maybe he had murdered Old Andrew Whitfield and shoved his carcass into the tomb. Maybe he was haunted by his father's ghost. That was why he seemed so happy to be leaving The Hill. He grinned inwardly. What a damn fool thing to imagine. Yet he knew something lay heavily on Cassius Whitfield's soul. It never occurred to him that it could be simple, as simple at it was.

They stopped at Asheville for lunch, a meal made almost uncomfortable by Cassius's eagerness to get going again. The journey was commonplace enough, but somehow he made an adventure of it, communicating his enthusiasm to Reese. Cary and Ann-Charlotte refused to enter into the pretense. They were openly bored with the whole business, and Cary was inclined to sulk because he hadn't been allowed to drive up in his own car, which was trailing behind under the proud hands of Tod who was bringing Clarissa and another girl from The Hill to take on the domestic chores at the lodge. Cassius had displayed an unexpected firmness over this arrangement, and Cary's ranting failed to move him.

"We'll all go together, Cary," he said. "Tod can bring up the girls."

It was almost as though, in leaving The Hill, he acquired new stature and decision, striking out as a person from the shadow of the gloomy house.

Outside of Asheville they took a branching, unpaved road that ducked and twisted through small ravines and over streams, forcing upward to the broad plateau where the lodge commanded the valley. Reese had never seen mountains before, and his imagination was captured by their brooding majesty and the sharp, heady crispness of the air. No wonder, he thought, Mr. Whitfield likes this better than Winton. From the lodge's porch his eyes could sweep the countryside, dotted with the homes of summer residents and small cabins of native folk who endured the annual invasion of visitors with unblinking stoicism.

Cassius paced the broad veranda, running on three sides of the house, with the comfortable assurance of a captain on his bridge and fastened on to Reese, pointing out the view, identifying houses and the country club with a genial air of proprietorship as though the valley was something he and God had arranged together. He made Reese feel a part of it.

In a glowering silence Cary had gone immediately to his room, waiting with bitter impatience for Tod to arrive with the La Salle. Ann-Charlotte, however, was enduring her father's temporary monopolization of Reese with grim fortitude.

"Reese can look at the view all summer long, Father," she complained finally.

Cassius halted his soaring enthusiasm in mid-flight with an embarrassed little cough and an almost apologetic smile. Looking at him, Reese thought of a child being rebuked unnecessarily. There was something pathetic about him at that moment. Reese wondered why he didn't bat Ann-Charlotte across the ears, someone ought to. Instead, Cassius nodded without protest.

"Why don't you and Reese take the station wagon," he offered the suggestion indifferently, "and ride around? He'll like to see the village and, maybe, meet some of the other folks."

Riding down into the small town of Harlen, as Ann-Charlotte drove with a wild abandon and complete disregard for curves, Reese clutched at the side of his door for support and wondered how any two people as nice as Cassius and Laura could bear the almost studied contempt of their children. Ann-Charlotte was worse than Cary. She seemed to delight in deliberately forcing a bad situation, testing authority, uncovering weak spots.

"What are you thinking about?" Ann-Charlotte slowed down and looked slantingly at him.

"I was thinking that someone ought to spank your behind," he said with complete honesty, "talking to your father the way you did."

"Well, what did I say?" Her eyes were wide with unfeigned surprise.

"Nothing. He was just being sort of proud of the scenery. I didn't mind looking at it. He was showing off a little, old people like to do such things."

They drove through the settlement, stopping for a coke. Several persons in the store greeted Ann-Charlotte with enthusiasm and, Reese thought, something close to respect. She waved a friendly hand but at the same time managed to remain coolly aloof, almost condescending. It was difficult to remember she was only fifteen years old, he told himself. After they had covered the main street of Harlen from one end to the other, Ann-Charlotte turned the car down a branching road and into a main highway. They passed a cluster of what seemed to be single-roomed cottages. At one end of the group of buildings was a larger structure with a sign: "Eats and Gas, Tourist Cottages."

"Some of the summer boys bring their girls here." She nodded at the row of cabins. "You can buy moonshine and get a cottage."

Reese looked back over his shoulder. "How do you know?" he asked.

"Everybody knows," she shrugged the question off. "That's what the cabins are for."

They made a tour of the vicinity, stopping at a large, rambling country club where Ann-Charlotte introduced him to several persons whose names he didn't remember. The boys were offhanded, friendly, and a couple of the girls, he thought, were more than mildly curious and interested by the sight of a new face. They clustered about Ann-Charlotte, exchanging invitations and promises to visit together along with an endless chatter of reminiscences of what had happened during the past summer. Reese was uncomfortable, feeling alien, and he was relieved when they left.

"They're all dopes," Ann-Charlotte said critically, "but some of them are fun when you get to know them. We'll come down to the dances." She sent the station wagon rocketing back over the road. "I'm going to have a car of my own this summer, even if Father doesn't know it yet." She paused, turning to him. "Did he really say you could have a Cadillac convertible?"

Reese laughed quickly. "No, I was only joking."

"Well," she was serious, "I guess you could get one if you asked for it. Father likes you. I can tell." She giggled. "I think it is because he expects you to be a good influence on Cary and me."

Where the road to the lodge branched off from the highway she turned the car into a filling station drive. Unconsciously Reese glanced at the gauges on the dashboard and noticed that the gasoline tank's needle was fluttering at the full mark. Ann-Charlotte bounced the heel of her palm on the horn button and a man appeared in the doorway of the small, stucco building.

"Hi! Donnie." Ann-Charlotte called.

He walked toward them across the graveled strip, wiping his hands on a soiled ball of waste; a tall, sun-hammered man with a ranging stride. He wore an old pair of oil-soaked moccasins, dungarees, and no shirt, and his skin was the color of walnut stain.

"Hey, you, Ann-Charlotte. When did you get back?"

"Today." She leaned slightly toward him over the door. "This is Reese Benton. Don Blake."

"Hello, Reese." The acknowledgment dismissed the introduction with almost insolent curtness. Reese only nodded.

"We get our gas from Donnie." Somehow Reese felt that the explanation was made in too much of a hurry.

"Cary come up, too?" Blake rested crossed arms on the door's top. The knuckles of one hand accidentally brushed against Ann-Charlotte's shoulder and remained there.

"The whole family." Ann-Charlotte didn't move, but she seemed to ripple as a snake might beneath the warming touch of the sun. "We'll be here all summer."

"That's good." The man smiled briefly. "I'll be seein' you all, then." His eyes traveled quickly over her with negligent possessiveness. "You're my best customers." He straightened up. "Want anything today?"

"No." There was a sleepy quality in her reply. "I just stopped by to say hello."

"Come in any time." He moved back from the car. "Glad to have seen you, Reese."

Back again on the road leading to the lodge, Ann-Charlotte turned to Reese. "He, Donnie," she said, "plays football for some professional team in the North during the winter and runs the filling station in the summer. He," she hesitated, "he's pretty old, I guess; probably thirty, but he's good-looking, don't you think?"

Reese grunted with noncommittal enthusiasm. Something about Blake, the way he lounged against the car, looking at Ann-Charlotte, left him with a vaguely uncomfortable feeling.

"I guess so," was all he said.

She darted a lightly amused glance his way. "What's the matter?"

"Nothing." He was angry without knowing why.

"You're jealous," she cried triumphantly.

"And you're crazy," he answered rebelliously. "Why should I be jealous over a kid like you?"

"I'm not a kid," she was serenely confident, "and you know it. If I were, you wouldn't be sitting there with your mouth drawn in like a dead fish." She swung the car to the side of the road, braking it against the steep incline, and turned quickly to him. "Oh, Reese," there was a throaty, pleading note in her voice, "let me be your girl. I'm not a child. You can't keep treating me like one. You know that." With a twisting motion she slid into the circle of his arm. Her hands crept upward to touch his face and then pulled with sudden fierceness at his head until she found his lips. Her mouth was creeping, inquisitively searching, and she gasped with a quick, small cry of pain.

Instinctively his arms closed about her. Something pounded relentlessly within him and for a moment they were locked in a breathless delirium. Her fingers fought silently over the front of his shirt, pressing against his chest.

In agony Reese pulled away, lifting his head, and her face buried itself in the hollow of his neck. This was crazy, all wrong.

"Oh, Reese!" She was trembling, her words were cloudy. "I want you to love me." Her breathing was a warm flutter on his throat. She slid her fingers to his mouth, they sought and then tugged gently at his lips. "It's always been this way."

Reese was frightened. A child couldn't talk this way. He didn't know much but he knew that.

"Look," he said shakily, "this is only going to cause trouble. You've got to stop it. You know what'll happen."

"I want it to." She clung to him and he could feel the hard tightness of her breasts through the soft sweater she was wearing. "I want to be your girl, Reese."

Gently he took her arms and lifted her shoulders until he could look down into her face. He couldn't keep pretending she was Cary's baby sister any longer. Maybe it was true, that a girl was always older than a boy, but just the same she wasn't that old. The sun on her bright hair lent a misty quality to her features. Her eyes were softly luminous.

"All right," he said and, somehow, the words didn't seem strange, "you'll be my girl. Maybe I can take care of you that way."

"Yes, Reese," she whispered, "and, and you won't be ashamed?"

"Ashamed of what?" He didn't understand.

"Ashamed to let people know it; Mother, Father, even Cary?"

"What do you expect me to do?"

"Nothing, just be natural. Stop trying to pretend I'm a baby. Do you love me, Reese?"

He touched the hair dropping so softly at her cheek. The question didn't seem unnatural. He bent his head and kissed her gently.

"Yes," he said helplessly, "I love you. It's hard to get used to."

They drove back to the lodge in silence. There seemed nothing to say. He smoked a cigarette jerkily and tossed it half-consumed to the road. Ann-Charlotte stopped the car and made him get out and tramp it down.

"You'll burn the whole mountain top off," she said patiently.

He watched her as she drove. There was a bright assurance about her handling of the wheel, the way she cocked her shoulders at an angle in the seat, the manner in which she glanced over at him now and then. I'll be damned, he thought with surprise, if she isn't older than I am.

He was momentarily embarrassed when they reached the house, feeling certain that something of what had happened must show on their faces. Laura and Cassius were on the porch, and as they walked toward them there was unmistakable pride and confidence in Laura's eyes as she watched them mount the steps. Reese was troubled, and then he cast the doubt away. Nothing had happened, not really. Maybe he shouldn't have kissed Ann-Charlotte that way, but how could he help it? Anyhow, it wasn't anything to be ashamed of. He kept repeating this to himself.

"Have a good drive?" Laura called.

"Uh-huh," Ann-Charlotte slipped her hand into Reese's, tightening her fingers as she felt his surprise.

"Cary drove down, looking for you. I think he was hurt because you left him."

"Well, he'll have to get used to it." Ann-Charlotte bounced herself to the porch railing, clinging to a pillar for support. "Hi! Pop," she added impudently.

Cassius smiled benevolently. He was happy. Clad in an old pair of flannels, wearing disreputable sneakers and a sweat shirt, he leaned back in his chair and surveyed his daughter with pleasure and satisfaction. Something, he thought, happened to them all in the mountains. They were closer to each other. He wondered why they just didn't stay here, leaving The Hill to Andrew Whitfield's tomb.

"I'm Reese's girl." Ann-Charlotte settled herself against the post. "Did you know that, Mother?"

"No, dear," Laura smiled indulgently, looking at Reese, who shifted awkwardly, "but I'm very happy to hear it."

Reese wanted to cry out, to tell her she didn't know what she was saying. That was the mistake they all made with Ann-Charlotte, dismissing her with a figurative pat on the head. He wondered what Mrs. Whitfield would have thought if she could have seen Ann-Charlotte in the car back there on the road. Just the way she talked was enough to scare the hell out of anyone.

"I thought," Ann-Charlotte said seriously, "you all ought to know it. That's why I said Cary would have to get used to our going off without him."

Reese marveled at the ease with which she was settling things to her own satisfaction. Being Reese's girl was a romantic fancy, a childish whim which Laura and Cassius would encourage and humor. Laura glanced slyly up at him to show she understood.

"When I'm eighteen," Ann-Charlotte continued, "I'll probably marry him if I still feel the same way."

"I'm sure Reese will wait," Laura said, pampering the idea. "Why don't the two of you go down to the pool and have a swim before supper? Cary said he was going over to the Claytons if he didn't find you. He'll probably bring Norma and Doris back with him. We'll all eat outdoors this evening. Your father wants to cook at the grill." She picked up her sewing. "Reese will like Norma, I think," she added dryly, hiding a smile.

Ann-Charlotte slid from the railing. She grinned knowingly, refusing to be provoked. "I'll take care of Reese," she said quietly, "and Norma Clayton, too, if she comes mewling around here."

They swam in the rock-lined pool behind the house, cavorting in its depths like two young porpoises, slicing into the icy water from the diving board, racing each other from one end to the other and crawling out, breathless and happy to lie in the warm afternoon sun. Ann-Charlotte wore a scanty, yellow suit and she was a radiant, flashing flame, arching from the board. Reese watched her with pleasure and a disturbingly tight sensation in his chest. He was seeing her as something vividly new.

"You see," she said, as they stretched on the warm, concrete lip of the pool, "how wonderful this is going to be, Just Reese."

"What?" He asked the question lazily, knowing the answer.

"My being your girl," she replied matter-of-factly. "Now you don't have to worry about going someplace for your date." She straightened up on one elbow, peering down into his face and then leaned over and gently brushed her lips against his. "See?"

Cary came down later with Doris and Norma Clayton who lived in an enormous, graystone, crenelated house on the opposite side of the small valley. Cary, Reese thought, had been drinking. He was sure of it later when Cary whispered to him.

"I've got some cool corn stashed in the car. We'll take Norma and Doris home after supper."

The Clayton girls were visibly interested in Reese and inclined to be slightly patronizing with Ann-Charlotte, three years their junior. Watching them, Reese smiled to himself. They stretched out with studied languor in the reclining chairs, with Cary sitting cross-legged at their feet.

"It's sure good to see a new face around here, Reese." Norma drawled the statement. "I hope you'll stay all summer."

"Why?" Ann-Charlotte regarded her with bright innocence.

"Well," Norma flushed, the directness of the question unbalanced her for a moment, "well, just because he looks nice. I get tired of seeing the same old boys every summer."

Cary leaned his head familiarly against Doris's leg. "The club is having the first summer dance on Saturday. Want to go, the four of us?"

"Well, I'd love it Cary." Doris pretended surprise at the invitation. "Norm?"

Her sister glanced at Reese. "I'm crazy to go, but," she assumed a provocative and shy air, "Reese hasn't asked me." She smiled.

"Reese has a date." Ann-Charlotte rose and tugged at her bathing suit. "He's taking me."

Cary emitted a shout of laughter which subsided with an uncertain gurgle as Ann-Charlotte stared bleakly at him. When he was quiet, she nodded as though satisfied.

"Well, my goodness," Norma was all honeyed surprise, "I didn't know you were old enough to go to dances with boys, Ann-Charlotte."

"Reese thinks so, don't you?" She looked down gravely.

He was embarrassed. It was silly of her to act this way, and yet, watching her, he felt a little proud. She was so completely self-possessed.

"Yes," he said, not too happy, "I'm taking Ann-Charlotte. We," he offered this desperately, "we could all go together, though. In Cary's car."

He could see the astonishment in the eyes of Cary and the girls, and for some reason it made him angry. He rose from the grass, standing beside Ann-Charlotte.

"We'd better get dressed. I'll," he turned to the others, "we'll see you later."

He walked away stiffly, conscious that he and Ann-Charlotte were being watched.

"You shouldn't talk that way," he said tightly.

"What did I do?" She was unconcerned.

"It made me feel foolish."

"I only said you had a date. That's true, isn't it?"

"Oh, hell. I guess so." He was helpless and realized it. "But you didn't have to say it the way you did."

"I didn't know there was any other way to say it." She refused to become ruffled or apologetic. "Norma Clayton's not going to come sucking around here this summer, and she might as well know it right now."

"All right." He wasn't satisfied. Without trying she had made him look a little ridiculous. His vanity was wounded, and he knew that back there by the pool Cary and the Clayton girls were laughing at him. "All right," he repeated the assertion with hollow vehemence, "but that's the last time."

Cassius made an event of their first meal at the lodge. Outfitting himself in a tall chef's cap and white apron, he flourished a gleaming knife and carved the thick steaks as they were taken sizzling from the grill. Potatoes had been baked in the oven built into the back of the fireplace, and the maids had set out a long table near the pool, bringing down a huge bowl of salad, baked beans, and pitchers of iced tea. Watching Cassius as he hovered over the grill, Reese experienced a strange feeling of guilt, as though he were peeking through someone's window. The man's eagerness to be necessary even in so small a matter as cooking a piece of meat was almost indecently revealing. He hummed as he bent over the grill, his face flushed from the heat, and he even took little dancing steps as he speared the steaks up on a long fork. Reese had been so long accustomed to seeing him as the uneasy master of The Hill that this new role disturbed him, although he didn't know why.

They ate in the deck chairs, filling their plates at the table and then holding them in their laps. An early twilight was brushing the mountains, the scent of the hickory coals was faint but compelling, and there was a sudden hush in the air as though the darkening hills waited for the night.

Seated next to Laura, Reese listened to the casual small talk. The Claytons, he gathered, were from somewhere in Alabama and they had been coming to the North Carolina mountains every summer for years. The girls talked continually in softly slurred accents that sounded pleasantly foreign to Reese's ears. Several times he caught Norma's eyes upon him, and once she winked as though to tell him they shared a secret. The talk was of people they all knew, things they had done together, parties they had attended. Once or twice Laura attempted to lead him into the rather aimless conversation. He didn't know what to say and felt awkward and embarrassed.

After supper they drove over the valley to take the Clayton girls home. Cary and Doris were in the front seat, with Ann-Charlotte, Norma, and Reese wedged into the rumble. Indifferent to his protesting shrug, Ann-Charlotte leaned her head on his shoulder with an attitude of possessiveness. He spread his arms out over the back of the seat, enclosing both girls and almost laughed out loud when Ann-Charlotte cocked one eye up quizzically as though she were saying: What the hell goes on here, anyhow?

"Who are you going with this summer, Norm?" Ann-Charlotte asked the question with sleepy indifference.

"Oh! I'm not goin' with any boy, yet." She pronounced the word boy as though it were spelled "bohy" and glanced with an air of shyness at Reese.

"That's too bad." Ann-Charlotte smiled faintly.

Cary stopped just outside the circle of light at a roadside stand and they each had a short nip from a quart of light, yellow moonshine, washing it down with fast gulps of coca-cola.

"My goodness," Norma giggled, "I don't know what mamma would say if she smelled that on my breath."

"My goodness," Ann-Charlotte deliberately mimicked her, "youah mamma would probably say, Normah, you've been drinkin'."

They had two more drinks apiece before they left the stand and by the time they reached the Clayton place were all feeling a little glow. There was an excited flurry of good-bys and promises to visit.

"You come over and play tennis, Reese." Norma looked beseechingly at him, implying a world in desolation if he failed her.

"Reese has a wooden leg," Ann-Charlotte said calmly.

XIII

THE days and weeks folded effortlessly into summer, and all of the things which in the beginning had been novel and exciting became dulled by repetition and turned commonplace. Time fell into a pattern, and Reese began to experience a fretful restlessness. This amused him at first. He used to lie out by the swimming pool, face buried in his arms, feeling the hot beat of the sun on his back, listening to Cary and Ann-Charlotte, and laugh silently to himself. This, he thought, was what most of the world envied or spent its time trying to capture, and it was no good. In the end it could become as wearying as chopping cotton, bending over a machine, or clerking in a dime store. Andrew Whitfield had had the best of it all. He knew now what harried the soul of Cassius. A man needed something to do. Mr. Whitfield proved that every day. He built a stone wall, slapping mortar happily, wearing his hands to blisters. He resurfaced a tennis court while two Negro yard boys stood by in astonished idleness, or daubed paint over discarded porch furniture and raked down the graveled walks. Cassius was a haunted man because his father had planned too well. There was nothing left for his son to do. That was why he liked the lodge. The Hill forced him into conformity with the idea of what a Whitfield could and could not do. Here he could saw and chop, build and tear down, not giving a damn. It wasn't good enough, though, and he knew it. Reality lay across the valleys in a paneled office in Winton's tallest building.

Sometimes Reese offered to help with the small tasks Cassius invented and the man, recognizing something of himself in the boy, made a place for him at his side. They erected a solid stone fence, an achievement Reese regarded as second only to the Panama Canal, and built a small forge at the far end of the estate with the idea of pounding out ornamental ironwork for the gate. Nothing much came of this, however, since once the forge had been set up, neither of them had the slightest idea how it should be used. In the end

Cassius ordered the gate and post lights from an ironworker in Asheville.

To these activities Cary adopted a supercilious attitude. He would stroll down to where Reese and his father were at work on the wall; stand, hands in pockets, watching with critical amusement, and then, shaking his head as a man might at the antics of the simple-minded, walk back to the lodge.

Reese found a curious companionship with Cassius Whitfield. The man treated him as an adult, according him respect and, sometimes, even deference. They could talk without embarrassment as they bent over the laying of a stone or lifted a fence rail into place. It was different, somehow, than sitting in chairs, facing each other.

"Have you ever thought about what you want to do, Reese?" Cassius put the question conversationally one day as they struggled with the intricacies of squaring the forge. Cary and Ann-Charlotte had gone to the country club in disgust, leaving them alone.

"I don't know." Reese was frankly puzzled. He was almost nineteen; by that time, he thought, he ought to have some plans. "I've thought some about studying law."

Cassius nodded. "Has Cary ever talked with you about, about himself?" He looked up and Reese understood he was appealing for help.

"No. I don't think Cary ever figured he'd have to do anything."

"Money is a damn bad thing, Reese." He shook his head with a gesture of resignation. "The worst part of it is that you can't convince anyone of the evil." He smiled a little self-consciously. "I suppose you think that's funny."

"No." Reese didn't think it was funny. "No, Mr. Whitfield. I don't."

Cassius hung a plumb from the top stone and nodded with satisfaction as it fell true. "It's a good thing for a boy to strike out for himself, Reese." He spoke slowly. "You'll never have to worry about money, I've taken care of that. I hope it is the right thing. Sometimes it's hard to know." He looked squarely at Reese. "I—I feel about you the way I do about Cary or," the admission was painful, "I could if he'd let me."

They allowed the matter to drop there, but Reese felt a new respect for the man. He began to like him as a person as he knew and understood him better. Sometimes he just liked to sit with him on the lodge steps, staring out over the valley without talking. He and Lance used to do that, only instead of mountains there was the brown stubble of the fields and the distant line of blue where the uplands began, but there was the same, silent communion; heart-warming and close.

It was Laura Whitfield, though, who touched him. Reese had never known his own mother. Lance found it difficult to talk about her, and so the boy hadn't been able to visualize the woman. Had she been dark or fair, gay or solemn, happy or troubled? As a child he tried to create an image, but it was shadowy and fleeting. Laura Whitfield, somehow, sensed Reese's need and her heart went out to him with quick affection.

"I wish," she said unhappily one afternoon, "we could find another name for me. I don't like ma'am, and when you say Mrs. Whitfield I want to weep. I know you couldn't call me Laura, and I suppose you wouldn't want to say mother. What are we going to do, Reese?"

"I don't know, ma'am." He smiled with appreciation at the unconscious joke.

"Neither do I. When you say Mrs. Whitfield I feel, somehow, that we have failed."

"I'll tell you what." He wasn't smiling. "I'll—I'll call you mother to myself and ma'am or Mrs. Whitfield out loud."

She kissed him, quickly, shyly, and then hurried inside the house while he stood looking after her and, for some reason, wanting to cry.

After these few weeks it was becoming increasingly difficult for him to remember any other way of life. Laura and Cassius made every effort to see that he was completely absorbed into the family. His allowance was the same as Cary's. He moved with the same freedom. The Whitfields' friends became his, he met them on an equal footing and their homes were as open to him as they were to Cary and Ann-Charlotte. It was pleasant to be liked, he discovered this with something close to astonishment, and he unfolded slowly under the warming influence of Laura's affection. There were rich, new things in life whose existence he hadn't suspected. The ramshackle cottage on Lance's pitifully few acres was taking on the aspect of a waystop.

If the days clung to a pattern, it was not unpleasing. Someone in the colony was always giving a party. There were overnight camping trips, long rides on horses along the mountain trails, dances three times a week at the country club. Reese learned tennis, despite Ann-Charlotte, tried golf, and became at ease in crowds, picking up the small talk which seemed so essential. He and Cary roamed with predatory intentness through the valley, dating as the fancy struck them. They uncovered the roadside speakeasies, divided the girls into those who would and those who wouldn't and making no other distinction. Boys were at a premium, and they soon discovered their worth. There was an intoxication in being sought after. Cary was accustomed to it, but Reese found it a heady draft. He discovered, also, that Ann-Charlotte's attachment had it drawbacks.

"You might as well be married to her," Cary had complained. "It's getting so you almost have to slip out of the house."

Reese fumbled with the problem. Ann-Charlotte didn't attach herself to him with the persistency of a kid sister, but she never allowed him to forget she was there. What actually bothered him was the fact that he would rather be with her than anyone else. When he took her to the club on dance nights, he was proud of her. She was as delicately beautiful as a snow crystal seen under a microscope. He no longer thought of her as being only fifteen. He knew Laura regarded Ann-Charlotte as a baby and was happy in the knowledge that Reese was fond of her. He even suspected she thought the relationship amusing.

Ann-Charlotte frightened him. When they were alone she dropped all pretense of being a starry-eyed adolescent experimenting with a first love.

"How much longer is this going on?" They had come home from the movies in Harlen and were sitting in the station wagon in the garage. Cary had gone to the Clayton place. "How much longer," she repeated, "are you going to be so damned noble? Oh, Reese!" She twisted up into his arms. "Why don't you, please. I—I never have before but I want to, now with you."

Her voice, the peculiar note of suffocation inflamed him. He almost believed her, kissing her fiercely while she writhed and whimpered.

"My God, Ann-Charlotte." He didn't want to be noble. "We can't do this, baby. You're smart enough to know it." It wasn't easy to remember anything. "Your mother, father, they're like my own people. You're almost my sister."

She jerked out of his arms, her eyes hard. "Like hell I am," she said. "If I were, you couldn't have kissed me the way you did just now. You make me sick. Do you think I'm going to beg you?" She slammed the door open and stepped out. "If you do, you're crazy."

He let her walk to the house alone and sat there, smoking one cigarette after another until his mouth was dry and bitter. He had never known anyone like Ann-Charlotte. There had been other girls; furtive love making, self-conscious excursions into the woods after school to a secret meeting place, but always they had been timid, frightened, clumsy. This was different. Nice girls didn't act the way Ann-Charlotte did. She was without shame. Her hands never left him, even when they danced together he could feel the insistent pressure of her fingers as they seemed to search beneath his coat for naked skin. Shame wasn't the word. Ann-Charlotte made it seem natural, sensible. He couldn't get her out of his mind. She was a torment, a fire, and sometimes he would lie face down on his bed, pulling at the corners of a pillow as he thought of her, choking on the agony of desire.

Sometimes he thought Cassius understood. He could remember that night on The Hill when he had said: "Take care of Ann-Charlotte, Reese." How could he take care of her? How could a man mind a witch? He pulled himself painfully from beneath the car's wheel and almost stumbled along the path to the lodge, not trusting himself to look up at the light in her room.

Ann-Charlotte sat on the edge of her bed, hands tightly clasped to still their trembling, staring with a helpless, blank intensity at the door. The thing tearing at her was vicious and silent, leaving her weak and nauseated. For a moment she thought she was going to vomit and didn't care. It would have been a relief. Always it had been this way and she couldn't help it.

She rose with an effort and walked slowly and without purpose to her dressing table, leaning against it for support, her head drooping limply between hunched shoulders. Distantly she heard steps in the hall and then the closing of a door. That would be Reese, he hadn't stopped. She had an almost overpowering desire to yell, to scream all the dirty, four-letter words she had ever heard or seen written on fences and sidewalks. Just the thought of them lashed the fury. Dimly she was conscious of a clock's ticking, there was an idiotic monotony in the sound. The small timepiece in its pigskin case was at her hand. Numbly she gripped it in her fingers, turning its face upward. It seemed a long time before the position of the hands registered themselves on her mind. She groped through the numerals, counting methodically. Nine-fifteen. They had gone to the early movie. Laura and Cassius were over at the Penimores' playing bridge. She toppled the clock over, pressing against its back with her palm, hearing the crush of glass as it was ground into the table.

Her body hurt. It was a dull, exhausting pain that left her limp. Why was it this way? What made her different? The eyes staring back at her from the mirror were dull, pain-shot. She turned and walked to the door, down the stairs and out into the black hole of night.

Her step along the path quickened. By the time she reached the garage she was running. She fumbled clumsily with the ignition key, kicking angrily at the starter pedal, and when the motor caught she backed out with a senseless roar, cutting into a half-circle with screaming tires. The station wagon dove at the opening made by the headlights and swooped out of the driveway.

Halfway down the mountain she eased the pressure of her foot on the accelerator, shivering against the enveloping chill. Reese would have heard her, probably even looked out of the window. Now he would be wondering. For a moment she hesitated. The road wasn't wide enough to turn around in; there was no place to turn anywhere along her road.

At the fork of the highway she swung in alongside the filling station, avoiding the floodlights above the pumps. There was a car there and Blake stood over the tank, feeding gas into it from the heavy hose. He looked up as the station wagon crunched over the pebbled yard, stopping in the shadows, and then turned his eyes to the heavy curved nozzle through which the gasoline spilled and gurgled. She could hear the meter bell tinkling the gallon count and she watched him in the rear view mirror as he hung the hose on its hook, carefully screwed the tank top on, and walked to the front of the car to collect. He stood beside the pump until the car rolled out of the driveway. Then he turned and crossed toward her, peering back once over his shoulder.

"Hello, Donnie." She looked up at him, both hands gripping tightly at the wheel. She tried to breathe. It was difficult and she experienced a feeling of suffocation.

He stood looking at her, bending slightly, shoulders and head thrust over the door. Then his hand reached out, sliding under her arm. He was grinning, amused contempt written on his face, and his touch was deliberately insolent as he half turned her about.

"Hello, kid. I've been wonderin' when you'd be around."

In the gloom her face was a tortured, ivory mask. She could only stare, her eyes hollow and imploring. He kept his hand tight against her breast and she was no longer able to control her trembling. She tried to speak but the words formed soundlessly on her lips.

Deliberately he took his hand away and his laugh was short and humiliating as she leaned forward instinctively, following it.

"I'm crazy to be foolin' with a kid like you." The words were brutal and she cringed beneath them. "Besides, it's too early."

Still she was unable to speak, her eyes were wide, begging. He pulled back, straightening up, and glanced quickly around.

"It's early. I'll lose a lot of business if I lock up now." He weighed the statement. "I don't know if it's worth it."

She waited, helpless, as he turned his back and strolled toward the front of the station. He was whistling as he found a key and locked the pumps, lugged two display racks of oil into the building, and took in a chair that was canted against the wall near the entrance. The floodlights snapped out, she could hear the door slam and the quick rattling of the knob as he tried the lock, then the hissing sound of his footsteps in the loose gravel.

There was no tenderness in his touch as he slid in beside her. His hands were rough, purposeful, but she clung to him with a small wail of distress, some of the torture spilling over the dam and engulfing her.

"Not here," she couldn't let him go, "not here in the car again. Take me someplace, Donnie. Please."

"You're crazy. I'll only get in a hell of a lot of trouble foolin' around with you." He bent her over into the corner.

"Please, Donnie. Not here like before." She twisted away and he followed.

"All right." He dropped her and for a moment she knew terror, afraid that he was going to get out of the car and leave her. "All right, only God damn it, I don't want to get into any trouble. Let's get out of here. I'll get in at Toomis' cabins, if they don't see you."

She waited in the car near the end of darkened cabins. There were small chinks of light showing through the tightly drawn curtains in some of the boxlike buildings. Others were dark, silent. Above each doorway there was an empty, rusting socket. Toomis' guests didn't want to be seen entering or leaving and the electric bulbs had been smashed long ago.

Donnie came back, carrying two bottles of coca-cola in his fingers and with a pint bottle of corn stuffed into his hip pocket.

"Number seven," he said. "It's the second one. You go first an' don't walk."

She slipped from the car and hurried across the rutted path, sliding through the doorway and waiting in the darkness. The single, narrow room was stuffy and smelled strongly of disinfectant. She backed away and saw Donnie's form outlined in the opening. Then the door closed and she could hear the key squeak with dry protest as he turned it in the lock. A single electric light bulb hung from a limp cord in the center of the room, glaring with a sickly yellow glow when he turned it on. Donnie walked to the window and pressed the sleazy, cracked shade tightly into the corners, then he turned and looked at her.

"Don't stand there like I dragged you here. This is what you wanted, isn't it?"

She nodded, her eyes darting around the room, taking in the ragged strip of faded carpet, the bare, flimsy wooden walls, and the rusting, springless bed with its chipped and blotched ironwork.

"Let's have a drink." He took the pint of moonshine from his pocket and unfolded a crushed paper cup. "Go on, sit down." He pushed her gently with his fingertips toward the bed. The colorless liquid splashed into the cup, seeping quickly through and turning the bottom soggy. "Drink it." He held out the uncapped bottle of coca-cola for a chaser.

She almost gagged on the raw whisky. It had an unpleasant, oily taste and she swallowed the coca-cola in hurried gulps. Donnie drank directly from the bottle and then placed it on the bureau, from which the veneer gaped in peeling strips. He walked over and sat beside her, drawing her unprotesting body into his arms and leaning back on the patchwork quilt. He kissed her, his mouth working over hers with greedy assurance, and as her breath quickened he laughed.

"You summer kids are all alike," he said harshly. "I guess you got nothin' else to do but run around like little sluts. What's the matter? Can't those fancy-pants boy friends take care of you?"

She opened her eyes slowly, they were smoldering, and then she laughed.

"Get me another drink, Donnie." She pushed against the heels of her slippers and they fell to the floor. He was surprised and she knew it.

"Sure," he said after a moment, "if you want one."

He watched her from the corners of his eyes as he poured a second drink. She slid back on the bed, tucking one leg beneath her and leaning against the cold wall. Her gaze was calculating, unhurried, and she took the paper cup from his hand without shifting her stare from his face. When she swallowed the drink she crumpled the wet container in her hand and tossed it into a corner.

"Come here, Donnie," she said huskily.

"What the hell's the matter with you?" He betrayed his uncertainty and when he sat beside her again, much of his swaggering assurance had evaporated.

She pulled him down, bending his head to hers, both hands fastened on his open shirt. His fingers fumbled with the yoke of her dress. They were clumsily eager now, almost supplicating.

"What the hell are we waiting for?" His words were strained.

"I don't know." She was devouring him with a cold confidence, biting savagely at his neck as his uneasiness was communicated to her. "Turn out the light, Donnie."

He rose shakily, reaching up to the bulb and snapping the square switch between his fingers.

"Call me a slut again, Donnie."

XIV

THE two state troopers were stiffly erect, standing close together and waiting in embarrassed silence as they pretended not to see the limp figure of Cassius Whitfield as he slumped in the armchair. They waited, fumbling with the cords of their broad-brimmed hats, fixing their gaze on the hewn beam above the fireplace and trying not to watch the terrifying horror mounting in Laura's eyes. The room was so quiet that when one of the men moved, the tiny rasp of his leather boot was startlingly explosive.

Ann-Charlotte sat in one corner of a divan, her feet and legs pressed tightly together, arms crossed in her lap. Her features were without expression, betraying neither concern nor indifference but only an ethereal detachment as though she had no part in the scene. Her mouth was immobile, but her fingers opened and closed with slow regularity as if she were trying to breathe through them.

"If there had been any other way," the sergeant made the statement seem an apology, "we wouldn't have come to you like this."

Cassius gave no indication he heard, but his body shook and the blood was so completely drained from his face that the shorn beard stubble seemed to be a dusting of black powder. His eyes were blank as though he hadn't been listening or didn't understand what the trooper had said.

"If she had been older, maybe"; the officer looked up at the ceiling. "But when we saw she was only a kid, we just had to bring her in. I'm sorry about this, Mr. Whitfield. When these things happen, they are hard for all of us. You understand?"

Cassius nodded, and after the first gesture of assent his head continued to move back and forth as though he could no longer control it.

"We've been watching Toomis' cabins for some time. Tonight we made the raid. And, well." He stopped, looked to his companion for assistance. "When we broke into the cabins we found—"

"Who was the boy?" Cassius didn't look up, but he rubbed a finger against his mouth, forcing the question back.

The silence seemed without end. The trooper brushed his hat against the flare of his breeches. He couldn't bear to look at the man. He seemed to be shrinking there in the chair.

"Well, it—it wasn't exactly a boy, Mr. Whitfield." Cassius looked up then.

"It," the trooper was having difficulty in speaking, "it was that Blake fellow, the one who runs the filling station."

Laura whimpered, cowering back from the knowledge. "Oh! No." The words formed a hopeless prayer.

"He's in jail now." The sergeant made the statement with an almost eager wistfulness, and he glanced over his shoulder at Ann-Charlotte, who pretended not to see him.

"I," the trooper twisted his hat, trying to find something of comfort in what he was about to say, "I don't know." He spoke to the floor. "I don't know if anything—if anything happened." The muscles in his jaw leaped beneath the skin. "He, Blake—the man still had his clothes on. I—I guess you'll have to ask her, your daughter, about that."

Laura's moan was the cry of heartbreak. The trooper looked miserably at her.

"You understand, Mrs. Whitfield," he said unhappily, "we only did what was right, what we had to do?"

The square, silver clock on the mantelpiece counted the hour of eleven on its muted bell. The troopers and Laura listened intently, seeking in the chime some relief from the tension. Cassius bowed his head. When the final note slipped from the room his eyes lifted.

"What's going to happen?" he asked dully.

"That depends on you, I guess." The trooper became crisply alert. "We've booked Blake on a disorderly charge, just to hold him. You can go farther; contributing to the delinquency of a minor, or," he flushed and looked uneasily at Laura, "or statutory rape if—if that's what happened." He swung his hat with a motioning gesture in the direction of Ann-Charlotte. "She wouldn't say anything."

"Thank you." Cassius's eyes were silently appealing.

The troopers shuffled uneasily. "I guess," the sergeant hesitated, "I guess that's all."

"Yes, thank you." Cassius nodded absently.

The men glanced at each other and then turned, striding from the room, eager to get out of the house. The sound of the front door closing behind them was sharply definite, and then silence locked itself with the Whitfields. Ann-Charlotte looked across at her mother and for a fraction of a second their eyes met and then darted apart, unable to endure the contact. Cassius sighed and the sound was a wrenching admission of despair. His hands went to the arms of the chair as he made an effort to rise, and then dropped away, falling without strength and dangling lifelessly over the sides.

Ann-Charlotte waited through the interminable quiet. Humiliation, not for what she had done, was bitter in her mouth. To have been hauled out of a scummy cabin, forced to walk past a snickering, slack-mouthed crowd of staring idiots who had to be pushed aside by the troopers before they would give way, was a form of degradation she hadn't thought possible.

The faint ticking of the clock became a hammer, pounding at their nerves, beating them into a screaming pulp. Unable to endure it longer, Ann-Charlotte rose. Slowly, as though she were testing her ability to walk, she moved toward her mother.

"Oh, my God. My beautiful, lovely baby. My little, shining one." Laura tore the words from her heart with a strangled cry.

"Mother." Ann-Charlotte put her hands out, trying to stay the agony, and Laura clutched at them, turning them over in her own as a bereaved woman might fondle the small clothes of a baby.

Ann-Charlotte couldn't cry, and she realized with a shock that she didn't want to. Her only emotion at the moment was pity for her mother, pity because her grief was so pointless. She was weeping for a daughter who needed no tears and who, instead of melting beneath them, was experiencing only an embarrassed impatience. She knew what Laura was thinking, that she had been hurt, soiled, violated; God, what a word. None of those things, of course, was true, but who knew the phrases with which to explain? Would it help to say: I went because I wanted to. Something tortures me. It wasn't the first time. It won't be the last. I go to a party or see men or boys on the street and I say to myself: I wonder what this or that one would be like. You wouldn't understand. I don't, myself. I only know it is there.

"Mother, you mustn't cry. It's—it's all right." The lie was not without its reward.

Laura lifted her face and Ann-Charlotte could see relief flood into it with substance and color. It seemed so small a thing to give, the counterfeit assurance, the easy denial.

"Good night, Mother."

She bent until their cheeks touched. Laura wept then, but without fright or hysteria. Relief lay in the tears, surcease in the sobs. Ann-Charlotte straightened up, slipping her hands from the confining grasp. Laura held her palms, face up, as though she had released a bird.

"Good night, Father." This was harder, witnessing the dulled reflexes, the worn stamp of suffering.

Cassius raised his head with an effort and he nodded. His lips twitched, and it was a few seconds before they could shape a sound.

"Good night, Ann-Charlotte."

She hesitated, he seemed to be on the point of saying more and she wanted him to have that release. He shook his head then, almost as if he understood why she waited, and wanted to tell her there was nothing left unsaid. She turned and walked slowly from the room and upstairs.

For a long time Cassius and Laura sat there without speaking. Looking across at his wife he wanted to comfort her, to say something gentle and reassuring, and he bowed helplessly beneath the obligation. There was nothing to say; a pat on the shoulder, a gesture of comfort, such things would be foolish and without meaning. Falteringly he tried to understand himself, to analyze his own confused emotions. If he could set them in place, maybe, he could help Laura. First, there was the desperate crying within him that what they had heard couldn't be true. She was a child, a youngster. Somehow, he knew this wasn't so. He was reaching out for hope and it was a phantom. Ann-Charlotte wasn't a child. She knew what she was doing. He felt no shame, really. His pride was touched by the tawdry assignation, but strangely enough he found himself thinking of it objectively, almost as something he had read in a newspaper. What hammered at him, beating at his brain until it ached, was the knowledge that this was not the end. There was a futility in challenging it as a man might shout against the wind. What happened to the blood of man? A fever fed upon it, thinning it out until there was neither the power nor desire left to fight against inherent weaknesses that grew with the persistency of a malignant tumor. It wasn't always so, though. Honesty compelled the admission. His mind raced over the names of a dozen families, born to great wealth and power. They ruled vast industrial empires. Their sons grew up, conscious of their responsibilities and took their places with pride and intelligence. That was where he had failed or Andrew had failed him. There was no

150

machine or mill or field to which his sons could turn. Idleness ate at him as it consumed Ann-Charlotte and Cary.

What evil lay within that bright, blonde girl who had walked so casually out of the room a few moments ago? From what secret well seeped the selfish indifference he saw in Cary?

Ann-Charlotte would never change. She would take what she wanted. He thought of Blake and knew blinding hatred for him and his kind. The Blakes of the world stood ready to foul and make dirty all they couldn't understand; instinctively able to seek out a weakness. He knew, had known, he thought now, ever since the day Vance Porter had come to him with the story of the trouble over Duke Reid that this night was inevitable. With a secret sense of shame he confessed to himself that, somehow, he had hoped to stay it with Reese Benton. There had been a moment tonight, as he asked the troopers for the name of the boy caught with Ann-Charlotte, when he had almost hoped it had been Reese, although he was certain in his heart it couldn't have been. So, he thought, here it is, and I am without the wisdom or courage to handle it.

He lurched heavily out of his chair and Laura looked up quickly. He tried to smile, hoping to offer her comfort and reassurance, but his mouth remained fixed.

"It's late," he spoke gently, "hadn't we better go upstairs?" His eyes turned to the clock. "Cary will be getting in soon. I'd rather not have to talk about it in front of him. If he sees us this way he will know something is wrong."

"Yes, of course." She was eager for guidance, taking his hand with childlike confidence.

Mechanically Cassius depressed the light switch on the wall as they passed from the living room and then, with their arms linked they ascended the staircase with the hesitant footsteps of two very old people. Without being quite conscious of what they were doing they both paused before Ann-Charlotte's door. Clearly in the house's silence they could hear the tumbling splash in her bathroom as the tub was filled. There was something almost reassuring in the sound. It was an everyday noise, a simple thing, easy to understand. Cassius felt Laura's fingers tighten in his. He knew what she was thinking and shook his head.

Cassius sat in a chair by the window. Laura came in from the dressing room, her heavy, still youthfully bright hair cascading about her shoulders. From long habit she settled herself on the low bench before a mirror and began brushing it with even, unhurried strokes.

"What will happen now?" She turned slightly, holding the brush in her lap. "I mean, will there have to be more?"

"No, not unless we want it."

"Oh! But we don't." She was pleading with him. "If—if there was a charge, wouldn't there have to be a trial?"

Cassius nodded.

"I couldn't bear it, the publicity, Ann-Charlotte's name in the papers, all the filth which would have to be spoken openly. You won't let them, Cass, promise me?"

"No." What did it matter if she had this moment of peace? Would it be better to tell her now that such a thing couldn't be hidden in a woman's heart? Too many people already knew what had happened, too many eager tongues were carrying the cry at this moment through the night. "No," he repeated the word, "there won't be any charge or trial. I promise."

"And Ann-Charlotte?" She wanted so desperately to hear him say everything was going to be all right. "Maybe she ought to go North or West to school. California." Laura was seeking distance as though it mattered.

Cassius stared into the rolling darkness of the hills. Somewhere out there the word was already tumbling through space. He could almost see it go, follow its path. First, the weekly newspaper in Harlen would toss it to Asheville and from there it flashed to every city room in the nation. Already mildly interested rewrite men on the lobster tricks of afternoon papers were calling for the Whitfield clippings in their morgues, padding the brief press association story with background. The files were being searched for photographs of Ann-Charlotte, and if they couldn't be found, then pictures of himself, Laura, even Old Andrew could be used. Tobacco Heiress in Brothel Raid. That wasn't exactly true, but it was close enough. What of Blake? He would fatten on it. Tourists would reroute their trips to pass his filling station. More of them would stop, straining from their seats to watch and wonder as he filled their tanks or checked the oil. Cassius shut his eyes but the nightmare danced with nimble feet across his brain.

"Maybe," he said slowly, "California might be nice this winter. Maybe, a cruise." He spoke without thinking, and a quick panic seized him for fear Laura might believe a cruise the solution. Aboard a ship they would be on exhibtion every hour of the day. He hoped she hadn't heard. He didn't want to explain.

"Mexico, Cass. We've never been there. They say it's lovely." Laura was seeking escape, hugging geography to her as a postulant might cling to a breviary at the gates of hell.

"We'll see, dear." He felt so much older and wiser at the moment. Walking to her side he looked down, his hands touching lightly at the rippling hair, and he tried not to see the mark of the hunted on her face.

In the yard below they could hear the crunch of gravel as a car rolled down to the garage.

"There's Cary. He's home." Laura reached up, clinging to his hand. "Let me talk, Cass. I know it's Cary. I know you know it's Cary. I just have to keep saying something. I'm afraid if I stop talking I'll scream. You wouldn't want me to scream, would you, Cass? It wouldn't be right. What would people think if they heard me? Maybe," her voice was playing along the border of madness, "maybe they would think you were beating me. We wouldn't want people to believe that, would we, Cass?"

He drew her head close. She was shaking with horrible, twitching spasms, and the sobs were dry and crackling in her throat.

"Everything will be all right, dear." The little comfort he had to offer was so inadequate to the moment. "Come to bed now." She allowed him to lead her across the room.

"You'll talk to me, Cass, won't you? You'll hold me the way you used to. Do you remember? I used to be a little ashamed. Somehow I didn't think it was right. I thought it wasn't quite decent for people to be happy in bed. Oh! My God. What am I talking about? He touched her, Cass, put his dirty, filthy hands on her. Maybe she cried and no one cared." She turned her face into the pillow and he could only sit there and listen.

Cassius waited in the dingy room adjoining Harlen's court. He hadn't wanted to attend the hearings, but the proceedings were relayed to him by the deputy marshal, a lanky youth who doubled as sort of a night watchman and errand boy. Toomis had been bound over on a charge of maintaining a public nuisance. The other cases had been dismissed. Ann-Charlotte's name hadn't been mentioned, but the story was loose. People had looked at him with undisguised curiosity as he walked from the car. On some of the faces, only a few, he had seen sympathy. Others displayed amusement, the sly satisfaction of small, mean souls who licked greedily at the misfortunes of others. There was double nourishment in today's dish, and they stuffed themselves with righteous vindictiveness. A Whitfield was no better than anyone else. For all her clothes, easy airs, and money, the Whitfield girl was a pushover, a quick jump for a guy in a filling station. They sucked at the knowledge, coating it with their imagination. Probably, if the truth were known, she'd been with most of the boys in the valley. They prodded each other with questions: What do you know about the Whitfield kid? How long do you suppose Donnie's been gettin' that? I always thought she looked like stuff, didn't you? They rolled her in the gutter, picking over her like buzzards.

The deputy marshal brought Blake into the room. He was uneasily defiant and he made a desperate effort to avoid Cassius' eyes. The deputy lingered. He didn't want to miss this.

"You can leave us alone," Cassius said quietly.

The deputy hesitated. "I guess so," he said reluctantly. "There ain't no charge against him." He stalled, hoping Cassius would change his mind. Cassius waited patiently and after a moment the marshal backed to the door. He laughed shortly and a furtive sneer curled itself on his mouth. He winked at Blake who was leaning negligently against the wall, plucking at his fingernails. The old man was probably going to offer him money to buy out the filling station and get him away from town. Maybe he might even try and make Donnie marry the little tramp. That would be something, wouldn't it? Donnie up there in the lodge, riding around in one of the big cars. He'd be a sucker if he didn't take it. What if she was a bum? Most rich girls were, anyhow. With all that dough they didn't have to worry. Catching the wink, Blake grinned back and dropped an eyelid in understanding. Regretfully the deputy closed the door behind him. He'd sure like to hear what old man Whitfield had to say. Donnie was no fool. He'd milk him for plenty. The guy would probably never have to work again as long as he lived.

Cassius sat and stared at the man, studying his insolent indifference. Blake looked at him and then dismissed the meeting with a contemptuous shrug. He wet one grease-coated nail with spit and dug at it with a studied and critical air.

"Why did you do it, Blake?" Cassius's voice was low.

Donnie dropped his hands to his pockets, thrusting them inside.

and lounged loosely against the boards. His eyes caught the level gaze of the man before him and then dropped.

"I ain't got all day here. What's on your mind?" He stared disinterestedly out of the window on the opposite side of the room.

"This won't take long." Cassius leaned slightly forward. "I asked you a question. Why?"

"Look, Mr. Whitfield. This isn't goin' to get us anyplace." He made the statement sound intimately confidential. "If there's somethin' you want to say, well, say it an' let's get out of here."

An angry color spread slowly over Cassius face. He tightened the grip of his interlocked fingers.

"I could send you to jail. That's where you belong."

Blake laughed scornfully. "You're not scarin' me," he said. "If you were goin' to make a charge you'd have done it already. I know you don't want the publicity, so stop sayin' Boo!"

Cassius stared incredulously at him. He experienced a sense of rising fury. With difficulty he kept his voice under control.

"But," he was thoughtful, "she's only a child."

Blake snorted. His mouth twisted. "That's what you think."

"She's fifteen." Cassius was trembling. "There must have been other, older girls you could have had. I—a man," he stumbled over the words, "ought to want to take care of a youngster even when she, when she's a little wild."

Blake chuckled softly. He was in a reminiscent humor. "All girls are the same to me when they're that way. A little wild?" He forced a burlesque look of surprise. He was confident, playing with the man before him, experiencing a savage delight in the torture. "You ought to put that kid away. She ain't hot, she's a ball of fire." He tossed his head back against the wall, laughing. "If it hadn't been me, it would have been somebody else." He stared at the ceiling, shaking his head gently, marveling.

The whispering scrape of Cassius' chair caused his eyes to slant across the room. They widened at what they saw.

The gun in Cassius' hand slammed viciously. The first shot caught Blake in the chest, throwing him against the wall. He screamed, a high animal cry. The second shot ripped into his side, beating him down, and his knees buckled. The third bullet tore into his guts. He didn't feel any pain there. It was as though someone had struck him with a club. He caught at the smooth boards as he slid to the floor, mechanically attempting to hold himself upright.

155

The door crashed into the corner and the young deputy plunged against a worn desk, the momentum of his charge carrying him across the room.

"Jesus Christ!" he yelled.

Deliberately Cassius laid the muzzle of the gun at a spot just below his ear and pulled the trigger, and in that terrible, final moment he looked down at Blake on the floor and smiled wearily before his head snapped and he crumpled across the chair, carrying it with him as he fell.

XV

THE murder of an obscure wayside filling-station attendant and Cassius Whitfield's suicide in the mountain hamlet of Harlen was fare of such robust character that even the press had to chew it several times before it could be swallowed. Reporters were tossed into the village by the carload. Photographers, lugging their black cases, roamed like beagles through the valley, taking pictures of anything that moved and much that couldn't. In a fruitless quest they besieged the lodge and were rewarded by nothing more than a fleeting glimpse of a maid at a back door. Laura refused to permit the telephone to be answered and kept the house locked against intrusion. In Winton a more enterprising member of the craft hired a car and drove out to Bluestone to see Joseph Whitfield. He discovered that gentleman, clad in pyjamas and a robe of starlight blue, happily engaged with brandy and soda on the terrace. Joe told the delighted reporter he couldn't understand the whole thing.

"It doesn't seem right." He meditated on the odd quirks of justice. "I always figured someone would shoot a Whitfield. It sort of upsets a man to see things happen the other way round."

When the reporter attempted to pry for details, Joe offered him a drink, opined that bird shooting would be fine in the fall, said he preferred Havana cigars to cigarettes, and asked the newsman if he knew a good remedy for athlete's foot. After the reporter left, he went inside, dressed carefully, packed a bag, and drove to Harlen. On the way he picked up an escort of State troopers, and five minutes after the lodge was reached its grounds were cleared and the news-gatherers, unabashed but overwhelmed, were straggling down the mountainside.

"Is there anything you want, Laurie?"

They sat in the bedroom she and Cassius had shared. Following the roar of the departing troopers' motorcycles the lodge was enveloped in silence, the quiet that always attaches itself to a house in time of tragedy. Even Joe, never overly sensitive, unconsciously lowered his voice when he spoke.

Laura shook her head. Her eyes were without luster, deadened by shock. It was still difficult for her to talk.

"No; no, thank you, Joe." Her lips moved automatically and the words were without feeling.

"I got rid of the newspaper people. That's the end of them." He tried to be comforting.

Her eyes were on her hands. "It'll never be the end, really, Joe."

She looked at him; grateful, somehow, that he had come. They were, she realized with astonishment, almost strangers. During all of the years of her marriage Joe had come to The Hill no more than a dozen times, while she and Cassius had never even been inside Bluestone. There had been no feud between the brothers. They simply didn't understand each other, had no interests in common, and were both too honest to contrive a pretense of sympathy. Sensing the question in her glance, Joe smiled lightly.

"Duty didn't send me, Laurie. I came up because I wanted to. Must be gettin' soft."

"I'm glad."

"There ain't any point in talkin' about it, Laurie."

She had to smile then. No one but Joe had ever called her Laurie. He made it sound comfortable; almost folksy, sort of back country. She relaxed slightly and her hands halted their nervous, fumbling movements.

"There ain't any point in talkin' about it," Joe repeated, smoothing down the satiny wrapper of a cigar with one finger, "because neither you nor I'll ever know why Cass did what he did. Oh!"—he shook his head—"I know what went on before. That might make some men reach for a gun, but not Cass. There was somethin' inside of him, Laurie, somethin' no one but Cass would understand. If you look at it that way, then you'll know he did what he thought was right and was satisfied. Maybe that'll make it easier. I don't know."

Laura gazed out of the window with a distant, puzzled expression on her face. She wanted so to talk with Joe, but the past and the present pushed in upon her, crowding her back and making speech difficult. Murder and violent death were things one read about in a newspaper. They didn't happen to people, only to names. Yet, here they were, companions with her on a mountaintop.

"I want to talk for a few moments, Joe." She didn't turn her face to him. "For two days now I have lived with it. Maybe if I just talk and you don't interrupt, I can get things straight in my own mind." She drew a deep breath. "Ann-Charlotte killed her father, Joe. I know it, so does she. I loved Cass. We were simple, nice people. As simple and as nice as we could be under the circumstances. I'm going to miss him." She dropped her eyes to her hands again. "But I love my daughter, also, Joe. Now, for the rest of our lives we will have to read what we each know in each other's eyes. I'll never be able to look at her without remembering she killed Cass, and I don't know whether I can stand it. She'll grow up, marry, and, probably, go away. I'll keep asking myself why? Why should I be alone? Why; because of you, Ann-Charlotte? And then I think I'll hate her, Joe. I don't want that to happen."

"Then you shouldn't let it," he interrupted brusquely. "Don't begin to borrow trouble for the years ahead, Laurie. Likely enough you'll find you're overstocked if you do. Ann-Charlotte didn't kill Cass any more than the man and woman who whelped the gas station fella did. If I tell you Cass has been a long time dyin', then you'll probably get mad, but it's the truth just the same."

She rose and walked to the window. "You probably think I don't know what you are talking about," she said softly, "but I do. You might have helped Cass. Sometimes it seemed to me he needed you."

Joe smoked thoughtfully, his eyes half closed. "I'm sorry you feel the way you do, Laurie." He spoke with sincere regret. "Cass wouldn't have understood me. He just wasn't made that way. You see, if this thing had happened to me, I might have shot Blake but I sure God wouldn't have felt it necessary to turn a gun on myself. That's brutal talk, maybe, but true. For Cass and me to get together was like two men lookin' through different ends of telescopes an' sayin' to each other: 'What do you see?' Probably they were seein' the same things, only the proportions were a hell of a lot different. That, though, is all over. What you've got to do now is think of yourself and the children; mostly, though, about yourself."

She turned from the window with a gesture of helplessness.

"I don't know where to start, Joe." Her eyes sought his. "I'm confused and afraid."

"Confusion is all right," he admitted soberly, "but bein' afraid don't make any sense."

"But what shall we do?" she cried desperately. "I don't want to go back to Winton, to The Hill, and I can't stay here."

"Why don't you go to Europe for a year?"

"I don't know." She pressed her hands to her forehead. "I've never had to think for myself before. So many things now; Cary and

Reese were going to college this winter. Ann-Charlotte? In the name of God. What am I going to do about Ann-Charlotte?"

Joe rose to stand beside her. "You can't carry the weight for her, also, Laurie. Pack them all up and go abroad. You'll be surprised how quickly people forget things. For my part, I'd let Cary and Ann-Charlotte sweat it out right here. It might do them good. It's kinda rough on young Reese, though."

Laura leaned slightly against the wall. "Cass liked Reese." She spoke with a lingering thoughtfulness. "They became very good friends this summer. In many ways Reese was closer to him than Cary. That's a strange thing to say, I know, but it's true. I'm afraid we haven't done so well by Reese. Maybe he was better off. It's hard to know."

Joe took her arm. "Would you like to go for a drive with me, get out of the house?"

She shook her head, touching his hand with her fingers. "I'm all right, or I will be. I suppose what you say is true. Maybe we ought to go away for a while." She glanced at him apologetically. "I don't know where to start; honestly. Reservations, passports, tickets..."

"I'll take care of everything for you."

She fumbled with her handkerchief. "I'm not going to have a funeral. I just couldn't bear it. The—Cass—the body has been sent to Winton. Will you take care of that for me, also?"

He gave her a reassuring pat. "Try and straighten yourself out. I'll handle the details."

She bowed her head in quiet assent. "Will there be much; papers to sign, a will, and all the other things you hear about?"

Joe led her to the door. "Probably not. If I know Cass, everything is down to the last comma. He was a great fella for detail. Maybe, now," he grinned down at her, "maybe you'd buy me a drink."

Reese and Cary walked aimlessly along the ridge back of the lodge. Reese had been out all morning, unable to bear the chilling silence of the house, slipping away before the newspaper people arrived to take up the early watch. He wanted to be alone, and yet the memory of Cassius Whitfield was a silent companion, following along the uneven paths, moving at his elbow, and disappearing only when Cary joined them.

Reese hadn't wanted to talk, and Cary seemed to understand. They strolled without purpose, kicking at small stones, fixing their eyes on the ground and now and then glancing up at the mountain line across the valley. Something hard and bitter was crystallizing within Reese. He had never hated anyone before, but now the thought of Ann-Charlotte moved him to a black, inarticulate fury. There was heart-break, also, and the dull ache that seemed to leave him without strength. It was funny, he thought, the things he remembered at a time like this. Take care of Ann-Charlotte. He wondered if Cassius had known what he was asking. You'll have to help, Reese. He had said that, too. And Ann-Charlotte, sitting beside him in the movies on the night before she went out to meet Blake. They were like a couple of kids, holding hands, leaning over to whisper to each other, their cheeks brushing in the half-light. She'd been different; softer, dropping the brittle impudence and scorn she affected in the presence of sentiment. Touching her fingers, feeling the soft pressure of her head as she leaned confidently against his shoulder, he had been engulfed in a surging wave of pride. He thought of Laura and Cassius, and how, on chilly evenings, they would sit by the fire; not talking very much but all with a quiet trust in each other; he, Ann-Charlotte, and, sometimes, Cary. For the first time he understood what a family meant and knew the warmth of being part of one, of being liked and wanted. Once he had caught Laura's eyes and they smiled a little as though she suspected what he was thinking. Now, things would never again be the same. Always what Ann-Charlotte had done would wedge itself between them. He hated her for what had happened to Laura and her father, to all of them.

Remembering Cassius was painfully easy. There had been un-suspected depths of gentleness in the man. In some ways he reminded him of Lance. They had had fun together. Sometimes it wasn't easy to talk to him. He was almost shy, but they understood each other.

"I think you're going to be a fine man, Reese," Cassius once said. "Lance will be proud of you."

Reese suspected Cassius was identifying Lance with himself, and the knowledge tugged at his heart, giving him confidence and assurance. He had never stopped to wonder why he had been so completely absorbed into the family. It was enough to know he was loved and respected. Now there was no family, just four people and a lonely woman back there in the lodge. He wondered if Ann-Charlotte cared or felt badly about what had happened. Somehow he didn't think so.

He had been seated on a huge boulder, chipping at a little space between his legs with a piece of stone, when Cary found him. He moved over without speaking, making room on the rock.

"You have breakfast?" Cary tapped his heels against the boulder, drumming with uneven rhythm.

"Yep. I ate in the kitchen."

"Uncle Joe came up. He's with Ma now."

"That's good." Reese spoke without enthusiasm.

Cary glanced obliquely at him. Reese was a funny guy sometimes. The way he was acting now, you'd think something had happened to him.

"It's a hell of a note, isn't it?" Cary waited but Reese only nodded. "Pa was always so easygoing. He was the last man in the world you'd suspect of pulling a gun. It's going to make a stink. I don't know how we can go back to Winton—or stay here, for that matter."

Reese looked up quickly. Cary was staring at the ground, his forehead wrinkled in a thoughtful frown. He really meant it. Reese couldn't believe it for a moment. Cary was worrying about what people were going to think or say. His father's suicide was embarrassing.

"Sometimes," Reese said slowly, "I wonder if you've got good sense." He slid from the rock. "I'm going for a walk."

Cary followed. "Say," he called defensively, "what"s the matter with you?"

"Nothing." Reese snapped the word. "I just feel like walking. You don't have to come."

Cary followed him along the narrow path. He was injured. Reese was acting as though he thought he didn't care. That was foolish. Anyone ought to know he cared. How could he help feeling badly when everyone in the state, probably the whole country, knew what had happened, how Ann-Charlotte was dragged out of a crib? That was going to be a fine thing to live down. It made the name of Whitfield something to be proud of. He knew people would expect him to feel badly over his father's death, but actually he was experiencing no sense of personal loss. He and his father hadn't even been good friends, not friends the way Reese and Lance used to be. He tried to remember any time when they had played or roughed around together. He couldn't even recall when they had talked much. Reese and Lance had been different. Sometimes they used to act like a couple of kids, almost as though Lance had been a big brother. The violence of his father's death shocked him, but so would the suicide of anyone he had known. It would seem strange, at first, not to see him around. Cassius had always been there, sitting in the position of authority, able to say yes or no. Thinking of this, he realized he was the only male Whitfield on

162

their side of the family. In three years he would be twenty-one. He couldn't help but wonder if he would be expected to go down to his father's offices or to know anything of the business. What did his father do anyhow? Was there really any business to take care of? Somehow, he didn't think so. It was only a sort of a game his father had played because he didn't have anything else to occupy his time. Uncle Joe would know about those things. Uncle Joe never worried about business, so there was probably nothing to it.

Reese had halted at a fork in the path, waiting for him to catch up.

"I didn't mean what I said back there, about your not having any sense. I just can't get over what happened. It sort of makes me sick when I think of it."

"That's all right." Cary tried to be nonchalant, hiding his surprise. Reese never said he was sorry about anything. "I didn't pay much attention."

"I guess we'd better go back down to the house. Maybe your mother wants us for something, now that Uncle Joe is here." Reese caught himself, realizing he was thinking as a member of the family. When he said Uncle Joe, he had the feeling he really was a relative. "I mean," he added, "she has probably made plans about going back to Winton or someplace."

They walked slowly toward the back of the house. From her window Ann-Charlotte watched them. She stood to one side, half concealed by the curtain, wanting to go down and be with them. She was desperately lonely. Reese should have understood. Maybe, she thought, he did but didn't care. She hadn't expected anything from Cary; but Reese ought to have known. Her mother's quiet grief terrified her. She had gone to her room, hesitating just inside the door, waiting to be spoken to. They hadn't been able to talk. What was there to say? She knew what her mother was thinking as she looked up and saw her standing timidly on the doorsill.

"Do you want to come in, dear?" Laura's voice had been toneless. It frightened her.

She crossed quickly, dropping on her knees at her mother's chair, reaching for her hands. Laura hadn't pulled away as she half expected.

"I don't think we can talk about it now, Ann-Charlotte, and even if we could, it wouldn't help."

"I know you hate me. Everyone will hate me." She was crying softly. "It wasn't all my fault, Mother."

Laura's hand touched wtih lingering tenderness at the top of her head. Ann-Charlotte trembled beneath its gentle stroke.

"I don't hate you, dear." It seemed to Ann-Charlotte that a stranger was speaking. "You're my baby. Maybe," she paused, "maybe your father and I didn't understand you. I guess it's our fault. I suppose it never occurred to either of us such a thing as this could happen, and so we didn't guard against it. There is so much we ought to say to each other, but I can't talk now."

For the first time in her life Ann-Charlotte experienced humility. She was frightened and lonely and helpless before her mother. Kneeling there, she needed something to cling to, and, reaching out, found nothing. When she finally rose, her mother made no motion to detain her, and she had hurried out, almost running to her own room across the hall.

Watching Reese and Cary as they came through the yard, she set her teeth against a desire to call out. They didn't even glance up at her windows. She had the feeling of being shut away, a prisoner. She thought angrily: I wont be treated this way, not by them. Reese couldn't ignore her as he had these past two days, staring at her as though she was a dirty rag someone had left in a corner. He had to understand. She hadn't killed her father. He didn't have to do what he had done. The knowledge hurt. It seemed so useless. Sometimes, as she thought of those last few minutes when he must have stood alone with Donnie in the courthouse room, the enormity of the act overwhelmed her. She had never thought her father capable of such violence. He had always been such a soft, quiet man. How could any act of hers have driven him to murder? She knew what he must have thought; that Donnie had forced her to something she didn't understand, that he had taken advantage of her, she was only fifteen, a child and couldn't have known what she was doing. But she had known. Maybe if he had realized that, things would have been different. There was no need to shoot Donnie or himself. If he had only stopped to think, maybe, it wouldn't have happened.

Uncle Joe decided to drive back to Winton that afternoon and they were all spared the necessity of gathering in the dining room for dinner. Laura wanted nothing but tea and toast sent to her room. The boys had sandwiches in the kitchen. Ann-Charlotte remained upstairs.

Reese waited until Cary was out of the house, and then he went to Laura's room. Her door was open and she looked up, startled by his knock.

164

"Oh." She was surprised. "Come in, Reese."

He sat uncomfortably on the edge of a chair. There was so much he wanted to say, and he didn't know where to begin. He was, suddenly, miserably conscious of his youth and inexperience.

"I've been thinking about a lot of things all day," he said slowly. "Maybe this isn't the time to talk about them, and if you don't want me to, I won't."

Laura couldn't help smiling. He was so solemn, trying with awkwardness to approach her as an adult. Her heart warmed for him.

"I'd like to talk with you, Reese," she said simply.

He flushed, twisting on the chair. "I've been thinking," he said with visible effort, "that since," he looked appealingly up at her, "that since Mr. Whitfield wouldn't, wouldn't be here any more, maybe I better go back to my own place." He finished the sentence with a rush.

Laura shook her head. She didn't trust herself to speak at the moment, feeling if she did the boy before her would break down and cry. She wanted to reach out for him. In some strange way she felt he needed her.

"You see," Reese was forcing himself to continue, "I know how you must feel, and when something like this happens, I guess a family is better off by itself. They need to be together, alone."

"That's right, Reese. I guess we do." Laura watched him.

"So I thought," he continued, "it would be better for everyone if I went home. I can probably find Pa. Maybe, sometime, when you come back to Winton I can come to The Hill and see you."

Laura waited, and then when she saw he had finished, she motioned to a place beside her.

"Come here, Reese. Bring your chair." She paused until he was seated again. "A family should be together, Reese. You're right; but don't you know you are part of one? Cass was very fond of you, and I—" She smiled tenderly. "Well, I guess I feel about you the way your own mother would." It was strange, she thought quickly, but I feel I can depend on him. It should be Cary, but it isn't. "I need you, Reese. That's selfish, if you're going to be unhappy."

"It isn't that, Mrs. Whitfield." He hoped she would understand. "Somehow, I'm afraid things will be different."

"You mustn't feel that way about Ann-Charlotte, Reese," she said. "I don't. I've been thinking it over for the past two days. The terrible thing that has happened to us can't leave hate and bitterness. Joe Whitfield convinced me today. You can't keep it in your heart."

165

"I," he hesitated, "I liked Mr. Whitfield."

"And I," she met his eyes, "I loved him, Reese."

He had the feeling of being trapped. She didn't know what she was asking. How could he look at Ann-Charlotte day after day without remembering what had happened?

"It isn't the same thing," he said doggedly.

Laura experienced a moment of uncertainty. Maybe she shouldn't ask him to stay. Perhaps he would be better off, happier, back on a small farm with his father. Sometimes people weren't meant to be transplanted.

"If I can forgive what has happened," she said, "you can. No one can live alone with tragedy, certainly not a fifteen-year-old girl. You've been something more than a big brother, Reese. I could see what was happening this summer, and it made me happy. It was a little foolish and, well, just a little wonderful. I want you to stay with us. Somehow you seem so much older and wiser than Cary. I need a man, Reese."

Reese stared unhappily at the carpet. She made him feel proud but troubled. Cary was all right. They understood each other; but Ann-Charlotte was different. She scared him. She was born for trouble.

"I don't think I'd be much help to you, Mrs. Whtifield. I'm just growing up myself." He smiled suddenly. "I've probably got a lot of hell to get out of my own system. I sure wouldn't want to burden you with that, too."

"You just be yourself, Reese. I'll take a chance if you think there is one."

He nodded. There didn't seem to be any way out.

"I," she spoke thoughtfully, "we wanted you and Cary to go to college this fall. Cass planned for it. I don't know, though, if it would be wise now. Would you," she took his hand, "would it make a great deal of difference if we postponed it for a year? I don't think it would do any harm."

He grinned quickly. "No'm. I can wait. I never did take it very seriously. Anyhow, I don't know what I want to study. Maybe it would be a good idea if we all thought it over for a few months."

"Joe Whitfield suggested we go away for the winter. I don't know. Perhaps it would be better if we went back to Winton. Europe is so far away. It frightens me to think about it. There is bound to be talk."

Reese didn't know what to say. There would be talk. Winton would cherish the scandal, keeping it alive.

"Uncle Joe Whitfield," he said after a moment, "usually knows

what he's saying, even if it doesn't sound that way sometimes." He
stood up. "I guess, though, you are the one to decide things."

"We'll all decide them." She turned to him. "Come here, Reese."

He approached her with hesitation, sensing what was going to happen, then he ducked his head quickly and kissed her lightly on the
cheek. She held his head for a second.

"Thank you, Reese. I'm glad you came. Maybe we understand things
better now." She released him and he straightened up.

"I guess so," he said. "I only wanted to do what would make it
easier for you."

"Reese—" She spoke with an effort. "I want you to try and understand Ann-Charlotte. Help her, won't you? She needs it. Don't be too
harsh, will you? And," she paused, "don't let Cary hurt her. He'll
probably want to, and you mustn't let him. Help me, all of us, Reese."

XVI

The withdrawal of The Hill from Winton was so gradual and unobtrusive in the year following Cassius Whitfield's death that few, and certainly not those who lived there, realized what was happening. There was no conscious effort to shut the big house away from the town. Its doors were open as always. At night it was an uneven cluster of light when seen from below. Laura hadn't sought seclusion, but it seemed almost as though the human tide receded until it lapped raggedly at the edges and then drained off, leaving the house in grim solitude like some great ship gale-driven, high on a lonely beach.

Confused and uncertain, knowing only that the mountains were unbearable at the moment, Laura had returned to The Hill with the boys and Ann-Charlotte. Her plans were without form, but she sought the house as sanctuary, finding shelter and relief from her doubts in its ugly shape. A few of their close friends telephoned. Others made formal calls, but the conversations were stilted and unhappy. Tragedy feeds upon itself, and the spectacle isn't pleasant. Visitors were uncomfortable and they hurried away, feeling a vague uneasiness as though they had looked upon decay unnoticed by those surrounded by it. Laura was cordial, offering a subdued friendliness, but misfortune whispered through the rooms like an invisible bat. People lowered their heads and hastened out into the sunlight.

Winton, of course, talked and gossiped behind its hands. Everyone knew Ann-Charlotte Whitfield had been taken in a raid on a group of unsavory tourist cabins near Harlen and drove her father to murder and suicide. The story was flung across the country with prodigal enthusiasm. If Laura realized the scope of its sensationalism, she gave no indication that the knowledge was an almost unbearable burden. Once they were settled again on The Hill, she made a determined effort not to hear the echoes of the scandal, allowing it to beat with empty sound and little meaning.

Ann-Charlotte heard it, though, and cringed. The telephone that used to clamor incessantly every fall when they returned from the lodge was silent, and the driveways where defiantly battered jalopies used to park were vacant. She used to wait, hoping, with hollow desperation, that someone would call; anxious even for a furtive word, a whispered conversation with one of the girls she had known. The ostracism was complete. Bright, young voices no longer fluttered in the yard or from the waiting deck chairs in the garden, and the boathouse balcony and the float in the lake were deserted. She progressed slowly from frightened humility to hysterical helplessness and finally to a bright, hard indifference and insolent mockery.

Cary turned to Reese with an almost pathetic eagerness, following him about with the apprehensive fervor of a dog that expects any moment to be sent home or confined to a leash. He was humbly grateful when, after they had been home a couple of days, Reese suggested they drive down into Winton and then out to his father's cottage. Reese had the feeling he had been afraid to go into town by himself. He was sure of this when Cary insisted he drive and then slid down into the seat as though reluctant to be recognized by anyone they passed.

Lance's house was vacant as he had left it. Somehow he had been hoping his father might have returned by now. The Hill made him uneasy, and he was tortured a dozen times a day by Laura's air of tight concentration. He walked through the weed-grown yard, around to the back, and stood looking at the narrow kitchen door. A key was hidden in a can beneath the steps. He and Lance always left it there. Reaching down, he felt the tin, shook it gently, and heard the sharp rattle of metal inside. Lance hadn't come back. Suddenly Reese felt old and a little weary. With bent head he kicked out through the matted and uncultivated field. Somehow it didn't seem right to have it this way. When a man neglected the land he owned, it did something to him. I'll put someone on it, he thought. I'll find a family. There isn't much here, but a family could work a living out of it if they all tried.

"What were you fooling out there in the field for?" Cary had been waiting in the car.

"Nothing." Reese couldn't have explained the action to himself. "I just wanted to go out and look around." He climbed into the car.

"Do you think your pa's been back this summer?"

"No." Reese turned the car around. "If he had been back he would have planted something even if it had only been a few rows of corn and beans. He couldn't have stood looking at that field the way it is."

They drove into Winton and Reese deliberately drew in at the curb

169

before the Rexall store. He looked at Cary and saw something close to fear in his eyes.

"Come on in," he suggested, "and we'll get a dope."

Cary shook his head quickly. "I'm not thirsty."

Reese leaned across the door toward him. "You better get over this. You've got to stop giving a damn what you think people are going to say. You have to say to yourself: The Hill is bigger than anything that can happen to it."

At his urging Cary reluctantly crawled out of the seat. The sliding doors of the drugstore were thrown open, making the fountain almost a part of the sidewalk. They drank their coca-colas unhurriedly, chewing on the slivers of ice. The boy behind the fountain made an unsuccessful effort to conceal his interest in Cary. Reese stared unemotionally at him until he flushed and dropped a glass. A dozen or so persons they both knew wandered in and out of the store. Reese was casual beneath their curious, sidelong glances. He called a greeting now and then with studied assurance. He was answered, but the eyes were upon Cary. This was the first time any of the Whitfields had been in town since the trouble.

When they finally drove away, there was a general turning of eyes as the La Salle shot up Memorial Avenue. Cary stared with silent bleakness straight ahead. He was shaking a little.

"Damn them to hell, anyhow," he said. "I didn't do anything. It isn't my fault."

"I guess," Reese spoke thoughtfully, "it isn't anyone's fault. Maybe not even Ann-Charlotte's."

"It's all right for you to talk!" Cary was experiencing a sense of futile rage. "It hasn't anything to do with you. It isn't your family."

Reese turned his head, looking at him for a moment. "I guess you're right," he said, and his eyes returned to the road.

Cary was instantly contrite. "I didn't mean it that way, Reese. You know I didn't. It's just, maybe, you couldn't feel the same. I don't know."

"Forget it."

Reese allowed the car to drift along. It had been a good idea to make Cary get out. It would be better if Ann-Charlotte came the next time. They couldn't shut themselves up on The Hill. Probably that was what Mrs. Whitfield wanted him to do. Well, he'd try. He grinned, thinking of what would happen if he, Cary, and Ann-Charlotte drove out to the country club tomorrow. People, he said to himself, would probably run like someone had turned a rattlesnake nest loose on the porch.

He turned through the gates to The Hill, looking up at the big house with a feeling of security.

Laura had tried to postpone or even avoid an inevitable meeting with the Whitfield lawyers. Whatever there was to be done, she thought, could wait. She still couldn't get used to the fact that Cassius was no longer with her, and she didn't want to put the final seal on his death with the details of his estate. The lawyers had been gently insistent, waiting impatiently in a suite at the New Winton Hotel and trying, by telephone, to make her understand there were certain legal conventions to be observed. In desperation she had finally agreed to a meeting.

It seemed barbarous, somehow, to sit in the high-ceilinged, oppressive living room while the firm's senior partner and a junior member rustled through a brief case filled with papers they had brought over from Raleigh. She waited unhappily, with Cary, Ann-Charlotte, and Reese seated stiffly in chairs.

She had never thought about money as it was being explained to her now. By comparison to the sums set down in Cassius' will their needs and desires had been ludicrously small. It seemed so foolish that no one had wanted more. What could anyone do with it all? The magnitude of Cassius' share of the fortune Old Andrew had established and safeguarded so well frightened her as she listened. There were bequests in millions to the schools, laboratories, and foundations Cassius had sponsored. She listened with mounting uneasiness as she tried to grasp the importance of what was being said. The trust funds Cassius had set up for herself and the children, the principal involved, shocked her. In a small way she was beginning to understand some of the apprehension Cassius had carried with him all through the years. No one needed or had any right, she thought desperately, to so much money. There was something so completely overpowering in the sums involved. They didn't seem real. Money in such proportion could have no value to its owners. Not even the Duke fortune had been as large. It seemed incomprehensible that they could have flowered from so ordinary a plant as tobacco.

"Mr. Whitfield"—with a start she realized the lawyer was addressing her directly—"made no provision for either Cary or Miss Ann-Charlotte until they became of age. A court order, if you wish, will establish a more than adequate allowance for them until their majorities are reached and the bulk of the estate is released. There is also provision for an annual income of $10,000, out of interest, or principal if it should become necessary, to Reese Benton. That, also, is not to start until Mr. Benton reaches the age of twenty-one but is to be continued thereafter for the period of his lifetime."

Reese listened to the mention of his name, only half understanding, at first, what was being said. Throughout the reading he had been uncomfortable, wondering why he was present. The meeting had seemed to be strictly a family affair. He had been filled with an increasing sense of amazement as he struggled to realize Mr. Whitfield had been one of the wealthiest men in the world. No one would ever have suspected it. Now Cary and Ann-Charlotte were inheriting it. It would make Ann-Charlotte as rich as Doris Duke or Barbara Hutton. He couldn't help looking at them, half expecting to see them change beneath his glance. They just sat there acting as though nothing had happened. His attention was snatched back as the lawyer repeated his name and he gathered the import of the bequest. $10,000 a year. That was about $200 a week. He looked guiltily at Mrs. Whitfield, feeling as if he had been caught in something dishonest. She only looked at him and smiled, so she must have known in advance.

Reese hunched himself in the chair. He had the sensation of suddenly being conspicuous, as though Mr. Whitfield's lawyers were peering at him over their spectacles and saying to themselves: How did he get in this? His mouth dried up unaccountably. He felt as ashamed as he would have been if someone had dragged him naked into the room. There was something he couldn't understand. Mr. Whitfield shouldn't have done it. It made him feel as though he were stealing. He wanted to say something, deny the gift, tell everyone it must be a mistake. He looked appealingly at Laura Whitfield, but she merely shook her head in a negative sign. He sank back in the chair then, not daring to look at Ann-Charlotte or Cary. The amount still refused to register itself completely. He contemplated the number ten thousand in a dazed fashion. In all of his life Lance Benton had never had a thousand dollars at one time. Now, he was to get not one but ten, ten thousand dollars, every year of his life for as long as he lived. He knew something must be wrong. The lawyers would go back over the will and discover the mistake.

There was a general rustle of papers and the two men at the table were closing up their brief cases. Dimly he heard Laura Whitfield speaking. Now, he thought, would be the time for someone to say:

I'm afraid that Mr. Whitfield didn't know what he was doing when he included Reese in his will. Reese is only a boy we know, a youngster who played with the children. He waited. No one mentioned his name.

"Thank you very much, Mr. Wharton." Laura was extending her hand to the lawyer. "I'm sorry I kept you in Winton so long, but I'm sure you will understand."

It seemed a long time before the two men finally gathered up their things, and longer still, to Reese at least, before they left. When their car ground out of the driveway, there was a moment's silence and then Laura rose. Ann-Charlotte and Cary, strangely subdued, stood with her, and Reese struggled to his feet. Without actually touching any of them Laura seemed to gather the three into her arms for comfort. Ann-Charlotte glanced up at her mother. Her lips trembled and then her eyes dropped.

"I never thought," Laura spoke with quiet reluctance, "it would be this way. I always counted so much on Cass. Now he isn't here. I hope I can do what is right. I'm afraid of the responsibility for you, Cary and Ann-Charlotte. It's hard for me to remember you are growing up." She turned to Reese. "I'm not worried about you. Both Cass and I wanted you to have the freedom. We talked it over a long time ago. When you're older, you can make your own life, only," she smiled, "somehow, I hope it will never be too far away from The Hill."

In a moment Reese knew he would be crying like a kid. The inside of his nose burned and he swallowed an uneasy lump. "I don't need anything, Mrs. Whitfield," he managed to say. "You and Mr. Whitfield didn't have to do anything for me."

Laura did put her arm around him then. "I know you don't need anything, Reese. You're part of the family. It's better this way, though. I suspect you'll understand someday." Her fingers tightened momentarily on his shoulder and then the hand dropped away. "We've all had a bad time." Ann-Charlotte looked at her as though to stay the words. "It won't be easy for any of us for a while. All we can do is try." She took Cary's and then Ann-Charlotte's arm, linking hers with them. "Let's go out on the terrace garden. We'll have lunch there, if you like. I thought we might go away from Winton for the winter. Let's talk about it."

Following them, Reese thought again of what the lawyer had said and of Laura Whitfield's words. "Make your own life, but I hope it will never be too far away from The Hill." I'm stuck, he said grimly to himself. No matter what happens now. He wondered if Cassius had known; realized what he was doing. I wish I could see Pa. He'd know what I ought to do. Maybe, though, Lance wouldn't know. Probably, he'd just see the $10,000 and say it was good. He tried to imagine what that amount of money would look like in one-dollar bills and grinned. Maybe, he said to himself, I'll get it all in a room and walk through it barefoot, picking up a handful whenever I want to buy something.

Over lunch in the garden Laura fought to make her words sound casual, striving to make them believe that there was nothing unusual in their leaving Winton. For long hours at a time she had paced her room trying to find an escape for Ann-Charlotte. Boarding school was no answer. Boarding school, she thought bitterly, was the problem. A good school, probably, wouldn't take Ann-Charlotte right now; not even the schools endowed by Whitfield money. Reese and Cary would be all right, but she couldn't let them go. Ann-Charlotte was in desperate need of companionship. The child, she realized, was on the brittle edge of a nervous collapse. The tight defiance and assumed indifference she struggled to maintain were shockingly transparent. It was no good for her to pretend she didn't care or was oblivious to the fact that not one of all the girls who used to come almost daily to The Hill had telephoned, or that the invitations to parties or picnics hadn't been extended this year. Laura had discovered pitiful evidence of her inner turmoil in a ragged column, torn from the newspaper, which listed the small social activities of Winton's teen-agers. The clipping, marked with pencil, was lying on the floor beside Ann-Charlotte's dressing table. Watching her daughter, Laura knew what was happening and felt powerless to set things right. Maybe in a year or two it would be different. Maybe, she thought wearily, nothing would ever be the same for Ann-Charlotte again.

"Uncle Joe," Laura said, "thought it might do us all good if we went abroad." She paused, finding it almost impossible to continue. "I don't know. It—it seems so far away."

Cary's eyes betrayed his excitement. Going away; ships, England, probably, France—the idea fired his imagination. Ann-Charlotte stared blankly at one corner of the tablecloth. Her features were impassive. Reese glanced at her and suddenly felt sorry for what he saw.

"We could go to New York," Laura continued reluctantly, feeling, somehow, that every word was taking her farther away, "and spend some time there. Would you like that, Ann-Charlotte?" She was almost pleading.

"No, Mother." Ann-Charlotte didn't compromise. "I wouldn't like it

174

at all and I know you wouldn't. I know why we're going, and so, whatever you decide will be all right."

Surprisingly enough it was Joe Whitfield who, in the end, offered a solution. At least, it surprised Laura, who hadn't looked to him for help. He telephoned a couple of days later.

"Laurie," he said, "why don't all of you come down here for dinner tonight." She heard him chuckle. "Don't think I'm gettin' a touch of family—it's just that there's a lot of stuff left over in the icebox I want to get rid of."

There was something so reassuring in the sound of his voice. Laura laughed spontaneously for the first time in a week. Joe was so wise, so confident. He'd seen so much of life. He must know what to do at a time like this.

"Are you," she asked, almost gaily, "going to provide a sturdy oak for me to lean on?"

There was a moment of silence. Joe was thinking this over. "Well," the tone was soberly thoughtful, "if I don't exactly let you lean on it, I'll try an' spare a little shade for you to sit in. How about six-thirty?"

For a long time after she replaced the receiver in its cradle Laura sat beside her desk, looking at the framed photograph of Cassius on one corner. It was a picture she had insisted he have taken, and as always, he managed to get that solemn, small-boy earnestness on his features.

"Whatever," she said aloud, "Joe tells me to do I'll do. Isn't that the way you would want it?"

They all felt better for getting away from the gloomy confinement of The Hill. Even Ann-Charlotte responded. They took Cary's open car, experiencing, although none of them said so, a sudden sense of unity in the casual companionship. Reese and Ann-Charlotte were in the rumble seat.

"Don't you think it's funny," she called to her mother against the rush of wind, "that Uncle Joe should invite us for dinner? He never did before."

"I stopped puzzling over Joe's actions years ago." Laura turned her head slightly. "Don't drive so fast, Cary."

Joe was waiting on the terrace overlooking the river, and as he came halfway down the broad, flaged steps to meet them, Laura found herself studying him with the interest she might have displayed toward a stranger. There was nothing about him to remind her of Cassius. No wonder, she thought, they were so different. They don't even look alike. Where Cassius had been heavy, unconsciously radiating solid, unimaginative prosperity, Joe was lean and hard, almost to the point of being gaunt. His face was weathered and lined, and there was a hint of subdued laughter in his eyes. Joe had always found life pleasant and mildly exciting, and he had cultivated it as he might a good companion, never asking more than he was willing to give. As a result he was in fine balance with the world, moving through it with assurance. Mounting the steps, Laura thought a little regretfully of the things Cassius had missed. It hardly seemed possible brothers could have been cast in such distinctively different molds. She also experienced a small touch of excitement at being at Bluestone. Cary, Ann-Charlotte, and Reese had been frequent visitors, feeling free to use Joe's stretch of the river and his boats whenever he was away, but she and Cassius had never been asked down. Now she glanced across the terrace with unconcealed admiration. There was a freedom and ease in the construction, the feeling of light and well-being. No wonder Joe had fled from The Hill the moment Old Andrew died.

"Hi, Laurie." He took her hand and called a greeting over her shoulder to Reese, Ann-Charlotte, and Cary. "I'm glad you could come." It really seemed as though he was. He led Laura to a chair on the terrace. "Let's have a drink out here and then see what's in the stew pot."

Sitting in a row on the wall with Cary and Ann-Charlotte, Reese thought how simple Joe Whitfield made everything. On The Hill or at the lodge when Cassius wanted a cocktail before supper he engaged in an elaborate pretense, pretending there was no one else around. Once he had even committed the unforgivable error of saying: "I don't suppose the children drink, yet," and then laughed a little self-consciously. Joe Whitfield just took it for granted that if they wanted a drink they'd have one. He darted a glance at Ann-Charlotte and saw she was regarding her uncle with a new and respectful interest.

They had sherry on the terrace; a dry, almost straw-colored wine, served in slender, cylindrical glasses without stems. It had a curious taste of earth, as though something of the land had been bottled with the grape.

As if he understood what was in their minds, Joe smiled appreciatively.

"That's clay," he said in explanation. "Not North Carolina clay but the soil of the Jerez district in Spain. They filter the wine through it. Hell of an idea, isn't it? Turns out all right, just the same."

Dinner was friendly and informal and to Laura a grateful release.

176

There was no struggle to make conversation. Talk flowed from Joe, an easy, effortless comment that didn't seem to be directed at anyone and so included them all. Nothing he said was particularly important, and yet, by a magic she couldn't understand, he made it seem interesting and entertaining. No wonder, she mused regretfully, Joe and Cassius hadn't understood each other.

She discovered she was tasting food again with honest pleasure. Unconsciously she relaxed and, glancing about the table, saw with gratified surprise that Ann-Charlotte was responding. Her eyes were bright again and she leaned slightly forward now and then eagerly following every word Joe uttered.

"I've always remembered that." Joe grinned reminiscently. He had been talking of Holland. "It's the great curiosity that sets an American apart. This little scrubwoman in the cathedral at Delft insisted on showing me through the building, although a blind man could have found his way. She talked and I kept answering. Finally she turned to me and said: 'You're an American, aren't you?' I told her yes, but it gave me a jolt. There I was, a hell of a lot younger, with my London clothes an' maybe even a try at a British accent because I thought it was smart in those days, an' the old woman was callin' the turn on me as an American. 'How do you know?' I asked. Well, she looked at me for a moment. 'I can always tell an American,' she said, an' I said: 'Is that so?' " He threw back his head and laughed. " 'Sure,' she said. 'I can always tell. No matter what you say to them they always say: "Is that so?" ' "

His delight in the story was so apparent, even Ann-Charlotte laughed, and she was still smiling when they all pushed their chairs away and strolled outside. She wondered why she had always thought of Uncle Joe as a rough, ill-tempered old man. He was fun to be with, and he hadn't treated her as a child. She was suddenly grateful.

Cary and Reese, without asking her to come along, walked from the porch and down beside the river. Joe sat smoking for a moment, and then when he did speak, his words were quietly reflective.

"I'm not goin' to talk in front of Ann-Charlotte like she was a baby, Laurie," he said. "We all know what happened, and there ain't any use in actin' as though we didn't. It's bad for you, but most of all it's bad for Ann-Charlotte. When I suggested up at the lodge you all go away for a while, I hadn't thought things out. Now, I don't think it would be any good."

Laura nodded. A trip was the straw of silent desperation and she had clutched at it, knowing, somehow, it wouldn't sustain them.

"I'm sailin' on the *Majestic* in a couple of weeks." Joe didn't turn his head but continued to stare out over the river. "I figured on spending the winter in France for a change. I have a lot of friends there. What would you think, Ann-Charlotte, of comin' with me, just the two of us?"

Ann-Charlotte looked up, wide-eyed, incredulous. He hadn't made it seem anything special; not as though they were running away, trying to hide. And he had asked her. He hadn't put the question to her mother. She experienced a suffocating gratitude for the understanding.

"Oh! Uncle Joe," she breathed, "I think it would be the most wonderful thing in the world."

"A lot of people don't think much of France in the winter." Joe acted as if he had to convince them of its advantages. "But there's a lot of France. Also," he smiled in the darkness, "there are some fine girls' schools in Paris."

"Oh!" Ann-Charlotte sagged. He was going to put her away.

"I only said," Joe continued, pretending he hadn't heard her gasp of disappointment, "there were some fine schools. You could make up your own mind. Well, Laurie?"

Laura couldn't speak at once. What Joe was proposing was so revolutionary she had difficulty in grasping its implications. Ann-Charlotte away, almost alone, all winter. She was still a baby, no matter what anyone thought or said.

"I want to go with you, Uncle Joe." Ann-Charlotte was quietly determined, and Laura somehow knew the decision had been taken away from her.

"I think," Joe said, "you an' me would get along. Maybe we're quite a bit alike, even if that don't give Laurie any comfort."

"Joe, I don't know." Laura couldn't keep the apprehension from her voice.

"After all," he was ridiculously solemn, "I'm her uncle. It ain't exactly like some rip askin' a young thing to run away for a life of sin in Paris. Besides," he added, "I'm gettin' too old, at least I think I am."

"But," Laura was protesting automatically although she knew what the final answer would be, "Ann-Charlotte, she..."

"She's old enough to dress herself, ain't she?" Joe interrupted, "an' she doesn't have to be fed at the table. That's all I'll ask. About school, if that interests her, an' I think it will, we can talk about it later. A finishing school in Paris isn't to be tossed over the shoulder. I think, maybe, Ann-Charlotte would respond to the Continental touch."

Laura looked across at her daughter. Ann-Charlotte was regarding her uncle with something close to awe, recognizing wonderful and unsuspected qualities in him.

"This afternoon, after you telephoned," Laura said, "I spoke to Cass's picture. I told him whatever you said I would do. So," she added weakly, "I guess I'll keep my word."

Ann-Charlotte rose from her chair. Watching her, Joe thought what a remarkably beautiful girl she was. The light from the living-room doors built a frame about her. He was afraid, now, that she was going to be overly demonstrative, maybe throw her arms about him, even cry. Instinctively he shied away; gratitude in any form always embarrassed him. Ann-Charlotte did none of the things he might have expected. Instead, she leaned over and kissed him on the cheek. It was a grave salute of appreciation, nothing more. The girl, Joe thought admiringly, didn't slop over.

"Thank you, Uncle Joe," she said simply. "We'll get along better than you think."

Reese stood at the window of his room in the Plaza looking out over the small lake and the ordered tangle of Central Park. Rain slanted across the trees and tore through tattered wisps of cloud tumbling along below building level, churning itself into steaming, hissing pools on the asphalt of Fifty-ninth Street. It was a city rain, he thought; a New York rain, sharp and well ordered, falling with tailored perfection. Through its curtain he could see the gilded equestrian statue of General Sherman with the figure of Victory marching ahead, and he laughed softly, thinking of the driver of one of the horse-drawn cabs. They had hired him for a tour through the park and later down Fifth Avenue. The coachman, recognizing a Southern accent, pointed at the statue with his whip.

"You can tell he was a Yankee," he said. "Look at him ridin' there an' lettin' the lady walk."

It was probably an old joke, Reese thought, but it struck him funny every time he said it over to himself. He wondered how many tourists the driver had told it to. It was his only joke, most likely, because he didn't have the face of a man of humor. New York was a funny place, anyhow. Driving through the park they had seen a crowd of fifty or more persons standing in silent wonder, gazing steadily at an ordinary milk cow. If you stopped on the sidewalk to tie a shoelace, half a dozen people would slow up or look back to see what you were doing. He thought the city was noisy in a patterned sort of a fashion, like a phonograph record. The rain outside now was an example. It came down as though someone had ordered so many inches, and not in the gusty, blowsy fashion of a rainstorm back home.

During the week they had been in New York, while Ann-Charlotte and Laura were completely absorbed in shopping, he and Cary had been left to their own fancies. They roamed from Battery Park to upper Riverside Drive. Because he had been here before, Cary pretended a great boredom with the business of sight-seeing, adopting the air of an original settler, but Reese discovered he didn't know as much as he thought he did, and whenever they lost themselves Cary covered his confusion by calling a taxicab. Privately, Reese thought New York an over-touted city. It was big and everyone was in a hell of a hurry, but it wasn't much more than Winton multiplied several thousand times. Broadway and Times Square jostled each other in a noisy, dirty clatter, and the Greenwich Village he had heard so much about seemed down-at-the-heel, across-the-railroad-tracks. He looked vainly for a velvet-coated artist or a few Bohemian girls he had read about. Joe Whitfield, on a rare afternoon when he took them to George White's Scandals, summed it up.

"Most of the people here," he said, "have spent half their lives trying to get to New York and the other half trying to get back to wherever they came from."

Joe was anxious to sail and he looked upon the mounting racks of Ann-Charlotte's purchases with skeptical impatience, assuring her, and Laura also, that there were a couple of good stores in Paris and London. He disappeared on mysterious business of his own during the day but kept his evenings free. Cary suggested to Reese that Uncle Joe probably had a few girls set up around town and spent his afternoons with them. At night he took them to the theater and later to such night clubs as Texas Guinan's or George Olsen's, where everyone seemed to get drunk right away.

"This is strictly tourist stuff," Joe explained, "but I suppose you wouldn't feel right going away without seeing it. New York's a great city if you catch it just right. It's no good for the very young or the very old."

Some of the things about the city Reese remembered and liked. There was the sweep of the Hudson River as seen from the top of a bus looking down from 125th Street; the hard, theatrical brilliance of a moon set at one corner of the Fisk Building near Columbus Circle; a strangely exciting and electric quality about Fifth Avenue in the late afternoon, and the ageless majesty of the library at Columbia University at dusk.

He and Cary had left a bus at 116th Street, walking up the sloping sidewalk, across Broadway to the polished, spherical sun dial set on its raised block by South Field. In the gathering twilight the buildings were silently massive, and here, in the short blocks between Morningside Drive and Broadway, the noises of the city were miraculously shut out. Looking up over the broad sweep of steps to the classic beauty of the library, Reese caught his breath. Nothing he had even seen before was comparable to this hushed perfection. There was something exalting in just standing there and looking.

"When I go to school," he said quietly, "I'm coming here."

Cary snorted at the idea. "You wouldn't have any fun here. People study too hard. We ought to go someplace down home, or maybe Cornell or Princeton. This looks like a factory to me."

Reese shook his head. "You go wherever you want. I'm going to come up here."

Cary was humoringly curious. "What do you want to study?"

"I don't know," Reese answered thoughtfully, "but by next year I will."

"I'll bet they won't even take Winton High School credits here."

"If they don't"—Reese was determined—"I'll make them up someplace first."

They strolled without purpose across Amsterdam Avenue, over Morningside to a circular plaza from where they could look down and across the ugly confusion of Harlem with its bewildering maze of human warrens.

"That's the Negrah section." Cary nodded below. "How would you like that, if you're so crazy about the city?"

Reese stared; there was something a little terrifying in the spectacle. He shook his head. "I just wonder how the Negrahs like it. How do you suppose a man must feel waking up to that every morning? Somebody must be crazy, either the white people down home or the Negrahs, I don't know which."

Riding back downtown in a cab, he couldn't erase the memory of that stone jungle from his mind. That was what the colored people down home looked to as the Promised Land. Somebody was awfully wrong, he thought, and wondered why.

"Still going to Columbia?" Cary imagined he was being funny.

"Yep." Reese smiled suddenly at him. "You too, lint-head, even if you don't know it now."

They both laughed then for no particular reason and grinned companionably at each other from their corners. Cary, Reese mused, had changed a lot since his father's death and Ann-Charlotte's trouble. He seemed to have grown older and wasn't always thinking about himself. For the past few weeks they had been able to talk and joke together the way they used to when they were kids in grammar school, before—he chuckled at the idea—before Cary began to realize he was a Whitfield.

"What are you laughing about?" Cary peered at him.

"I was just thinking," Reese was deliberately serious, "even a stranger might like you now." He was sorry for a moment because he realized Cary didn't have any idea what he was talking about. Mystification was plain on his face.

"What the hell do you mean?"

"Nothing. I was only thinking out loud. Give me a cigarette."

Cary fumbled with a package. He wasn't satisfied, but then it was hard to tell what Reese meant sometimes. Now and then he felt as though he was standing off to one side and watching him, wondering what he was going to do next but really not caring; the way a man might watch a raccoon playing in a pen. More than anything else, though, he was puzzled over Reese's attitude toward Ann-Charlotte. For a while it seemed as if things were the same as they always had been. Ann-Charlotte wasn't as fresh as she used to be, she was quieter. Well, she damn well ought to be after what had happened. But Reese, Reese didn't laugh the way he used to when they were together. He couldn't remember when he first began noticing that, but now he watched for it. A stranger wouldn't see any difference, but it was there; and he could tell Ann-Charlotte knew it, and he thought maybe she was helplessly frightened by what she saw. There was nothing to be afraid of. Reese had a right to be sore, and she ought to know it.

"Here." He tossed the cigarettes across the seat to Reese. "You've got some stock in the company now. Maybe you better begin buying your own."

Staring out of the hotel window now, Reese thought of that afternoon. Cary hadn't believed him when he said he was coming back to New York next year and go to Columbia. Cary didn't want to go to college, not if it meant any work. A nice country club would suit him better. Well, that was all right, but he wanted more. This confused him sometimes. Why did he want more, and what was it? When he was twenty-one, he'd never have to work for a living. Ten thousand dollars a year wouldn't be much the way Cary would be looking at things when he came of age, but it was more than plenty. He could sit on his backside in Winton for the rest of his life and not even go near The Hill if he didn't want to. He shook his head. It wasn't really his money. It never would be. I guess, he thought, it's no good coming this way. Probably that was what used to worry Mr. Whitfield. I'm damned if I'm going to end up building stone fences just to give myself something to do.

The opening of a door caused him to turn from the window. Ann-Charlotte stood in the hall and then stepped inside, closing the door behind her.

"I wanted to say good-by, Reese," she almost whispered. "I know you all are coming down to the ship with Uncle Joe and me, but it wouldn't be the same there on the dock with a lot of people." She walked over to the window and looked down into the street.

Standing beside her, facing the rain, Reese waited and wondered what he was going to say when he had to speak.

"I'm going to be gone a long time." She didn't look at him. "No one but you knows that. Mother thinks I'll be back next summer, but I've talked with Uncle Joe. I'm going to school in Paris for the next three years, until I'm eighteen."

The rain brushed against the windowpanes, bouncing and scattering with a faint, drumming sound. He didn't turn his head, but he was acutely conscious of her as her sleeve touched his. She was wearing a grayish-blue suit. It made her look older and poised. He caught a faint scent of perfume and wondered how perfume could smell like damp grass with hot sun on it.

"I'll be different then, and so will you." She lifted her fingers to touch the glass. "Maybe it will be better." She turned suddenly, her face lifted slightly. She was almost as tall as he. "Will you kiss me good-by, now, Reese?"

He looked at her for a moment and realized he was beginning to tremble. In another moment she would notice it. Then he touched her cheek with his lips.

"I was afraid it would be that way," she said, turning back. "I guess that's why I thought for a long time before I came in. Oh, Reese!" Her voice broke ever so faintly. "I wish it had been you, from the very beginning. Maybe, then, you'd understand." She wheeled and walked away.

He waited until he heard the door close. I'd be crazy, he said to himself. It would be about the craziest thing a man could do. His hand shook as he plucked at the foil of a pack of cigarettes. I could beat my heart out and it would always be the same. He jammed the cigarettes back in his coat. To hell with it. Maybe when people are tough and don't give a damn they're better off.

The luggage had gone down from the hotel to the pier earlier in the day, and so they all crowded into a single taxicab with Reese and Cary on the two folding seats. No one seemed to want to talk and so they rode in silence, their heads turned toward the windows. The cab bucked and slithered through the crosstown traffic and then down West Street to the Cunard–White Star Line piers.

"For God's sake," Uncle Joe said as they walked through the long, cavernous shed, "don't stand around out here waiting for the ship to sail and expecting me to be leaning by a rail waving good-by. Do you want to come aboard, Laurie, and look around?"

Laura shook her head and make no attempt to hide the fact she was ready to cry. "No," she said, "it would only drag things out." She looked tremulously at Ann-Charlotte. "I can't believe you're really leaving."

At the desk where Joe checked in with their passports and tickets they all seemed silently embarrassed. Ann-Charlotte kissed Cary good-by and then turned to her mother. They clung together for a moment.

"You'll be careful, dear," Laura was unashamed of her tears, "and write me, baby."

Ann-Charlotte was troubled by the demonstration and drew away. "Good-by, Reese."

They shook hands and he thought how foolish it looked. "Good-by, Ann-Charlotte. Take care of yourself and," he grinned for the first time, "and Uncle Joe."

They waited in a tight little knot until Joe and Ann-Charlotte crossed the gangplank and vanished with almost startling suddenness through the yawning port.

XVII

On that autumn day when Ann-Charlotte sailed with Joe Whitfield for Europe, Laura felt that she stood alone. Cary and Reese hurried down to the pierhead for a final glimpse of the *Majestic* as she swung, midstream in the North River, pointing her towering bows toward the Narrows and open sea. Laura waited, caught in the grip of an almost overpowering sense of desolation and helplessness. Her world, once so secure and unshakable, was dissolving, and she was unable to close her hands upon any part of it. Now that Ann-Charlotte had gone she wanted to call her back, desperately anxious to hold what she could. The thought of Winton and The Hill and the reponsibility of attempting to control Cary and discharge her obligation to Reese filled her with mounting terror. Perhaps, she thought with a quick stab of despair, it would have been better not to have allowed Ann-Charlotte to go away. With all of them together, they might have achieved a balance. The family was disentegrating, chipped at by forces she was unable to master. She watched as people streamed past on their way to the street, laughing, talking, so obviously carefree. She stood, a lonely figure, waiting, as Cary and Reese came toward her. Cary was laughing excitedly, and she felt a quick resentment. Didn't he know what had happened or was happening, or didn't he care?

The ride back to the hotel was dreary. Rain beat furiously against the cab's windows, and a chill wind wriggled through the cracks. Without warning, the season wound them all in its melancholy. Staring out of the cloudy window, Laura wondered what they should do. She tried to reassure herself, repeating over and over that both boys were almost grown and capable of shouldering some of the burden if they wished. The thought brought no comfort. Fantastic notions flitted through her brain. In a moment Cary would hail the cab into the curb, step out and say: Well, good-by. She would awaken in the morning and find herself alone in a hotel room.

They stayed in New York a week, Laura finding anonymity in its millions, seeking to occupy her mind, striving to postpone a return to Winton. One day she suddenly realized there was nothing to call her back to The Hill. The idea shocked her at first, and then brought a blessed feeling of relief as she thought it over. She wasn't alone. Cary and Reese weren't going away to school. They would all spend the winter someplace; keep traveling, if necessary, putting time and distance between them and what had happened. She became almost cheerful again.

To Cary and Reese, who had been fidgeting unhappily, wandering disconsolately through the suite and lobby, her decision not to return to Winton was electrifying. They both felt that the possibilities of New York had been exhausted, and Cary didn't want to go home. As for Reese, he was unable to shake off the uncomfortable sensation of intruding where he had no business. Any diversion was welcome. Several times he had been on the point of asking Laura if he couldn't go back to Winton by himself, but he knew in his heart this would only make her unhappy. As a release they all seized upon the simple question of where to go with furious enthusiasm, pretending it was a matter of such weight as could only be decided after long consultation. They read every line in the many travel folders sent up from the porter's desk. The merits of Mexico over Cuba, California compared to Florida were debated with little knowledge on anyone's part. In the good-natured wrangling Laura lost herself. She laughed frequently, and something of the hollow deadness left her eyes.

"I'll tell you what," she said one evening. "Let's start with Florida. If we don't like it there, we'll go to Cuba. Those islands, the Bahamas, sound attractive. We'll sort of be tramps, tramps with wardrobe trunks. Whenever we get tired of a place, we'll go to another."

"Where 'bouts in Florida?" Cary was disappointed. He had been entertaining visions of great distances.

"I don't know." Laura wouldn't permit her enthusiasm to be quenched. "We'll start right at the top, Jacksonville, and work our way down. How's that?"

Reese knew he would always remember that winter. First there was the, apparently, limitless novelty of traveling. More than anything else, though, he was conscious of growing up. In a sense the sensation was mystifying, something achieved without effort. He found a new confidence which surprised him in so many little ways. He discovered he was walking through cars and hotel lobbies filled with people, without the unbearable feeling that all eyes were turned upon him. He could sit in a dining car across from a stranger and not experience a fumbling awkwardness as he tried to eat. Because Laura relegated so many small duties to him, the handling of porters, checking of bags, payment of restaurant checks, he achieved an almost solemn dignity. Also, he had his own bank account. Laura made the arrangements.

"There's no point in your having to ask me for money, Reese. It's yours and you might as well have what you want of it now. It will make it easier for all of us."

The winter was kaleidoscopic. They hadn't liked Jacksonville. It was too much of a city. St. Augustine was better. They registered at the Alcazar, and after the first two days, when Laura, feeling morally obligated to expose them to history, insisted they go sight-seeing, Cary and Reese were left to find amusement for themselves. The sleepy, ancient city seemed to drowse in its past, wrapped in a warm blanket of the years and nodding in the sunlight. Cary, tiring of Reese's enthusiasm for the old fort and the water front along the Matanzas River, sought a livelier diversion.

"I've found out where the cathouses are," he confided to Reese. "Fellow who drives one of those surreys told me. Take us out for two dollars." He was condescendingly elated with his knowledge.

Neither of them had known exactly what to expect. After dinner they made an elaborate pretense of coaxing Laura to go to the movies and were secretly delighted when she preferred to stay at home. Outside, Cary located his coachman, and after several minutes of furtive whispering they clattered off to gaze into the unashamed face of sin as displayed in a dismal line of cribs hunched together on an unlighted dirt road.

From the carriage they surveyed the crooked little street and the tightly drawn blinds of the single-room cottages, and then they both laughed. The spectacle was so dismally pathetic. Both, somehow, felt vice should wear glittering raiment, and even Cary, whose sense of the ridiculous was never acute, howled with unaffected hilarity at the gloomy, poverty-ridden line. Still laughing, Reese ordered the mystified driver to turn around and take them to town.

Back on King Street they found a couple of girls idling along in the block near the old slave market and eventually spent a quiet and decorous evening at the movies, eating popcorn, holding butter-smeared hands in the darkness, and later walking arm in arm along the sea wall, listening to the heavy booming of the surf as it pounded at Anastasia Island across the narrow river.

The days of the month they spent in St. Augustine were pleasant if unexciting. They hired a boat for fishing outside Matanzas Inlet, swam in the ocean off the island, visited the Alligator Farm, peered dutifully at America's oldest house, chipped their initials in the coquina battlements of Fort Marion and stared from its towers out to the open sea. Laura regarded them both with approving pride. Cary had changed. He was thoughtful and attentive and actually seemed happy when she went on an excursion with them. Some of the lonely ache left her, and she found great comfort in the boys. Reese, though, was a source of almost constant surprise. He's elastic, she thought. It made her a little happy to witness the flowering of a personality and see in him now what Cassius must have glimpsed. He was good for Cary. There was something steady about him.

Reese and Cary mentioned Ann-Charlotte only once. They were seated on the wall by the river, tossing small stones at the blue crabs feeding in the shallow water.

"Did you ever see a letter from Ann-Charlotte?" Cary asked the question.

"No." Reese shook his head. "I never figured she'd write me," he said slowly.

"I didn't mean that." Cary squinted up at the sun. "I don't think she even wrote Mother. If she had, we would have heard something about it."

"I suppose so." Reese tried to sound indifferent.

Cary leaned over and aimed a rock at a scuttling crab. "What do you suppose is wrong with her?" He didn't lift his head, and the words were muffled. "Do you suppose it's the way you hear about people, girls I mean? They can't help it. She was always sort of crazy, like that time in Vance Porter's, but I just thought she was trying to be smart."

"Oh, shut up!" Reese was furious. "You don't know what you're talking about." He rose quickly and without another word strode off down the street, leaving Cary angry and puzzled.

He watched until Reese turned the corner and then stood up, tossing a final piece of coquina into the water. Walking slowly along the embankment, he felt a sudden resentment. Reese didn't have to act the way he did. They both knew what had happened, and he was glad when Ann-Charlotte went away with Uncle Joe. Maybe Joe would put her in a French convent or some place where she could keep out of trouble until she grew up. It was a hell of a thing, having your sister running around until everyone in the county knew about her. Reese didn't have to tell him to shut up. Ann-Charlotte wasn't his sister.

He dawdled along, stopping to watch some old men playing checkers in the little park where the tourists sat all day. It was silly. They just hunched there like mummies. Suddenly he was tired of St. Augustine. It wasn't fun any longer; nothing to do.

Laura was reading in the shady patio of the hotel when he strolled in. She looked up, smiling.

"Where's Reese—didn't he go with you?"

"I don't know." The more he thought about Reese, the angrier he became; treating him like he was a kid, telling him to shut up and then walking away. He was getting too damned smart. "He got sore about something." He threw himself in a chair, chewing at his lower lip. "I wish Father hadn't left him that money." He blurted out the words without thinking.

Laura closed her book with a snap. "I don't know what happened," she said, "but I never want to hear you say a thing like that again. Do you understand, Cary?"

He had never seen his mother angry before. "Well, it's true." He adopted a doggedly defensive attitude. "He thinks now he can act any way he likes. You help him, too. It's always 'Reese, take care of this,' or 'Reese do that.' I ought to be the man of the family."

Laura relaxed. The boy was jealous. "I'm sorry, Cary." She was sincerely concerned. "I hadn't thought about it. I keep pretending you're still a small boy. Maybe it's because I don't want you to grow up and away from me."

"Well"—he was slightly mollified—"I get tired of it. I'm tired of St. Augustine, too. It's all right for old people who only want to sit around and talk or read. I'd like to have some fun."

Laura wanted to be fair. St. Augustine probably wasn't the liveliest resort in Florida. She had been almost happy here. As the days went by, the town's peaceful, unhurried charm impressed itself upon her. She was beginning to think in normal channels again. It wasn't too much to expect Cary to understand.

"I'd like to have some fun," Cary continued. He was beginning to enjoy the suffering of exile. "I don't see why we couldn't go to Palm Beach or Miami. If I had known it was going to be like this, I would have stayed in New York or gone back to Winton. No one cares by now what happened in Harlen. I don't see why we have to keep remembering it."

"All right, dear." Laura sighed. Every instinct rebelled against this spineless acquiescence. It wasn't that she minded leaving St. Augustine now. What outraged her was the knowledge he would have his way or become so unpleasant as to make staying longer unbearable. "We'll go to Palm Beach if you wish. Now, what happened between you and Reese?"

"Nothing." He was in a mood to be generous. "I said something about Ann-Charlotte and he told me to shut up and walked away."

Laura rose. "You know," she said, and her face clouded, "we decided not to discuss, to talk about, what happened. I think Reese feels he should have taken better care of Ann-Charlotte. She was always pretending she was his girl, and I guess he thought he was too grown up."

"Why should Reese think he ought to take care of Ann-Charlotte?" Cary's indignation exploded. "I'm her brother!"

Laura nodded. "I hope you'll always remember it, dear. Now," she took his arm, "Let's go in and find out about Palm Beach, shall we?"

They spent a month at Palm Beach before Cary wearied of the resort. Then they went on down to Miami. From there they took the small overnight ship to Nassau, but Cary soon tired of the island. He exhausted the limited diversions of Bay Street, excursions in glass-bottomed boats over the coral gardens, and the quaint atmosphere of the out-island boats packed along the quay.

"Wait until I'm twenty-one," he confided to Reese as they sprawled in the sun on the beach before their hotel, "I'll buy a yacht and we'll fill it up with people and go around the world. I'm going to get some fun out of things."

"You'll get tired of it, the same as this." Reese watched a pretty, blonde girl as she came out of the water toward them.

"That's what you think. I'm going to live the way Uncle Joe used to, just hell over the world."

"All right." Reese was lazily indifferent. "The world is only so big, and the amount of hell you can raise without getting into trouble is limited." He was wishing the girl would come over and sit near them. Last night she had smiled at him. Maybe it was just being friendly, maybe not.

He never found out. The next day Cary decided he was tired of Nassau. Laura was willing to leave. There was a hunger within her for familiar things; The Hill, Winton, home. At their best, hotel rooms were cheerless, and this wandering was without purpose. It accomplished little save a momentary distraction. She understood what The Hill would be without Cassius, and yet she longed for its ugly, comfortable security. Thinking of it made her feel a little breathless. The need for home brought a sensation close to physical pain.

190

Cary wasn't satisfied to take the direct route to Winton. First they must cross the state, spend a few days in Tampa. She allowed him to have his way because it was easier than arguing. Once she had considered going home by herself and having Cary and Reese follow. They were old enough to take care of themselves. As badly as she wanted to be home, though, she found the prospect of entering the house by herself almost frightening, and so she endured the seemingly endless trek, knowing Winton was getting closer all the time. When they finally left Jacksonville on their way north, she settled back in her seat, tiredly grateful and confident she would never want to see a train again.

The Hill seemed to crouch like some great, friendly old animal waiting to welcome them. Nothing had changed, although all of them secretly imagined it would be different.

Reese wanted to go out to his father's place, and he wanted to make the trip alone. Avoiding Cary, he took one of the cars and slipped away. The house was deserted. Somehow he knew it would be, but there was something comforting in its weatherbeaten sides and the sagging line of the narrow porch. He didn't go inside. It was easy enough to tell, just by looking at the yard, that Lance hadn't returned. The house had the empty, neglected appearance of being unused and unwanted, and when he walked across the porch the boards echoed boomingly to his footsteps.

Sitting on the rickety steps, he smoked a cigarette. The afternoon was powdered with a golden, purple haze; suspended in silence. He was alone.

There were things to be thought about and decided. If I'm going to go, he said to himself, it'd better be now. I could find a job, or maybe work enough of this land to make a living. The whole business was crazy; Mr. Whitfield leaving him money, Mrs. Whitfield treating him as though he were her own son, living on The Hill and pretending to be something he wasn't. The idea filled him with a confused feeling of uneasiness. He was being hedged in and given too much responsibility. It had been different when Mr. Whitfield was alive. He wished he could talk with Mrs. Whitfield. Maybe she'd understand, but he doubted it. She'd only be hurt, and maybe think it was her fault.

He rose regretfully and walked around the yard, kicking indifferently at small mounds of earth, trying to convince himself he was lucky.

"You're being a damn fool," he said aloud, but there was no conviction in the statement. "Someone takes you by the seat of your pants and lifts you out of a shack and you bellyache. What do you want to be, a factory hand, or a clerk downtown in one of the stores?"

There were no answers to the questions. Lance, he thought, must have known what he was doing to let him go. Lance hadn't much education, but he wasn't a fool. If he had known it was all right, then it must be. He knew what was wrong but couldn't explain it to himself. He was supposed to take care of Cary. That was the truth of the matter. No one had ever put it in so many words. He was Cary's friend and they were supposed to have fun together. The trouble was, being with Cary all of the time exhausted him. It was as though he kept saying: Now think of something for us to do. Hell, Reese snorted silently, I don't want to be in a lather all the time. Maybe I've hookworm, but I just like to sit.

They could have had fun in Nassau, but Cary wouldn't take it easy. He wanted a girl, and when they met two from New York he was anxious to get rid of them. Reese had to make excuses when he broke a date. If they went out in a boat, Cary wanted to go back to the hotel. If they were at the hotel, he wanted to hire a car and drive around the island.

"He's bad enough now," Reese spoke accusingly to the mulberry tree; "what's going to happen when he comes into all of that money? He'll drive everyone crazy, me along with them."

What plagued him was the knowledge that he didn't have to remain on The Hill. I could leave, he thought. I could pack up tomorrow and get out, and if I wanted the money Mr. Whitefield left me, I could have it too. There was nothing in the will saying he had to stay on The Hill to get the money. Maybe, he turned the thought dourly over in his mind, maybe Mr. Whitfield was a whole hell of a lot smarter than anyone gave him credit for being. He must have known how the bequest would tie him. He shook his head. Mr. Whitfield wouldn't have done a thing like that, and, anyhow, he didn't have any idea of dying right away when he made the will. After all—he couldn't help but grin—$10,000 a year was a lot of money to pay just to have Reese Benton around. No, Mr. Whitfield had done what he had because he wanted to and because he liked him.

"All right," he was arguing with himself, speaking aloud and not realizing how foolish it would have sounded if anyone had been listening. "Suppose I don't want either, the money or The Hill. I'll be Just Reese the way I was meant to be. I'll farm this place a little and take a job uptown in the winter. Maybe Pa will come back one of these days."

If Lance came back, it would only be to tell him he was crazy. He knew what Lance would say. He climbed into the car and drove slowly back through Winton and to The Hill. The house was so large that with only the three of them in it now, it seemed abandoned. You had to hunt, he thought wryly, to find anyone. Maybe we ought to play some sort of a game, drop pieces of paper when we walk and leave a trail.

He went upstairs and after a moment's hesitation knocked softly on the door of Laura's sitting room.

"I went out to Pa's place," he said in explanation. He knew she hadn't known he had been away, and if she had it would never have occurred to her to question his movements. "Do you mind if I close the door?"

"Of course not, Reese." She waited, a mystified look on her face. "Of course not. Come in and sit down."

"I've been thinking," he said after he was settled in a chair across from her. "I don't feel right about things." Talking to her was more difficult than he imagined it would be. The carefully rehearsed speech was lost.

"I'm sorry, Reese." Laura spoke with simple regret.

"It's hard to say." He hesitated with a silent appeal for help. "Now that we're home and some time has passed, I think maybe I ought to go back to my place. There isn't really anything you need me for."

"It isn't a question of that, Reese," she interrupted.

"Well, anyhow . . ." He couldn't continue.

"We talked about this once before, don't you remember?" Laura spoke thoughtfully. "After, after Mr. Whitfield's death. I hoped then it was settled for all time. I don't want to make you stay, Reese. I had hoped you would want to. I," she twisted her fingers, "I feel so desperately alone. Somehow, I couldn't say that to Cary. I can to you, and I wonder why."

"Another thing." He spoke hurriedly. "The money Mr. Whitfield left. I don't feel right about it."

"You mean," Laura seemed to want to help him, "you mean you feel it ties you to, to us?"

"Well"—he was miserable—"I guess so."

"Believe me, Reese. It isn't important. There isn't enough money in the world to do that."

"And then," he was trying to make a case for himself, "I might not always do the things you want. There's no way of knowing how I'm going to turn out. I might just be a lot of trouble to you in the end."

She laughed then. "You aren't frightening me, Reese." Her smile touched him briefly.

He felt he was losing, being outmaneuvered. How could he say: Cary's a damn fool. Sometimes I don't think he has good sense. I still want to cry when I remember Ann-Charlotte and Mr. Whitfield. Everything here makes me think of them, and I feel sorry for you and you sort of break my heart when you look at me the way you are looking now. No one could say those things. He had been halfwitted to imagine he could.

"All right," he said. "Maybe I don't make much sense. I guess it was getting back to The Hill and all." He was licked.

"I hope so." She regarded him with affection. "If you were a little older, I wouldn't say anything. I'd let you make your own decisions. Right now, though, I think you may be upset. You couldn't go back home and live there alone. I want you to have an education, everything Mr. Whitfield and, yes, your own father planned. It won't be so many years, Reese. If it's too bad, then you can always make other arrangements. Finish school first. Will you do it for me?"

He stood up. "I don't know how you can make it sound as if I was doing you a favor." He had to smile then. "But you do."

"That," her eyes were gentle, "that comes under the head of a woman's wiles. Men rarely understand, and perhaps it is a very good thing they don't."

He closed her door behind him and stood there for a moment, hand on the knob. Then he released it and walked thoughtfully along the hall and downstairs. Nothing he had meant to say had been said, and if some things had, then they didn't sound the same as when he said them to himself.

"I'll be damned." He spoke confidentially to the newel post at the foot of the staircase. "I'll just be damned."

XVIII

"You look mighty silly to me, but then so does everyone else." Reese flipped a sheet across the scarred mission table to Cary. Morning and afternoon newspapers were scattered about the floor, and Cary had a small stack of torn sections before him. "Going to start a scrapbook?" Reese chuckled.

"Go to the devil." Cary held a two-column picture of himself at arm's length and regarded it critically.

"Tobacco Heir In Columbia's Freshman Class." He read the words with a stately cadence. "Did you know I was a tobacco heir, Mr. Benton?"

"I'm learning." Reese leaned back in the heavy chair. "Now if you'll catch on to the idea of reading without moving your lips, they'll probably let you stay here."

Cary had been honestly surprised over the fact that his matriculation at Columbia received the attention it did. Until the photographers sought him out, he had been only one of a large entering class, compressed into uniformity with a dinky skullcap perched on his head and a copy of rules for freshmen printed on green cardboard sticking conspicuously out of his coat breast pocket. In Winton he had only been Cary Whitfield. Here, in New York, he was suddenly elevated to a temporary position of prominence. The idea that he was news hadn't occurred to him.

At first he had felt foolish and miserably self-conscious. The photographers, indifferent to his embarrassed protests, had almost dragged him out to stand awkwardly before the Alma Mater statue on the library steps. He smiled with weak apology as other students looked on curiously, and he could see them asking each other who the freshman causing so much excitement was. Later he had to pose with an opened book at the study table in the rooms he and Reese had been assigned to in Hartley Hall. Then, abruptly, and with what he thought was a surprising lack of ceremony, the newspapermen trooped out, leaving them alone. He had answered a few stock questions. How had he happened to select Columbia? What was he going to study?

Even Reese had come in for a minor share of attention, but he had passed lightly over the queries. He was only a friend and roommate.

"I never figured it would cause so much fuss." Cary arranged the clippings into a neat pile. "How do you suppose they knew I was here?"

Reese grinned. "It's mighty hard to keep the sound of fifty million dollars moving around quiet."

Cary digested this slowly. Being important was a novelty and not entirely unpleasant. Already he was feeling better about Columbia. No one would have paid much attention to him if he had gone to Chapel Hill or even Duke. He had argued, sulked, and stormed over Reese's determination to enter Columbia. Reese had been unmoved by his protests.

"You go wherever you want," he said. "I'm going to Columbia if I can get in. I liked what I saw of it when we were in New York. They mean business there." Somehow he felt this was his last chance. He knew what Cary had in mind. It was a raccoon coat, Stutz Bearcat, feather-in-the-hat, prom-trotting notion of college. Something he had seen in the movies.

"You won't have any fun up there." Cary was stubborn. "The school looks like a mill. How can there be any college spirit in a place sitting right in the middle of a city?"

"You can probably buy a pennant to wave on the corner of Broadway if that's what you want." Reese was unimpressed by the argument.

Cary tried all the methods of persuasion he could think of. In his heart he blamed his father and mother for Reese's obstinacy. If he hadn't known he would have money of his own and could afford to be independent, Reese wouldn't have been so determined to have his own way. He attempted flattery, assumed an air of dependence, resorted to days of silent indifference. None of these things, apparently, had any effect upon Reese. In the end he gave in.

"I'll try it for a year," he said angrily, "but if I don't like it I'm going to quit."

Reese nodded without enthusiasm or encouragement. "Columbia is going to be mighty flattered over your decision. I wouldn't tell them, though, that you're sort of taking them on trial."

Laura had hoped to delay what she knew was inevitable. A letter from Ann-Charlotte telling her of the decision to continue school in Paris hadn't actually been a surprise. Somehow she had felt she wouldn't return at the end of summer. Joe had written her. Ann-

Charlotte was happy, or she seemed to be. He advised against forcing her to return. "I know," he wrote, "if the boys go away to college you'll be alone. I thought, maybe, it would be a good idea if you came over here and spent the winter near Ann-Charlotte. But now I think she would be better off without you or anyone for a while. She's a strange girl, Laurie. I thought I had known all kinds in my life, but Ann-Charlotte is something new. I'll be here in Paris until November, and then I'm going to Scotland for a few weeks before I come home. Of course, Ann-Charlotte is something you'll have to decide for yourself, but I think my advice is good."

Laura hadn't read that portion of the letter to Cary and Reese. She skipped through it, picking out a paragraph here and there. While the argument over Columbia was going on, she had remained silent. Reese should have the chance he wanted. She had hoped they might decide on a school nearer home, leaving open the possibility of getting back to The Hill for week ends. When Cary ungraciously gave in, she experienced a momentary panic. The thought of being alone in Winton frightened her.

"I think," she told them, "I'll go to Raleigh for the winter. If you like, we'll come back to The Hill for Christmas, or you can join me there." She smiled with wistful sadness. "There isn't much left of the family, is there?"

Reese understood what she was thinking as she waved good-by from the station platform, but his feeling of regret in leaving her there, a solitary and lonely figure, was overshadowed by the excitement of going away to school and, he admitted to himself, getting off of The Hill.

"Take good care of Cary, Reese." She whispered as she kissed him.

"I'll do my best." He smiled at her with a happy confidence. "Don't worry. We'll both be all right."

During the first few days of getting settled neither of them had had much time to think of home. Everything was new and excitingly novel. Their rooms in Hartley Hall, two bedrooms and a study overlooking South Field, were comfortable, if sparsely furnished. Cary went out to remedy this and returned from the bookstore with an assortment of plaques, shields, pennants, and a four-foot banner with the word Columbia spelled out in white letters on a light blue background. With a hammer and noisy enthusiasm he had cluttered the walls of the suite with these spotty decorations.

"You're getting to be quite a college dick." Reese was quietly

197

amused by these domestic touches. "It looks better, though," he admitted. "Takes some of the fine academic chill off the place."

Along with most of the other freshmen they were being treated to an intensive period of rushing by the fraternities. Cary Whitfield was the year's prize; at least the competing houses, scanning their bank balances and lists of needed repairs, hoped he would be. Both he and Reese were constantly booked for smokers, luncheons, dinners, and theater dates. The competing groups brought in their most urbane old boys. Photographs of past football heroes were prominently displayed, and there were impressively casual references to campus prestige and departed glories. The best china and manners were on display as the bewildered and excited freshmen were scrambled over, their ears ringing with thinly disguised warnings of the irreparable consequences of a faulty decision.

Reese found the rushing season exciting and stimulating. It was pleasant to sit in the window seats of the houses along 114th Street, talking, exchanging jokes, and making plans. He felt he was part of a great school; a personality and no longer simply an unidentified member of a large class. He was being sought after, his opinions accepted with grave understanding, his wishes deferred to. College was no longer a contest between himself and a relentless passing mark. These were friends who would stand by when he needed them.

Cary had been firm in his determination not to accept a pledge unless Reese went to the same house. They talked this over in their rooms, weighing the not fully explored merits of the different fraternities against each other and feeling, somehow, they were making a choice which would effect the rest of their lives. Reese wanted Cary to decide for himself.

"Just because I like one crowd doesn't mean you have to go there. It wouldn't make any difference between us."

Cary had refused to accept this. "We'll go together," he argued, "the same as we always have."

In the end they both took the small blue and white pledge pin of Theta Xi, fixing it in their lapels with the proud conviction that they were firmly set apart from those hapless misfits, the subway students and wistful undesirables who missed out during the rushing period. It was something of a shock to learn, once the pledge had been taken, they were no longer pearls of great price, and the brothers who had once hung so eagerly on their every word were not above thrusting a broom into their hands with an order to sweep out the lower hallway. Cary accepted his new status with bad grace, sulking over tasks he considered menial until Reese wanted to kick him.

"Why don't you stop remembering you are Cary Whitfield?" he exploded one night. "You're not being asked to do anything that'll maim you for life."

"It's silly, that's all." Cary brooded over the indignity of having to polish the round brass Greek-letter seal on the outside of the house. "If they need help, I'll hire a porter and pay his salary."

Reese looked up from his book. "I'll bet you would," he said thoughtfully and then laughed. "I'd sure hate to be your rear end on initiation night."

They hadn't discussed the matter again, but Cary remained defiantly balky. He rebelled against wearing the ridiculously small frosh cap, refused to display the freshman rules, avoided the fraternity house at noon and ate, instead, in the Commons or at one of the cafeterias on Amsterdam Avenue. Reese knew he was going out of his way to make himself unpopular, and he wasn't surprised when three upper classmen from the house called on them one evening in Hartley Hall.

The meeting was so gravely studied and ponderously handled that it might have been funny to an outsider. Reese felt almost miserably apologetic.

"We"—the spokesman for the visitors was finding it difficult to handle an unhappy situation—"thought we ought to come over and talk with you." He looked at Reese but his words were directed to Cary. "Somehow the brothers have the idea that you aren't satisfied with the decision you made. We wanted you, Whitfield, but if you think the choice was wrong, maybe we ought to think it over."

"I'm not used to sweeping off steps and polishing brass." Cary was white and tense. "It's silly. What good does it do?"

"All the pledges take turns at such jobs. It's just the way things are run. No one ever objected before." The boy was making the best of a thankless task.

"Well," Cary refused to be placated, "I object to it and I'm not going to do it."

"That's what we thought." The spokesman tried to smile understandingly. "It's just a difference of opinion."

"You can have your pledge pin back." Cary fumbled with the small button and then slapped it down on the table. "If belonging to a fraternity means I have to scrub floors, I don't want to join."

The boy nodded and picked up the pin, holding it for a moment before dropping it into his coat pocket.

"Well," he spoke with regret, "I guess there isn't much more to say if you feel that way. Maybe it sounds foolish to you to make an issue over anything so trivial, but we look at it differently."

Even as he reached for his lapel, Reese was furious with himself over what he was about to do. He had liked the TX house; looked forward to the friendly, boisterous bull sessions, found a warm and satisfying companionship in belonging. He liked the easy exchange of ideas around the tables at noon and the quiet pleasure of sitting on the front steps in the evening, smoking and talking. It was part of being in college. He hadn't resented the small chores given him. When he swept down the front steps, he was sweeping steps that belonged to him. Giving up this pledge pin hurt, and he hesitated, unable to bring himself to the act. Instead of this ridiculous gesture of loyalty to Cary he ought to take the damn fool's head and beat it against the wall until some sense was knocked into it.

"I guess you better take this, too." He turned the button over between his fingers, reluctant to let it go. Cary didn't protest. He hadn't really expected he would. "If Cary isn't going TX, I guess it would be better if I didn't." He held the pin out, face up in the palm of his hand. "You see," he wondered why he was bothering to explain, "Cary and I have sort of grown up together. I guess it wouldn't be right for me to go with a house that didn't want him."

"You sure you don't want to think it over, Reese?"

He shook his head. "No. I guess not. Thanks just the same."

When they were alone, he tried to concentrate on the next day's French assignment. The words meant nothing and he read and reread them without profit. Cary pretended to be deeply engrossed in his own work, but now and then Reese was conscious of his questioning glances across the table. Finally he slapped the grammar closed and rose.

"I'm going out for a walk." He went to a closet for a topcoat and strode out of the door before Cary could offer to come along.

The air made him feel better. It was wetly fresh, smelling faintly of the sea. At least he liked to think of it as being whipped up somewhere out beyond where the Hudson ran through the Narrows. He was angry with himself. The decision had been his own, and he felt cheated by it. It was a ridiculous and helpless affection for Laura Whitfield. She would never have understood why he had joined a fraternity when Cary hadn't been asked. At least, he knew she would assume he hadn't received a bid and no one would explain exactly what had happened.

Walking slowly up Claremont Avenue, he tried to tell himself it didn't make any difference. The only important thing was to get what he had come to college for and be rid of The Hill. I'll pay it back, he thought. I'll save so much every year after I am out and return it, and they can keep what Mr. Whitfield wanted me to have. He didn't identify "they" to himself. No one but a god-damn fool, he assured himself bitterly, would go on the way I am.

Huddled against the chill, he sat on a bench near Grant's Tomb, looking across the river at the electric signs on the New Jersey side and the winking progress of the trolleycars as they crept up the inclines of the steep west bank. Something of his enthusiasm for school had vanished. He felt a little lonely, almost an outcast. That's crazy, he said to himself without conviction. There are a lot of other things in college besides fraternities. It would have been fun, though; tea dances after the Saturday football games, late Sunday breakfast, sitting around and talking, reading the papers. To hell with it. What was done couldn't be recalled. It was something to forget.

He had a glass of milk and a piece of pie at the dairy lunch on Broadway near 115th Street and went back to his room, hoping Cary had gone to bed. There would only be an argument if they tried to talk about it now.

Cary wasn't asleep. He was stretched out on the couch in the study thumbing through a new copy of *Judge*.

"Want to go for something to eat?"

"I just had something." Reese tossed his coat into a chair. "I've still a French assignment to get." He sat down at the table.

"You didn't have to do what you did tonight." Cary wasn't satisfied to allow the matter to drop. "I don't give a damn about their silly fraternity, anyhow."

"Shut up, won't you? Let's forget about it. It doesn't make any difference now." Reese adjusted the goose-neck lamp over his book. "I've a nine o'clock class in the morning."

"It's kid stuff, anyhow; initiations, pledge pins, mystery hocus-pocus." Cary dropped the magazine on the floor and yawned with an elaborate pretense at boredom. "I'm going down and buy a car tomorrow. Then we'll have some fun on week ends, get some girls, there's some nice stuff over at Barnard."

Reese turned slowly in his chair. "I think I'll poke you in the nose in just about a minute."

Cary laughed uncertainly and then subsided at the look on Reese's face. "All right," he mumbled, "if you want to get sore about it."

"I'm not sore, but it won't take much to get me that way. I suppose I've got to go on being a damn fool with you for the rest of my life. Now, keep quiet and let me finish my work."

For days he was unable to glance down at the unblinking slit in his lapel without experiencing the quick, empty feeling of having lost something. Walking to or from classes, he looked covertly at the jackets of other students and it seemed everyone he met was wearing the pledge of one of the houses. He alone was without the little button. It set him apart, an untouchable. The boy working at the adjoining sink in chemistry class noticed the pin's absence.

"I thought you were pledged," he said.

Reese nodded. "I was."

"Forget your pin? They make us wash dishes over at Sigma Nu if we don't keep it in." He was being chummily confidential, brother to brother, Greek to Greek.

Reese hadn't bothered to explain. Words were a broken crutch. Maybe Cary was right. It was kid stuff, horseplay and abracadabra and not worth worrying about. What difference would it make five years from now? He tormented himself with this sterile philosophy. It made a hell of a lot of difference right now, even if he pretended to Cary he didn't care. He avoided walking down 114th Street. In the late afternoons he and Cary would stroll down to Riverside Drive, sit on the stone wall and contrive awkward flirtations with the girls who idled along in pairs and responded with maddening enthusiasm to an occasional wave from a group on the steps of the Sigma Chi house across the street but paid little attention to the park's railbirds, who might be anything and who were probably only extension students at best. Looking ahead he could see only years of hard work. The glamor of college had vanished, slipped out of his hands. Some of the time, he thought bitterly, it is supposed to be fun. Now and then he was forced to laugh a little sheepishly to himself, half amused by the doleful self-commiseration. Anyhow, he assured himself solemnly, you have Cary. Yes, sir, you've Cary, all to yourself.

College fooled him at first. The deceptively unsupervised schedules seemed too easy. No one, apparently, was concerned if a class was cut or an assignment unprepared. It was several weeks before it occurred to him that the problem of his remaining in school was being put squarely up to him. The work was more difficult than he had expected, and he was forced to long hours bent over the study table with a container of milk and a sandwich for supper. What actually surprised him, however, was the ease with which Cary seemed to drift through the studies. He was never brilliant, but somehow he absorbed enough to maintain a fair average, and he could always find time to go downtown to a show or take in an uptown movie. Reese used to stare at the door after it had closed behind him and wonder what the secret was. Maybe, he thought a little wonderingly, he is just smarter than I am.

Cary was becoming a man of many social affairs. Friends of the Whitfields, business associates, and mere acquaintances seized upon him. His week ends were always filled, and he was constantly being invited out to dinner, theater, and cocktail parties.

"I never knew Pa had so many friends in New York," he confessed his surprise to Reese. "Hell, I never heard of half these people, but I might as well go out with them if you're going to keep your nose stuck in a book night after night."

In addition to buying a new Paige coupe, which he kept in a garage on 110th Street, Cary refurnished their rooms. They had a thick carpet in the study, warm, soft rugs in the two small bedrooms, leather easy chairs and stand lamps. Reese was a little embarrassed at first by the ostentation, but he felt better about it after a few of their neighbors from down the hall dropped in and were so visibly, if silently, impressed.

"You ought to get a couple of those Turkish water pipes," he said facetiously to Cary one night, "and we could lie around on a tigerskin and listen to the bubbles."

"You'll have to admit it's more comfortable." Cary was unabashed. "Looked like a monk's cell before."

Among his new acquaintances Cary now numbered a bootlegger who made his deliveries in person, bringing his wares in a suitcase. Cary set aside part of his clothes closet as "the cellar," purchased a bartender's manual, cocktail shaker, and an assortment of glasses, and managed to get himself foggily potted in the afternoons experimenting with various recipes.

"They'll kick you out of here if they find that stuff." Reese was fascinated by the idea of cocktails in the afternoon, but openly worried.

Cary laughed at the warning. He passed the word of the bar, gathering the eager and faithful to him. Night after night the rooms were crowded, smoky, and almost intolerable to Reese, who shut himself in a bedroom, trying to study there over the persistent hum of boozy conversation. He had the uneasy suspicion that Cary's friends considered him a stupid grind, unable to understand the worldly sophistication of the gatherings, and probably wondered how Cary stood him. Now and then he would put aside the books and join them, but such drinking struck him as just short of ridiculous. They were small boys playing at being grown up, and liquor did nothing to sharpen the few poor wits they brought with them to the rooms.

"You ought to mix in things more," Cary complained.

"I suppose so." Reese hadn't felt he was missing anything. "I like to drink the way we used to at home. You know, get a pint of shine and a couple of girls and go out helling around. This is kind of silly, and," he hesitated, smiling, reflectively, "you have to keep too quiet. I like to let out a whoop an' a holler now and then. What's the point in getting drunk if all you are going to do is sit down and argue whether there is a God and a hereafter. None of them knows, drunk or sober."

"Well—" Cary wouldn't argue the point. "We'll get some girls. I've met a lot of nice stuff." He had, Reese knew. There were always half a dozen telephone messages in his box. "What are you going to say when your son asks: Daddy, what did you do at Columbia? All you'll be able to tell him is: Son, I passed the examination."

"Will that be bad?" Reese cocked an eye at him. Cary was getting fun out of college, at least he acted as though he was.

"No." Cary was serious. "But you could have a little fun, too."

"Maybe you're right." Reese closed the book he had been trying to read. "I'll go along part of the way with you, anyhow."

It was better. He made the admission to himself later. Cary had introduced him to half a dozen girls he had met, bright-lipped, perky youngsters who attended Miss Spence's school or came home from out of town for the week ends. They drove over to Princeton or up to New Haven for football games on Saturdays, met at the Lorraine Grill for tea and a flask of gin under the table, or drove to West Point on Sunday to watch retreat and have dinner at an old roadhouse set high on the Palisades overlooking the Hudson. They talked of Michael Arlen and Cabell's *Jurgen* and *The High Place,* and necked with sophisticated detachment whenever the opportunity afforded itself. He made friends, through Cary, outside of school and off the campus, meeting people of his own age and their parents, all of whom, for some reason, seemed to think his attendance at Columbia instead of Princeton, Yale, or Harvard slightly on the quaint side, referring to it as "the garment-center annex." It was pleasantly exciting, though, to be called to the telephone or find a message in his box with now and then an invitation for a week end in the country. He began to feel less of a stranger in New York and even acquired a surface familiarity with places that had only been names in the newspapers before.

Cary blossomed in the city. He carried a wallet filled with speakeasy cards, had a notebook with the names and telephone numbers of half a dozen ladies of call, had been arrested twice for speeding on the Boston Post Road. The last-named was almost considered to be a necessary credit toward graduation. He also became a conspicuous member of a small group of worldly men who slid into their seats at a nine o'clock class wearing slightly disheveled dinner jackets and the weary expressions of those who found life so tiresome as to be practically unendurable. Reese was never able to figure out when and where he studied, and day after day expected him to be called to the dean's office or summarily bounced out of school without even the benefit of a conversation. Nothing of the sort happened. Cary went his airy, satisfied way, and Reese was impressed and a trifle envious.

"I don't know how you do it." He made the admission to Cary one Saturday afternoon as they were driving up to Greenwich, Connecticut.

"What?"

"Get through your classes, studying as little as you do. Sometimes I think you may be smarter than I am—but," he laughed, "it's hard to believe, or at least admit. What do you do, write the answers in invisible ink on your chest?"

"Oh!" Cary was pleased. That was about as close to a compliment as Reese had ever come. "I just remember some of the stuff."

"So do I." Reese was frankly curious. "But I have to study it first. I never see you crack a book, not very often, anyhow."

"I'm not smart." Cary was serious. "I only remember the answers, not what they really mean. When you get out, you'll know something. I only study enough to get by."

The weeks, for Reese, were so fully packed that there was Christmas and the talk of Christmas vacation in the air before he realized the first half of the year was gone. Laura had written asking if they wanted to join her with her family in Raleigh or meet in Winton.

He hadn't looked forward to the holiday. It had never meant much. Usually he and Lance had gone on a hunting trip for the two weeks when he would be out of school. Out in the woods they would cut their own tree, or maybe just pick out a small standing sapling and Lance would whittle small slivers of fat pine, frosty with their hardened resin, and tie them as candles to the branches. Usually he had brought along a new knife or a box of 12-gauge smokeless shells for Reese's single-barreled shotgun, as a present. With what money he could save, Reese bought his father socks, or perhaps a necktie. They would put the small gifts beneath the tree and later open them with solemn expressions as part of a necessary ritual, feeling embarrassed in each other's presence and acting as though they had been caught at some particularly childish game. If he could make the choice now, he would have preferred to remain in New York and allow Cary to be with his mother and her relatives in Raleigh. It wouldn't be much of a Christmas, anyhow, with only the three of them on The Hill. He tried desperately to think of an excuse Laura would believe.

"I shouldn't take time off," he said lamely to Cary, "to go away for Christmas. I'd like to get ahead on some of my work so I won't have to bang at it so hard next term. I'm tired out."

Cary refused to listen, and in the end they talked to Laura in Raleigh and decided to meet there. Reese knew she must want to avoid Winton this first Christmas after Mr. Whitfield's death. With Ann-Charlotte in Europe it would be a grim season on The Hill.

He wondered, as he packed, whether Lance would think it a time to go back to Winton, and decided that wherever his father was, he wouldn't be thinking much about Christmas. He might, Reese smiled to himself, go out and shoot a turkey, but that wouldn't be in observance of the season. Lance would shoot a turkey in July if he felt like it and could find a turkey.

Snow had been falling heavily for the past three days. South Field lay under a heavy, woolly-white blanket, and the sounds of automobiles and trucks in the streets were deadened by the cushion. The quantity of the snow amazed Reese. He couldn't accustom himself to the hush it seemed to create. The bells on the Broadway and Amsterdam cars seemed to peal with a holiday jingle, and there was an expectant look on the faces of everyone he met. His bags had already gone downstairs with Cary's, and he stood at the windows looking out over the small bowl of the football field.

"Hey," Cary called from the other room, "if you're ready, let's have a drink and get going." He held up a half-filled bottle of alleged bourbon.

Reese turned back almost regretfully. There was nothing to call him home or to Raleigh. Actually, he wouldn't have minded spending Christmas here in the dormitory. There were many students who either lived too far away or who, for reasons of their own, were not going home. Big trees had been set up and decorated in the lobbies of Hartley and Livingston Halls. Christmas in New York would probably be more fun than in Raleigh with Mrs. Whitfield's people. When I finish here, he promised himself, I'm going to be a hermit. I'm going to find a lonesome cave on a deserted mountain and do just as I damn please.

Cary thrust a glass and the bottle into his hands. "Merry Christmas."

"Merry Christmas." Reese poured himself a large drink. "It's a week off, but Merry Christmas just the same. We're lucky we're this far."

Cary watched him for a moment. "You really mean it, don't you?"

"Mean what?" Reese lowered the glass and looked up in surprise.

"About being in college and staying here. Sometimes I thought you were kidding, but I guess you're serious. You'll never have to work for a living after what the old man did. What the hell makes you so set on getting ready for nothing?"

Reese put the glass on the table. Cary meant what he had said, and any explanation now wouldn't make sense. "I just want to be able to sign my name on a hotel register," he said. "Let's get going."

XIX

AT BEST it had been an idiot's puzzle. The pieces had neither matched nor fitted, and no one, apparently, ever believed they would. Reese could understand this now, and he felt no hasty anger over what had happened. Actually, as he looked back, he was moved to a sardonic amusement at his innocence in imagining a pattern might be arranged.

The train burst out of the tunnel beneath the Hudson and drew itself into an eager, straining line between the Jersey marshes. Stretched out on the narrow bench of their drawing room, Cary thumbed through a copy of *Vanity Fair,* reaching down now and then to pick his drink up from the floor. Reese touched the wall button near his seat. They needed more ice and soda.

"Want anything to eat? I'm ringing for the porter."

Cary looked across his magazine and shook his head. "I'm carrying an awful hangover for someone. I'll have another drink, though."

"I'll order some ice."

Reese settled back, his feet resting on the opposite seat, and stared out of the window as the train drummed it way through the scummy flats. He tried to remember how the Jersey meadows had looked to him on that day, almost three years ago, when he and Cary came to New York for the first time alone. He had been absurdly excited, seeing only a narrow stretch of wasteland separating him from his goal. Since that time he and Cary had recrossed the flats often on their way down to Winton for Christmas or Spring vacations. Today they were different.

After three years, short of a few months, he and Cary had been booted out of college. Expelled was the word. Booted seemed to suit the action better. The expulsion had been accomplished quietly but with a firmness that had an almost physical impact. He felt uncomfortable just thinking about it.

In a way it had been his fault. If, when they went back in their sophomore year, he had agreed with Cary that an apartment somewhere around Columbia would suit them better than dormitory

208

rooms the trouble need never have arisen. He had insisted on their old quarters, holding out against Cary's arguments of more freedom. The discipline, he thought, was good for them both. An apartment with Cary would be a madhouse, overrun with women, noisy and impossible to study in. He used to wonder why Cary had finally consented and allowed him to have his way. He had even urged separate places of residence.

"You go ahead and rent an apartment. I'll stay here in the hall, and when I feel like a party I'll drop over."

Cary didn't agree. "That wouldn't be any fun. If you want to stay here, I'll stick it out with you, but it seems damn silly. We could have a place of our own, a couple of bedrooms. If you wanted to work you could shut yourself in one of them. If I had people up, we'd keep quiet."

At the beginning of each term Reese had been surprised when Cary continued in school. He wasn't getting anything out of college and he slicked through it, doing only what was required, and forever threatening to drop out. When Reese asked him why he stayed, Cary was hurt.

"What would I do with myself until you finish?" He asked.

They had gone back to the dormitory, Cary taking the term with the bitter expression of a man swallowing epsom salts after being told it would be good for him.

In a way, Reese reflected, I must have known all along something would happen. The years hadn't seemed real. He had never actually recovered from the initial astonishment of finding himself in college, of making passing grades and discovering a new and wonderful world. For the past two years he, Laura, and Cary had gone abroad each summer. They met Ann-Charlotte in Paris that first year. She was a new and startlingly different girl, who seemed to be so much older than any of them. The second year she had been in Switzerland. Laura left them alone in London and went to see her there. He always thought that perhaps Ann-Charlotte hadn't wanted to see Cary or him, and wrote her mother. Laura had only said that she was well and sent her love.

Now he and Cary were on their way back to Winton. Things had happened so quickly they still needed thinking about.

He had been asleep, half asleep, at least, when he heard someone fumbling at the door. He listened drowsily as it creaked open and was closed. For a moment there had been silence and then the sound of Cary's voice in a cautioning whisper. He thought Cary had probably brought someone in with him for a quick drink, and burrowed beneath the blankets, pulling the comforter over his head to shut out the light. Dimly he heard Cary stumbling through the study, and then he realized someone was in his room and a moment later sitting on the edge of his bed. A hand slid down beneath the covers, across his chest. He caught the heavy scent of perfume, and then his visitor giggled and pulled the blanket away from his face.

"Wake up, sugar. You have company."

Reese snapped up in the bed and saw the girl sitting beside him. She was laughing, happily pleased by the consternation on his face.

"What are you doing here? Cary!" He swung out of the bed, almost upsetting the girl, and took the few steps to the door.

A second girl was slouched in a chair, and Cary was solemnly holding a bottle to the light, trying to read the label. He looked up and grinned at Reese.

"I'm color blind," he said with stupid good-nature. "I can't tell whether it's gin or bourbon."

"You damn fool!" Reese was across the room, pulling down the window shades. "You know better than to bring girls up here."

"They're not girls." Cary was very drunk. He weaved and leaned against the table for support. "They're, they're jus' little pigeons from Riverside Drive who were cold an' I brought 'em up to get warm before they fly away, fly away, fly away home." He regarded Reese with glassy-eyed brightness and waved at the girl in the chair. "This is my brother," he said.

"How're you, brother?" The girl flipped her hand in recognition. "What about a drink now, John?"

"She calls me John." Cary was pleased. "Did you ev' hear a pigeon talk before?"

The second girl joined them, sliding up to Reese, taking his arm.

"Look," Reese appealed desperately to her, "I don't know how you got up here, but you've got to get out."

"Now," Cary waggled his head reprovingly, "you don't want to spoil a party. We'll just have a few drinks an' maybe a little fun, an' then the pigeons will fly off home."

"How did you get here, past the elevator man?" Reese ignored him and spoke to the girl in the chair who was watching Cary's efforts with the bottle.

"They walked up. Six flights." Cary seemed proud of the achievement. "I went in an' took the elevator. While Tom was taking me up they scampered like little pigeons up the stairs. I shoulda thought of this before."

There was a sudden, heavily impatient knock on the door.

Remembering the night, he couldn't help but think that the fist of doom should have had more thunder in it. The night watchman had caught a glimpse of the girls. Before he reached the building they had disappeared. It had been a simple matter for him to check with the elevator operator and find out who had gone up within the past few minutes. The trail led directly to their door.

Later, at the investigation, Cary had insisted it was all his fault. Reese, he said, didn't know the girls and wasn't a party to their being in the room. He wasn't to blame for what had happened. Reese thought the dean probably believed him; but: "For the good of the college." Those were the words, stark, unsympathetic. They had packed the same day and moved down to the Biltmore.

Cary made one or two ridiculously feeble attempts to be conscious-stricken over what had happened. He tried to appear concerned and thoughtfully grave. Finally he stopped pretending.

"It was crazy to begin with. A year at college is enough, just so you can say you were there. What did you want to be a lawyer for? Now we can have some fun."

The porter knocked at the door as the train eased into Manhattan Transfer, and Reese ordered more ice and soda. Maybe Cary was right. They'd have some fun. This time, though, it would be on different terms. We are now about to show you, he said to himself, the evolution of a heel. I'm not going to give a damn about anyone, not even Reese Benton.

Cary yawned and allowed the magazine to drop from his fingers. "Did you look through the train?"

"Not yet."

"Well, as soon as I get a drink we could mosey back and see if there is anything to be picked up."

Reese nodded. He was concerned at the moment only with his own thoughts. In two months both he and Cary would be twenty-one. I'm going to take Mr. Whitfield's money, every penny he left me, and I'm going to live on The Hill as though it belonged to me, also. I'm going to stop worrying about Laura Whitfield and think some about Reese Benton. Maybe I should have done that long ago. Someone was due for a hell of a surprise.

"What are you grinning about?" Cary was regarding him with a curious stare.

"Something I just thought of." Reese couldn't help but smile.

"Well, if it's funny, tell me. I could use a laugh if it didn't shake my head."

Reese didn't believe it was funny. He could confess to himself that what he was feeling at the moment frightened him, but there was grim humor in it. Good old Reese who had believed everything he was told, the nice kid who was supposed to look out for Ann-Charlotte and keep an eye on Cary. What was he crying about? He had been well paid, hadn't he? Ten thousand dollars was a lot of money when it came in every year. Maybe now, though, it wouldn't be enough. Ten thousand dollars a year was a lot of money if there were no strings to it. This way he was the dope who reached down to pick up a pocketbook and had it jerked from beneath his hand. Every day was April Fools' Day.

He watched Cary pouring a drink. His hand shook and the neck of the bottle scraped against the glass. He wondered what Laura Whitfield would think about that. She'd look at him and say: "Reese, can't you do something with Cary?"

There were probably a lot of things he could do with Cary. It was a little too early to think of them all. Besides, he shrugged inwardly, being a real heel wasn't easy. It was something to be worked at and practiced.

"I don't feel very well." Cary looked up and across the small room. "I think maybe I'm going to be sick."

"You'll be all right with a couple of drinks." As he spoke the words Reese thought them silly. A really professional heel would know better.

He watched Cary and wondered if he'd ever feel any satisfaction in seeing him make a complete fool of himself. He wasn't angry. That was the trouble. He should be. Cary had kicked everything he had really wanted out of the window, and instead of hating him he only experienced a feeling of regret for what might have been.

"I'll learn." He spoke the words aloud before he could catch himself.

Cary halted his struggle to replace the cork and looked up. "What do you want to learn now?"

"How to be a no-good bastard. It ought to be easy. There are so many in the world. I guess it's like anything else, though. You have to work at it. Anyhow, there's plenty of time. I'll pick it up as I go along."

Cary allowed the bottle to hang limply between his knees. "I don't know what you're talking about; probably you don't either. And," he shook his head stubbornly, "I don't know what we're doing on this train. Now we'll have to do a lot of explaining. It would have been just as easy to stay north until spring. Why are you in such a hurry to get back to The Hill?"

Reese had wondered himself, deciding finally that he had insisted on going to Winton because Cary hadn't wanted to leave New York. It was sort of a practice run.

"I started on The Hill," he answered reflectively. "It seemed a good idea now to go back to it and get going all over again."

"Are you drunk?" Cary looked suspiciously at him. "Sounds that way to me."

Reese punched a hollow in the pillow with his head and settled back at a comfortable angle. Laura Whitfield would want to know what had happened. This time she could have the whole story. No one was going to cover up for Cary. He'd tell her and wouldn't pretend it didn't make any difference. Now and then she ought to understand he was earning that ten thousand dollars. Even as the thought formed itself, he knew it was a resolution of little substance.

He would talk with Laura as he always had, never being able to say what he should. He laughed suddenly and turned to Cary, who was watching him with uncomprehending surprise.

"Give me the bottle and I'll have a drink. We're a couple of cutters, aren't we? Two city dudes drinkin' whisky-liquor in a Pull-man train an' ridin' on green cushions."

He took the bottle, still laughing. Everything was funny now, I'm not, he thought, going to make a success of being a heel. The Whitfields won't even let me do that.

Laura made no attempt to minimize her concern over their expulsion, and Reese, as he knew he would, tried to cushion the story—pretending it was the result of a thoughtless joke. Laura didn't believe him.

"It was something you wanted, wasn't it, Reese? Graduation meant something to you."

Reese was startled by the change in her. The years and what

213

had come with them weighed heavily upon her shoulders. She had the fragile, almost translucent quality of porcelain, and when he had taken her hand in greeting it was cold, resting in his own with a brittle chill.

"I've changed my mind." Something in the tone of her voice caused Cary to glance up from his end of the table. "I wish you'd go away, Reese. I'm sorry I tried to keep you."

"What are you talking about?" Cary interrupted without an apology. "Why should Reese want to leave?"

"Because . . ." she paused and then her slender shoulders straightened. "I don't think you are any good, Cary. I think you're weak and selfish, without an honest emotion in your body, and I'm afraid of what will happen to Reese if he stays here."

"That's a fine way to talk!" Cary was angrily defiant. "Reese is my only friend."

"And we've used him badly; haven't we, Reese?" Laura ignored her son.

Now, Reese thought soberly, I can start being a heel. There'll never be a better chance. I can say yes. I can tell her Cary is a drunk and Ann-Charlotte a nymphomaniac. I can explain I never wanted anything from the Whitfields and would have been better off if they had left me alone with Lance. I can say sure, I know why Mr. Whitfield brought me to The Hill. He wasn't man enough to take care of his own children and hoped I could do it for him, but I was only a kid and needed taking care of myself. I didn't know anything about girls like Ann-Charlotte, someone should have told me and then I wouldn't have acted as I did and it wouldn't tear the guts from me now every time I think of her. I don't think I want to go away now, Mrs. Whitfield. I think I'll just stay here and watch The Hill fall apart. Maybe, I'll even give it a kick now and then. Cary will never know what to do with his time. He'll load himself and the place with liquor and whores because he hasn't imagination enough to do anything else, and I think I'll wait around. It will be all right for the sort of a louse I'm going to be. There'll be plenty of women and money and I'll never have to think beyond the day itself. That sounds pretty good to me, Mrs. Whitfield. No one else would put up with Cary. Oh, there'll be plenty to hang around to get what they can, because he's Cary Whitfield, but he's already beginning to worry about that. He whines a little, sometimes, when he's drunk. There isn't anyone he can trust. That's

214

what he says, and he knows he hasn't anything to offer except his money. I'm his only friend, Mrs. Whitfield, and you can see it puts me in a nice spot. Right now Cary is afraid I'm going to walk out. What would you think about that, Mrs. Whitfield, if you were Reese Benton and used to go to school barefooted because there was never enough money around the house to buy more than the Sunday pair of shoes? You see, I was willing to finish school and go to work, but I was kicked out because of Cary and a couple of tarts. I think I'll stick around now and see what happens.

"Why are you smiling, Reese?"

His head jerked up at the sound of her voice. For a moment he had been lost in the possibilities of the elaborate fabrication.

"I'm sorry." He leaned back in the chair. "I was only thinking about something. I don't want you to worry about what happened. It doesn't make any difference. I probably wouldn't have made much of a lawyer anyhow."

Laura shook her head gently. "That isn't the point, Reese." She rose and they pushed back their chairs and followed her from the room.

In the morning she told them of her decision to leave Winton.

"There is nothing here for me." She spoke without an accent of self-pity. "I'm going to Raleigh and live with my sister. Maybe the two of us will travel. Her children are grown now and there is nothing to hold her at home." She turned to Cary. "You'll be twenty-one in a couple of months, Cary. If you would like to keep The Hill open, I would be pleased. Otherwise I'll have to make some provision for the help. They've all been here for so many years." She paused and then continued, a wistful smile of half-remembered things hovering about her lips. "I don't suppose you would care to come to Raleigh with me."

Cary didn't attempt to hide his eagerness. "No, I wouldn't know what to do in Raleigh. I don't think Aunt Dorah likes me, anyhow. I'll keep The Hill open in case you should change your mind. After all, it's home."

Laura nodded. "That's thoughtful of you. I've been very lonely here, Cary, these past three years." She placed her delicate hand on his shoulder with an almost appealing gesture. "It's strange, thinking of you as a man, and you are one, aren't you? The law says so. Yet it's hard for me to believe you are grown and ready to assume the responsibility of The Hill. I still imagine you, you and Reese, to be children."

Listening to her, Reese had the uneasy feeling that she was crying her loneliness out to Cary, who couldn't hear. She wanted him to say: We'll keep our home together. You don't have to go away. Cary said nothing and her hand slipped regretfully from his arm.

Laura turned from The Hill without regret. She was even happy in the thought of leaving. Winton no longer meant anything to her. She was a stranger. Sometimes she had felt, almost wildly, that the town was beginning to regard her as an eccentric who had voluntarily buried herself somewhere within the gloomy pile. It wasn't at all what she wanted. Even the death of Cassius could have been borne if she had felt either Cary or Ann-Charlotte needed her.

The night before she was to leave she went to Reese's room, thinking, as she tapped lightly on his door, how strange it was that she should be seeking him out instead of her own son.

Reese was reading in bed and turned hastily as she entered.

"Stay where you are, Reese." Laura laughed at his embarrassment. "You're not that old, yet." She shut the door and came to sit at his side.

He wriggled uncomfortably, feeling ridiculously young, as though she had come to tuck him in for the night.

"Do you know," she confessed with an attitude of surprise, "the only thing I feel badly about is leaving you, and it is not because I don't think you can take care of yourself. Do you know what I'm afraid of? I'm frightened at the thought you will be able to take care of yourself too well. You know what I mean Reese, don't you?"

He was surprised, startled by the thought that she must have known some of the things he had once imagined he might say. He nodded.

"Would you like a job?" He felt she was pleading. "There must be openings in some of the many companies and corporations. I've never inquired, but I know you could have what you want. A man needs something to do, Reese. Have you any idea of the deadly monotony Cary faces? I can't do anything about him, but there's time for you. Don't allow it to slip by."

"I haven't thought much about it." He didn't look up to meet her eyes.

"I suppose not." She rose and then smiled down at him as he raised his eyes. "If you do, you'll let me know, and if I shouldn't be near, talk with Mr. Wharton, Mr. Whitfield's lawyer. Promise me?"

He nodded, feeling she was waiting for him to say something. He didn't speak.

"Well," she hesitated, "we'll have breakfast together in the morning. I sort of feel that I am leaving you both on a strange doorstep. Foolish, isn't it?"

XX

Lillith sat on the edge of Ann-Charlotte's bed, hunched into a gnomelike figure, with arms wrapped tightly around her ankles and knees drawn beneath a lowered chin. She watched her sister-in-law with an impish air of delight.

"You look like something out of La Vie Parisienne, in color," she finally said.

Ann-Charlotte, clad only in a couple of wisps of lacy spindrift, turned on the seat before her dressing table and, leaning back on her hands, stretched out her long legs for a critical inspection.

"A little on the naked side," she admitted, "yet I am but a simple maid at heart. Aren't you going to dress?"

"Pretty soon." Lillith looked at her watch. "There's no hurry."

"Let's have a drink then." Ann-Charlotte crossed to the door, flung it open, and her scream slashed through the house. "Whisky, ice, and water, ye sons and daughters of Ethiopia!"

From far below Lillith could hear the delighted giggle of Clarissa as the summons bounced through the halls.

"Why don't you use that fancy bellpull?" she asked as Ann-Charlotte came back to the table.

"Ah! That wouldn't be any fun for Lissa. She likes to think all white people are crazy. Who am I to destroy her faith?" She flung herself into the chaise longue, lolling back in an attitude of complete abandon. "If I rang a bell, it would scare the hell out of them." She paused. "What are you going to wear tonight?"

"I don't know." Lillith straightened up, dangling her feet over the side of the bed.

"Don't feel like making little girl talk?" Ann-Charlotte cocked one eye at her.

Lillith smiled. "Not particularly. I was wondering if you wouldn't change your mind and come up to the mountains with us instead of going someplace else by yourself this summer."

"What's the matter, afraid?" Ann-Charlotte's glance was shrewdly speculative.

Lillith's fingers closed imperceptibly, curling into the fleecy pile of the counterpane. Her eyes didn't waver and there was no break in the rhythm of her feet as they swung gently back and forth.

"No," she said quietly, "I'm not afraid."

"That's good." Ann-Charlotte reached for a cigarette and lit it. "I was afraid you might say"—her voice rose to a quavering pitch of astonishment—" 'Whatever are you talking about?' "

"You know me better."

"Yep," tendrils of smoke curled lazily from Ann-Charlotte's nostrils, "I guess I do."

Clarissa, grinning broadly, came in with a tray and put it carefully on a low table.

"Dis heah fraish fram Ethiopia, Miz Ann-Charlut."

"And so are you." She kicked one of her mules at her and Clarissa fled, cackling happily. Ann-Charlotte mixed a couple of stiff highballs and handed one to Lillith. "Here's scum in your eye."

Lillith drank slowly, and the ice in the glass tinkled with the clear sharp sound of Oriental wind bells. "Where are you going?" she asked indifferently, "Paris?"

"Maybe; I don't know." Ann-Charlotte stretched back into the pillows and stared at the ceiling. "Someplace. Say," she turned indolently on one elbow, "I've been meaning to ask you for years, why do you spell your name with two *l*'s?"

Lillith laughed, and the almost too casually cautious look in her eyes vanished. "Everyone asks me sooner or later. I don't know." She rested the glass on one knee. "It's an ugly name to begin with, and it used to look uglier when I wrote it with one *l*, sort of grim and stubby so I just added an *l* for size."

"Adam's first wife, wasn't she?"

Lillith nodded. "Sounds like a radio serial, doesn't it? Adam's First Wife. With an extra *l* it's sort of Lillian with a lisp."

"People give their children the damnedest names. Look at mine. You have to stuff it in your mouth like dressing in a turkey. Ann-Charlotte, flowah of the South, creepin' magnolia. Are you in love with Reese?"

"No."

Ann-Charlotte yawned. "You didn't have to answer in such a hurry. I only wondered."

"Why?"

"Just an idle mind intent upon mischief, I guess."

"I want to be in love with my husband."

"Well, that's fine then." She put her glass on the floor. "We can make tonight sort of a bon voyage party for me. I think I'll get stinkin'."

"I'll dress now." Lillith set her empty glass on the tray. "Come in when you're ready, and bring a drink with you. Maybe I'll get stinkin', also."

"I'll bring the jug." Ann-Charlotte watched her with sleepy, half-shut eyes.

At the door Lillith paused and then turned, almost reluctantly. "I still think that was a funny question to ask," she said.

With an easy grace Ann-Charlotte uncurled herself and stood up, balancing on the balls of her feet, posing for a moment like a wind-blown sprite.

"Maybe you're right. If it wasn't funny it was at least foolish," she said. "There's no sense in putting ideas into a girl's head, is there?"

"I'm not very susceptible to suggestion." Lillith was smiling again.

"And I'm a sex-ridden hag. Go make yourself pretty and I'll be along with a snort in a little while."

Lillith walked slowly down the long hall to her room. Once inside she closed the door and stood with her back pressed against the panels. Finally she shrugged. It was a small gesture of uncertainty. Then she began to undress.

Cary wanted to go out to the country club for dinner, just a small party for the four of them. That meant an all night binge, ending back on The Hill with everyone they could collect or who wanted to come. It might be fun, she thought. It would do them good to get away from the house. Winton didn't have much to offer; the movies, bridge at someone's home. Cary didn't care for bridge. Actually, she thought, he didn't like people but he wanted them around, deriving some sort of bleak comfort from being part of a crowd. Sometimes his fear of being alone was almost frightening. She remembered now how surprised she had been when their wedding party on The Hill dragged on for two, three days and finally a week, until at the end there were none of the original guests present and the entire character of the party had changed. It was as though they had worked through the successive layers of Cary's friends and acquaintances until they reached the point where the people who were eating, drinking, and sleeping in the house didn't even have a nodding interest in each other. Half of them, she was sure, didn't know Cary. The reception degenerated into a shrill revel. It had been Reese who finally cleaned them out. He took over with a quiet efficiency, nudging the drunks into their cars and sending the others down from The Hill in taxicabs. She had been almost hysterically grateful to him.

She halted in the act of kicking a leg out of the slacks she was wearing and for a moment stood on one foot, half bent over in an attitude of meditation. In a way that had been the beginning of her own unconscious dependency. Little things came up after that, and somehow Reese was always around to manage them. Without realizing it, she found herself relying on him. It seemed so natural. The other night, for instance; going to Reese's room and asking him to take care of Cary, she hadn't given it any thought. She straightened up and tossed the slacks into a chair. It was funny, now that she thought about it. After three years of marriage there were times when she almost felt as though she and Cary were Reese's guests on The Hill.

She was in her shower when Cary came up to dress. He knocked on the heavy glass of the stall and pressed his nose against it like some street urchin before a bakery window, peering in at her with owl-like solemnity. She cut off the taps and yelled:

"You'll have to marry me, now."

Cary shook his head in a vigorous no. "It's too late," he called. "I have a wife."

Lillith stepped out of the shower and swathed herself in a voluminous towel. "She ought to know then that you go around peeking at other women in their baths. What have you been doing besides that?"

"Talking. Had a couple of drinks with Reese. Going to have a party tonight?"

"I guess so, dear." She slipped into a robe. "The bathroom is yours."

As she dressed leisurely, Cary splashed and snorted in the next room, and she wondered, as always, why men felt it necessary to make those distinctively animal-like sounds whenever they touched water. In a bathtub they gurgled and grunted. In swimming they rolled and splashed, blowing and spouting.

He stuck his head out of the bathroom, holding the squat mouthwash bottle. "Have a little straight snort?"

"Not now." She smoothed a stocking over her calf. "Ann-Charlotte and I had one in her room. Later, maybe."

A tiny frown of worry leaped to her forehead and she brushed her hand against her temple, smoothing it away. It wasn't Cary's drinking that bothered her. Everyone drank, few of them with any judgment. With Cary, though, there was something unhealthy in the way he sought out a bottle. It wouldn't be so bad if he actually found pleasure in drinking. He didn't. Instead, he progressed from a brief gaiety to expansive demonstrativeness when he wanted to call the entire world brother, to morose introspection, and finally to a maudlin state of helplessness when he was tormented by grotesque fears and a sense of inadequacy. What was it Reese had said the other night? "He always drank this way, only you never noticed it before you were married."

It was difficult to remember. Actually, they had spent so little time together, and even then there were always other people around. From that first winter they met until they were married, the occasions when just the two of them had been alone together could be counted on the fingers of one hand. Week ends they would go streaking up to Connecticut or Pennsylvania to be guests at house parties of friends whose sole mission in life, it seemed, was to crowd their homes from Saturday until Monday. Cary would pick her up at the theater after the curtain Saturday night. Usually he had others in the car with him. Always there was Reese.

She had been amused at first. It all seemed something out of the tabloids. Cary Whitfield, heir to the Whitfield tobacco fortune. Cary Whitfield at Belmont Park. Cary Whitfield at the opera. Cary Whitfield at the Embassy night club. Up the river with Cary Whitfield and the Rover Boys. Cary Whitfield and Lillith Payne lunching at the Savoy-Plaza. It was all exciting and a little unreal. New York had suddenly discovered Lillith Payne. She walked out on the opening night of a bright, new, and unheralded play by an unknown author, *The Highroad*. The next morning the town was hers. It had been as simple as that. One day she had been a student at Hunter College intent upon her degree, making an occasional appearance in amateur theatricals. The next day she held that part of Broadway between Forty-fourth and Fiftieth Streets in her hand. *The Highroad* had done that for her and half a dozen others, all eager youngsters who were sick of the pretentious plush of over-produced scripts. *The Highroad* was a sensation, and the back of the theater was packed nightly with standees. Lillith Payne became the carriage trade's darling. It began to be smart to leave wherever you were and drop in at *The Highroad* to stand in the dark rear aisle and listen in reverent silence, furtively eying your fellow worshipers for effect, while Lillith took over the stage. She became the dusky high priestess of a cult, borne aloft by the same hysterical mass nonsense that nightly packed one of the dingiest speakeasies on Fifty-second Street to the everlasting profit and wonder of its proprietor, Tony. She was approached by the representative of a syndicate who unfolded plans for an intimate night spot on Fifty-fourth Street, just off of Madison Avenue. The Payne Club opened, and thereafter Lillith, sitting on a piano, talked once each night for more money than she had ever dreamed of earning. She made a flying trip to Hollywood to appear in a lavish musical. All of it was in the spectacular tradition. Sometimes she would sit in her dressing room, staring at herself in the mirror, and shake her head bewilderedly at Lillith Payne who had once wanted to be a research chemist. That, also, was part of the fable. No one, apparently, had ever heard of a research chemist who was both young and beautiful. Certainly, research chemists didn't do little inimitable monologues from the tops of pianos. If for no other reason, her nightly appearance on the stage must be regarded as only short of the Second Coming.

Cary Whitfield fitted superbly into the dizzy mosaic of her life. Tobacco Heir and Broadway Star. Cary was a playboy; the word gave her a slight feeling of nausea. Lillith Payne was glamor. Their association was chronicled with such meticulous attention to detail that Lillith began to wonder if Cary was expected to accompany her to the bathroom.

Oddly enough, though, she was finding it more and more difficult to see Cary now as he had been. The past was blurred and fuzzy. What sort of man had Cary Whitfield been only four or five years ago? Much more to the point, she thought, what sort of man was he now? She lifted her head and listened as he shuffled about in the adjoining room, whistling unmusically, clattering glasses and bottles.

Most people, she knew, assumed that their marriage had been little more than the natural conclusion to a success story. It was part of the Cinderella legend. A young actress, finding an early place among the stars, should marry into great wealth. It provided

223

the proper background, rounded out the story. Broadway didn't know Lillith Payne very well. She had married Cary Whitfield because she had honestly believed herself to be in love for the first time. Something about him had drawn her. In his speech and manner there was an absence of the hard, polished assurance so characteristic of the other men she met. The appeal, she realized, was subtle and deceptive. What once had seemed compellingly gentle revealed itself with the years as a baffling weakness. Tenderness, she was beginning to understand, could flower from uncertainty. She left the stage for Cary without regret or a backward glance. It had never meant much, anyhow. Nothing about it had seemed real. It was a lark, sort of a Christmas holiday to be enjoyed and remembered, but certainly nothing to be pursued.

Cary had told her about Winton, the old house on the hill, something of Andrew Whitfield. It sounded comfortable, secure, and a little old-fashioned, a pleasant anachronism that fitted so well with her own ideas of a home and children in a small, drowsy Southern town. She made a lithograph of her fancy, a family group. There would be friends and good companions, pleasant days and comfortable evenings. She was the young matron, and her children, of course, would be handsome and popular. She and Cary would be part of a community. They would represent something solid, honest, fine and durable. Her first glimpse of The Hill had done nothing to alter the picture so clearly drawn in her mind. The house was as she imagined it must be, with its rolling grounds and terraced gardens; the lake and boathouse, the carefully tended paths and drives, all of the outward signs of entrenched wealth. There was a fine air of respectability about The Hill; a little grim, perhaps, and unassailable in its homely virtue, but something immutable in a transitory world.

In the beginning it had seemed natural there should be a period of adjustment. Cary was overanxious that she meet all of his friends. One party followed in the confusion of another. They both drank more than they should, and The Hill seemed to crawl with comparative strangers who roamed about with the casual attitude of guests at a summer resort. She was appalled, sometimes, by the spectacle of the maids gathering dozens of empty whisky, gin and rum bottles from all parts of the house, and by a kitchen that, apparently, was providing meals at all hours of the day and night. The servants didn't seem to know who she was, and if they did, the knowledge left them unimpressed. They performed their duties with unsmiling determination and not as people who were part of a family. She felt resentful, bewildered, and, somehow, humiliated.

"How many servants are there here?" She asked Cary once when they were alone for a few minutes.

"I don't know." He wasn't concerned. "I never paid much attention. Clarissa sort of looks after them, but Reese knows. He could tell you."

"When"—she hadn't wanted to sound impatient—"when does all of this end?" She looked unhappily about. "I mean, this isn't a party any longer. It's an endurance contest. Couldn't we sort of coax everyone outside and then lock the doors in a hurry before they could get back in?" She tried to make the suggestion with a light humor, hoping he would understand.

"Why," he was frankly puzzled, "I thought you would like everybody. I was afraid you'd be lonely."

For a moment she couldn't believe he was serious and looked up quickly, hoping to discover he was making a joke out of a bad situation. She realized with a shock that Cary was actually baffled by her request. There was an expression of hurt surprise on his face. In desperation she had appealed to Reese, furious but conscious of her own inability to handle the situation. Her position was without dignity.

It seemed days before the house was thoroughly aired out and the echoes of confusion silenced. Lillith moved cautiously, hardly daring to believe they were alone. Cary had been maddeningly casual about everything, seeming to think she would sustain herself on The Hill without any help from him. She hadn't expected him to line the servants up or bring them to her one by one, establishing their identity and her own position. Something could have been done, though. As it was, she had the feeling that her presence in the house was ambiguous, as though she ought to apologize for intruding.

During that first week or so, she also had time to wonder about Reese. She had known, of course, he and Cary lived together, but without anything ever having been said, she felt Reese would probably want to make other arrangements. Ann-Charlotte was away; she had never met her, but when her name was mentioned it was always in the sense that she, too, would spend part of the year at home. Lillith hadn't minded. She was fond of Reese and looked forward to being friends with Ann-Charlotte. Families did live together, and certainly there was no question of their being crowded here on The Hill. What really annoyed her was the bland, self-assured attitude of Cary and Reese, whose every act implied she would want things to continue as they always had. Her family chromo became something of a galling joke. The group was there, but she didn't recognize it. It had been handed to her, made to order.

Thinking back now, she could see how effortlessly the seal of a permanent arrangement had been placed upon what, at first, had seemed to her to be a confused and confusing situation. For a while she had the uncomfortable feeling of being the uninvited guest, something left over from the wedding party. After that initial period of uncertainty she began to understand how completely Reese fitted into the establishment. Actually, he ran it. Sometimes she believed he was more deeply rooted on The Hill than either Cary or Ann-Charlotte.

She wanted her own home and intended to be mistress of it; ready, if necessary, to contest its management with Reese. His immediate reaction to her arrival on The Hill was so disarming as to make her feel foolish. Diffidently, almost shyly, he approached her.

"There is a lot you ought to know, Lil. I've sort of had to look out for things; see that the servants were paid, bills settled, accounts kept straight. There are a lot of people working around here. You never see them all at once. Someone had to manage things, and Cary wouldn't, so I had to. I wish you'd take it off my hands. It's really your job." He smiled quickly. "It never was mine."

He explained everything then, how the servants were paid, how the ordering was done, Clarissa's unofficial position as head of the household staff, and the status of the yard help.

"You'll get along," he assured her. "All of the people working here have been with the Whitfields for years. Most of them are children or relatives of original help. You may have to feed discipline to them with a spoon at first, but they'll like it."

She had been grateful for his consideration and a little ashamed of her own attitude. Things had gone well after that, but whenever she needed advice she had turned to Reese and not to Cary. After a while this didn't seem odd either.

It all seemed so long ago now. She slid a gown of silver lamé from a rack in her closet, slipping into it with an expert twist. It was a favorite dress, a good-luck dress, she thought. Whenever she wore it she always had fun, probably because she knew she looked so well in it. Her dark hair fell with a heavy looseness about her bare shoulders. She touched it lightly with a brush and stepped away from the mirror to study the effect. It was good. Turning, she saw Cary standing in the doorway watching her. He held an empty glass in his hand.

"You look very beautiful for an old married woman," he said.

"Oh, I try to keep up an appearance of youth. It isn't always easy." She raised her eyebrows. "Aren't you going to get dressed, or is it going to be that kind of a party?"

She thought he might laugh. Instead he looked troubled, backing out of sight through the doorway.

"You go on down," he called. "Reese is probably waiting. I'll be dressed in a few minutes. I'm a couple of drinks up on you anyhow."

Ann-Charlotte and Reese were on the porch. She walked toward them.

"I thought you were going to stop by my room with a jug?"

Ann-Charlotte shook her head. "It's such a waste of time and liquor to drink with another woman, although I'll have to admit Mr. Benton doesn't give me much encouragement."

"I never knew you needed it." Reese looked at her with a faint smile. The words were without malice.

Ann-Charlotte sighed. "You're a doll, pet, just a doll, but I'm getting too old for dolls." She turned to Lillith. "Come on Lil, have a drink. We'll get stinkin'. There'll be no one at the club to stay sober for, either out of hope or fear."

They all had a couple of drinks before Cary came down. He was flushed and a little unsteady, pretending an almost defiant enthusiasm. Lillith knew the mouthwash bottle in the bathroom was empty.

"If it isn't any fun at the club, after dinner, let's bring some people back here." He looked to Lillith for encouragement.

"I suppose so," she agreed without spirit. "If you'd like to have them."

"You ought to join the Salvation Army." Ann-Charlotte was being deliberately unpleasant. "I never saw anyone so anxious to drum up a crowd."

Lillith slowly and carefully placed her empty glass on the railing. It was strange, she thought, that peculiar baiting note in Ann-Charlotte's voice whenever she spoke to Cary. It was something new.

"Well," Cary shrugged, "it gets damn dull around here sometimes. Lil and I both like people. Is there any reason why we shouldn't have them up?"

"No." Ann-Charlotte rose. "By all means let us seek them out in glen and glade, in fen and on the highway. To horse."

XXI

On the way out to the club, sitting in the back of the car beside Cary who had suddenly turned glum and uncommunicative, Lillith thought a little desperately that she would need more than the silver lamé dress to pull them through this evening. She slipped her hand confidingly, comfortingly beneath Cary's arm. He didn't pull away, but there was no responding pressure in his touch.

"Ann-Charlotte," he muttered pettishly, "wants everything her own way."

Lillith sighed. There was no point, she realized, in trying to wheedle him out of the mood; lights, a few drinks at the bar, the sight of people would do the trick better than a thousand words. She wondered again, trying to find the reason for the open antagonism Ann-Charlotte displayed toward him recently. It was almost as though she were blaming him for something, holding him responsible. I wish I knew, she thought. I wish someone would tell me. There was something poisonously secret between them. It included Reese, of that she was sure, although he masked it so carefully. Cary was transparent. His emotions were surface riffles, agitated by every passing breath, and he was too vulnerable to Ann-Charlotte's oral stoning. Reese treated them both with an air of amused tolerance, and yet, the fancy persisted, sometimes she thought he regarded them with a veiled alertness, waiting to see what they would do next.

"I don't see why we can't have a party." Cary chewed on his discontent. "If Ann-Charlotte doesn't want people around, she can get the hell out of the house."

Lillith experienced impatience. "Ann-Charlotte was only joking." She lowered her voice. "Don't take every word so seriously, Cary."

"I don't like the way she talks to me, almost as if I was a halfwit. I know what I want."

For a moment she was tempted to ask the question: What is it, Cary? What do you want? Instead, she said: "Light a cigarette for me, will you?"

The Glen Rock Country Club was an artfully fabricated triumph of man over nature. It stood in no glen, and the sight of a rock would have thrown the grounds keeper into a minor panic. As a result of skillful grading, cunning planting, and continual care, the effect of a lush, rolling countryside had been created out of a terrain that, at best, was only slightly undulating. Artificial brooks wandered with chuckling lack of purpose, and during the hot summer days the acres provided a brilliantly green oasis. The building itself was a comfortable, rambling structure with broad porches, high-ceilinged rooms, and gracious proportions. Its membership maintained an aggravating attitude of superiority toward the numerous other golf clubs that had sprung up around Winton to take care of the city's ever-increasing population. Glen Rock was the redoubt of the old guard, the citadel of Winton's power. Glen Rock even refused to compete in intra-Winton tournaments and felt itself so secure that it didn't bother with the pretense of liquor lockers for the membership. The bar was open and unscreened in the face of a militantly dry county.

Lillith liked the club, and she still entertained the wistful idea that she and Cary might use it oftener and to some purpose. Cary kept promising he would brush up on his golf, but he rarely managed to get past the bar. Now and then Lillith came out by herself, but it wasn't much fun. Most of the younger members found companionship within their own age circle. The older crowd was inclined to be stuffy, talking too much about each other and nursing incipient high blood pressure. The in-between group, those of her age and Cary's, were frequent guests on The Hill, but she had never thought of them as intimates. They drank too much and with little actual concern for conviviality. There was something machined, brassily hard and too perfect about them, for all their softly accented words and exaggerated courtesies. As they pursued a legend, they all seemed to be perpetually engaged in intrigue, striving to get in or out of bed with each other without disturbing the family equilibrium. Secretly Lillith thought it all a little on the dirty side, completely lacking finesse or discrimination. They were Cary's friends, or so he said, and she tried desperately to fit herself into their lives. Despising intellectual snobbery above all other forms, she nevertheless rebelled against conversations which never rose above comic strips, radio programs, and motion pictures. What surprised her was the fact that most of the men were college graduates and the women had all attended well-known girls' schools, yet they seemed satisfied to live in a mental vacuum. When they went to New York, their theater-going was limited to musical comedies. Their reading was delivered each month through a subscription club. She recalled the storm of abuse H. L. Mencken had provoked when he once referred to the South as an intellectual Sahara. They tore at the prophet's beard, but he remained unmoved.

As they turned into the driveway, Cary began to display a revived interest in the evening. Lights, music, and the presence of other people made him seem almost brightly eager. Watching him, Lillith had the uneasy feeling that they were, somehow, trapped. It was a squirrel cage, forcing a senseless chase.

They had a couple of drinks at the bar, seated on high stools. The room was crowded and noisy with a constant exchange of greetings, snatches of conversation, and the steady clatter of cocktail shakers. Cary wandered up and down the bar, stopping to talk and buy a drink, laughing a little too loudly at someone's joke, bending over to whisper one of his own.

"Bubber ought to buy himself a night club," Ann-Charlotte said without humor, "then he'd really be happy. Order me another drink, Reese."

Lillith fished for the olive in the bottom of her martini, stabbing at it with a toothpick. "I guess," she said seriously, "if you were supposed to eat these they'd fix it so they would be easier to get out. I'll have another drink, also. The same."

Cary broke away from a group at the far end of the room and rejoined them, wedging himself in between Lillith and Ann-Charlotte.

"Tom Payson, Janice, and her sister are coming up to the lodge this summer. I've just asked them."

"That's a major achievement," Ann-Charlotte said admiringly. "Now all Lil will have to do is get rid of them. Are we going to get stinkin', sister?"

Lillith smiled. "I don't know. I'll try. Sometimes it just seems to turn to water."

"That's your blood." Cary leaned over and looked earnestly up into her face. "The white corpuscles eat the red corpuscles, or maybe it's the other way around. Then your blood all turns to water."

"And you use it for a chaser." Lillith nodded. "I guess that's what happens to me, so I end up with nothing but water and never get drunk. Where are we eating, outside?"

"I don't know." Cary looked over at Reese. "Where is our table?"

"Outside, sir." Reese tossed down a straight bourbon. "Your usual table, sir." He grinned. "And I hope everything is satisfactory. The ladies with you, Mr. Whitfield, if I may say so, look particularly charming."

"Thank you, Benton. Remind me and I'll mention your name to the chief steward."

It was foolish, almost childish banter, Lillith knew, and yet there was something comfortable about it. Too often, when they were together, she was uneasily aware of fiercely silent undercurrents that strained to burst and engulf them all. She wanted to say: Let's always be this way, just a little silly, if you want, but liking each other. For a moment, as they crowded into a small group at the bar, she felt they were a tight, self-sufficient unit able to withstand assault from any direction. The room seemed brighter, and the people who pushed past through the narrow lane seeking tables or space, friendlier. When the men paused to clap a hand on Cary's or Reese's back and say hello, she smiled up at them with sincere warmth. The couples who halted to exchange a few commonplace words of greeting awakened a new interest. The women looked prettier than they had a moment ago, the music was gayer.

"I think I'll have a good time," she said suddenly.

They had dinner outside, beneath a sky so star-filled that it looked as though it had been dusted by a giant atomizer. A summer wind was an airy vagrant, halting to touch a candle's flame or whisper to a flower, waltzing with the music past the tables and then disappearing, off on business of its own.

Lillith danced, first with Cary and later with Reese. Ann-Charlotte pushed with a straw at the encrusted ice over white mint and brandy.

"Want to dance?" Cary asked without enthusiasm. He fidgeted unhappily in his chair, looking back over his shoulder now and then at a noisy crowd in the bar.

Ann-Charlotte shook her head. "No, thanks."

"When are you sailing?"

"Don't tell me we have to make conversation, Cary."

She drew a strawful of the sharply tingling frappé and allowed the liquor to roll on her tongue before swallowing. Her eyes followed the movements of the dancers with lazy interest.

Cary stared at the tablecloth, turning an empty glass slowly between two fingers. He was uncomfortable alone with Ann-Charlotte. She made him feel ridiculously small, relegating him to the position of a child who was being allowed to sit up with adults. To cover his uneasiness, he called a waiter and ordered another bourbon.

"You drink like a washwoman with a bottle of gin on Saturday night." Ann-Charlotte continued to look out over the heads of the people seated near them. "I wonder how Lil stands you." She contrived to ignore and talk to him at the same time. The pose was infuriating.

"Lil hasn't complained." He drew his mouth into a sullen line.

"I never knew Reese danced so well." She ignored his challenge.

The waiter brought the bourbon. Cary watered it with a few drops, tossed it down in a single gulp, and then pushed the glass aside.

"You're making an awful mess out of your life, aren't you?" She turned her head slightly.

"It's as good as yours." He felt slightly better. The bourbon was warming.

"I don't cry over mine at night." The words, low, almost whispered, slapped him across the mouth.

"You bitch." He leaned across the table, his face drained of all color.

Ann-Charlotte laughed softly. "Don't talk like a character in a cheap melodrama." She picked up her cigarette case. "How long do you think you can hold Lil this way? She's a normal woman, or hasn't anyone ever bothered to explain the facts of life to you?"

"Get away from me." He choked on the words.

Ann-Charlotte stood looking down at him. "Do you imagine you can go on getting yourself drunk every night, using that as an excuse for not being a man? What do you suppose she thinks about, lying there in bed—by herself?"

Cary wilted. He was a waxen figure dissolving beneath the fire of her quiet scorn. "I ought to kill you," he said thickly.

"You ought to take your wife away. Give her the home and the things she wants." She pushed her chair back and then turned. "Don't forget to take Reese with you, though, when you go." The suggestion was a contemptuous afterthought.

Cary stared after her as she threaded her way with a quick, nervous grace past the tables. There was no strength in the arms resting before him. He tried to push himself upright and his muscles wouldn't respond. Somewhere a woman laughed. He turned his head slowly, certain it was meant for him. No one was watching or looking his way. Slowly, painfully he forced his back against the chair and then stood up unsteadily.

"I think I'll get a drink." He spoke aloud to the deserted table.

Lillith looked up at Reese as the music stopped and his arm released

233

her. The echo of the chanting, half-barbaric rumba drummed lightly through the room.

"Gracias, senor," she said. "You dance one hell of a hot rumba."

They made their way out through the folded doors which made the dance floor part of the veranda. There was no one at their table, and they strolled the length of the porch. Lillith sighed happily.

"I feel like a gypsy," she said.

"There's no truth in it." Reese still held her hand.

"No truth in what?"

"That gypsies are happy. I made an investigation of the story. It's a myth without substance. Gypsies are not gay or carefree. They're dirty and usually pretty tired out. The only time they jangle a tambourine or dance in the streets is when they get paid for it. Usually they stay at home and beat their wives."

"I don't believe you." Lillith crooked his arm and slid her own beneath it.

"All right. Run away with the gypsies sometime and find out for yourself."

"Next time I see some gypsies, I will." She looked about. "I wonder where Cary and Ann-Charlotte went?"

"Oh, they're around." He led her to a shadowed section of the porch.

Lillith glanced at him. "Are you fixin' to spark me out heah in the dark, suh?" She feigned a tremulous sigh. "Ah'll beg to remind you, suh, mah husban's a faih to middlin' shot with a derringer."

"Well, then, maybe, we better just sit down out here." He pulled two deep wicker chairs to the railing. "We'll whistle and clap our hands just to let everyone know we're all right."

They smoked in companionable silence for a moment. Lillith slid down into the chair, hugging the night to her, fearing it might slip away before she could enjoy it. The silver lamé was a good-luck dress, she thought. Everything had been perfect. Cary had been careful with his drinking. He had even tried to be entertaining. She smiled to herself. Cary's humor and efforts to be sprightly were sometimes a little on the elephantine side, but they had become so rare. She realized with a start she was being grateful. For a moment she was worried. Gratitude, for what? She looked up, conscious that Reese was watching her.

"I just feel good," she said without explanation, knowing, somehow, he would understand.

234

"That's fine." He spun his cigarette out over the lawn. "So do I. Want a drink?"

She shook her head. "Don't need one."

"Come to think of it, neither do I." He settled back in the chair, propping his feet on the railing.

"Reese." Her voice was small.

"Uh huh."

"Reese, why haven't you ever married?" She looked up, almost apprehensively, as though realizing it wasn't a question she should have asked.

"Never had two dollars for a license."

"Couldn't you get it done for free?"

"I never thought to ask."

"You ought to look into it someday." She tilted her head against the cushion, turning slightly to watch him. "You know," her smile flashed through the shadows, "when I first met Cary, and you both used to take me out, I thought it was some sort of a joke. I mean, always the three of us. No matter where we went; to the country for week ends, out to dinner or a cocktail party. I had an idea I was being double-courted. That sounds nice and old-fashioned, doesn't it?"

"It was nice."

"But," she persisted, making no attempt to hide her curiosity, "if you weren't courting me, why did you come along?"

"I had nothing else to do, and Cary always paid the check."

"I'm glad to know, after all of these years. It's been worrying me."

"That's all. It was only a matter of a free ride and a free drink. Beside, you were beautiful and everyone knew who you were. I liked being with a celebrity."

"You're a liar and not a very nice one at that." She watched him from beneath lowered eyelids.

"Want to dance?" He dropped his feet from the rail and made a movement to rise.

"Please." Her hand touched his. He sank back, almost reluctantly, she thought. "I don't want to dance and neither do you. Stop trying to run away from me." Her hand remained on his. She was suddenly conscious of the strength in it, ridged, hard and full-muscled. It was a surprise.

"I wasn't running." He spoke thoughtfully. "It was only going to be a slow walk."

"Reese. There's so much you could tell me. Why won't you?"

235

"Little girls usually ask their mothers about such things." He re-settled himself in the chair.

"I ran away from home, so I never had a chance to ask." She laughed, but her eyes were serious.

"That's too bad." He deliberately avoided looking at her.

"Why won't Ann-Charlotte come up to the mountains? Why doesn't she ever come? What's the matter? Why do you stay in Winton? I don't think you are happy." The questions tumbled from her lips and she was unable to stay them. "Why is Ann-Charlotte running away to Europe? Why does she hate Cary?" She stopped, feeling spent.

Reese lit a cigarette, holding the match between his fingers, watching as the flame crept down and then snapped out. "Ann-Charlotte likes Europe. She went to school there and has a lot of friends on the Continent. Everyone she has any interest in goes abroad every summer. Why don't you and Cary try it instead of the lodge?"

"You're not answering me," she said with a gentle persistency.

"Of course not." The cigarette glowed briefly between his lips.

"And that means you don't intend to?"

"I don't think there are any answers to those questions, Lil; or maybe, they answer themselves."

"I don't believe Ann-Charlotte wants to go away this summer." Lillith withdrew her hand. "I think she'd stay here if you asked her to. She's in love with you, Reese."

"That's damn bad luck for everybody, then." The statement was made simply and without emotion.

"What do you mean by that?" She sat upright, looking at him with a puzzled frown on her face. "Why should it be damn bad luck for anyone except Ann-Charlotte, assuming you're not in love with her?"

Reese nodded soberly. "Somehow, Ann-Charlotte's troubles become community property. It has always been that way."

"Oh"—Lillith was impatient—"I detest evasiveness. Why don't you say it's none of my business?"

"Because it wouldn't be true. Only," he stared thoughtfully at the porch railing, "you need a family historian. I'm only a guy who hangs around the place."

"Why?"

His smile was lazy, gentle, and inscrutable. "It's a nice life and I like it."

Lillith rose. "Let's find Cary and Ann-Charlotte," she said a little hastily.

XXII

CARY was at the far end of the bar, the center of a noisy group, shaking poker dice for the drinks. He looked up as Lillith and Reese entered, and for a moment his eyes held an uncertain, almost puzzled look, as though he were trying to remember something. Then he spilled the dice in a clattering roll, indifferent to the triumphant shouts of the winners.

"Better get in on this, Reese." Johnny Parker, standing next to Cary, called the invitation. "It's all free. You can't lose."

"The Whitfield luck?" Lillith smiled up at Cary and inched in beside him. "Are you in a den of thieves?"

His face cleared instantly at her touch and the small frown of worry disappeared. "I think they're cheating," he said.

"Then I'll have champagne as long as you are going to pay for it anyhow." She looked back over her shoulder. "Reese?"

"It's a sissy drink, but it'll do to start with." He glanced down the room to a corner table where Ann-Charlotte sat with a foursome. She flicked her head with a mocking, gamin-like gesture, indicating a place beside her, and when he nodded, she allowed her mouth to drop open with a doltish expression of disbelief.

"Not afraid?" She called.

He walked over to the table. "I'll hate myself for this in the morning," he remarked sadly and nodded to the others. "How are you, Lucy, Phyllis, Tom?"

They moved around on the semicircular seat to make room for him, and Ann-Charlotte patted at the few inches of space uncovered.

"Here, pet. This is all for you, and if you start to slide off you may clutch at my knee, happy thought."

Lucy Blake giggled. She thought Ann-Charlotte was funny. "You say the craziest things. After all, you and Reese must be like brother and sister."

Ann-Charlotte regarded her with simulated delight. "We are, dear," she said finally, "only there's a touch of incest in the family."

Reese smiled to himself, listening unattentively to the small talk,

237

dropping in a few words now and then, and wondering why people like Lucy Blake insisted on talking when there was nothing to say. He also was wondering why he had come over to the table when it wasn't at all what he wanted to do. He turned, feeling the impact of Ann-Charlotte's questioning glance, and realized he had been staring at the group at the bar where Lillith was sitting.

"Forget something, Just Reese?" She asked the question so softly he barely heard her.

"Be funny if I had, wouldn't it?" He matched her impersonal tone.

"Maybe, if you laugh easily."

Lucy was leaning across the table, tapping at Ann-Charlotte's arm. "You weren't listening, Ann-Charlotte," she said reprovingly.

"Oh, yes, I was, dear. Go ahead. I think it's fascinating." She turned her attention to the table with obvious reluctance.

Reese was momentarily annoyed, not over what Ann-Charlotte had said, but rather at his own transparency in provoking the question. He looked across the room again and caught Lillith's eyes. She laughed and shrugged a little helplessly, indicating Cary, who was shaking the dice cup with unnecessary vigor.

"He keeps losing and so I have to keep drinking," she called, "otherwise we'd never get even."

At the sound of her voice Cary turned, still holding the leather container, and saw Reese. For the fraction of a second, the interval was almost imperceptible, he paused, and then winked with an elaborate gesture of secrecy.

"Sucker night," he yelled. "Better have some." He swung about and allowed the dice to spill across the mahogany, following their chattering course with rapt attention.

He was playing with the concentrated eagerness of a child, insisting upon continuing although the bar steward had enough rounds chalked up against him to keep the room supplied until closing hour. He moaned and lamented over his evil luck and kept the group together through sheer persistency despite the fact that the others had long ago wearied of the contest.

Sitting beside him, Lillith felt a small tug of compassion. Why should he be so desperately concerned that other people like him? Now and then, when he wasn't holding the dice, he would turn and touch her fingers, reassuring himself that she was still there. She caught herself abruptly. I shouldn't be feeling this way, she thought. I'm almost ashamed because he tries so hard. It makes people uneasy.

Her eyes wandered around the room, straying inevitably to the corner table. Reese wasn't even looking at her, yet she had the odd sensation of being watched. He looked up then. Their glances met quickly. She shivered and drank too hastily, laughing nervously when a drop of the wine dribbled down her chin. I must be getting tight, she thought, and imagining things. She slid about on the stool, facing herself in the mirror behind the bar. You don't look tight, she reassured herself. You look the way Lillith Whitfield always looks, but you don't feel the same, do you, my girl? She motioned with her glass to the steward.

"Another noggin o' grog, Harry, please." She commanded.

"You're three bottles behind now, Mrs. Whitfield." The steward smiled.

Cary was drinking straight bourbon, tossing it down from a bottle at his elbow, splashing it over the bar when he tried to pour into the small glass. He was pretending to himself that he had to take a drink every time he lost.

She nudged him gently. "Will you take time off to have a drink with me?"

He looked up. His face was flushed, and for a moment he seemed to be trying to place her. "Oh! Sure." He caught at the edge of the bar as he turned. "I'm sorry." He called to the steward. "Harry."

"No. I have plenty." She touched her glass. "What I really wanted was a little attention. I'm beginning to feel like a lone barfly."

"I thought you were dancing," he said uncertainly.

"That was hours ago, Cary."

"Oh!" His face brightened. "Then let's have a drink." He reached for the bourbon.

I'm going to scream in a moment, Lillith thought. She struggled to keep her voice normal.

"Would you like to walk out on the porch?"

"There's no one out there now." He was surprised by the suggestion.

"I guess you're right." She turned to the steward. "Harry, how does brandy mix with champagne?"

"Like a club on the back of your head, Mrs. Whitfield."

"I think I'll try it then. No one has beaten me recently. I've missed it. No," she stopped the bartender as he reached for a brandy glass, "pour it right in here." She pushed her glass across to him.

"That's a hell of a drink." Cary regarded the mixture with interested speculation.

Lillith drained the glass with a defiant gesture. It's probably my fault, she thought. Maybe we ought to drink together.

"Let's take some people back to The Hill," Cary said hopefully, "and have a party."

"Why not? Go and gather them in." She turned to the steward. "I'll have some more of that there stuff, Harry."

"You sure you want them, people I mean." Cary peered doubtfully at her.

"Certainly. We'll have drowning in the lake, falling down the stairs, hitting over the heads with bottles, and scrambled eggs and ham in the kitchen later. You're right," she looked up at Harry, "that's not only a club on the head but also a little man to swing it."

Reese had been wondering how he could break away from the table. Lucy Blake's inane chatter was something to take in small doses.

"When are you sailing, dear?" He heard her ask the question.

"I don't think I'll go," Ann-Charlotte answered thoughtfully.

He looked up then, half turning his head to stare at her.

"But you just said—" Lucy couldn't control her surprise.

"I know," Ann-Charlotte drawled the words, her eyes slanting up at Reese, "but I changed my mind. There's such a thing as staying away too long, don't you think?"

Cary stumbled against the table then, diverting their attention.

"Come on," he urged, "we're all goin' up to The Hill. Lil wants to have a party." He laughed almost complacently. "I think she's gettin' drunk." He weaved away, calling invitations indiscriminately.

"I'd love it." Lucy was excited. "I haven't been to The Hill in years. We used to have so much fun there, Ann-Charlotte. Don't you remember?"

"We still do." Ann-Charlotte made a motion to rise. "Don't we, Reese?"

He moved out, standing away from the table to make room for them to pass. "Night and day," he said gravely. "It goes on like a carnival."

Lillith's eyes were unnaturally bright, and there was an air of suppressed excitement about her. I am tight now, she assured herself, and it's not bad either. Cary leaned over the bar, laboriously scrawling his name on a chit.

"Was I making a noise like a wife a little while ago?" She bent toward him and tugged at his ear. "Well, I'll never do it again."

Reese drove with Ann-Charlotte beside him and Lillith and Cary in the back seat. Looking into the mirror he could see the lights of half a dozen cars as they followed. If Cary had missed anyone, he thought with amusement, it was because he hadn't looked in the toilets.

"You haven't said how delighted you were to know I'm not going away this summer." Ann-Charlotte snuggled into her corner, regarding him with quiet interest.

"Uh huh." He was watching the road.

Ann-Charlotte turned and called back to Cary and Lillith. "I've changed my mind," she said. "Instead of going to Europe I'm coming to the lodge with you, you all, you all."

Reese couldn't be certain, but it seemed as though Lillith hesitated before she replied. Her response when it came, however, was warm and sincere.

"That'll be wonderful. We will have fun now. Cary? He's asleep," she added. "Hey, wake up." She shook him gently. "Mamma's giving a party for you."

Cary only grunted and leaned his head against her arm. She looked down. His eyes were closed and there was an expression of beatific contentment on his face.

"Hey!" She spoke with an injured tone. "I baked a cake and everything for you. That's wonderful stuff," she added half to herself.

"What's wonderful stuff?" Ann-Charlotte turned, looking over the rim of the seat.

"Champagne and brandy." Lillith sighed happily.

"Is that what you've been drinking?"

"Guzzling it, darling. Don't I sound theatrical? Everyone in the theater always calls everyone else darling."

"I believe you're a little tight." Ann-Charlotte was surprised.

"I know damn well I'm tight." Lillith smacked her lips with satisfaction. "You are witnessing the renaissance of Lillith Whitfield nee Payne. From now on I'm going to be hell on wheels." She paused. "I wonder what that means?" She pushed Cary gently into the corner. "How are you, sport? Lean on that other lady for a while."

They opened up the bar in the boathouse and turned the floodlights on the lake. From the window of her room Lillith could look down to the water. She was experiencing a sudden, almost magical sense of freedom. I'm going to stop worrying about things or people or stuff or what. She spoke to her reflection in the mirror and then picked up a light robe to cover her bathing suit. I don't know what's happened, she told herself, but I like it.

From the lake came the sound of music, and voices were startlingly clear. She paused for a moment to listen. Maybe Cary was right. The Hill cried out to have people on it. I've been looking for something that isn't here, she reflected. I'm not going to try to take care of anyone. She hadn't even bothered to welcome the people Cary had asked up. Let them find their own way around, and if they don't like it, to hell with them.

She bounced out of the room and down the hall, leaping astride the bannister and sliding with an ear-splitting whoop to the bottom and into the arms of a man who turned to catch her. She looked up, not attempting to release herself.

"Who are you?" She asked.

"Bob Forbes. Who are you?"

"Just one of the help. Come on, Bob. I'll buy you a drink." She nodded to half a dozen people who seemed to be waiting for someone to tell them what to do. "Make yourself at home. If you want to swim, there are plenty of suits down at the boathouse. If you want a drink, just follow your noses. The lady what lives here usually sees to the guests, but she's away." She tugged at Forbes's hand. "Come on, I'll take you to the servants' quarters."

From the pantry she passed bottles out indiscriminately, laughing at the look of surprise on the face of one of the women as she pressed a quart of Scotch into her hands.

"We always do this. You'll need the empty to protect yourself later. By the way," she tossed the information over her shoulder, "I'm Lil Whitfield, just in case anyone wondered. I don't know any of you but I'm glad you could come. Don't expect to be taken care of, though. We only supply the incentive."

The general air of restraint disappeared beneath her chatter. Introductions were offered with the explanation that Cary had invited them. Lillith led them into the big kitchen. For a moment she wondered if she ought to send for Clarissa and a couple of the girls, and then she discarded the idea. I'm damned if I will, she thought. That's what Lillith Whitfield used to do, worry and wonder if everything was all right.

"I'm a new woman." She gazed up at Forbes who was regarding her with a quizzical smile. "Do you know how to open champagne?"

She thrust an unchilled bottle at him. "I've discovered a new drink, brandy floating on champagne. It makes you feel so vi-rile."

"I remember you, Mrs. Whitfield." Forbes twisted the wire from the bottle's neck. "You're Lillith Payne, aren't you?"

She didn't try to hide her pleasure. "Yes," she said, "and you can't imagine what it does to me to hear you say that."

"How do you want this wine?" He pointed the neck over the lip of the sink as the cork blew out.

"Here," she handed him a highball glass.

"That way?"

"All the way to the top but leave room for the brandy. What are you drinking, and how did you know I was Lillith Payne?"

"I'll take the straight brandy, and I knew you were Lillith Payne because I used to watch and listen to you almost every night for most of a season in New York."

She seated herself on the edge of the table, looking at him with bright attention. "Do you know," she finally said, "I don't know why that should make me feel good, but it does."

"I'm glad I said it, then."

"You're very nice," she said, "and I'm glad you came to our party. What are you doing in Winton?"

"I'm here on business."

She shook her head incredulously. "That's something else I haven't heard for a long time. You mean, you really have something to do; have to get up in the morning, see people about something, do things about things?"

He was laughing at her. "Not every morning."

"And how does it make you feel?"

"What?" Forbes was slightly puzzled by her seriousness.

"Having something, work—a job, I guess."

"Exciting now and then, but usually it's pretty routine."

"Don't you believe it," she said with solemn intensity. "Don't you ever believe it." She slid down from the table. "Walk down to the lake with me?" She called to the other couples from the door. "If there is anything you want and don't see, set fire to the house. The fire department comes then, and you can ask the men to get it for you."

As Lillith and Forbes walked down the sloping path to the lake, the blended hum of music and voices, punctuated by calls from swimmers on the dock, rose in irregular waves to meet them. Floodlights beat out over the water and the near shore with a hard and unwavering brilliance.

"Those lights," Lillith explained, "make you feel a little like a performing seal in a tank, but we had to install them after a couple of guests disappeared at the bottom and almost stayed there."

"It's a bit chilly for swimming, isn't it?" Forbes gazed out over the scene with interest.

Lillith laughed. "Not if you're properly fortified."

The large central room of the boathouse was paneled in knotted cypress with hewn overhead beams and portholes serving as windows. They walked through the crowd toward the bar, Lillith waving or calling a greeting as she passed.

"Quite a gathering for an impromptu party!" Forbes glanced about with curiosity.

"This could just be the beginning. They used to go on for days. Would you like to meet some people?" She smiled up at him. "I'll make an exception in your case. I wasn't going to do anything about anyone."

"No. I'll find my way around."

Lillith strained upward on tiptoes in an effort to see over the crowd at the bar and spied Ann-Charlotte.

"Hey," she called, "can you make room for a girl and sailor?"

"Will he show us his tattooing?" Ann-Charlotte yelled through the noise. "There are a couple of inches here if you can beat your way across."

Lillith and Forbes pushed and shoved good-naturedly until they reached the bar.

"This is Bob Forbes," she said a little breathlessly. "Miss Whitfield, Mr. Forbes. He catches people when they slide down the bannister."

"That's fine," Ann-Charlotte said. "Glad to have you aboard or whatever it is you say to a sailor. Shove in or shove off. Which is it?"

Lillith extended her half-filled glass triumphantly across to Tod Wilson who was trapped behind the bar.

"Look in one of those cupboards, Tod, and see if there is any champagne. How did you get behind the bar and where's your wife?"

"I only came back to fix myself a drink and now I'm stuck," he replied ruefully. "Zoe is out there someplace." He bent down and hauled out two bottles of wine. "It's warm, Lil," he said doubtfully.

"I put brandy in it and it gets red hot." She turned to hear Forbes say to Ann-Charlotte:

"I'm a guest of the Ralph Harmons."

"You mustn't try and explain how you got here," Lillith remarked. "No one does." She spoke to Ann-Charlotte. "Where's Cary?"

"I saw him around." She glanced at the robe Lillith was wearing. "Are you going swimming or just modeling the body beautiful?"

"Swimming," Lillith replied emphatically. "Just to prove it I'll leave you two together." Holding her glass high above her head she wormed her way back out. "Make way for a woman with child."

Outside she looked down the length of the dock and shivered slightly. The night was cooler than she had thought. She swallowed half of her drink and placed the glass atop a post. The mixture, for some reason, now seemed flat and tasteless. She heard Cary's high, nervous laughter and saw he was seated with a group at the end of the pier. They were shouting down at someone in the water. For a moment she thought of joining them, and then the sound of a step caused her to turn. She looked up to see Reese.

"You don't have to go in the water," he said, "just because it's there."

"I was thinking the same thing," she confessed. "It must have been the brandy and champagne. A few minutes ago it seemed like a good idea."

"It looks cold to me." He nodded out toward the float where half a dozen swimmers were huddled around a bottle, passing it about for straight nips.

"Do you suppose they're going to be marooned?" Lillith smiled at the picture.

"We'll get a note in a bottle if they are." He looked down at her, thinking how ridiculously small she appeared in flat-heeled slippers. "The second section of the party is under way in the kitchen. Maybe they'll give us some scrambled eggs if we appear properly famished."

"Sounds good." She hesitated and then dropped the robe to the dock. "Just one quick dive for the sake of appearances," she said.

Before Reese could answer she had curved out and into the water with only the barest splash. A moment later she scrambled up the ladder, blowing and shivering. He draped the robe across her shoulders.

Cary was standing at the far end, shading his eyes against the glare. "Lil?" he called uncertainly.

·"Yes, Cary?" She turned, waiting.

"Oh!" There was a long, almost embarrassing pause. "Nothin'." The word was thickly slurred. "I jus' wondered." He sat down abruptly.

Lillith bit at her lip and then shrugged her arms into the robe's sleeves. "That water," she said with half a laugh, "ruined all my drinking. Silly, isn't it? Will you walk up with me?"

They moved slowly down the dock and up the hill toward the house. With a simple, almost confiding gesture, she slipped her hand into his.

"Cold?"

She shook her head. "No." The shadows hid her features but he thought she must be smiling. "Do I need an excuse to hold your hand?"

They halted at the edge of the driveway as two cars swung out, capturing them for a moment in the glaring beams of the headlights. The drivers punched out departing salutes on their horns, and someone called good night.

"Must be off on a temperance lecture," Reese remarked dryly.

Lights blazed in the rear of the house, and they could see shadows move against the curtains in the kitchen.

"Let's go through the front." Lillith gave his hand a small tug.

There were more people on the long, dark porch, seated on the railings and steps. They called to Reese and Lillith, and they stood talking for a moment.

"You'll have to take care of yourselves," she said. "This is hostess night, the night when she doesn't do anything."

They pushed past a group near the door and into the house. Clarissa and Francie were up, doing their best to keep pace with the demands for glasses, ice, liquor, and soda.

"Ef you could he'p me cleah out the kitchen, Miz Whitfield," she said desperately to Lillith, "ahl try an' git some food ready."

"Don't bother, Lissa. Just do the best you can."

"An' that won't be nothin'. Theah settin' on the range an' on the tables, an' theah ain' room to crack an aig in." The girl wasn't concerned.

Lillith started up the stairs and then turned impulsively. "Come and talk with me, Reese?"

He regarded her with mild surprise and then nodded, following deliberately as she bounced up the steps. She opened the door to his room and snapped on the lights.

"I'll smoke a cigarette here with you," she said, "if you'll break out one."

He lit a cigarette, handed it to her, and then went into the bathroom and returned with a large, heavy towel.

"That robe's all wet, give it to me." He took the soggy garment, tossed it over a chair, and draped the towel about her. It trailed to the floor, lending a raffish air to her slender figure. He laughed.

"What's so funny?" She sat on a corner of the bed; the towel was wrapped like a burnoose, enclosing her completely save for the small oval of her face.

"You look like a desert rat."

"A million thanks, effendi." The tip of her tongue stuck out at him. She drew heavily at her cigarette. "I don't want to go back downstairs again," she said.

"Then don't." He walked across the room and stood looking out of the window.

"What am I going to do, Reese?" Her voice was small, frightened.

He didn't turn but rested his palms on either side of the window frame. He seemed to be bracing himself.

"When you know something isn't right, what's the honest thing to do? I'm only half alive and it doesn't get any better. I keep pretending it is something that can be worked out, when I know I'm lying. I—I think I'm too smart to fool myself much longer."

"Did you ever?" His words were muffled.

"I don't know. That's a rotten thing to say, isn't it?" She stared with haunted eyes across the room, feeling the words bounce back from his broad, unyielding shoulders.

"It's a little late to wonder, isn't it?" He seemed to be asking the question of himself.

"I don't know." Her low cry tore at him. "Don't you understand? That is what I am asking."

"How was it in the beginning?"

She had the strange feeling he was attempting to lead her by the hand, walking slowly along an obscure path, and she hesitated.

"It's difficult to explain to anyone else, Reese."

"Are you sure you know?"

"I," the words came reluctantly, "I think I did once. It's all a little mixed up. There was a gentleness, a consideration; something of laughter and a small-boy eagerness to please. I wasn't very smart about men, I guess. He seemed to want me so badly, to need me. Maybe I was flattered. The appeal isn't something a man would understand. At least, I don't think so because it isn't always clear to a woman. Perhaps that is why so many of us make a mess of things. Now I know what once seemed gentle is only frail, and what was appealing is weak."

"Now you want to call it off?" He turned to face her.

For a long moment she studied him. "You don't call something like this off, Reese. Some of it you have to carry the rest of your life."

Laughter from somewhere in the yard flew up through the open window. At the moment it was a shrill obscenity. Lillith winced at the sound. Reaching behind him Reese slid the sash down and walked over to where she sat.

"You had better get out of that suit," he said matter-of-factly and touched her gently on the shoulder.

She rose obediently and stood facing him, her face tilted, eyes searching his.

"Something has happened to you, Reese," she said. "I used to be a little frightened at what I couldn't understand. It was there, in your speech and manner. It's gone now, Reese. You wouldn't make love to me now, here in this house, would you?"

"No."

"But you would have once?"

"And laughed like hell to myself when it was over." His voice was flat, hard.

"I know." She smiled, gently and with wise tolerance. "I think that was what used to terrify me. It doesn't any longer."

"It's worse now. Can't you understand?"

She shook her head with compassionate tenderness. "No, it isn't. You'll see." Her hands rested gently on his chest and then she turned and slipped through the doorway.

He stood as she had left him until he heard the door of her room close. Then he walked over and switched on a small table lamp and cut the harsh wall lights. From downstairs came the sounds made by many people; indefinite, purposeless noises, the milling of shuffling feet and snatches of conversation. Why the hell don't they clear out? He phrased the question to himself with angry impatience.

Settling in the comfortable depths of a chair beside the table, he fumbled in the drawer until his hands located a pipe and pouch. He packed the blackened bowl carefully, nursing each grain from his palm with concentrated patience. When the tobacco was glowing he kicked absently at the door until it swung shut, dulling the downstairs clamor.

Why the hell don't they get out? He laughed shortly. Why don't you get out? It could be that simple. Don't you know when you are licked? He held the pipe in both hands at waist level, watching through half-opened eyes the small spiral of blue smoke as it curled toward him.

XXIII

WEAVING slightly and clutching at the handrail with a grotesque effort to maintain both equilibrium and dignity, Cary plodded down the dock toward the boathouse. Someone called and he flapped one hand in a weak greeting but kept his eyes steadfastly ahead.

To hell with them all. Parties on The Hill used to be fun. They weren't any more, just a lot of damn fools and half the time it wasn't possible to understand what they were saying. When he and Lil first came to Winton, they'd really had parties and the guests had sense enough to go home without being told. That was because Lil sort of took charge of things. Now he didn't know where she was and it was nothing but a brawl. If he had any sense he'd clear out tonight, just he and Lillith. The others would damn well go home when they couldn't find anything more to drink. He couldn't leave until he found Lil. He halted, clinging to the rail, looking out over the water. Lil was here just a few minutes ago. He drew a deep breath. He'd stop and get a drink at the bar and then go and look for Lil. She'd know what to do about all of these people, strangers, most of them.

At the side door of the boathouse he straightened his shoulders. They all thought he drank too much. He pushed with both hands against the panels, but someone must have pulled the door away. He spun into the room, half falling. A figure caught his arm. He steadied himself against it and heard a distant voice say: "Hey, take it easy. You'll be all right in a minute."

He pulled away angrily and squinted, attempting to focus his eyes to the sudden glare of lights. His entrance brought no interruption to the babbling voices. Someone had a damn queer sense of humor, jerking a door open that way. He shook off the restraining hands and plowed toward the bar. If he could find Lil, she'd get rid of these people.

"Hello, Junior." Ann-Charlotte eyed him from one corner of the bar.

"I want a drink," he mumbled defensively. He was angry at her, something she had said. He glowered, trying to remember.

"Of course you do, pet." She smiled at him with bright innocence. "Enjoying your party?"

"Oh, shut up!" There was a half-filled bottle of bourbon on the bar, just out of reach. He stared at it.

"This is my brother, Mr. Forbes."

A man standing next to Ann-Charlotte thrust out his hand. Cary took it mechanically and then clutched it with enthusiasm.

"See if—if you can reach that bottle." He almost whispered the words.

"Sure." Forbes was surprised. He reached out and slid the bourbon across the damp bar.

Cary took the bottle with a triumphant smirk, delighted at having outwitted Ann-Charlotte. Now he wouldn't have to ask her for anything. He appropriated a used glass, spilled what remained of the drink on the floor. Holding the glass before his eyes, he shakily splashed whisky to the halfway mark and then drank it in two hurried gulps. He waited a moment, as if to gauge its effect, and then replaced the bottle and glass before him on the bar. It was better now. A new strength seemed to gather somewhere within him. The noise and smoke of the room no longer beat furiously about his head. That was the way to drink; take a good one, let it almost wear off before you took another. No one could get drunk that way. He regarded Forbes with a friendly interest.

"You acted as though you needed one." The man smiled understandingly.

"It's chilly outside." He made the explanation with a lofty conviction of its validity.

"There are ghosts out there, also," Ann-Charlotte drawled, "and Junior sees them."

Forbes looked a little uncomfortable. He hesitated. "I think," he said, "I'd better find the Harmons. It's getting late. We ought to be running along. It's been a nice party."

"I think it stinks." Ann-Charlotte looked out over the room.

Forbes laughed uncertainly. "Well," he paused, "thank you just the same and, and good night." He turned and walked toward the door.

"Why did you say that?" Cary glared at his sister. "Why are you always trying to make a fool out of me? Do you think it's smart?"

251

She ducked beneath one end of the bar and hunted in the lockers until she found a bottle of brandy. Without bothering to reply she made a drink. Cary watched her in glowering silence. She turned and, with glass in hand, leaned across the counter. Cary waited, expecting her to reply. He fidgeted beneath her stare and then reached for the bourbon.

The party was breaking up. Several persons came over to say good night. The rest began scattering, drifting outside in couples or small groups. In passing someone reached out and turned down the radio.

"Your guests are leaving." Ann-Charlotte rested on her elbows, holding the glass in both hands and staring meditatively over its rim.

"To hell with 'em." He felt weary and disconsolate. He remembered then. "Where's Lil? Have you seen her?"

"Where she usually is when you get drunk." Ann-Charlotte touched the tip of her tongue to the glass. "In bed, I imagine."

He gazed irresolutely at the door, half-hearing the straggling voices as people outside left the dock and moved up the hill.

"Where's Reese?"

Ann-Charlotte tasted her drink. "Have you started looking for them together, now?" The question was softly innocent.

Cary fumbled in his pocket for a cigarette and then, as though he suddenly understood what her words implied, turned.

"What did you say?" He was puzzled.

"I didn't say anything." She lifted her shoulders with a small shrug. "You asked where Lil was, and then you wanted to know about Reese."

"You're a liar," he said slowly. "Maybe I'm not so damned smart, but I know you well enough to recognize a bitch when I hear one."

"Don't be an ass, pet." She was tenderly solicitous. "I know you can't help being a bore. If you want to go witch hunting, do it on your own." She looked up and called to a couple at the door. "Wait a minute, Johnnie. I'll walk up with you."

Cary stood alone at the bar. The room was empty. The radio hummed softly against the whine of the ventilator fan as it sucked ravenously at the few remaining pennants of smoke. He poured the rest of the bourbon into his glass and then, with savage impulsiveness, hurled the empty bottle through a window and felt a vague satisfaction at the gaping hole it left in the screen. There was no fun in anything. Not even in drinking. He drained the glass and threw it after the bottle. It missed the hole and bounced back from the wire mesh, splintering on the floor.

There were only two cars left in the driveway when he reached the house, and Clarissa was taking in a tray of jumbled glasses. He waited until she disappeared and then followed, ducking inside furtively. He crept to the dining room as though he had no business there and hurriedly poured himself a drink at the buffet. He could hear people in the kitchen and stood with silent attention, hoping to recognize Lillith's voice. The sounds were without identity. He turned and walked down the long hall and then upstairs, stumbling once on the steps. I'm not drunk, he thought with surprise. What made me do that?

Their room was empty. He turned on all the lights with the foolish idea that it was too dark to see well and even stepped into the bathroom although the door was open and he knew Lillith wasn't there. He experienced an almost irresistible desire to call her name. Sitting on the edge of the bed he found a cigarette in his pocket and had difficulty in lighting it. After a moment he rose and went down the corridor to Ann-Charlotte's room. He knocked once, and when there was no answer opened the door and looked hurriedly around. Ann-Charlotte hadn't come upstairs. For a moment he was on the verge of panic. They had all gone away and left him; Lillith and Reese and Ann-Charlotte. Lil wouldn't go without telling him. Ann-Charlotte didn't give a damn. She hated him, always had. What was it she had said in the boathouse, something about Lil, Lil and Reese? She had said something else, on the porch at the club earlier. Be sure and take Reese with you.

I must be drunk, he thought a little wildly, otherwise I wouldn't be talking this way to myself. He sagged against the door. I'm going to be sick in a minute. Nausea clotted in his throat and he fought against it. I'll find Reese. I'll find him and I'll ask him. That didn't make any sense. How could you ask a man such a question?

He shuffled back down the hall, head drooping between his shoulders. He halted at Reese's door, knocked with one hand and turned the knob at the same time with the other, stepping inside without waiting for a reply.

Reese was seated in a chair by the table, holding a cold pipe in his fingers. He looked up at Cary but didn't speak.

"Turn on some lights," Cary muttered and fumbled with the switch. The shaded wall brackets sprang out in relief.

Reese lowered the pipe and watched him as he stumbled across the room and peered into the bathroom with exaggerated indifference.

"What's the matter with you?" Reese eyed him with undisguised interest.

"Nothin'." Cary rubbed a hand across his lips. They felt thick and lifeless.

"Well," Reese was unsmilingly alert, "you have the damndest case of nothing I ever saw. You'd better sit down."

Cary sank to the bed as though his legs no longer had the power to sustain him. "I was trying to find Lil," he said after a moment.

"Did you expect to find her in the bathroom?"

"Oh, I didn't mean here! I—I went down to the room, and on the way back just, just stopped in." The excuse sounded lame even to his own ears, and he attempted to smile a weak apology, hoping Reese would understand.

Reese knocked out the pipe and scraped at the inside of the bowl with the twisted end of a match tab. Cary followed his hands with solemn attention as if Reese were, somehow, shaping their destiny instead of cleaning a pipe.

"Everyone gone home?" Reese asked the question without any particular interest.

"I don't know." Cary turned, bending slightly forward in an attitude of pleading desperation. "What's the matter with me, with everything, Reese?"

"Nothing that sticking a finger down your throat wouldn't cure." Reese smiled for the first time.

"That isn't it." Cary shook his head.

"It might do for a starter."

"No. I'm sick inside, Reese. I don't ever feel good." He licked at his lips. "Do you have a drink up here?"

Reese hesitated and then rose and went to a closet. "Scotch?" He said, turning inquiringly.

"Yes, sure, anything. Have one with me, will you?"

He gulped the straight Scotch hurriedly. "You see, this is what I mean. I only like to sit around and have a few drinks with people, but most of the time I have to do it alone. I worry, too. I wake up sort of scared, trying to remember. I keep thinking something is wrong. Then I say to myself: What could be wrong? I don't know."

Reese leaned back in the chair and closed his eyes. He heard Cary stand, go to the bureau and pour himself another drink.

"Do you remember, when we were kids?" Cary's voice took an edge of excitement. "We used to think it was fun to get a bottle of corn and go out in the car with a couple of girls. Now," the words trailed away, "it isn't fun the way it was. I wonder why." There was an interval of silence. "You're not paying any attention."

Reese looked up. "I wouldn't drink any more tonight," he said.

Cary was staring at a small chair in a corner. Reese followed his eyes. After a moment Cary rose, walked unsteadily across the room and picked up the light robe. It was still damp and he rubbed it between his fingers.

"This is Lil's," he said and turned to look at Reese.

"She left it here."

"When?" Cary spoke with an empty sound.

"Tonight when she stopped in for a cigarette." Reese was annoyed. "What the hell's the matter with you?"

"Where did she go then?"

"Oh, for God's sake!" Reese sat up quickly. "She probably went to her room, dressed, and went back downstairs. How do I know?"

"Yes, sure. I guess that's what happened. I must have missed her. Maybe she was in the kitchen. I didn't look." He was attempting an apology for things unsaid.

"Look," Reese was almost gentle, "I'm tired and so are you. Let's call it a night." He took Cary's arm and half led him to the door. "Get a good night's sleep, and maybe you might feel a little like climbing up on that wagon tomorrow. If—if you want me to I'll go downstairs and find Lil for you."

"No." There was a hurried plea in Cary's voice. "She, Lil doesn't like to see me this way. I'll go in and go to sleep and then she won't know anything about it when she comes up."

"All right." Reese steadied him.

"I," something muddled and inarticulate within Cary struggled for expression, "I want Ann-Charlotte to go away from The Hill. She's tryin' to drive me crazy, Reese. She says things an' then she doesn't say 'em."

Reese's fingers tightened on the limp arm. "What does she say?"

"I don't know, exactly. I—can't remember." Cary wasn't shamming. "You, you wouldn't let anything happen, would you, Reese?" He rubbed the back of his hand against his mouth with a weak, fumbling motion. "I—sometimes," he continued, "there are things you can't talk about. Even if Lil," he stared with blank despair, "you wouldn't let her leave me even if ... ?" The words died.

For a moment Reese was caught by the furious temptation to step back and lash out with his open hands in an effort to beat understanding, or at least pain, into the vacillating face confronting him. Do this for me, Reese. Good Christ, didn't the words ever change? Sleep with my wife if that will keep her here, but don't let her go away.

"Come on," he said wearily, "I'll take you down to the room."

He moved with patient care down the long hall, catching most of Cary's limp weight on his shoulder and paying little attention to his garbled muttering. Via Doloroso, he thought with grim sarcasm. Lord, the way is long.

Inside the room he shifted Cary to the edge of the bed, propping his back against the headboard and stepping away to look at him. Left alone he'd sleep as he was until Lil came up and found him.

"Let's get it over with." He struggled with the white dinner jacket, rumpled and stained, turning Cary's unresisting body from one side to the other until he had stripped him down to his shorts. He tossed the clothing into a chair and slid Cary beneath the sheets.

"Oh."

He turned from the bed and saw Lillith standing in the doorway. Her face was white and strained.

"Thank you, Reese." She spoke with an effort and then a wan smile of resignation trembled at the corners of her mouth. "I guess I didn't keep my good luck dress on long enough."

Cary moaned unhappily, turning halfway over and burying his face in the pillow.

"Was he bad?" She looked up.

Reese shook his head. "Just limp. He was worried about you."

She leaned against the door. "I was helping to speed the parting guests."

"Have they all gone?

"All except Tom and Milly Jason. Ann-Charlotte's sharing a stirrup cup with them in the kitchen." She stared down at Cary. "It started out to be fun, too." She spoke with a tinge of wonder. "I almost believed it, there, for a moment, at the club. Childish, wasn't it?" She raised her eyes to meet his.

"It was a good rumba," he answered, making an attempt to give the words a touch of lightness.

Lillith reached down and took a cigarette from a box on the table. "It was a good rumba," she said over the flame of the lighter he held for her. "It was a good dance and a better talk later." A hint of laughter flared briefly in her eyes. "Even if I did ask a lot of questions when I knew some of the answers."

"That fooled me at first." He matched the even tone. "It doesn't any longer."

"I didn't think it did."

Cary whimpered, the sound muffled in the pillow. He flung one arm across the bed and the fingers stretched as though they were searching for something just beyond his reach.

"Don't let him cry again tonight." Lillith breathed the prayer. "I couldn't stand it."

As though he had heard the words Cary's faint sounds of misery, springing from some secret torment, trailed off into a moaning sigh, bubbling as if it came from below water. Reese had an irresistible desire to get out of the room.

"Good night, Lil."

"If," she bent her head slightly, "if it's bad, may I ... ?" She looked up quickly, allowing him to finish the sentence.

"No." The word almost exploded although he didn't raise his voice. "No, God damn it. How much do you think I can take?"

He knew she was watching as he strode back down the hall and to his room. Inside he shut the door and after a moment's reflection turned the key in the lock.

He undressed with methodical care, reflecting sardonically that he became neat only when disturbed. Always when something troubled him he wanted order to be visible. Shoes with trees in them, trousers clamped in a hanger, jacket on a rack, everything must go in its proper place.

A distant but sustained roll of thunder swept in through the open windows. The night was growing sultry, and there was rain in the heavy clouds piling up beyond the ridge. He stretched out in the dark and smoked a cigarette.

He tried not to think of Lillith as she stood in the doorway, yet her image persisted, refusing to be brushed aside. He could feel her eyes, hurt and staring, as he turned away. She hadn't said it, but he knew

257

what she had been thinking. You're Cary's friend, Reese. Why don't you help him?

He started and then relaxed as a light tattoo, beaten out by invisible fingernails, sounded on his door. There was an interval of questioning silence and then he heard Ann-Charlotte's faint, inquiring call.

"Reese, are you awake?"

He didn't answer, and after a moment sensed she had walked on. The last of the guests must have left. The old house now closed itself in upon the four of them, mumbling and talking.

Over the bright tip of his cigarette he repeated one of the things Cary had said earlier. "Ann-Charlotte is trying to drive me crazy." That was foolish. Ann-Charlotte didn't care enough to make the effort. She had never liked her brother, recognizing something uncertain and weak in his nature. Indecision, Cary's inability or refusal to take what he wanted and be indifferent to the consequences, aroused only an amused contempt within her and she never allowed him to be unaware of it. Even as a youngster she had flicked with delicate precision, scoring him with the small, sharp blades of a nimbler wit, and and he was helpless before her. Ann-Charlotte, it seemed, had always known what she wanted, and her approach to the fulfillment of her wishes was cool and direct.

Thinking of her now Reese could see her clearly, outlined in precise detail, as she had appeared upon her return from Paris at the time of Laura Whitfield's death. Poised, exquisitely groomed and with an indefinable foreign air about her, she came back for the first time in almost five years. She had the hard perfection of a rare gem, brilliant and glowing but essentially cold. He and Cary had been in Colorado that summer when Laura's sister wired, asking that they come to Raleigh at once. They took the first train, Cary reluctantly turning his back on the camp he had leased and the dozen or more guests who had been invited for the summer. He seemed to consider his mother's illness as a personal inconvenience.

Laura was more than ill. She was dying. Reese knew this the moment he stood by her bed. Laura had no wish to linger. Life was no wonderful, shining thing to which she wanted to cling.

"How are you, Just Reese?" she whispered and ventured a tiny smile at the old, old joke. "You never did," she spoke with an effort, "get a chance to be just Reese, did you?"

Ann-Charlotte was late by several days and never saw her mother. Looking at her Reese had to wonder why she bothered to make the voyage. Sentiment, he knew, had small place in her nature. She was even slightly amused and surprised by the impulse which had sent her traveling over four thousand miles.

Instead of returning to Colorado, Reese and Cary went down to The Hill and Ann-Charlotte joined them there, coming directly from New York after talking with her aunt on the telephone and learning that the funeral had been held. The three met on the front porch of the old house, Ann-Charlotte driving up in a cab from the station without bothering to let them know in advance when she was to arrive.

Save for that one day in Paris four years ago, they had seen nothing of each other, and so, for a moment, they waited, each with a certain wariness, and then Ann-Charlotte flung a quick hello to her brother and strode over briskly to stare up into Reese's face.

"Mmm." She made an approving sound. "I should have come back before. I had an idea you'd turn out this way, Just Reese. How are you?"

A thousand memories flooded over him as he looked at her with unsmiling attention. It was difficult to remember this was Ann-Charlotte, and yet there was something achingly familiar in the small gestures she made with her hands or in the impudent cocking of her head as she asked a commonplace question.

"I'm fine," he said after a pause. "No wonder Paris is such a popular city."

"Darling," she reproved him gently, "compliments don't become you. I prefer you rugged and a little on the insolent side. Don't change and spoil everything."

"What's left to spoil?"

"That's better," she said happily, "let's have a drink. Come on, Stinker." She turned to Cary. "Put on a hospitality act for the prodigal."

Cary made no attempt to be gracious or even pretend he was glad to see her, and, Reese thought, this was one of the reasons she decided to stay. That night at dinner she leaned over and sent a fine stream of cigarette smoke down the table in Cary's direction.

"I think maybe you need a woman around here," she said. "Not necessarily a good woman, just a woman, and so I'll stay for a while, or for as long as I can stand you." She turned her face to Reese. "Will we have fun, darling?"

"Not if you continue to call me darling."

259

"I forget," she apologized. "I've been hanging around with a lot of actors."

"Pimps, too, I hear." Cary snorted. "What happened to that toy count or duke you bought? I read about it in the papers."

"My God," she gave him the full benefit of her amazement, "can you read?" Her lips pursed thoughtfully. "Never let me hear another word against our educational system. The results are too obviously marvelous."

Without further comment Ann-Charlotte established herself on The Hill, and for the first few days she was a strident-voiced harridan until she brought the servants into a slightly hysterical state of order. Reese was quietly surprised by her capacity for management and organization although her methods were anything but orthodox. He listened to her one morning after she had cornered Francine, one of the upstairs maids. He never learned what dereliction on the girl's part touched off the fury, but he was certain little, skinny Francie would never forget.

"I won't fire you, Francine." Ann-Charlotte spoke with quiet venom. "No one was ever fired from The Hill, but if I ever catch you doing that again I'll take my bare hands and beat the living hell out of you."

Francine had disappeared with a terrified yelp, and she must have carried the warning to the kitchen and the yards, for Reese couldn't help but notice the slovenly attitude vanished with magical promptness. Thereafter the house functioned with quiet efficiency. He even commented on the change, and Ann-Charlotte laughed.

"In Paris I'm really the madam of a bawdy house. That's how I learned to handle maids and count change."

It took Reese some time before he realized to what extent Ann-Charlotte had become something of an international figure. Over the years he had seen pictures of her, in the rotogravure sections or in Sunday supplements, taken in Switzerland or along the French and Italian Riviera. Now and again there had been highly colored reports of her rumored engagements, and always, or whenever possible, she had been referred to as "the Tobacco Princess" to distinguish her from the Tin Plate Duchess, the Poor-Little-Rich-Girl of the Five and Ten Cent Store, the Asbestos Queen, or the Oil Heiress, whose spectacular flights from continent to continent provided week-end reading for an avid public or shelfpaper in a share-cropper's cabin, or, possibly, some less delicate use to which old newspapers are frequently put. Once established again on The Hill, Ann-Charlotte set up a small communications center. She called Paris, London, and Rome on the telephone with the same casual attitude she might display in asking Clarissa for the morning paper. Friends in New York and points east and west dropped in on The Hill for week ends and stayed for weeks. They were well-dressed and well-bred people who somehow seemed to be neither American nor European, having achieved a status and nationality of their own.

"I know I'm just a country boy," he said to Ann-Charlotte one evening, "but what do all of these people do?"

"What's the matter?" She looked up quickly over a martini. "Don't you like them?"

"As a matter of fact," he confessed, "I do; most of them, at any rate. They seem to get a lot of fun out of life without trying very hard."

"Don't you believe it." She was emphatic and serious. "It's a profession, and has to be worked at twenty-four hours a day. Anyhow, you pick out the ones you don't like and we'll throw them off The Hill, you and I."

At first Cary had been inclined to resent Ann-Charlotte's guests, adopting an attitude of churlishness or openly scoffing at what he considered their pretensions.

"Fortune hunters." He blurted out the words with superior ill-humor.

Ann-Charlotte looked at him for a moment. "That's something you read in a cheap magazine," she said quietly. "Everyone's a fortune hunter. Some have sense enough to go to a good tailor first."

By summer's end, though, Cary was enjoying himself. After a couple of surprisingly easy conquests when compliant young women hoped they might find, at least, part of the Whitfield fortune in his bed, he began to take a lively interest in Ann-Charlotte's friends and added some of his own. The Hill took on the appearance of a country club. They even shuttled back and forth from the lodge in the mountains to Winton. Reese had wondered a little about this at first, curious to see if Ann-Charlotte would betray any emotion at the sight of Harlen, the lodge, or other scenes which should have been tragically familiar. Not a turn in the road, a house or ridge broke the effortless rhythm of her composure. She even drove into the filling station at the bend in the lodge road and sat talking with indifferent attention while a strange boy filled the tank. Watching her, Reese was compelled to admiration. She, she or her pose, was flawless. Nothing, he was certain, had ever touched her save when she willed it.

The months of summer and autumn Ann-Charlotte spent on The Hill that year were crowded. There never seemed to be enough time for anything, and certainly no backward glances over the shoulder. Only on the day before she was to leave for Cuba to join friends on a yacht there did Ann-Charlotte intimate she, also, had been remembering. They stood together, alone, for a few minutes on the boathouse dock.

"I thought you ought to get used to me again, Reese," she said. "That's why I came back and stayed so long."

He shook his head. "It's no good."

She smiled then, quickly and with understanding. "I'm not so sure." Her words were whispered. "Maybe we'll have to wait around a while and even get a little shopworn. Perhaps that is the way it was meant to be, to have some of the fuzz rubbed off first. I'll be back every now and then to see, Just Reese."

She left the following morning. Now and then she sent a brief note. They came with the postmarks of South America, China, India, and always one or two from Rome or Paris. Sometimes the letters contained nothing more than a single sentence, scrawled diagonally across a page, rarely followed by a signature: "Are you ready to give in?" He had never replied, knowing she did not expect an answer. The notes, though, supplied a strange, tenuous link between them. Sometimes he imagined the question, repeated so many times, was a wistful expression of homesickness. Whatever her feelings, Ann-Charlotte made no effort to return to New York or to Winton until after Cary's marriage to Lillith Payne.

Locked now with the darkness in his room, Reese was free to examine Ann-Charlotte's attitude toward her brother. Never had she pretended to care for him, yet her dislike had once born an almost impersonal quality. She flayed his smug selfishness with an air of detachment, as a small boy might throw a rock at a stray cat. It was a target to shoot at, but also a target to be ignored if she didn't feel like playing. Now it was different. For months he had sensed an undercurrent of vindictiveness, and, seeking the reason, it occurred to him that its beginning lay so far back all of them, save perhaps Ann-Charlotte herself, had forgotten where it was hidden. Once she had allowed Cary the doubtful privilege of making himself vulnerable and if he was caught and had to squirm, the fault had been his own. Now, however, it seemed to Reese she sought and stalked her victim. "She's trying to drive me crazy." Cary's words repeated themselves.

Reese knew he was wrong. She was, though, engaged in a campaign of torment which was making Cary miserable, filling his drunken dreams with terror.

This quiet but relentless pursuit of her brother began, Reese understood now, almost from the day Ann-Charlotte had returned to Winton and found Lillith installed on The Hill. It wasn't a question of authority; Ann-Charlotte didn't want the responsibility of The Hill. Lillith, though, stood and walked now where her feet had once been so determinedly planted. This shadowed, beautiful girl who, so surprisingly, had married Cary was far too intelligent and attractive to be ignored. With the unreasoning perversity that was her own, or perhaps just feminine, Ann-Charlotte became Lillith's friend while secretly blaming Cary for her presence.

She's jealous, Reese thought with surprise. He reached for and found a fresh cigarette, pressing one end into the coal of the stub burning his fingers. Never had he imagined Ann-Charlotte could succumb to the small fears or emotions that plagued and harassed others. She had been too aloof, too coldly remote. Jealousy was for small people whose lives she dimly understood. Yet, Reese pondered, there it was; plain enough to be read by anyone who would take the trouble. She was transferring some of the evil stench of fear to Cary. No wonder he cried aloud at night.

XXIV

ONLY after he had admitted to himself that he was little more than a rheumy-eyed ancient prying into the affairs of others and matters which did not concern him, did Joe Whitfield make good his promise to Lillith and ask them all to Bluestone for a barbecue.

Joe was curious. Something was happening on The Hill and he wanted to know what it was. Not, he assured his reflection in the shaving mirror, that it is any of your business. If you had a particle of the sense your years are supposed to bring, you would oil your guns, calk the rowboat, spade a garden, or do anything but meddle or even take a fast look at what goes on at The Hill. As it is you are a prying old dodderer who is difficult to amuse. Now, pick up the telephone, call Lil and get it over with.

He did just that. "I told you," he said to Lillith, "I wanted to give a party."

"You'd better do it soon, then," her voice rippled over the wire. "We're going up to the lodge."

"All of you?" He waited and wasn't disappointed. There was a brief silence and he knew she was thinking quickly.

"All of us, Reese, Ann-Charlotte, Cary, and I."

"Well," he didn't want to pursue the subject too obviously, "come down tomorrow night an' we'll roast a shote or two."

"We will come and eat and spend the week." She was laughing at him and he knew it.

"To hell with that." His reply was a rumbling growl. "Just come an' eat an' then leave. I'll tell you when."

With an interest he couldn't quite explain Joe spent most of the day supervising the barbecue prepartions in the pine grove behind the house. The fire in the pit had to glow with a precise cherry-red richness. The young pig and a venison haunch, marinated in Burgundy with onion and freshly ground black pepper, must be handled in just such a fashion before it could be laid on the rack. The table had to face in a certain direction. The details kept him busy, and he had time to wonder no more than once or twice why he was bothering to give a dinner for four persons whose collective company he had taken especial pains to avoid.

It's because I like that Lillith girl, even if she does have a damn silly name, he convinced himself after much silent argument. I like her, an' in a way, a mighty small one, Ann-Charlotte. I even like Reese or would once I figured out whether he's all no good or just part good an' part bad like the rest of us. Cary, I suppose, is blood kin an' has to eat. After examining these details, he tucked them away for reference if the necessity arose.

By the time they had finished dinner Joe was thoroughly pleased with himself as he always was with perfection. Even the moon had behaved as it should, rising at dusk on the soft river wind and hanging behind the pines with the warming light of a Halloween pumpkin. Joe was kindly disposed toward Nature when she behaved herself. They talked of inconsequential things, and although his attention seemed to wander without purpose about the table, resting impartially on them all, he kept a sensitive ear tuned whenever Lillith or Reese spoke. People said things with their voices. It was an unfortunate weakness even he had had to watch at times. Now, as he listened to Lillith, he caught the tight note of quiet desperation, and he wanted to reach across the table and tell her not to speak again.

Over coffee and brandy Joe watched Reese and had the uncomfortable feeling that he, in turn, was under a keen scrutiny. It wouldn't have surprised him in the slightest if the younger man had risen from the table and told him to go to hell. "We'll work this out." He could almost hear Reese's quiet but decisive drawl. "We'll work this out without any interference, so mind your own damn business." The fancy was so acute he unconsciously stiffened, waiting for the words. Instead of speaking Reese was thoughtfully spreading a slice of pear with ripe Gorgonzola and, apparently, devoting his full attention to Ann-Charlotte.

In his own fashion Cary, also, was aware of things unsaid and of fugitive overtones. The liquor tonight at Bluestone was the first he had touched in three days and his nerves were raw, responding slowly to the anesthetic of alcohol. Perhaps, he thought, that was why he was imagining things; the way Lil's voice dropped when she spoke directly to Reese, and Reese's studied avoidance of her eyes when she looked up in reply to something said. I am going crazy, he thought. This damn foolishness. Ann-Charlotte started it. She thought he didn't understand or pretended to say one thing and mean another. And now, Uncle Joe, watching them all across his cigar tip as though he was waiting for something to happen.

"Kinda unusual for you to spend the summer in North Carolina, ain't it?" Joe pushed the decanter of brandy across the table in Ann-Charlotte's direction.

She accepted both the bottle and the challenge with an enigmatic smile. "No more so," she said, "than your inviting us to Bluestone for dinner. You tell me and I'll tell you. By the way, this is wonderful brandy."

Joe couldn't restrain an appreciative chuckle. If there was anything he liked about this niece, it was her willingness to stand toe to toe and slug it out. She might have the tongue of a fishwoman and the conscience of a ferret, but, by God, she was honest.

"It's been let alone." He nodded at the squat crystal bottle.

"That," her eyes sparkled frostily, "sounds like a great recipe for a grape or," her voice dropped, "or a man."

"Let's don't overdo it." Cary reached up and took the brandy from in front of Ann-Charlotte. He was a little pleased with himself over the remark and happy when Lillith laughed. He filled his glass, emptying it slowly in his mouth and holding the liquor there for a moment with the critical air of a connoisseur. No one seemed to notice he refilled the glass before putting the bottle down again. It was nonsense that a man couldn't have a few drinks. All he had to do was be careful and space them properly the way he was doing tonight. Liquor was made to be drunk. The wisdom of the silent observation pleased him, and he beamed with sudden friendliness at Reese.

Later, after the fire had been reduced to a dark and flameless bed, the brandy bottle emptied and table candles gutted, they strolled back along the narrow path with its cushioning carpet of pine needles. Standing on the terrace, they looked with silent appreciation at the swath of hammered silver laid down by the moon. Along the banks the oaks bent like gnarled crones, striving to catch their reflection in the water, and the wind hunted through their crooked branches. No sound intruded as the night claimed its own.

"How do you hang the world up this way so only you can look at it?" Lillith took Joe's arm.

"It came on a Christmas tree when I was a youngster." He glanced across the terrace to where Reese and Ann-Charlotte sat. Cary had disappeared inside the house, heading for the decanters on Joe's sideboard.

"You keep it nice and well polished," she answered absently.

With a guiding pressure Joe turned her from the river and down the porch, and they walked without speaking to the far end.

"It was a wonderful evening, Uncle Joe." She had the certain knowledge he was about to say something and, somehow, sought to divert his attention.

"I keep a few like this on tap for my friends," he replied, "and only take them out for a special occasion." He cut the end from a fresh cigar, folded the bright blade of a small gold knife and dropped it into his pocket. "Get out," he spoke with quiet determination, "get out, both of you and run like hell. Don't stop to look back or wonder about Cary or Ann-Charlotte. If you do, you'll never go."

They stood by a huge stone flower urn serving as a corner post. Lillith reached out and plucked a small blossom, tucking it into her hair.

"I suppose," she meditated, "it would be easier to say I don't know what you are talking about."

"If I thought you were that stupid, I wouldn't bother to talk with you."

"Is it so apparent?" she waited.

Joe drew lightly upon the cigar. "Maybe not," he said. "I was looking for it."

"Why?" She asked the question with solemn attention.

"I'm damned if I know." He regarded her with an attitude of quizzical amusement. "Probably I was just curious to see if human nature was changing. Also, I sort of like you. Maybe leaving wouldn't be the best thing, but you couldn't be any worse off, could you?"

"But," there was wonder in her voice, "I don't think I knew it myself until a few days ago. Either that or I've known it for so long."

"What the hell difference does it make?" His words were uncompromisingly rough. "You know now."

"Yes." The admission was a sigh. "I know now."

"Well," Joe plainly thought the subject closed, "do something about it."

She had to laugh then. He reduced everything to the simplest terms. If you wanted something, you took it. If you didn't like something, you said so.

"A girl," her eyes were bright, "a girl has to wait until she's asked." With an unconscious gesture of regret she touched the tips of her fingers to her lips. The words shocked her. It didn't seem decent, somehow, that the two of them could be standing here, discussing the lives or at least the futures of three persons, and pretending what they were saying had no importance.

"If girls wait until they are asked," Joe peered down at his cigar, "then they must have changed some since I knew them."

The scraping of wood on the flagged stones of the terrace caused her to glance in its direction. Reese was seated on the low wall, facing Ann-Charlotte, who was slumped comfortably on the end of her spine in one of the heavy, broad-armed chairs. Reese leaned forward to say something, and Ann-Charlotte laughed with lazy confidence. A sudden doubt flashed through Lillith's mind. Suppose she was imagining things? I'm taking a lot for granted, she thought. Maybe a girl *had* better wait until she's asked. Even as the idea formed itself, she discarded it. No one has to say those things, block them out in words. One day you are talking as usual and something happens. It is swift, electric, and a little breath-taking, but you know and don't have to be told.

"It beats me," the sound of Joe's voice snatched at her wandering attention, "what you both see in him, since you an' Ann-Charlotte are so different. Maybe he's just one of those men who are all things to all women. It's excitin' but enervatin'."

It's odd, she thought quickly, how we have avoided mentioning him by name. It is almost as though we were afraid to say it.

"He," she set herself, determined to end this oral sparring. "Reese has changed. I used to think he walked around with a sullen anger locked within him. Maybe I was wrong. Anyhow, it isn't there now."

Joe snorted; the sound might have implied disgust or impatience. "Love," he said, "sort of softens a fella up."

"Is that what we were talking about?" She regarded him with an expression of surprised innocence.

"Well," he was serious, "whatever it is, don't let it lead him into any of those scruples folks like to think of as honorable."

"Do you know," she attempted to work the thought out as she spoke, "I think there was a time when the idea of making love to Cary's wife would have appealed to him as a fantastic joke. Sometimes," she hesitated, "sometimes I even think that is one of the reasons why he wanted Cary to marry me."

Joe stared at her in amazement. "That's pretty long-range plannin' for any fella."

"No." She followed the suggestion, worrying and pursuing it to

268

the end, suddenly convinced it was not untenable. "No. It wouldn't have been to anyone who knew Cary as well as Reese did."

"And . . . it's all changed now?" Joe waited.

"I—I think so. Oh, that's nonsense! I know so. It's a little ironic, isn't it? Now he wouldn't take what he could have because he has stopped thinking about himself."

"You make a little sense," Joe admitted grudgingly, "but not a hell of a lot."

"With all of this talk," she looked appealingly up at him, "we haven't said much about Cary, have we?"

"No one ever talks about the husband in such cases." Joe was laughing silently. "Sometimes he doesn't even have the doubtful privilege of being felt sorry for. When one dog runs off with another dog's bone, the rest of the pack chases after him. They don't sit around commiseratin' with the one who got stole from."

"Do you know"—there was a hushed appreciation in the question—"there is a certain, lacy delicacy in your conversation at times; a charm so elusive it damn near escapes me."

"Like hell it does." Joe was enjoying himself, then he sobered. "I wouldn't worry much about Cary. He'll get over it and even take a small amount of gloomy satisfaction in what happened. It ain't every day a fella's wife runs off with his best friend. Usually she takes up with some stranger she met at a bar or had the stateroom next to hers or even stood close to in an elevator. The husband don't generally get the benefit of a noddin' acquaintance with the other man."

"So," she suppressed a smile with difficulty, "it would actually be something of a favor to Cary?"

Joe scratched thoughtfully at his ear, matching her serious expression. "I guess you might say so. There may be a few conflictin' opinions on the subject, but generally speakin' you'd all be better off."

Lillith turned her back on the river. Through the broad, leaded panes of the windows she could see Cary, glass in hand, talking with Joe's Negro, Tom. He seemed happy, almost animated, and she felt a sharp tug of sympathy.

"Buy a girl a drink, will you, Joe?" She said impudently.

"Don't want to talk any more?"

"Not about the same thing." She took his hand. "It will take a little thinking from now on."

"Don't fool yourself." They moved toward the front doors. "You've already made up your mind. From this point on, it's only a question of the modus operandi."

"I still think a girl ought to wait until she's asked. No one has yet said: "Flee with me, wench. Maybe I'm taking a whole lot for granted."

Cary had been enjoying himself. Joe's Scotch had a fine, smoky flavor and there was plenty of it at hand. Tom, between mixing drinks for him, had been flatteringly attentive to such observations on life and politics as he cared to make. It had been a damn sight better than sitting outside with Ann-Charlotte around, and Lillith seemed to get along well with Uncle Joe. This was the way to spend an evening, with no one interfering with what the other person wanted to do. He glowed with the thought. Uncle Joe understood how to live. He never filled his house with a lot of damn fools. From now on this was the way things were going to be run on The Hill; just a few friends who knew how to behave and drink quietly. Lillith would like that, too. That was the trouble with the parties they had, always so many people he had to take care of. The first thing he knew he was tight, trying to drink with everyone. He considered the problem somewhere in the bottom of his glass and then thrust it into Tom's waiting hand for refilling.

"Yessuh." Tom took the glass doubtfully. "Yessuh, right away," he added without enthusiasm.

This young Mistuh Whitfiel', he thought, was about the drinkines' man he'd ever seen at Bluestone. He never did seem to know when he was gettin' drunk. He was a-swayin' right now like one o' them river reeds with a breeze on it. All the time he kep' drinkin' he kep' talkin' slow nonsense about how a man should only have a few drinks after dinner for his stummick's sake, an' all the time he was polishin' off a whole quart. White people were crazy with their kin. As he padded off in the direction of the buffet, he glanced back and was relieved to see Joe and Lillith in the doorway. It's time, he muttered to himself. It's sure God time they was gettin' in to take care of him.

Cary looked up at the sound of Lillith's voice and smiled. It was a frightening grimace, twitching and uncertain. He was glad Lil was coming in. He wanted her to understand he didn't have to get drunk just because he decided to go off the wagon. Anyhow—he straightened his shoulders with a touch of belligerency—going on the wagon was something a man could decide for himself.

"I was jus' comin' out. Tom's fixin' me a short drink." The words were fuzzy.

270

"Let's sit down, shall we?" Lillith took his arm and led him un-protestingly to a couch. "Uncle Joe and I were going to have a drink. Now we can have one together."

After one shrewd glance Joe ignored Cary, pretending not to see the unsteady trembling of his legs as he attempted to walk across the room. He felt sorry for Lillith, though. There was something degrading in having to take care of a lush when he was so certain he wasn't drunk.

Something is wrong, Lillith thought, but I don't feel anything. It's all gone. Where? It's gone and I can't feel badly. I don't even care. This is my husband. I married him. I've shared his bed and known ecstasy with his body. I've spent a thousand intimate and tender moments in his arms. I ought to feel something now. I should at least be angry, but I'm not. Cary's head drooped and he caught it with a convulsive jerk. Even this helpless gesture failed to move her. There had been times, as she watched him nodding in a chair, when she experienced disgust or impatience. There was something terrify-ing about a body without normal reflexes. The halting movements of a spastic made her shudder. Gently she eased Cary into a corner of the couch. He settled there with a small grunt of satisfaction. But, she said to herself, I would have done that for a stranger. That is how he felt when I touched him. A stranger. But things don't end that way. They can't be snapped off. They trail away in little agonies.

She looked up. Tom was standing before her with a frosted high-ball on a silver tray. She took it, pressing the cold glass into her palm. Joe came in from the dining room carrying a drink. He looked down at Cary, who was nodding, chin touching his shirt front.

"I'm sorry," he said and there was no mistaking his concern.

"But," she wanted him to understand, "it isn't your fault. It isn't anyone's fault, not even his. I don't know when I learned that, but I did."

"It's part of growing up. Some people catch on sooner than others. After you've absorbed enough of it, you become known as a charitable character."

Half asleep, Cary murmured. It was a small and fretful sound, the meaningless whimper of a child. His hand groped without purpose, a fumbling, indefinite motion, and after a moment Lillith slipped her fingers through his. It was a gesture of friendly comfort. It is queer, she thought, but I can like him now when a personal issue no longer exists. There was relief in the knowledge. She wanted to say: Hey, chum. Wake up. You're tight again. Those were the words she might have used in dealing with an old and close acquaintance whose weakness she understood but didn't have to live with. It's so easy, she thought. Why did I ever imagine it would have to be complicated. She looked at Joe, believing, somehow, he must understand what had happened.

Reese and Ann-Charlotte came in from the porch at that moment. "Have you two settled the world's problems yet?" Ann-Charlotte called from the doorway and then her eyes fell upon Cary. "Not quite, I can see that," she added.

The tone of her voice angered Lillith for a minute. It was unnecessarily contemptuous. She glanced past her at Reese. His presence seemed to fill the room. My God, she thought, I'm beginning to feel like a schoolgirl.

"Have a drink or some coffee?" Joe broke the lengthening silence.

"I think we'd better get back to The Hill." Lillith shook her head. She nudged Cary's shoulder. "Cary?"

In his sleep Cary's mouth puckered into the helpless expression of a lost child. "Lil." The name was uttered as a distant call. "Lil?" He repeated her name with rising insistence.

If he cries now or calls again, she thought frantically, I won't be able to stand it. I'll go mad.

"Yes, Cary." She answered him soothingly, and recognizing her voice, he nodded and went back to sleep.

"I'll take care of him." Reese came over and slipped a hand beneath Cary's arm. "You go and powder your nose, or something. I'll meet you in the car."

Grateful and relieved, she rose and hurried from the room. Somehow, she felt, it wouldn't be so bad if just she, Uncle Joe, and Reese were witnesses to Cary's collapse. Ann-Charlotte's cold, unspoken scorn made it seem sordid; something that should be taking place in a gutter.

She waited in the dining room, pressing her forehead against the cool glass of a window and fighting against following, in her mind, Reese's slow progress with Cary across the porch, down the steps, and finally to the car. The dragging scrape of Cary's feet; the peculiar, twisting position they took as he tried to walk, that made them seemed deformed; the limp heaviness of his body as he leaned against Reese—these things she had seen too many times. She pounded

272

the heel of her fists lightly on the window frame, shutting her eyes against the picture.

Not until she was certain Reese had reached the car and Cary was settled in the seat did she turn and walk from her hiding place. This doesn't make any sense, she assured herself. It's all over and can't make any difference now. We'll sit down and discuss it as intelligent, sensible adults. No one can be expected to live through one nightmare after another.

Ann-Charlotte and Reese were in the front seat of the car when she came down to the driveway, and Joe was standing by the rear door, holding it open for her. Cary was snoring lightly in the far corner. She hesitated, reluctant to enter and wanting to ask Ann-Charlotte to move over so she might ride with them. Instead she turned to Joe.

"Thank you for the handout." She took his hand. "It's been a nice evening."

He closed the door after her. "You come again whenever you like." She caught his smile in the gloom. "I don't suppose I've said that to more than half a dozen people in my entire life." He turned to Ann-Charlotte. "I don't have to ask you," he said pleasantly. "You'd come whether I liked it or not and," the confession seemed to surprise him, "I usually do. Good night, Reese."

An uncomfortable silence closed about them as Reese drove out and to the highway. It was as though all three realized something had happened that needed to be thought over, each in his or her way. They were in Winton's outskirts before anyone spoke, and then Ann-Charlotte rested her chin on the back of the seat and looked at Lillith.

"I'm lonely," she said and there was a subdued note of surprise in her voice. "All of a sudden I'm lonely. I haven't felt this way since I was a little girl and used to dream I was floating down a great, muddy, churning river. I never seemed to get wet, but there was nothing but dirty yellow water and bobbing pieces of driftwood all about me. The dream had no end. I was just there, alone. That's how I feel tonight."

"That's a curious dream." As she spoke Lillith knew the remark was inane, but there seemed nothing else to say.

"Probably filthily Freudian," something of the usual flippancy crept into Ann-Charlotte's tone, "but I never bothered to find out."

Lillith lit a cigarette, conscious that Ann-Charlotte was studying her expression as it was caught briefly in the match's glow. She leaned back in the corner and wondered what Reese was thinking about.

"Chatty bitch, aren't you?" Ann-Charlotte said after a moment and turned abruptly about to face the road. "All right, then, I'll just be an old stick floating down a dirty river."

XXV

I'm going to be sick, Lillith said incredulously to herself. I'm going to be sick, now. She was. The spasm came without warning. One moment she had been brushing her teeth, feeling fine and humming a ridiculous, bubbling tune through the toothpaste's foam. Then this gripping, overpowering sense of nausea. It left her as it had come; quickly. After a moment she straightened up and walked weakly to the basin and stared at her reflection in the bathroom mirror.

I don't believe it. The face in the glass echoed her words without conviction. I won't believe it. She leaned slightly forward. Do you understand? It's some crazy mistake. Something we had for dinner last night has upset my stomach. This, this other thing. Well, I'm late, that's all. There isn't anything unusual about that, is there? Those things happen. It could happen to anyone. Maybe, her silent argument gathered madness, maybe it's the water up here in the mountains, the altitude. Maybe. Oh, my God! Desperation clouded her eyes. Maybe you're pregnant as you knew you were.

She held on to the sides of the porcelain bowl and looked helplessly at the girl in the glass. It's fantastic, she assured the image. After all these years. He stayed sober one night a month ago. One night out of six months he didn't drink, and so when you came to bed he was awake. You didn't try to pretend. You just lay there because you were his wife and he asked you so desperately, and when it was all over you wanted to cry and did, later. Do you remember how you cried? You wept, not because of what had happened, but because you were ashamed it could mean so little. It would have been honest and decent to have said: No. It's all over. It's been over for such a long time. You wouldn't do that, though. You had to take the easy way.

With a gesture of weariness she thrust her hair back with one hand, angry when the girl in the mirror mimicked the motion.

You see, she said earnestly, it couldn't be. You're nervous and upset. The doctor told you a long time ago. What did the doctor tell you? He said: There's nothing wrong with you, Mrs. Whitfield.

275

Perhaps you'd better ask Cary to come and see me. You never did, though, did you? You just took it for granted that it couldn't happen. Now, what in the name of God are you going to do?

She backed away from the mirror and automatically took a robe from a hook on the door. From the window she could look down at the sloping lawn behind the lodge. The pool glinted icily beneath the morning's sun. One of the boys was cutting flowers for the breakfast table. She had intended to put on a bathing suit and go down and help him before taking a swim. He was a stupid Negro, cutting whatever was close at hand and too lazy to make a selection. She had an insane desire to scream down now and tell him he was a shiftless idiot.

Hastily she turned from the window. I'll be talking to myself in a minute, she warned. I'll be walking around muttering and mumbling. She went out into the dressing room adjoining their bedroom and snatched a scanty bathing suit from a chair.

I'll go swimming. I'll dive off the tower. I'll do back flips from the board. I'll take one of the horses and ride up and down these damned mountains. I won't have a baby. I won't. I won't. I won't.

Cary was asleep. They had been over at the Cranstons last night. She hadn't wanted to go to a party. For the week they had all been at the lodge she had tried to make an opportunity to talk with him. We're going to be sensible; adult. The phrase rang in her head now. I'm going to be adult, she thought wildly. I'm going to be a mother. That's adult enough. She looked through the connecting door. Cary was sprawled on one of the beds, an arm flung across his eyes to block out the light. She tiptoed in and lowered the shades. I don't want him to awaken now, she breathed the words. I don't want to talk to anyone for a few minutes. Please, God, don't let Ann-Charlotte or Reese or Cary wake up for a little while until I've had a chance to think.

Usually she stopped in the kitchen to say hello to the girls on her way to the pool. This morning she ducked quickly out a side door. The gravel on the driveway cut into her feet, and she realized she had come out without slippers. When she tried to walk through the grass, the ground was cold and wet, soggy with dew. She hurried, possessed by the notion that something or someone was following. The boy with the flowers looked up, tugged at a ragged straw hat and called good morning. She didn't answer.

The first plunge into the pool hit her with a stunning, icy shock.

She gasped for breath and then swam with hard, decisive strokes from one end to the other until her body had thrown off the chill and left her glowing with warm vitality. Now, she thought, take your time. You're too old for hysterics; and anyhow, you could be wrong. Peeling off the tight rubber cap she shook out her heavy hair with a confident, almost gay toss of her head and then searched for a cigarette through the pockets of her robe. These simple, commonplace actions, somehow, gave her a new feeling of confidence. Drawing heavily on the cigarette, she stood at the edge of the pool and watched the garden boy as he plodded up the hill to the house.

They had come to the lodge two days after Joe Whitfield's barbecue. She tried to delay the trip, desperately seeking a reasonable excuse to keep them on The Hill. She was afraid once they reached the mountains the summer would drag through the weeks leaving everything as it was and, she was certain, could not remain. It was dangerous to temporize and falter; dangerous and pathetically futile for them all. Cary had been so eager to get away from Winton, and he couldn't, or wouldn't, understand her reluctance to leave.

"But you've always liked the mountains." He was puzzled by her indecision. "It's going to get pretty hot here in a couple of weeks. You won't like that."

Because she could think of no valid excuse for not going to the lodge, she finally agreed. Simple things had suddenly become so complex. Even saying yes or no was difficult. Time after time she had steeled herself to the point of saying: Let's sit down and talk things over, Cary. The opportunity never seemed to present itself. After a while she became obsessed by the notion Cary was anticipating her resolutions and cunningly avoided being left alone with her. With one innocently deceptive subterfuge after another he made an exchange of confidences impossible. It was as though he had keyed himself to the idea that once they were away from The Hill, matters would resolve themselves and everything would be as it had been. There was apprehension, something close to fear, in his eyes when he looked at her. He had about him the air of a man condemned but uncertain of the sentence. She wondered how he knew. Outwardly nothing had changed. At least, she tried constantly to maintain a surface calm; alert to the reflections of everything she did or said. Perhaps, she thought, I'm trying too hard. It must show.

Ann-Charlotte wasn't fooled for a moment. She regarded her sister-in-law with an eager attitude of humorous speculation, watching her as a mother might note the first, uncertain steps of an infant.

"Some women are born for intrigue," Ann-Charlotte smiled knowingly one morning across her coffee cup. "I'm afraid it isn't your metier, darling."

"I wasn't thinking of adopting it as a career." Lillith refused to be pushed off balance by the suddenness of the assault or the innocence in which Ann-Charlotte cloaked it. If the thing was to come out, she thought quickly, it had better be now while we are alone.

Ann-Charlotte yawned. "Even as a temporary diversion it's likely to be unprofitable," she said. "You're competing with the old master."

Lillith extinguished her cigarette in the remaining coffee. "The technique does creak sometimes at that," she said quietly.

Ann-Charlotte brightened. "And I love you, too, dear. Isn't it vile how bitchy women can get?"

Lillith couldn't resist a smile. "Without even trying, either," she admitted proudly.

They left the table arm in arm, chatting amiably, and went out to join Cary and Reese on the porch.

Lillith dropped her half-smoked cigarette to the ground and reached for her robe. The wind, seeping down through the small ravines, was chilly. She shivered and looked at the pool. It was leaden and cold. There must be easier ways of doing this, she thought. Anyhow, I'm hungry. She caught herself. My God. What am I saying? I'm never hungry in the morning. This is what they must mean about eating for two. She covered her mouth with her hand; a gesture of mock astonishment. I can't make a joke out of this; she felt an almost uncontrollable desire to laugh a little wildly. It isn't funny. I want to run back to the house, awaken everyone and say: Listen, I'm pregnant. We've got to do something about it. You've got to help me. I'm trapped. She shook her head, trying to clear it of the insane fancy.

On the way up the path she glanced at the empty windows and thought angrily of Cary, Ann-Charlotte, and Reese. Behind those curtains they were sleeping, probably even snoring. No one gave a damn what was happening to her. Surreptitiously, trying to pretend to herself she wasn't conscious of what she was doing, she slid her hand beneath the robe and laid it, for a moment, on her abdomen. It was flat, normal. She sighed with unaffected relief and straightened her shoulders with a defiant gesture. I'm crazy; she adopted a firm attitude toward herself. The whole thing is nothing more than imagination. Imagination and a little case of indigestion. Oh, I wish I could talk with Reese! I wish he would talk to me.

That was the trouble. Reese hadn't said anything, not even after that night at Uncle Joe's when he must have known or needed only to look at her to see. He must understand. When two persons are in love, they don't have to resort to words. Her footsteps lagged. Who, she asked herself, who said Reese was in love with you? Has he ever said anything or done so much as to touch your hand when it wasn't necessary? The thought startled and frightened her. Uncle Joe had said it, but how did Joseph Whitfield know what Reese Benton was thinking? I said it. She repeated the statement. I said it. There was no conviction in the small voice speaking within her. But I know. What do I want?—a lace surrounded heart on Valentine's day? Maybe someone ought to chalk on a wall: Reese Loves Lil.

She reconstructed the morning after the dinner at Bluestone. Both Cary and Ann-Charlotte had slept late, and when she came out of her room Reese was just turning at the stairs.

"If you're going swimming, I'll go with you," she called softly, and he nodded.

"I'll wait for you down on the porch," he said.

They had been swimming in the morning before breakfast a hundred or more times. Cary preferred a shower. There wasn't anything different about this morning, but she approached it with almost breathless expectancy and was vaguely disappointed when Reese seemed indifferent to its possibilities. As they walked to the lake she took his hand, not coquettishly but with a buoyant feeling of confidence. Their locked fingers swung between them, but he dropped her hand as casually as he had accepted it when they reached the dock.

Later, as she was dressing, she hummed softly to herself and was almost guiltily conscious of the fact she was moving with extra care in order not to awaken Cary. Leaving the room, she paused and hoped Ann-Charlotte would have breakfast upstairs as she usually did. This was a day to be held cherishingly, and too many hands must not be allowed to touch it. Then—she could remember her surprised regret—nothing happened.

After breakfast Reese had said he was going down into Winton for cigarettes. Before she thought, she almost said there were plenty upstairs.

"Take me with you?" She waited, almost afraid he would say no.

"Sure. Ready?"

They picked up half a dozen cartons of cigarettes in the town and then drove out along the river road. The morning air was fresh and exhilarating, sweeping through the rushing open car with steady pressure. She tucked one foot beneath her and sat straight in the seat, tilting her face back to look up at the sky.

"You look like a radiator cap ornament." Reese darted a quick look at the clean line of her profile.

"I guess that's a compliment." Her head dropped. "This is sort of fun. Most of the time I ride down here by myself in the mornings."

"I had an idea you slipped away to meet a hermit."

"I used to look, but the only one I could find was Uncle Joe." She straightened her leg and stretched beneath the dash. "He's too smart for me."

Reese nodded and turned his attention to the road. Last night, she thought, Uncle Joe had said run away. Run away both of you and never look back. How can you run away with a man who seems to be more than satisfied to stay where he is? Dropping her cheek against the upholstery she could snatch a glimpse of Reese's face now and then without his being aware of the inspection.

"Reese?" Her voice was faint.

"Uh-huh?"

She didn't answer immediately and he tossed a quick glance her way. There was a mild, almost amused, curiosity in the look as if he knew what she wanted to say and was betting with himself she wouldn't.

"Nothing." She made the reply unnecessarily short. Men, she thought, have the better of things all the way. A man could say: Listen, baby, let's get the hell out of this place. We'll just keep on going in the car. It will create one big scandal and everyone will say Reese Benton is the louse who ran away with his best friend's wife, but we won't have to be around to listen. He could say that and she could say yes and there would be an end to this nonsense. How could a woman say such a thing? And, if she did, suppose the man said: But I don't want to run away with you. What does she do then?

"Will you eat a second breakfast?" He slowed the car as they approached a dirt road running off toward the river.

"Here?" She sat up and looked around with interest.

Reese drove up alongside a small whitewashed shack leaning a little drunkenly on the shore. A thin blue vine of smoke curled up from a rusty tin pipe, and the air was rich with the scent of burning pine.

A couple of Negro children, wearing nothing but ragged shirts, sat in the dirt near the cabin and eyed them with finger-sucking, unblinking gravity. Above the building was a crudely scrawled sign: Fresh Fish. Cafe.

They sat on the top of the back rest, their feet on the seat, and ate sandwiches made with thick, highly seasoned sausage cakes, and drank coffee from heavy mugs. A heavy-breasted colored woman wearing a faded calico print dress sat in a rowboat moored to the shore and watched the cork float on the end of her line.

"I'll bet she doesn't catch anything there," Lillith whispered.

"There are always a couple of lazy fish hanging around the bank," he said, "and if you can catch them it saves the trouble of rowing out into the river and back again." He took her empty cup. "Hey, you chillun," he called. The larger of the two came over and shyly accepted the mugs. When Reese dropped a dollar in her palm she stared at it unbelievingly for a moment and then shut her hand around it and dashed inside the house without a word.

They drove back to The Hill without hurrying, and Lillith wondered a little sadly why such a simple thing as a ride and a cup of coffee at a Negro's riverbank shack could have the flavor of adventure.

"That was fun, Reese," she said thoughtfully. "Just fun without any reason. I'd sort of forgotten about it."

"The place has been there as long as I can remember." She realized he was evading her unexpressed question. "I think I'm the only customer."

"Will you take me again sometime?"

He looked at her then, steadily, until she dropped her eyes. "I'll take you," was all he said, and somehow, for the moment it seemed enough.

They were in the driveway to The Hill before she spoke again, and even as the words were shaped she realized how perversely she was attempting to force something from him.

"Do you think we ought to go to the lodge this summer, Reese?"

He dropped into second gear and allowed the car to creep along the incline.

"I don't think it will make any difference, Lil. Time is running out. You know that and so do I."

"You're being a little overgenerous, aren't you?" Her voice was low but edged.

"No, just realistic. I don't think geography has anything to do with it."

There it was. She went over the words as she walked up the wide stone steps to the lodge's rear door. In the kitchen she could hear the girls at work, and there was a cheerful clatter in the sounds they made. She sniffed at the scent of coffee and bacon and realized she was ravenous. The maid Lucy came out on the porch, and she called to her.

"I'm starving, Lucy. Do something about it, will you?"

"Yes'm." The girl grinned broadly. "Whinevah youah riddy."

Cary turned over heavily when she entered the room and looked without recognition for a moment. Then his face cleared as the sight of her drove the sleep from his eyes.

"Where did you go? I woke up a little while ago and you weren't here." His attitude was almost petulant.

"Swimming. It's cold." She slipped into the other room and stripped out of the damp suit.

"Why didn't you wake me?" He was nagging and the call was querulous.

"You know you never like the pool in the morning." I'm not going to be annoyed, she said firmly to herself as she dressed. I'm not going to allow him to make me angry. I can't be upset. I'm—I'm a woman with child. She stiffened. Good God. Why do I have to try and make a joke of it?

"Did you go alone?" Cary's voice hammered at her.

"No, dear. I went with the Seventh Confederate Regiment. They are all downstairs now, waiting to escort me to breakfast. After that we are going to shoot a Yankee spy as target practice."

There was a momentary silence. "I only asked." Cary was weakly apologetic, sensing her gathering impatience. "You don't have to get sore."

She came into the bedroom, smoothing at the waist of the brightly colored peasant dress she wore. "I'm not angry, Cary. It just seemed silly. Where did you go? Who was with you? What did you do?"

"I didn't mean anything." He pulled himself out of the bed and stood, tousled and uncertain. He ventured a smile. "I'll have a shower and come down to eat with you and the Seventh Confederate Cavalry."

"Regiment," she corrected from the door, "and hurry. They have a date to save Richmond this morning."

Dancing lightly down the steps, she kept asking herself: What am

I feeling so good about? Don't tell me I am going to like this? The thoughts sobered her to a sedate walk. This is simply one hell of a note, Lillith Payne Whitfield, and if you think you can laugh it off, you're crazy.

The table was set on the east porch overlooking the valley. Places had been laid for four. I'll have company, she mused, and somewhere between the fruit and eggs I'll put aside my spoon and announce with lowered and fluttering eyelashes: I am caught.—What a ghastly expression!

She walked over to the railing, wrapped her arms about one of the posts and leaned her head against its rough natural surface, staring down through the folded hills over which the morning mist floated like a trembling scarf.

I'll go to Winton, she told herself, and see Dr. Cochrane. Then I'll know. I have to know, and there is no sense in waiting.

She was having her first cup of coffee when Cary joined her. He was drawn and the skin seemed to be stretched tightly over his cheekbones, giving him a lean, almost saturnine appearance.

"What become of the Seventh Regiment?" he asked, making a feeble attempt to perpetuate the meaningless joke.

"Sherman's around the bend, yonder," she answered, "an' they had to get out fustust. Coffee?"

He accepted the cup and his spoon rattled against the lip. He put it down with an exclamation of impatience and tried to smile.

"What time did we get home last night?"

"I don't know. It wasn't much fun. I didn't pay any attention to the time." She braced herself mentally. "I'm going back to Winton this morning." She tried to make the statement sound matter-of-fact.

Cary nodded with unattentive affability, and then, as he realized what she had said, he halted in the act of raising the cup to his lips.

"Winton?" He repeated the word as though he had never heard it before. "Why do you want to go to Winton? We just came up here."

"I'll be back, late this evening or tomorrow."

"But why are you going to Winton?"

"There's something I want to do, Cary." She tried to keep a note of exasperation from her voice. After all, his question wasn't unreasonable.

"Can't you get what you want in Asheville?"

"No."

"Well," he considered this for a moment, "I'll go with you then."

"I don't want anyone to go with me." She was being patient, displaying an exasperating forbearance. "I'm simply going into Winton and coming back. Is there anything so unusual about that?"

"Of course there is." His voice rose and she knew he was right. "If there is something you want, we can send for it or have one of the boys from The Hill bring it up. There's no reason for you to go."

"I have a lover there and he can only see me on Tuesdays." She knew she was being ridiculous. It would have been simpler to say she didn't feel well and wanted to see Dr. Cochrane.

Reese came out then and put an end to the foolish spitefulness nagging at her.

"Hi." He pulled up a chair. "Can I get a handout?"

"Lil's going over to Winton today." Cary made the statement and then seemed to wait for an expression of surprise. When Reese only nodded, he frowned. "Alone," he added.

"It's not a bad drive." Reese took the cup from Lillith and then lit a cigarette.

She experienced a sudden impatience with him. Didn't he care? Didn't anything ever move him to interest? Oh, she thought with horror, I am becoming absurd! Maybe it has something to do with, well, with IT. Next thing anyone knows I will be wanting a cold quince or whatever it is women ask for in the middle of the night. I wonder why anyone would want a cold quince?

Ann-Charlotte joined them, and Lillith looked at her with a little twinge of envy. She wore crisp white slacks, a soft cream-colored shirt, small sandals of gilded leather, and had a bright blue bandanna over her blonde hair. She's exquisite, Lillith thought, and makes me feel like a dusty wren.

"What were you doing in the pool at daybreak?" Ann-Charlotte kicked out a chair and dropped into it. "Or did you spend the night there?"

You'd be up early yourself, my girl, Lillith thought, if you had what I have. She smiled. "No. I woke up and a swim seemed a good idea. It was cold, though."

"Lil's going to Winton." Cary made the announcement glumly, and Lillith felt like reaching over and shaking him.

"Bored?" Ann-Charlotte dropped a lump of sugar in her cup.

"No." This is preposterous, Lillith thought. "No, I only want to go to Winton."

"Nice day for it." Ann-Charlotte stretched her legs comfortably. "Want company?"

For a moment Lillith was tempted to say yes, but she changed her mind. "No. It's sort of an Eagle Scout test to see if I can find my way there and back alone."

"Do you get a medal or a scoutmaster if you win?" Ann-Charlotte sampled her coffee.

"I'm going over to the club." Cary rose. He was angry. "Damn foolishness, running off to Winton. I don't know what can be such a secret." He pushed past the table and walked away.

"Daddy's mad, Daddy's mad," Ann-Charlotte chanted.

"Go to the devil." He hurried down the steps without a backward glance.

Lillith went upstairs and packed a small bag on the chance she might break the trip back by spending the night in Asheville. When she came downstairs again, Reese was in the hall.

"Be careful," he said.

She nodded and picked up a light coat from a chair. He walked across and held it for her and for a moment his hands remained on her shoulders.

"You're coming back?" He spoke quietly, but there was no disguising the concern in his voice.

Lillith didn't move, although she wanted to lean backward against him and have him hold her there, gently but firmly.

"I'll be back," she whispered.

"Getting up a parade?"

Reese dropped his hands and they both turned. Ann-Charlotte was standing in the doorway watching them with unsmiling interest.

"A snake dance," Reese answered with matching flippancy.

Ann-Charlotte nodded and tapped the butt from her cigarette holder into an ash stand. "There's probably some Biblical allegory in that remark," she said calmly, "but its significance escapes me at the moment."

Lillith picked up her bag. She wanted to get out of the house. Tempers were a little too obvious and ugly. "If I decide to stay overnight," she said, "I'll telephone."

"Do, dear." Ann-Charlotte said. "We'll be worried."

Reese walked to the car with her. "Watch yourself on the curves," he said, closing the door.

Lillith grinned, thinking of Ann-Charlotte. "That's good advice

285

even if you aren't in an automobile." She backed slowly around. "At least the Highway Department puts up warning signs."

She drove with furious concentration for the first ten miles. The top was down, and the wind snatched and worried at her hair. I'll bet I look like hell, she thought and derived a morbid satisfaction from the idea. Next your face gets pasty and then something happens. I forget what, but it isn't good. After that it's up to the doctor and Lane Bryant.

It was early afternoon before she reached Winton. Coming into it alone this way made the town seem new and unfamiliar, and she drove down Monument Avenue with the interest of a tourist. I must visit here again sometime, she said to herself, and meet some of the people.

Dr. Cochrane's nurse had been comfortingly unimpressed by Lillith's recital of impending catastrophe as she prepared her for examination. When she was wound in a sheet Lillith took one look at herself in a mirror and wailed:

"Can't they do this with rabbits or something? Do you mean I have to be poked and peered at?"

"I'm afraid so, Mrs. Whitfield. Now, if you'll come with me."

The examination had been easier than she imagined it would be. Later she sat in Cochrane's office, perched on the edge of her chair like some truant child in the principal's office.

"Well," Cochrane was cheerily complacent, "congratulations, Mrs. Whitfield."

You idiot, Lillith wanted to shout. You pink-faced foxy-grandpa! Don't sit there and beam at me. What in the name of God am I going to do?

Concern must have displayed itself on her face, and the doctor leaned over and patted her gently on the hand.

"Now," he was professionally soothing, "don't you worry. There's no reason why it shouldn't be a perfectly normal, easy experience. You come in and see me once a month for a check."

She left the office, unable to do more than nod her understanding of the instructions, and for a long time sat in her car at the curb, staring blankly down the busy street. I suppose, she thought desperately, I could go to another doctor and have something done about it. Why, why, *why* did it have to happen now?

She looked at her watch and debated the problem of returning to the lodge. It would be late before she reached Harlen, and she didn't

286

like to drive at night. I'll go to The Hill, she decided, get a jug and crawl in the tomb with Old Andy. It's all his fault anyhow. Why did he have children?

She had dinner in the big dining room, feeling small and desperately alone and just a little ridiculous as though she were the only guest at a masquerade. Even the three cocktails before the meal hadn't seemed to help. I'll pretend I'm Queen Victoria, or was it Elizabeth or Bloody Mary who used to eat by herself? I'm going to get drunk, so it couldn't be Victoria. I'm sure she was never tight and pregnant at the same time.

She called the lodge and left word she wouldn't be back. Lucy told her everyone had gone to the club. Later she walked down to the lake, opened the boathouse, turned on all the lights and tuned in the radio. Then she mixed a tall brandy and soda and sat on a stool at the bar.

"A bunch of the boys were whoopin' it up," she caroled with a dismal croak. "A bunch of the boys were whoopin' it up. I forget where. And the kid that tickled the music box. Hey!" she yelled at her reflection in the mirror. "Don't let's talk about kids."

The brandy was pleasantly assuasive, and after a second one she was calmer and able to think clearly. There's no point in turning and twisting, she philosophized; you're going to have a baby. You can tell Cary and leave him, or you tell him nothing and leave with your unborn child. Good God, what a phrase. It sounds like an advertisement for a Persian lamb coat. What are you going to tell Reese? Are you going to say: Beg pardon, sir, but would you mind waiting while I have a baby? But maybe Reese wouldn't expect her to tell him anything. Hadn't he asked her, though, if she would be back? That had to mean something; or did it?

She went behind the bar and mixed herself a fresh drink. I'll get potted and go reeling around the grounds until Tod or one of the boys finds me in the morning.

Returning to the stool, she hunched over the drink, holding it in both hands and peering down through the ice cubes.

"If you can read tea leaves," she said aloud, "there ought to be something in ice cubes." She looked accusingly at her reflection. "You're getting drunk. I am a maiden all forlorn blessed with a child as yet unborn." She chanted the dirge. "Bottoms up."

She went behind the bar a third time, but instead of mixing a drink she placed bottle, siphon, and a small bucket of ice before her stool.

"You have to conserve your strength, Lil," she cautioned solemnly and reseated herself; "mustn't overdo things. Remember your delicate condition."

With a sudden gesture she swept out with both hands, clearing the bar of bottles and glass in a crashing fling, then buried her head in her arms and cried, her sobs echoing with dry and empty misery.

After a few minutes she rose, thrusting the back of her arm against her forehead with a motion of despair. Dully she flicked off the radio switch and then the lights, and walked silently across the dock and up the slope toward the house.

288

XXVI

THE return trip to the mountains the next morning seemed disconcertingly short. Dawdle as she would, the car ground steadily away at the miles with exasperating efficiency. In an attempt to delay the inevitable Lillith stopped over in Asheville for lunch, which she didn't want and couldn't eat. Later she spent a couple of hours shopping for things she didn't need. Finally, when she could think of no more excuses, she gave in and settled down for the short run to Harlen.

I'm a gal with a load of mischief, she thought as the stone gates to the lodge grounds loomed before her. There was no escape now. She left the car in the front driveway and mounted the steps with reluctant feet.

All the way back from Winton she had been fighting against this moment. Reese will have to know. Before anyone else I will have to tell him. She couldn't rid herself of the notion that there was something shameful in what had happened. Once, and once only, her sense of humor made a brief rescue. I am acting as though I have been unfaithful to a man who has yet to kiss me. It's legal, by the book and the ring it is. How can a woman commit adultery with her husband?

Behind the tangled emotions crouched small, dark fears. Will he want me now? Can things be the same? Does a man run away with another man's wife under such circumstances? No longer was it a question of how Cary would accept the break when it came. His feelings had suddenly become unimportant. Once the act of leaving him had seemed an almost insurmountable obstacle. So many things were involved. Now she could only ask herself what Reese would do. Ethics, morals, however they might be tagged, were without value. *If he'll only take me.* The reckless cry within her would not be stilled.

Inside the lower hall she called, and after a moment Lucy's sister, Dorah, came from a room to the upstairs balcony.

"Miz Ann-Cha'lut ain' home. Mistuh Cary say he at the club ef you come in. Mistuh Reese out ridin' a horse someplace." Having dutifully accounted for the family, Dorah waited.

Lillith stripped the gloves from her hands and thrust them in her coat pocket. "How long has Mr. Reese been gone?" Self-consciously she tried to make the words sound indifferent.

"Raight aftah lunch."

Lillith nodded. Reese would probably come down over the ridge through the back trail. He usually rode in that direction when he went out. Without hesitation she went outside and walked slowly down past the pool and the stables and began climbing up the slope to the ridge. He'll think I'm crazy, coming to meet him this way. Perhaps I am. If I'm not, I will go mad sitting in the house waiting.

A broad trail snaked over the ridge's spine, twisting in a gradual descent to the valley. Unless he had gone in the direction of Harlen, he would have to come back this way. With the feeling of being both conspicuous and foolish she found a seat on a dead and fallen pine beside the path and waited.

Mrs. Cary Whitfield entertained this afternoon in the copse behind her home. The ridiculous words raced through her mind. The affair was intimate. Mr. Reese Benton, of Winton, was the only guest.

She lit a cigarette. Her foot swung back and forth and the toe of her slipper caught at the ground, gouging out a small hole. Maybe, she thought, I can dig it deep enough to crawl in and hide. Maybe, maybe it will only be big enough to bury a dream.

Through the tangled growth on the ridge she could look down at the lodge and orderly grounds. By contrast to her confused maunderings it seemed revoltingly neat and perfectly managed. Somehow this was all wrong. The world ought to be in a turmoil.

The dead ends of half a dozen cigarettes lay in the hollow at her feet before she heard the steady clop of a horse down the trail. She waited with everything tightly balled within her, struggling against a desire to run into the bushes and hide.

Reese pulled up at the sight of her. He was astonished at finding her on the ridge and made no effort to pretend otherwise. After a moment he swung down and, leading his horse, walked to where she sat.

"Are you lost, little girl?" He watched her eyes.

"No. I was waiting to run off with those gypsies we talked about."

"You ought to go down to the highway. No one but Reese Benton ever comes this way."

"I guess he'll have to do, then." She moved a foot or so on the trunk. "Sit down and I'll tell your fortune."

This isn't the way, she thought frantically. We won't get anyplace if I try to kid about it. Where are all of those bright, brave speeches you memorized on the way back from The Hill? Go ahead, tell him.

Reese dropped the reins over his mount's head and came over, sitting astride the tree in order to confront her. He wasn't smiling.

"Something wrong?" He asked quietly, but he searched her face with eyes sharp and concerned.

"Everything." The hands jammed into the pockets of her loose coat were clenched. "I—I wasn't just taking a walk. I came up to wait for you."

He shook a cigarette from a pack. Offered it to her and allowed it to dangle between his fingers when she refused.

"Before we came to the lodge..." Talking was so difficult and she stared at the ground. "You, you said time was running out for—for both of us. I know what you meant, Reese. Anyhow, I think I do, but I want—I almost have to hear you say it in simple words. It's important."

"Don't you know I would have said it long before this if I hadn't thought it was important?"

"It won't wait any longer, Reese." She lifted her head and met his eyes.

"I love you." His gaze was level, as steady as the word themselves. "That is why I said time was running out, and time is about all we have at the moment."

"And, what were you going to do about it?"

"I'm going to take you away with me." He made it sound so simple she almost believed it. "There was never anything good in it, not even from the beginning. I could have told you then, but I didn't. Sometimes I used to think it was too late and I could only wait and see."

He threw one leg over the trunk and stood up. After a moment he reached down and, with hands beneath her elbows, lifted her. She caught at him, clinging to the rough tweed of his jacket.

"My God, darling. Don't cry." He gathered her to him.

"Kiss me, Reese." The words were torn from her throat. When he bent his face to hers, her mouth was fiercely possessive. "All of this time." The words were muffled. "Where have you been?"

His hand was at her cheek, tilting her face up, and his knuckles wiped tenderly at the tear stain close to her nose.

"Your face is dirty," he said.

"No, Reese." She shook her head sadly. "I have to tell you something. Just hold me this way and I want to look at you as I say it. I think I have to look at you, otherwise I'd never know."

His hand was softly caressing as it reached up and pushed the small hat from her head. It fell to the ground unheeded, and her hair covered his fingers.

"All right," he said and she could feel his arms tighten. There was something protective in their strength, as though he wanted to share it with her. "All right. Now, tell me."

Her eyes held his and she could see herself reflected in them. "I'm going to have a baby. Cary's baby, Reese."

For a moment she felt certain he either hadn't heard or didn't understand. The pressure of his arms was constant and reassuring. The torment was becoming unbearable. She experienced a frantic desire to pound with her fists against his chest and cry: Don't you know what I am saying? As you hold me here and I say I love you I am carrying Cary's child. You don't find them beneath rose bushes no matter what people tell their children. Can you understand how, loving you as I do, I have conceived a child by Cary? Can't you realize what it means, or don't you care?

A finely drawn muscle at the corner of Reese's mouth trembled. It was the only indication of the torture to which she had exposed him. The sight of it made her want to weep and she was almost compelled to touch a soothing finger to the leaping ripple.

"It's strange," his voice and the words were unhurried, "but I think I knew. I can't tell you how, but I even had an idea why you went to Winton."

"I thought of you every moment. When I called I hoped you would answer the telephone. Not because there was anything I wanted to tell you but simply to hear you speak."

"Do you," he seemed to be thinking aloud, "do you want to do it now or later?"

She was uncertain. "What, Reese? What should I do?" There was fear in the question.

He smiled then. It wasn't his usual smile; a little careless, indifferent, springing from a secret well. Instead, it was delicately kind and understanding.

"We just can't pretend it hasn't happened. Do you want to ask Cary for a divorce now or would you rather wait until after the baby is born?"

I'll die here as he holds me, she thought. This way, standing beside him and looking at that almost homely face that is suddenly beautiful.

"And," she hesitated to answer, "and it doesn't make any difference, Reese? If you sensed what had happened, then you know how and, maybe, why?"

"I think so."

She breathed with deep gratitude. "Then I'd like to stay, Reese. I'll stay, not as Cary's wife. He will have to be told. To go away now and then have a baby born . . ." Her eyes sought his, seeking help.

"You'll feel better about things that way? It is going to be difficult."

"I don't know how I am going to feel," she said honestly. "That doesn't make so much difference right now. I think the baby should be born here or on The Hill as Cary's child. I wouldn't want there to be any question about it. Somehow," her words were shadowed, "I think it would make it cleaner and decent. I don't want any loose ends, Reese. They have a way of getting soiled."

"But you'll tell him?"

"Tonight. Will you be with me? I want everything out in the open."

He kissed her eyes shut and she kept them that way, dropping her head against his coat, rubbing her face into the cloth. He held her without moving, and, somehow, she knew he was staring off across the valley, attempting to measure a reply.

"I'll be with you," he said at last.

She was experiencing the exhaustion of great mental strain. It was difficult to speak, words required effort. "I want to talk with Cary, alone. I—I don't suppose there is any sense in hoping he will understand."

He shook his head. "No, Cary won't understand. What is worse, he won't try."

"You—you won't let him make me stay, Reese?"

His laugh was short and incredulous. "You know better. Come on now." He released her. "Let's go home."

They walked hand in hand down the trail, Reese's horse following with docile obedience. At the stables they stopped for a moment while one of the boys took the animal. Clinging to Reese's hand, Lillith took a deep breath, looked up at him, and smiled suddenly.

"If I had known being in love was like this I would have tried it long ago."

"This is the easy part. Wait until I get you out in the fields planting tobacco."

She looked up quickly and with immediate concern. "That is something." She made the admission with amazement. "Where do we go from here?"

"Does it make any difference?"

"No," she reflected soberly, "no, of course not. I just never stopped to think. You've always seemed so much a part of everything here and on The Hill."

"I'll try not to miss it too much." His fingers tightened through hers and she clung to them confidently. "I imagine I can even support you."

She halted then and gazed earnestly up at him. "It's funny, but I never considered that. It just never occurred to me before. Is it something we should think about?"

He gave her arm a slight tug. "Not to the exclusion of anything else." I'll bet, he thought with tempered humor, Cassius Whitfield never expected I would use his money to support Cary's wife.

As they neared the lodge, their footsteps slowed until they barely moved across the lawn.

"I wish we could just go now, Reese, without saying anything to anyone." She scuffed through the thick carpet of grass, head averted, unwilling to meet his eyes.

"That would be too simple. You don't expect this to be easy, do you?"

"It's strange," her voice was pitched so low the words were almost indistinguishable, "but I do. I don't mean that exactly," she added quickly. "What I'm trying to say is, it means so little, now that I know you want me, it is difficult to believe Cary will care."

"Did you ever imagine I wouldn't want you?"

"It—it isn't quite the same. I mean, what I told you on the ridge has to make a difference."

"No." He didn't attempt to evade the question since she insisted upon raising it. "No. It isn't quite the same. Cary's child will always be there, but not between us. That you can believe."

She turned halfway around, holding his arm with her one free hand. "I'll have to, Reese. I'll keep saying it over and over to myself."

"I won't let you forget." He glanced at his watch. "I'll buy you a drink if you'll wait until I catch a quick shower."

"Go ahead. I'll change." She trotted up the side steps and held the door for him. "Do you know," she leaned over to whisper and her lips brushed his cheek, "I have the feeling this place belongs to us and no one else has any business coming in. I feel extremely bridish, sort of checked-gingham-apronish."

"Your husband and," the small smile broadened into a grin, "and his sister are likely to ruffle those feelings. I'd keep them to myself for a while."

Lillith widened her eyes. "Ooo! What Ann-Charlotte is going to do to you." The laughter died quickly. "Is it wrong, Reese? Is it wrong to feel this way? Shouldn't my conscience be bothering me?"

"Go upstairs," he turned her about and cracked her rear smartly, "and ask it. I lost mine along the road someplace years ago."

"Uncle Joe put me up to this," she called back over her shoulder.
"What?"

"He said run. Run like hell, the two of you, and never look to see who is following."

"That's good advice. In the meantime go and wash your dirty face. I'll meet you down here in fifteen minutes. We'll go over to the club for a drink."

She halted on the first landing and turned to look down. "Dorah said Cary was at the club. He—he left word."

"I know." He watched her. "That's why we are going."

Lillith hesitated, doubt and apprehension appearing on her face. Finally she nodded, turned, and with measured steps continued to the second floor. Holding to the balcony railing with both hands she looked down into his upturned face.

"I suppose you know what is right?" The question was tossed to him.

"Nope. I haven't the slightest idea what is right. I can only guess what would be wrong. Running away from things would be wrong."

"All right." Her smile was fast, trustfully assured. "Be sure and wash behind your ears and don't forget your neck."

Reese waited until she had disappeared into her room. For a few seconds he stood, tapping thoughtfully at the lower step with the toe of his boot, and then his shoulders shrugged with a gesture of acceptance. The words sounded fine when he spoke them to Lillith.

In the shower, and later, as he was dressing, Reese tried to imagine what he was going to say to Cary. There would be no point in attempting to cushion the blow, because Cary would never see where he had failed. It would be Reese who had let him down. Reese who had undermined and betrayed him. I'm going to let him stand up alone and take this, Reese thought. I'm going to say: Lillith and I are going away together because she'll never be happy with you and I think she may have a chance with me. All of my life I have carried the heavy end for you. From this point on you'll have to forget everything that has gone before. This isn't good old Reese talking. I'm not your friend. You have something I want and something you couldn't keep anyhow. I'm going to take it. Now, you can be the bastard I know you are or try and be a man for a few minutes. It wasn't easy. Just saying those things to himself was difficult. Lord, he whispered almost fervently, don't let me develop into a noble character.

Lillith was waiting in the hall. She looked up as he came down the steps, following him with her eyes. When he bent and kissed her, she strained up on her toes and then buried her face in his neck.

"I can't get over the idea this is wrong," she whispered. "Do you suppose this is what they mean by illicit love?"

"No." He laughed at her. "I think there's more to it."

"This is just necking, then?" She pulled away and regarded him with grave concern.

"That's right. Sort of a preliminary warm-up."

"You make it sound so earthy. Oh, Reese," she breathed happily, "it has been so long since I've been able to laugh this way."

He took her by the hand. "Let's go and find the drink I promised you."

"We could have it here." She made the suggestion doubtfully.

"It tastes better when you have to pay for it."

"Everything?"

"Uh-huh. Let's go."

Cary sat alone at a corner table in the club's bar, steeping himself in a dark brew of melancholy and self-commiseration. The sensation was not entirely unpleasant. He had occupied the same chair throughout most of the afternoon with the pained expression of a martyr who wants to be certain his suffering does not pass unnoticed. He drank with moody concentration, shunning companionship and conversation. Drink as he would, the whisky turned to sawdust in his mouth.

No one gave a damn about him, not even his wife who ran away to Winton without a word of explanation. Reese went riding by himself and didn't ask him if he wanted to come along. I'm not a bad guy, he assured himself, but suddenly everything has gone wrong. I'm a good husband, too. Lillith could have anything in the world she wanted. That was part of the trouble. She didn't want anything. Lillith, Reese, and Ann-Charlotte had ganged up the way kids did, and wouldn't let him share in their fun.

He ordered another drink. Reese had changed. You never knew what he was thinking. I wish to God he would marry Ann-Charlotte or go someplace and live with her. I'm sick of seeing her around.

He swallowed the bourbon and shuddered. I'm not feeling well, he said. That's the trouble. I'm sick and no one cares. I'm sick inside. It doesn't show, but it's there. He looked up to call for another drink and saw Ann-Charlotte in the doorway.

She walked the length of the bar, leaned over and patted the top of the bartender's bald head.

"Fix me a little Scotch and soda, Fred."

With the drink in one hand she turned, her back against the bar, and stared at Cary, pretending she didn't recognize him. He made an attempt to ignore her presence and effected an elaborate ceremony of lighting a cigarette. Ann-Charlotte sipped her drink and her glance was level and unwavering across the glass's rim.

"How's business, 'Fred?'" She spoke to the bartender without turning.

"Slow at the moment, Miss Whitfield." He was glad to have someone to talk with.

"That's too bad. I'll do something about it for you." Carrying her drink, she walked to the corner and pulled out a chair across the table from Cary.

"I'll have a drink, Fred," he called to the bartender without looking at her.

"Bring the jug, Fred. We'll be here for a spell," Ann-Charlotte amended the order, and leaned contentedly back in the chair. "Hello, darling. How's the self-immolation racket today?"

"Do you have to drink here?" He regarded her with frank disfavor.

"Someone ought to stay around to help carry you out." She stamped a small series of circles on the table with the damp end of her glass. "Why don't you take up golf or the ouija board?"

Fred brought a bottle of bourbon and a small pitcher of ice water. "Do you want something else, Miss Whitfield?"

She waved him away. "I'll drink straight bourbon with Cary from now on." She pushed the bottle toward Cary. "Here, darling."

"What do you want?" He refused to notice the bottle.

"Don't be coarse, sweetheart. I come to you, dewy-eyed and palpitant, seeking only your charming company. Heard from Lillith?"

"No." He eyed the bottle and then, with assumed indifference, picked it up and poured a drink.

"Have you seen Reese?"

He swallowed the bourbon and felt better immediately. He hoped his laugh was as unpleasant as it sounded to him. "I guess," he said, "Reese is your problem."

"I wonder." Ann-Charlotte was serene. "I'll make a deal with you."

"Why?"

She ignored the question. "I have a home in France. I'll make you a present of it. The summers are wonderful there. You and Lil would have a lot of fun out of the place."

"Why?" He was beginning to like the sound of the word. Also, he could tell it annoyed Ann-Charlotte.

"Since," she said evenly, "subtlety would be wasted at the moment, I'll make it simple and easy to understand. I think Lil is in love with Reese."

For a moment she experienced a feeling of compassion. The frightened panic in his eyes was terrifyingly naked. The sight of it almost made her ashamed.

"You oughtn't to talk that way." He could only whisper. "Even if you don't like me. I know you try to get me sore. You always have, but you shouldn't say such a thing, Ann-Charlotte, even as a joke."

"It wasn't a joke." She waited.

Cary shook his head and a smile tried to force its way to his lips. The effect was pitiful.

"I know. You always try to do this to me. You're, you're sort of the way Uncle Joe used to be when we were kids. He used to say things. I guess he was joking, too." He was pleading for confirmation. "Why," his expression was one of injured bewilderment, "why Lil and Reese; she's all I've ever had. The only person who liked me for myself. The others never counted. I knew what they wanted and it didn't make any difference. Reese. Reese is my friend." He leaned forward and then the argument died in his throat.

I can't do this, Ann-Charlotte told herself, and the thought surprised her. I can't do it. I despise him, but I just can't do it.

"I guess maybe you're right." She slumped in the chair, defeated and secretly reviling herself.

"Sure, I'm right." Cary was trying to convince her. "I know you

298

get sore because Reese," he paused, "well, you know what I mean. But," his eyes sought hers, begging for agreement, "you oughtn't to have said what you did."

"All right, Cary." She sighed.

He poured a drink eagerly and the whisky slopped over the glass and made a small, glistening pool on the table.

"I'm not going to drink any more after tonight." He was proud of the resolution. "I know I've been sort of foolish, but you've never understood how I felt about things. You never needed anyone but yourself." He rested both hands on the table and bent toward her in confidence. "I don't know why, but I've never been sure of things the way you, you and Reese have. That's why, sometimes, I drank too much. Lil understanods."

Ann-Charlotte stared at him with mounting amazement. Why, she thought, he's a little crazy. It's almost sad. My God. What's happening to me? I've never felt sorry for anyone in my life before.

"Here." She was harshly impatient, annoyed with herself and unable to endure the childish supplication in his eyes. "I'll take a drink." She poured the bourbon into the remainder of her Scotch and soda, indifferent to the mixture.

At the sound of voices in the doorway, Cary looked up and his features were momentarily illuminated. Reese and Lillith stood at the entrance. Her arm was linked through his and she had locked it firmly with the other hand. Cary half rose, stumbling against the table, and then he sank back in the seat and dropped his glance to the table.

"Hey, you two." Lillith saw them and called. Her voice was singing. "A man picked me up and said he'd buy me a drink here. Is it all right to come in?"

Ann-Charlotte turned. The buoyant note in the voice wasn't lost upon her, and in one quick glance she caught the full significance of Lillith's attitude and mood. Her confidence and happiness were so plainly the reactions of a woman loved and in love.

"Why not?" she answered. "If his dues are paid."

Lillith dropped Reese's arm and walked quickly to the table. She was dancing.

"Hello, darling." Her fingertips touched Cary's chin lightly. He looked up falteringly. "Been a good boy?"

"Hello." It wasn't at all what he wanted to say. He knew she thought he was sulking; still angry; but he wasn't. If I could only talk to her as I once did, he thought despairingly. The words are here, but they won't come out and so she never knows. "When, when did you get back?"

"A little after two. Are you going to let me sit down?"

"Sure." He rose with jerky awkwardness and held a chair for her. "I'm sorry."

Reese dropped into a seat next to Ann-Charlotte. She slanted a fleeting glance his way and grinned with mocking shrewdness.

"Good ride?"

"So-so." He refused to be disturbed by her tone or the fact that she made a point of glancing at her watch. "What will you drink?" He included all of them in the question.

"I don't know." Lillith communicated an air of supressed excitement. "Something new. Is there such a thing?" She looked at the bottle of bourbon and her nose wrinkled. "I managed to get potted all by myself last night on The Hill. We had a hell of a time, Lil and the drunken stranger."

"You feel pretty good, don't you?" Cary tried to make the question jocular but succeeded only in sounding morosely abused.

"I feel wonderful, Cary." She slid her hand atop his for a moment. "Really. If I could only begin to tell you. Now," she straightened up, "what about this drink?"

"You don't need one, baby." Ann-Charlotte was thoughtfully subdued. "If I had what you have I'd bottle it for future use."

Lillith subsided abruptly. It isn't right, she assured herself, for me to feel this way. I want to stand up and yell: Reese loves me. We're going away together. Life is such a good and marvelous thing I wish I could share it with you. Without meaning to do so she watched Cary as he poured himself a drink and tossed it down ungraciously. Some of the whisky clung to the corner of his mouth and he wiped at it with the knuckle of his thumb. Suddenly the ebullient sparkle within her was extinguished. I don't want a drink, she thought. I only want to get out of here and talk with Cary before he is too drunk to understand what I am saying. I want to tell him tonight and get it over.

"I've changed my mind about a drink." She spoke directly to Reese. "I think I'd like to go back home." She turned in her chair. "Will you come, Cary?"

He didn't seem to understand at first and stared uncomprehendingly at her. When he finally grasped what she was saying, he scowled.

"You just got here. I—I thought we might have dinner and . . ."

"I know," she finished the thought for him, "then take some people

300

back to the lodge. Not tonight, Cary." There was a new note of determination in her voice.

Ann-Charlotte rose. "Let's all go," she suggested. "I'm beginning to hear the death rattle of something."

Cary stood up, clutching at the table for support. His eyes clouded. "Will you ride with me, Lil?"

"Of course. I'll drive." She turned to Reese and Ann-Charlotte. "We'll see you later?"

"I always go to wakes," Ann-Charlotte replied. "This one I could miss, though, given any encouragement. I have a little private interment of my own to take care of."

Cary started to reach for the bottle when Lillith took his arm. "Not now, Cary, please. You don't need another drink."

"Sure." He had difficulty with the word. "Sure, Lil, whatever you say." There was a dispirited, fawning note in his voice. She shuddered and turned quickly away.

Ann-Charlotte yawned deliberately. "I've changed my mind," she said indifferently, "I think I'll stay here and find a couple of toss-pots to spend the evening with." She looked at Reese. "Will you join me in the greenwood with some nut brown ale?"

Reese hesitated. "No," he finally said, "I think I'll go back to the lodge."

"Oh!" Ann-Charlotte was tolerant. "A community sing?"

Reese ignored the thrust. "I'll take my car back," he told Lillith. "You go along."

XXVII

Wɪᴛʜ Cary lounging in miserable silence beside her, Lillith drove back to the lodge through the steel-blue twilight. The top was down and there was a keen bite in the air. When he made an attempt to raise the window at his side, she stopped him, thinking grimly of the wonders of a mechanical age. Once you walked a drunk around the block until he was sober. Now the sobering up process was accomplished at fifty miles an hour. She pulled up in front of a roadside barbecue stand and ordered a cup of black coffee. When the girl brought it out, she nodded toward Cary.

Cary held the thick mug gingerly in his hands and peered distastefully at the steaming liquid.

"I'm not drunk," he complained. "What's this for?"

"I don't think you know any more when you're drunk, Cary." She forced herself to be decisive. "Drink it." As she spoke, she kept repeating to herself: I mustn't be impatient. This is important.

After the second cup of coffee and a cigarette he brightened perceptibly. "Maybe it wasn't a bad idea," he admitted.

"Feel better?" She turned out of the driveway onto the road.

"I was all right to begin with." He was edgy, ready to argue the point. "I only went to the club because you weren't home."

"I came back as soon as I could." This was ridiculous; petty accusations. What difference did it make why he had been drinking alone all day?

"Let's don't go home." He sat up with renewed interest, trying to catch her fancy. "Suppose we went on down to Asheville and spent the night, just the two of us. We can pick up a couple of toothbrushes and whatever else we need. It would be fun."

Lillith shook her head. It would have been fun once. That was the sort of thing they had done when they were first married, flying to Cuba at a moment's notice in a chartered plane or catching a boat to Bermuda on an hour's decision. Spontaneity was flavorless now.

"I'd rather not." She let her refusal drop there.

"There's nothing to do at the lodge." He was struggling against

302

returning home. "Ann-Charlotte asked me if we wanted to use her place in France this summer. We, we could drive right on to Winton tonight and catch a train out for New York tomorrow or the next day—?" He waited for a moment. "Maybe," he was eager, "maybe you might like to go West. There's a place in Wyoming I know; Jackson's Hole; or we could go to a ranch in Colorado." He babbled with a rising note of false enthusiasm, hoping, somehow, to tag her imagination.

"No, Cary." She was weary of sound. "I don't want to go away."

He was worried now, concerned and perplexed by her inflexibility, and as though he understood they both were at a moment of truth and resolution, tried to squirm away.

"I feel better now. Maybe, maybe I was a little drunk"—he offered the admission as a generous gift—"but I'm all right now. We could go back to the club for dinner. Ann-Charlotte and Reese are probably still there." He searched her face for a response.

If I can only get home, Lillith thought, and put an end to this. The words dribbled away like the spittle of an idiot. She cut off the highway to the lodge road. Two miles now. If he will only keep quiet until we get there.

"There is something different about you," Cary persisted. "You're not yourself. Something has happened."

Reese's car was in the driveway; she parked behind it and turned the ignition key, feeling worn and exhausted. She rested for a couple of seconds, hands on the steering wheel. This is the end, she thought gratefully. It was the sensation she used to experience as a youngster when she had to go to the dentist. In a few minutes it will all be over. She realized with a start that Cary was staring at her.

"Let's go in, shall we?" She made the suggestion with casual interest.

As he stepped from the car, Cary staggered slightly and held to the door for a moment. He smiled a little foolishly.

"Fresh air," he explained limply. "I didn't notice it while we were moving." He straightened up and waited until she came around from the other side. "Lil." He clutched at her arm. "Let's not go in." There was despair in the request, a plea for commutation. His eyes were misery-filled as he watched her.

Lillith pretended she had not heard, mounting the steps with assumed briskness. She knew Cary was standing there by the car, waiting and watching. I'm not going to be a schoolmistress, she decided, and lead him by the hand. The night will wait.

Reese was in the broad sunken living room staring out across the valley. He turned at her step and lifted the glass in his hand.

"This is the drink I didn't have time to get at the club."

"I'll take one, double." She walked toward him. I'm being brisk, she thought with a forlorn grimace, I'm acting like the chairman of a board of directors calling a meeting to order.

"Scotch?" Reese stood over the wheeled tray.

"Please." She sagged a little. "Oh, darling," she didn't move toward him, "I don't know what to do, how to say what must be said. I can't think honestly. I want you to be here with me, but then I wonder if it would be better to talk with him alone."

"If you look that way at me," he said quietly, "I'll pick you up and carry you out of the house without a word to anyone. Do you want me to talk with Cary?"

She took the drink from his hand and their fingers touched. "No. I'll do it, but don't leave me."

He was doubtful. "There ought to be a better way, but I can't think of it."

She heard Cary as he came down into the room, but didn't turn.

"I thought you were at the club with Ann-Charlotte," he spoke to Reese, and there was surprise and relief in his voice as if he was reassured by his presence.

"She's staying with the Jamesons for dinner."

"That's good." Cary went directly to the wagon and poured himself a stiff drink of bourbon. "Lil's been giving me a coffee cure. I need this to get over the stuff."

Lillith went over to the windows and sat on the ledge. She took a deep breath. How, the question raced through her brain, how am I going to start? I wish I'd read more books, but there probably isn't a book on this. How to tell your husband in six easy lessons.

Cary took a second drink. He was feeling better. The dejected look on his face drew away, but he was still uncertain. There was a mystifying air of tension in the room. It made him uncomfortable. He glanced at Lillith.

"I guess we could have done this at the club." He made an attempt to laugh.

"Cary," Lillith placed her glass on the seat, "Cary, I have something to tell you. It—it isn't easy." She stared unhappily at him. "I don't know where to begin. You'll have to try and understand. I'm going to leave you."

304

The words were out, and for a moment Lillith was appalled by what she had said. There was a terrible, breath-taking finality in that simple, unequivocal statement. What, she wondered in the second before Cary would answer, can a man say?

He laughed and the sound was so startling she jumped, unable to believe her senses. A man might do anything, but he doesn't laugh. Then she realized he did not or would not understand.

"Why," try as he would be couldn't hide the slight tremor in his voice, "why, you had me scared for a minute. I never saw you so solemn before. You don't have to go away." He turned to Reese. "Does she, Reese?" His eyes sought hers again. "I know you haven't been happy in Winton. We'll go away. Just the two of us. The way it used to be. You remember."

He knows better, Lillith thought desperately. He's doing this on purpose.

"You don't understand, Cary. I'm leaving you. Not with you. Oh!" She tore the cry out with difficulty. "You must know. Don't make me say it all." Where, she thought frantically, are those crisp, clear-cut things people are supposed to say to each other?

"Oh...no! You don't know what you are saying, Lil." He was wilting, abjectly. "Tell her, Reese." He wiped the back of his hand against his mouth. "Tell her, Reese. You know she doesn't mean what she said. Look," his voice was rising. "I won't drink any more. I'll swear I'll never take another drop. I—I know it's been bad, but you'll see. I can stop. You know that," his head turned from Lillith to Reese and back again. He was being hunted, driven into a corner, and sought escape. "I—I wouldn't know what to do, how to live without you, Lil. You don't know what you are saying. It's some sort of a joke; punishment, maybe, but good Christ, don't do this to me, Lil." Even from that distance he seemed to be pawing at her hands, begging.

Lillith couldn't remain seated. She stood up and realized she was unaccountably weak. Her knees trembled and she put one hand to the window sash for support.

"I'm going to have a baby, Cary." Her voice seemed to be coming from someone standing beside her. "That's why I went to Winton, to see Dr. Cochrane and be sure."

"No, no." He repeated the word in a strangled monotone and his head bounced in limp cadence. "No." There was the groggy, hurt plea of a punch-drunk fighter who knows he is going to be hit again,

305

in the protest. "No." His voice didn't lift. "No, Lil, you couldn't have done that to me. Not to us. You know how we've been."

For a moment she didn't understand. He was breaking up before her eyes. It wasn't what she had expected. She turned to look at Reese, who was watching Cary with an expression of complete amazement. "I'm going to stay until after the baby is born." He didn't seem to hear. "Cary. After the baby I am going away, for good." I'm going to scream if he doesn't answer.

Cary's head was almost hunched between his shoulders, and in this attitude he turned to Reese and there was a maddened glare over his eyes, a milky film of fury.

"You no-good son of a bitch." He panted over the words. "You share-cropper's bastard!"

"Cary." She knew now what he was thinking and flung herself at him, trying to turn him about. "You don't know what you're saying." He shrugged her off with such violence that she stumbled and almost fell. This, she thought wildly, is the way murder is committed.

"Get out of my house!" He was shaking, and a small trickle of saliva formed at one corner of his mouth. "Do you think you can have your crooked, little offal here and then run away together?"

Reese slapped him across the mouth then with the back of his hand. It was a brutally vicious blow; cold and deadly in its delivery. Cary slumped beneath it, and blood seeped between his parted lips. The colored maid, Lucy, who had just started in with a small silver bucket of ice, screamed, a loud, wailing note of terror, and dropped the container to the floor as she fled back to the kitchen. In her horror Lillith noticed how the frozen cubes slithered across the polished boards like small bright fish.

"I ought to kill you." Reese bent forward, arms hanging loosely at his sides.

Without realizing what she was doing, Lillith placed her hands on Cary's shoulders, supporting him as he seemed to crumple.

"You can't believe what you said, Cary. You know it couldn't be true. Never until today has Reese even kissed me. It's your child, Cary. In your heart you know it."

Cary smeared his bleeding mouth with his fingers, trailing the stain across his chin and shirt collar. He pushed past Lillith, not hearing or caring what she said, and poured half a water-tumbler-full of whisky and gulped it. Hot pain flashed in his eyes as the alcohol seared his split lips and bleeding teeth.

"All of your miserable life," Cary was drooling the words with slavering rage, "the Whitfields have taken care of you. You've lived off of us."

Reese interrupted him. "Cary," his voice was so low it became a whisper, but shocking in its intensity, "Cary, if you say it again I'll kill you."

"What do I care?" He screamed a hysterical defiance. "You've already done that. After four years we are going to have a baby!" He glared at Lillith. "Is that what you want me to believe? When? How? You think I'm a drunken fool but I know." He made an attempt to laugh, but the sound was a hideous croak.

He believes what he is saying. He doesn't remember. She was stunned by the violence of his accusations and felt shame and degradation in the memory of how he had crawled, whimpering, with hot, searching hands, pleading and crying his need. This is shameful and dirty, she thought wretchedly, and I wanted to be honest.

"I'm not that drunk." The words spewed through the blood and saliva and he kept rubbing with the fingers of both hands at his mouth. "Sure, you liked The Hill," he shrieked insensately at Reese. "Why not? My sister and my wife when you wanted them, and no one to care but drunken, old Cary. But you never knew why I drank, did you? It was because I was afraid and I have dreams at night. Sure, you liked The Hill, but you never gave a damn what happened after you got the money my father left you. Oh, you were nice enough until then! You got what you wanted, didn't you? Well, take your bastard, but don't try and pretend it's mine." He coughed with a choking spasm and a crimson spray covered his hands.

Reese stood in bitter silence, and the balled fists at his side relaxed. I ought to hit him, he thought wonderingly, but he's crazy. You can't hit an imbecile.

Lillith backed away in slow horror, unable to take her eyes from Cary's face. She moved, haltingly and confused, with the uncertain step of a blind person.

"No, you mustn't." She seemed to be speaking to a frightened child, admonishing and at the same time quieting him. "You don't know what you are saying. Reese is the only honor you have known."

"Whoremaster!" Cary shrilled the word with crazy defiance.

I can't help it, Reese thought dumbly. It has to stop here. He was suddenly weary, emotion had drained from him. The words Cary was mouthing no longer had significance. They were only dirty; the senseless obscenities found scribbled on toilet walls. He walked toward him almost regretfully.

"All of my life," he said emptily, "I've lied and covered up for you. Everything I ever wanted to do has been ruined while you've had your way. You've cheated and wriggled out of everything and I've taken it, pretending I didn't care. Do you think your lousy money can buy that? Now I'm going to kill you."

"Whoremaster!" Cary screeched and hurled a glass from behind the bar cart.

Reese didn't shift his body. His almost easy stride was relentless and the tumbler shattered against the opposite wall. With a frenzied yell Cary bounded forward, his shoulders hunched, twisting himself into a taunting, demoniacal figure.

"Reese, for God's sake!" Lillith screamed helplessly. I'm looking at murder, she thought desperately. I'm standing here, seeing it done.

Reese's hands shot out as Cary rushed toward him, fastening on the lapels of his coat. "I want to look at you for a minute," he said hoarsely. "I want to see what I am doing."

Cary's hands beat about his face. He yelped in the fluting tones of hysteria, but the blows were without strength. Amazement gathered in Reese's eyes. He shook Cary and the man was collapsing in his hands. His flailing arms were the harmless spinning of a paper windmill. I can't do this, Reese thought bleakly. I ought to, but I can't. It would be like twisting the neck of a baby. Damn you to hell. I can't even kill you.

Without effort he swung Cary about, fingers still caught in his coat, and flung him away with a gesture of disgust. Cary spun lightly and crashed into a light chair, falling face down over it, arms trailing on each side. He sprawled there for a moment, his breath coming in gusty, heaving sighs, and then he began to cry. He blubbered, weeping with miserable despair; unashamed and abject.

Lillith shut her eyes against the spectacle. She was trembling with uncontrollable violence and could barely stand. Feeling Reese near, she looked up with mute supplication and then crept into his arms for shelter.

"It's all right now." His voice was steady, comforting and strong. He kissed her eyes and held his lips gently against her cheek. "It's all right, Lil. Nothing is going to happen; believe me."

She could only nod and cling to him, and in the silence Cary's sobs

308

were frightfully distinct, spilling out with his shattered manhood. I'll hear those sounds as long as I live, Lillith thought.

"I didn't mean it. I didn't mean it." Cary lamented over and over and the unhappy wail echoed in the depths of his agony.

Lillith turned in Reese's arms and looked quickly across the room. Cary had pulled himself from the chair and was huddled on his hands and knees, staring at them. Blood made a tortured mask of his face, and then, as Reese and Lillith gazed at him, he began dragging himself across the room with a crawling, broken motion. As he crept across the floor he seemed more animal than man, and his upturned face reflected a desperate plea. As he scratched his way over the boards, his eyes never left them. There was something monstrous in the spectacle.

"I didn't mean it. I didn't mean it." His mouth writhed with the words.

I'm going crazy, Lillith thought. That—that thing on the floor can't be Cary. It isn't anything human. It's something out of hell, a tormented soul seeking escape.

"Help him, Reese. In God's name don't let him crawl that way."

Reese was already on his way to Cary's side as she spoke. He bent down and lifted him from the floor and then half carried him to a couch.

"I didn't know what I was saying, Reese." The entreaty was shattered by a bubbling moan. "I didn't mean it. You know I didn't mean it."

"Bring me a drink." Reese called over his shoulder to Lillith who was standing transfixed. She had to force herself to move.

Reese took the glass and held it for Cary while he gulped eagerly at the whisky. Lillith stood at his side and Cary gazed up at her with dumb intensity. He shook with a sudden spasm.

"You don't have to go away, Lil. I can't get along without you. Reese—you and Reese are the only ones who understand me. I'm lost if you go away. I'll be all alone, don't you understand?"

"Don't talk now, Cary." There was a horrible fascination in the depths he was plumbing, and she was unable to turn from it.

He drank the balance of the whisky, and the empty glass dropped from his fingers. "Tell me you're not going away. I want to hear you say it. We'll go back to The Hill. You and—Reese and I. I'll never say anything again."

She shook her head. "No, Cary, but don't try to talk now."

"But," his hands reached for her dress, trying to fasten upon the hem, "if you'll just stay with me. It will be all right. I—I can't sleep when I know you're not in the house. Things bother me, but when you're there I don't hear them."

"Cary, please." I can't stand it, Lillith told herself. Don't let him say anything more.

"You don't understand." His fingers caught her dress and clung there. She wanted to snatch it away. "It will be all right from now on." His voice gathered a new and eager note, and speech was coming rapidly. "I'll never say another word. You and Reese. The three of us. We'll go on and no one will have to know. The baby. The baby will be all right. I don't care, if you just won't leave me. We'll pretend. That's it," he tried to smile reassuringly, "we'll pretend, don't you see. I'll pretend and so will you and Reese, and no one will have to know. It will be like it was before, and after I'm asleep—" He was becoming incoherent and his tongue constantly flicked in and out as he tried to moisten his dry lips. "After I'm asleep." He became foxily intent and there was something sly in his manner. "No one will know anything. We'll send Ann-Charlotte away, then there'll just be the three of us." He waited, drooling small bubbles.

With a sharp cry Lillith tore her skirt from his grasp. Stark horror leaped into her eyes. He still believed what he had said, but now it was all right. A pimp trying to sell his whore couldn't be more ingratiating.

"Take me out of here, Reese." She backed away.

As though he hadn't heard, Cary rose and stumbled across the room. He fumbled with the bottles on the tray, knocking them over, and finally clutched the bourbon triumphantly, pressing it into his waist with a silly cackle of glee. He looked at Reese and Lillith, and then, half bent over in a miserly attitude, hurried from the room.

They stood in stupefied silence for a moment. Heard the front door slam and then the crashing of a car door.

"He'll kill himself," Lillith said dumbly.

A starter whined, and a second later they could hear the scream of a car in low gear as it whipped out of the driveway.

"Reese." She looked at him and then broke completely. She laughed and cried, tugging and pulling at his arms, calling his name over and over.

"My baby," she moaned. "My God, my baby." She fainted then, slipping against him, and he gathered her quickly into his arms and carried her upstairs.

XXVIII

BUD CRAMER dropped a damp rag on the bar and rubbed thoughtfully at the smooth yellow pine boards. He was worried, and fine lines of concern crinkled about his eyes as he considered Cary's crouched figure at a table in a narrow booth on the opposite side of the room. There was the smell of trouble about him, and it made Bud uneasy.

Cary held an empty glass tightly before him and tapped its bottom with stupid monotony on the table. After a moment Bud sighed, dropped the rag, and walked around to the end of the short bar. He glanced down the room. It was a quiet night. Had Mason and his girl were in one of the booths. Parks Tatum, Ronnie Weaver, and a couple of waitresses from the hotel had another table, and two girls, summer people, Bud thought, were on stools at the bar drinking rum and coca-cola. Bud was glad there weren't many people in the place, because Whitfield was going to be hard to handle before he was through. He'd staggered in looking like something that had come out of a meat grinder; blood all over his face and shirt. Bud wouldn't have let him in if he hadn't pounded and yelled outside the door, and Bud liked to keep his place quiet and orderly.

At first Cary had acted as though he didn't know where he was, standing just inside with his head weaving back and forth. For a moment Bud thought he was badly hurt.

"Jesus," he said in alarm, "what's happened to you, Mr. Whitfield? Been in an accident?"

The two girls at the bar had taken a short look and one of them yipped with a quick squeak. Turned halfway on the stool, she stared at Cary. Tatum and his party glanced up and went on talking. Had Mason, who was warming his girl up beneath the table, hadn't even noticed the disheveled specter. Bud led Cary to the back of the room and eased him into the last booth.

"Gimme a drink." Cary was speaking with difficulty. His mouth was puffed like a mushroom.

"Maybe," Bud was uncertain, "you ought to see a doctor. Was it an automobile crack-up?"

311

"Someone tried to kill me." Cary touched at the corners of his swollen lips with thumb and first finger.

Bud looked at him. Save for a split mouth he wasn't in bad shape. If anyone had tried to kill him, he'd given up mighty easily.

"Want a drink, now? It'll hurt to drink." He half hoped Cary would change his mind and leave.

"Gimme some of that corn you keep an' plain water." Cary kept his eyes fixed on the table and fumblingly tried to light a cigarette.

Bud brought the whisky and a damp cloth, wrung out in the cold water of the beer ice. "Here." He put down the drink and forced the towel into Cary's hands. "Try this. It'll get the blood off, anyhow. You look like hell." While Cary mopped tenderly at his face, Bud leaned against the booth and watched. He and Cary were about the same age, and he remembered what a stink old man Whitfield had caused by shooting Donnie Blake years back. Harlen never had forgotten. They still talked about it in the town. Cary, probably, had been mixed up with someone's girl and had a poke taken at him.

"Who'd you say tried to kill you?" he asked conversationally.

A sly, cautious light appeared in Cary's eyes, and Bud had the uneasy feeling that he was gazing upon distilled evil. It gave him the creeps. Cary drank the moonshine in a single gulp and handed the glass up to Bud.

"Bring two at a time. It'll save your arches."

He hadn't moved from the booth save once when he went to the toilet. When he wanted a drink he summoned Bud by knocking against the wood with an empty glass. Bud hadn't minded as long as he kept quiet. Sooner or later the corn would catch up with him. No one could drink the stuff that fast without something happening. Now and then, as he worked behind the bar or passed down the corridor to carry a tray of fresh drinks to the tables, Bud glanced at him out of the corner of his eye. It was funny a fellow like Whitfield would let himself get in such shape. You'd think a man with so much money, fifty million dollars some said, would find time to be decent; raise a family and be proud of who he was. Instead he burned himself out. The town had heard stories of what went on at the summer lodges in the mountains; men and girls swimming naked in the pools, fellows laying each other's wives. When people don't have to scramble for a living, that's probably all they have to think about. Bud kept wondering who had torn into Cary. It couldn't have been serious or he would have more than a split mouth.

312

Walking over now in response to the tapped signal, Bud wondered what was going to happen when Cary tried to stand up. Funny thing, he didn't seem to be getting drunk.

Bud picked up the empty glass and started to turn away.

"What would you do if a man tried to kill you?" Cary's mouth sagged as it shaped the question, and Bud noticed he was shaking the way a man with a chill might tremble.

"I'd sure keep the hell out of his way."

Cary leaned slightly out of the seat and made an attempt to spit. The saliva was thick, almost mucous, and it hung over his lips in a slimy string. Bud picked up the towel and wiped it roughly across Cary's face. The son of a bitch. Where did he think he was, spitting on the floor. Almost roughly he pushed the slanting body into a sitting position. If he had acted this way wherever he had been, it was no wonder someone had taken a poke at him.

"Buy a drink for everybody." Cary waved his hand to indicate the room.

"They're all right." Bud spoke with angry impatience. "They'll buy their own."

Cary stared uncomprehendingly up at him. "Where's my drink?"

"You oughtn't to have any more, Cary." Bud had stopped calling him Mr. Whitfield.

"I want another drink." Uncontrolled rage flushed the sallow face. "Don't tell me what I ought to have."

Bud hesitated. "The hell I won't," he said and reached down, lifting and sliding Cary from the seat with one strong motion. "This is my place and I'll run it the way I like. Now you get the hell out of here." Without giving Cary a chance to argue he hustled him down the center of the room and out the front door. "I ought to toss you right into the gutter," Bud was breathing heavily, "that's where you belong." He released his hold and Cary sagged against the wall. "Go ahead," Bud shouted, "fall on your ass for all I care." It was late. A couple of the boys from Yeager's pool hall watched with idle curiosity.

"Havin' trouble, Bud?" one of them called.

"Not in my place." Cramer experienced the pleasant glow of outraged virtue. "Tryin' to spit an' puke all over my floor." He turned, slammed and locked the door behind him. Walking back to the bar, he glanced significantly at Ronnie Weaver.

"Gettin' too much for you?" Weaver was amused.

Bud set his shoulders with a swagger. "Don't make any difference to me who they are." He was a little proud of throwing Cary out so neatly.

Behind the bar again he leaned confidentially toward the two summer girls. "See that fellow?" He pushed a toothpick to one side of his mouth. "The one I tossed out? Cary Whitfield."

"You mean the Winton Whitfields?" The girls were excitedly interested. "The tobacco family?"

"Yep." Bud grinned slowly.

"Gee! What do you know? I thought he was some bum." The girl was wistfully impressed. "How do you like that?"

"Cary Whitfield." Bud rolled the name over on his tongue. "What'll you have to drink?" He suddenly felt generous and swept up the two glasses. "The same? I'll buy this one. Here." He took three nickels from the cash register ledge. "Drop these in the juke box."

Cary leaned against the front of Cramer's place, his head bursting with multicolored lights, and without strength enough to pull himself into an upright position. There was a cackling snicker and he turned with painful slowness, peering with lowered head at the two men standing in front of the pool hall. They were watching him with complacent amusement, whispering from the sides of their mouths to each other.

"Shut your damn mouths." Cary made a feeble effort to straighten up.

"Shut up, you drunken punk." They didn't move toward him but stood faintly menacing in the rectangle of light.

Cary wanted to reply, but speech came painfully. He could think of the words but couldn't say them. Laboringly he forced himself to stand and then began a stumbling walk across the sidewalk to where his car was parked. He lifted his feet high with the grotesque dignity of a crane, and once he almost spun completely around on one foot. At the roadster's side he clung to the door for a few minutes before he could force his fingers to thrust down the handle. Once in the seat he had to wait for a long time until he was able to reach back and close the door.

The two youths walked across and stood watching him. There was a quietly eager speculation in their manner, and they darted quick, nervous glances up and down the silent street.

"How about takin' us up to your place for a drink, Whitfield?" The boy wet his lips and leaned against the door. His companion waited, lounging indifferently.

"Get away from this car." Cary saw him distantly through a red haze.

The youth measured his capacity to resist. "How about takin' us up to see your sister?" The small, mean eyes were aflame with envy and malice.

"Joe," his companion called softly. "It's Marty. Let's beat it."

Joe turned and saw the solitary figure of the night marshal halfway down the block. He leaned over and slapped Cary viciously across the shattered mouth. "Why don't you go where you belong, you bum?" He laughed and backed away and the pair strolled down the street.

Marty Dunne hesitated as he drew opposite the car and peered at its lone occupant. Finally he walked over and looked at Cary.

"You all right, Mr. Whitfield?"

Cary nodded. His mouth was bleeding again. He could feel the warmth streaming from his teeth and kept his lips closed. Dunne considered him doubtfully for a moment and then shook his head.

"Better be careful driving home." He hesitated. "Want me to get someone to drive you up?"

Cary waggled his head in silence and groped along the dash until he found the ignition switch. When the motor caught he forced himself to think what must be done next. First the clutch, then the shift lever. The car bucked away, and as it left the curb Cary opened his mouth, allowing it to hang slackly, and the blood spilled down across his chin and shirt. I wonder why he hit me, he thought, with miserable shame.

He couldn't remember turning off the highway to the lodge road and was halfway up the mountain before he realized he was no longer at Bud Cramer's. The brilliant lights fanned out across the narrow road, and he hunched over the wheel fighting the ruts every inch of the way. Somewhere in the car was the bottle he had brought with him from the lodge. He kicked with one foot around the floorboards until he located it and then pulled it toward him with the toe of his shoe. The night was filled with a curious whining sound. He listened as he held the bottle between his knees and worked at the cork with the fingers of one hand. It was a hell of a noise, a wailing cry in the mountains. The car jumped and slithered as his foot rested unevenly on the accelerator.

He took a long drink straight from the bottle. It didn't taste like anything. He wondered if he could light a cigarette. The unearthly screech pierced his ears, and then he realized he had been keeping the car in low gear all the way from Harlen. He started to shift into second and then changed his mind. It was better this way. Go off the road and down the side of the mountain. No time to get killed that way now.

I mustn't forget. He repeated the admonition over and over to himself. Got to remember what it was I wanted to do. His fingers were fastened so tightly to the rim of the wheel that they ached, but he refused to allow them to relax. He knew a moment of terror when he thought he might have taken the wrong road. I'll never get back down the hill and up another. The car crept slowly and erratically up the steep incline. This had to be the road to the lodge. He was crying in anticipation of frustration. There wasn't any other road like this.

Yard by yard the car gained on the incline, and when Cary could make out the stone gateposts marking the lodge's entrance he chortled foolishly and tramped heavily on the gas as the tires spun into the raked gravel.

In one of the guest rooms at the front of the house Lillith heard his clumsy entrance and gripped her hands tightly. Just the knowledge that he was in the house frightened her. She was prone on the bed, lying hot-eyed and feverish in the darkness, struggling against the night's horror. Reese had been at her side when she regained consciousness, and she stared uncomprehendingly at him until the full memory of what had happened returned.

"I want to get out of here, Reese. Tonight. Take me away." Her eyes were starkly pleading.

With one hand he held both of hers, smoothing lightly at her forehead with the other. She had never known he could be tender, worried.

"I brought you up to one of the front rooms. You'll be all right here. We'll leave the first thing in the morning. I don't think you ought to try and make the trip tonight."

She struggled to rise, panic on her face. He held her gently. "I'll go on my hands and knees," she pleaded. "I'll crawl, if necessary. Don't make me stay."

"Believe me," he cradled her in one arm, "it's better this way. Nothing is going to happen."

She nodded without the strength to argue and he had remained at her side for hours; talking in a low, easy voice, holding her with strong confidence. She was drowsy and wakeful by turns; nodding off to quick, uneasy dreams and awakening with a start. Once she

316

knew a moment of panic when she awakened and found him gone, but before she could cry his name he was back, carrying a tall glass of warm milk and brandy.

"Warm milk makes me sick," she protested after the first experimental sip. "Do I have to drink it?"

"Just drink the brandy. Forget it is mixed with milk."

She nodded with childish confidence. "I'm sorry I passed out. It's a little old-fashioned, isn't it?"

He smiled and bent to kiss her. "I remembered reading that when a lady faints the first thing you do is loosen her stays." He grinned and she felt better. "You don't have any, though."

"Did you look?"

He shook his head. "No. I felt."

She sighed. "I'm sorry I wasn't awake."

The brandy took hold with lenitive insistence, and she could almost feel it creep through her veins, calming and pampering her nerves until they no longer jumped at every sound or quivered at Reese's touch.

"It was pretty terrible, wasn't it?" Try as she would, she couldn't entirely erase the scene with Cary from her mind. Every time she closed her eyes she could see him crawling and slobbering across the living room floor.

"He has had a lot of practice," Reese answered. "That's where he has the advantage."

"We'll leave first thing in the morning, won't we, Reese? Early, before anyone is awake?"

"You get some sleep if you can. I'll be ready when you wake up."

"And," she hesitated, "we won't have to see anyone or say anything?"

"No." He was reassuringly confident, and a small, pensive smile danced across her mouth. He was good to be with, she thought.

She must have slept, although she fought against the release it would bring, for when she opened her eyes again the room was dark save for a tiny chink of light where the bathroom door was not quite closed. Reese was gone, and for a moment she struggled against the desire to scream his name. You have to stop this, she warned herself sternly. You're grown up and the boogie-man can't get you.

Her fingers searched across the bed table until they found cigarettes and matches. Something was wrong. She was vaguely conscious of feeling different. It was a few seconds before she realized she was tucked neatly beneath the covers and clad, now, in pajamas. When

317

did he do that? She groped beneath the sheet and light blanket. They're mine, too, she thought with surprise. Mr. Benton is a very handy man to have around the house. I love you, darling. She whispered the words, half believing he would hear.

She heard Ann-Charlotte come in, listened as the car rolled down to the garage. For a moment she was afraid it might be Cary and turned quickly out of bed to lock her door. A few moments later she caught the sound of a screen banging and then a light step. It must be Ann-Charlotte, she reassured herself. Cary would make more noise if he was able to walk at all by now.

She finished her cigarette, drawing it down to a small end. What of this strangely tortured man who was her husband? What was to become of him? How had he reached this state of confusion and what sort of world did he see through that distorted mind?

After awhile she heard Ann-Charlotte come upstairs and pass down the hall to her room. The house was quiet then; secure and reassuringly peaceful. Lillith mashed out her cigarette butt and wondered if Reese was awake. I wish he would come back, she thought a little desperately. I could sleep again if he was here to hold me.

She closed her eyes, screwing them up into tight knots. If I can go to sleep, then morning will come quickly. She tried to remember all the inducements for courting sleep she had ever heard about. Most of them were foolish. Counting silly sheep was no good. They would never stay in line and jump properly. After a while they began doing back-flips, double-Gaynors, or just went floating off in the air, and trying to follow their flights kept her awake.

Exhaustion tugged at her and she did sleep, awakening with a convulsive start at the sound of Cary's car. She waited a little breathlessly, attempting to trace his course in her mind. She heard his stumbling feet on the steps below her window, then the banging of the front door. There was a tinkling crash and she tried to imagine what was broken. He was careening from room to room, turning on lights, for their pattern was reflected upward from the ground to her window. Then he turned on the radio and music boomed through the house. A moment later an addition was made to the swelling sound. He must have set the victrola going since the thumping, unmusical beat of "Sweet Sue," an old Whiteman record they had kept, was added to the cacophony. There was an automatic return on the machine, and she knew "Sweet Sue" would be dinned into all their ears until someone went down and turned it off. She could no longer distinguish

318

Cary's movements. He had probably found himself a drink and was waiting with malicious satisfaction for someone to take notice of his return.

Lillith waited. It was senseless, being terrorized this way. There was nothing he could do. He might come looking for her, but the door was locked. She wasn't afraid of physical violence. Reese was across the hall, and anyhow, Cary would only be maudlin and supplicating. The idea disgusted her and she turned her face into the pillow in an attempt to shut out the sound.

There was no escape from the witless confusion downstairs; it pounded with relentless fury, and Lillith wondered how long Ann-Charlotte would stand it before she went down and kicked the instrument into silence or added her screaming vituperation to the din. Cary had probably shut himself away in the kitchen where he could escape part of the noise. She could almost see him there, sitting and waiting.

Suddenly Lillith was frightened. There had been no sound above the clamor, but somehow she was certain Reese had left his room. She could almost feel his presence as he walked past, just outside.

"No, please, Reese." She spoke in hushed and prayerful accents. "Don't go down. It will only mean trouble. I don't mind. He'll get tired soon and go to sleep. Let him alone."

She was unable to stay the words even though she knew he couldn't possibly hear. Cold panic seized her as she remembered the unmistakable fury on Reese's face earlier as Cary screamed and frothed. She lay rigid, strapped to the bed by a dread she no longer tried to explain. Only after a tremendous effort could she force herself to rise. She tiptoed to her door with unnecessary caution and opened it. Across the hall Reese's door was ajar. He had gone out. For a moment she hesitated, reasoning frantically with herself. Let them alone. Reese will be able to take care of him. There isn't anything you can or should do.

She waited at the door, straining to catch the sound of voices over the harshly blended music from the two instruments. Reese, she thought, must have gone to the kitchen. He probably was with Cary now, talking to him as he always did.

Uncertain, tormented by fears as formless as they were real, she relocked her door and went back to bed. They wouldn't fight, she was certain. The time for that had passed. Reese would either quiet him or come back upstairs, leaving Cary to wear himself out.

He was gone a long time. She turned to watch the sweeping second hand of the small electric clock beside her bed. Its silent swing was hypnotic. Maybe he was putting Cary to sleep on one of the couches. She sat on the edge of the bed, unable to tear her eyes from the clock, and then, suddenly, the music stopped, and for a moment the silence was unbearable. She rose and started for the door, unable to control her movements.

The house was without sound. With her hand on the knob she leaned her cheek against the door's panel and waited. She counted slowly in what she imagined to be seconds. One minute, two minutes and then she heard a step. Without looking, she knew it was Reese. The stride was measured, deliberate, almost thoughtful.

She felt him pass her door, pause and stand for a moment. He was looking at her through the wall. Then, although there was no sound, he moved away.

Although she was certain, she had to reassure herself. Trying to avoid a revealing click of the lock and latch, she turned knob and key at the same time and then inched the door back, peeking furtively out. Reese's door was closed again.

In bed she slid cautiously beneath the covers, unable to rid herself of the fancy that any sound or movement would awaken Cary and start the whole ridiculous proceedings over again. With relief and a feeling of security she burrowed beneath the blanket, drawing it tightly around her as though this simple act had the power to ward off further unpleasantness.

The room was dark. Reese had turned the lights out downstairs before he came up. Somewhere outside a lonely whippoorwill called with plaintive insistence; waited and called again with heartbreaking melancholy.

XXIX

THE stable boy, Cletus, stumbled sleepily past the paddock and through the back yard on his way to the kitchen with the hope of wheedling some coffee and breakfast from Lucy or one of the girls at the lodge. There was a damp, clinging chill in the early morning air and the mist was in unwilling movement in the hollows, hiding from the sun. Cletus hunched his shoulders beneath an old mackinaw, thrust his hands into the breast pockets and walked with averted head. It was cold and uncomfortable, and he hadn't wanted to get up.

Following a familiar path, he was halfway across the back grounds near the swimming pool before he looked up. From a distance the dark object, flung loosely near the pool's edge, was without shape. Someone from the lodge had left a coat out all night. He looked again. His eyes widened and he stiffened.

"Mighty col' mawnin' to be lyin' aroun' thataway in the yahd." He spoke aloud, hesitated, and then walked slowly forward, his feet squashing heavily in the soggy grass. He paused again, halted by a nameless dread, and then circled the object, his head canted to one side and his eyes slanted with wary suspicion. He had an impulse to run. Instead he stopped and considered the figure.

The man was sprawled on the cropped grass. The arms were outstretched and one cheek buried on the ground. A leg was drawn up slightly and the foot of the other hung over the pool's concrete lip. Cletus shivered and backed away while he argued audibly with himself.

"Ef Mistuh Cahry is a-sleepin' theah he goin' t' give you hell foah wakin', oah, maybe, jus' lookin' at him. Ef you don' wake him, Miz Whitfiel' goin' t' give you hell foah leavin' him lay. Maybe you bettah go back t' th' bahn an' lit youah stummik grumble foah hits breakfus' till someone else finds him."

The colored boy rolled his eyes as he debated the problem. Finally, and with great effort, he inched forward. As he walked, he called with soft persistency.

"Mistuh Cahry, suh? Mistuh Cahry?"

He waited and then raised his voice. A boy could get himself into all sorts of unknown trouble this way. White people didn't like to be found dead drunk in the yard. He called again with mounting apprehensiveness, and when there was no reply he looked up at the lodge with silent appeal. A stable boy didn't have any business here, anyhow. Someone from the big house ought to come down and take charge.

"Mistuh Cahry, suh?" His voice adopted a pleading note. "Ain' you col' out heah? That grass is raight damp, hit suah enough is."

He paused hopefully. If the man would only move a little or yell a curse at him the way he did sometimes, he could go on about his business.

"Mistuh Cahry." He was whimpering uneasily now and there was panic in his eyes. "Lord God, you suah enough hadn' ought to be sleepin' thataway."

Each forward step was a form of torture, and the boy's head darted from side to side, tugged by fear. Finally he stood above the crumpled figure. Without bending he could see the small, powder-singed wound in the temple and the dirty brown line curving down across the pallid cheek. Cletus wanted to yell, but no sound issued from his throat. He was unable to tear his eyes away and stood in horrified fascination.

"Deah Jesus, Mistuh Cahry, you ain' sleepin', is you?"

He saw the gun then, lying a few inches from the outstretched fingers, and screamed with a loud wail of terror. Without stopping for a second look he ran wildly toward the kitchen door, shouting at the top of his lungs with every bounding step. The shrouded hills picked up the call and tossed it back until the valley was filled with a yammering, ghostly clamor.

XXX

THE whisper ran lightly at first; rippling as a small flame might creep with bright innocence along a fringe of leaves in the forest it meant to destroy. There was no halting the murmur. It died here but sprang up there, gathering force as it spread. The town of Harlen heard it first and gave it voice. It appeared between the lines of the sensational newspaper stories and clung to the lips of gossips. It was heard in Winton and New York; San Francisco and London. Chris Mayberry, the County Solicitor, listened and pondered. They heard it at the mountaintop lodge, and the word was murder.

Who was there to say when it had first been given tongue? Bud Cramer said: "He told me a man had tried to kill him. He was beat up some, not real bad, you understand, but sort of slapped around." The colored maid, Lucy, shot her eyes about, until they seemed all white, and trembled. "I heah Mistuh Reese say, 'I'm goin' to kill you,' an' Mistuh Cahry screamin': 'Git out of my house!'"

The whisper gained strength and began pounding at the bolted doors of the lodge. It knocked on the panels of Chris Mayberry's office and he let it in.

Mayberry was shrewd and ambitious. So shrewd and ambitious he was afraid to listen to the whisper, for if it was a liar and he took its hand, the road led to political suicide, and Chris Mayberry wasn't interested in self-destruction. The coroner's jury, also, heard the word but was afraid. Finally, the verdict was a compromise. It could have been murder. It might have been suicide.

Chris Mayberry shut himself in his office and studied the two roads. A Whitfield murder trial would be a sensation. A conviction might start him on the way to the Governor's mansion. Failure? He didn't like to think about it. That road was marked with the graves of public officials who overreached themselves. When he walked down the street, people stopped to ask him what he was going to do. His wife nagged, sensing the opportunity. Friends dropped in to question him. Always Chris listened, and finally he sent word to the lodge.

Reese sat in a straight-backed, uncomfortable chair across the desk from Mayberry and waited. He was tight and drawn, and there were dark hollows beneath his eyes from the sleepless night.

"You don't look very well, Benton." Chris leaned back in his soft leather chair and touched a match to the end of a fat cigar. He watched Reese across the flame.

"That isn't surprising." Reese was shaking inside, but he kept his voice steady.

"Do you know what I think, Benton?" Deliberately, Mayberry ignored a prefix.

"I guess so." Reese watched him carefully.

"I think," Mayberry's face appeared through a heavy cloud of smoke, "I think you shot and killed Cary Whitfield."

"You have a lot of company." Reese smiled faintly.

"Why did you do it?" The question had the savage attack of a rocket. Mayberry threw it over the table, not because he expected an answer but rather to see its effect.

"I didn't do it." Reese kept his hands steady and in sight as he took a cigarette from a flat leather case. "But," he paused, "if you think I did, then you must have already figured out a motive. Why ask me?"

Mayberry shook his head. "You won't get anyplace trying to be funny."

"I'm not being funny." An edge was apparent on Reese's voice. "Also, I'm not going to be pushed around. If you're going to bring a charge, make it."

Mayberry slid a little deeper into his chair. He was a good lawyer and a competent prosecutor. Usually he could tell when someone was lying. You can smell a lie, he always said, the same as a dog can smell fear. It's just there, and after a while you get so you can recognize it. Now, he wasn't certain, and the knowledge worried him.

"Your fingerprints were on the gun." He was using a casual, friendly approach.

"That isn't remarkable." An inner voice was warning Reese to be cautious. "It was a twenty-two-caliber gun. Cary and I were shooting with it that morning."

Mayberry nodded. "I figured you'd say so." He swung the chair about and raised both feet to the desk. There was a speculative light in his eyes. "Do you want me to tell you what I think happened?"

Reese laughed shortly. "That's a rhetorical question, isn't it?"

Mayberry half dropped the heavy lids over his eyes and allowed the smoke from his cigar to drift out through his nostrils.

"Maybe," he admitted after a moment. "This is the way I see it. I think you were having an affair with Lillith Whitfield."

Reese spun his chair about and rose in a crouch, both hands resting on the desk and his head thrust toward Mayberry. "I'll push those words down your throat with my fist," he said with deadly earnestness.

"Sit down." Mayberry wasn't disturbed. "This isn't personal. I'm building a case. The public already believes that without my saying so, and you're a fool if you don't know it."

Reese sank reluctantly back. He knew what the County Solicitor had said was true. Wet tongues were spreading the talk. He could feel it.

"I think," Mayberry continued dreamily, "there had already been some argument about this. That afternoon you took Mrs. Whitfield to the country club and met her husband and sister-in-law. There was an argument and Cary took his wife home. You followed after a few minutes and there was a fight in the house. One of the maids saw you hit Whitfield and heard you say you were going to kill him."

Mayberry carefully laid his cigar in the small trough of the ashtray and stared up at the ceiling. He folded his big hands across the suggestion of a paunch and whistled moodily.

"Later in the evening Cary Whitfield went to Bud Cramer's bar. There was blood on his face, and when Cramer asked him what had happened he said: 'Someone tried to kill me.'"

"Get it right." Reese snapped. "He said: 'A man tried to kill me.' Just a little help," he added sarcastically.

Mayberry's head moved slowly up and down. "That's right. A man. Makes a difference, doesn't it?" He smiled pleasantly. "After that," he resumed the story, "he went home. He was drunk and wanted company. He turned on the radio and phonograph and made a hell of a noise in the hope, probably, his wife would awaken and come down. Instead," the County Solicitor's face was grave, "you went down. You had an argument, picking up where you left earlier in the day."

Reese's scornful laugh was harsh. "Then, I suppose," he carried the imaginary tale, "I said, 'Come on out, down by the swimming pool where I can shoot you'?"

Mayberry's expression was bland. "You know, that worried me for a while; but I don't think you'd have to say it in those words. Suppose," he considered Reese shrewdly, "just suppose you were acting as Cary Whitfield's friend. It would be easy enough to take his arm and suggest a little air. Down by the swimming pool, with the radio and

325

phonograph going, no one would be likely to hear the report of a twenty-two if it was held close to the head as this one was."

"You're crazy." Reese tried desperately to sound convincing, but the words rang with a hollow futility. What Mayberry was saying was on the lips of the entire state and much of the country. It made sense no matter how he tried to beat it down.

"I don't think so." Mayberry was unruffled. "Now, Mrs. Whitfield comes into one of the largest fortunes in the United States, and if what I think has been going on is true, it looks like a good deal for you. Murder has been committed for a hell of a lot less."

"Well?" Reese could only wait. Nothing he could say would alter the irresistible course of the tragedy.

"I could get an indictment without any trouble," Mayberry was thinking aloud; "I'm just wondering if I could get a conviction."

"Don't take any chances." Reese was bitter.

Mayberry smiled understandingly. "You know, that's just what I haven't any intention of doing. You, maybe, have some idea what this would mean if I can pin you down and stake you out?"

"I can guess," Reese answered helplessly. There was a dull, nagging ache within him.

Mayberry scratched thoughtfully at one ear, his eyes unwaveringly on the opposite wall. After a few moments he turned with a reluctant grunt and pressed a button. When his secretary came to the door, he glanced up.

"Ask Mrs. and Miss Whitfield if they'll step in for a moment, John." His eyes slanted toward Reese.

They both rose when Lillith and Ann-Charlotte entered, and Reese watched silently as she came toward him, then he pulled out his chair and brought another one from near the wall for Ann-Charlotte.

"They ought to throw you in the can oftener." Ann-Charlotte grinned at him. "It improves your manners."

Reese had to smile although Lillith's stricken eyes haunted him. Ann-Charlotte would laugh on the lip of hell.

"How do you do, Mrs. Whitfield? Thank you for coming down." Mayberry was heavily polite. "Good morning, Miss Whitfield."

"How are you, Chris?" Ann-Charlotte stretched her slender legs comfortably. Lillith only nodded. She wanted Reese to speak, to say something reassuring. He moved closer to her chair, and she could feel the warmth of his hand near her shoulder. Without seeming to

326

shift her body she leaned back to touch his fingers with her arm. Mayberry pretended to ignore the gesture.

"Nice day?" Mayberry spoke vaguely.

"Nuts." Ann-Charlotte yawned in his face. "I know a better word," she warned. "Also in four letters."

Mayberry settled himself in the chair again and drummed against the desk with his fingers. "This is sort of unusual," he spoke with false humility, "but I had an idea it would be better." He paused and then looked directly at Lillith. "Do you think Reese Benton shot and killed your husband, Mrs. Whitfield?"

Lillith didn't display any emotion. "That is absurd," she said with quiet dignity.

Mayberry nodded as though satisfied, and directed his gaze at Ann-Charlotte. "And you, Miss Whitfield," he persisted softly, "do you think Reese Benton killed your brother?"

"No," she drawled the reply with studied insolence, "but it was a hell of a good idea."

Mayberry was actually shocked, and he made no effort to hide his surprise. He was momentarily uncertain. "Well," he said with hushed determination, "I do, and so do most of the people in this state and a great part of the world, if you can believe what the newspapers only hint at. I'm going to take my suspicion to a grand jury," he almost whispered, "and ask for a first degree murder indictment. Now," there was something close to triumph in his voice, "what do you think of that?"

Ann-Charlotte found a cigarette and lit it with a bored air. "I tell you what I think, Chris." She deliberately blew a cloud of smoke his way. "I think you better be sure you can get a conviction, because," she dropped the word with infinite care, "if you just raise a dirty stink with an indictment and fail to prove it, I'll spend a million dollars or more of the Whitfield money to ruin you politically. I'll fix it so you couldn't even get a job tacking signs on outdoor toilets. What do you know about that?" She beamed with the innocent expression of a person who expects to be complimented.

Mayberry flushed and coughed. This wasn't at all what he had expected.

"I should think," he said with uneasy aggressiveness, "you would be one of the first to want to see justice done."

"One more time," Ann-Charlotte warned lazily, "and I'll let you hear that other four-letter word I know."

"But if your brother was killed ..." Mayberry spread his hands helplessly, indicating there was nothing more to say.

"If my brother was killed," Ann-Charlotte replied, "I'm only surprised it didn't happen a long time ago."

"How," Lillith's voice was so gently pitched it was almost startling, "how do you think Mr. Benton killed my—Mr. Whitfield?" She was watching Mayberry carefully.

The County Solicitor brightened as though he had found an unexpected ally, and he seemed to be trying to pull his chair closer to her in a confidential mood.

"I think," he said, his eyes watching her eagerly, "Reese Benton went downstairs after your husband came home, lured him outside on one pretext or another, and then shot him." He waited, practically sniffing with excitement.

"Is that what you would tell a jury?" She seemed to be gathering herself together.

"It's the only time it could have happened, Mrs. Whitfield. Don't you see?" He was growing confident. What a case this would be, with her help.

"Well," Lillith idly picked up the gloves in her lap and sighed regretfully, "I'm afraid your case wouldn't stand up then, Mr. Mayberry." She looked gravely at him.

"Why?" Mayberry blew out his cheeks.

"Because," Lillith rose with seeming reluctance, "Mr. Benton couldn't have gone downstairs and shot my husband. He—" She slipped her hand beneath Reese's arm. "I was with him in his room."

"Lil!" Reese couldn't still the exclamation.

Mayberry could only stare at her, and when he found his voice it was shaky.

"That isn't true, Mrs. Whitfield, is it?"

Lillith regarded him steadily for a moment. "No," she said finally, "it isn't."

"But," Mayberry was trying to hold himself under control, "you'd swear publicly in an open court that Reese Benton was in bed with you when, and after, your husband came back to the lodge? You know what that means?"

Lillith's laughter was the spilling of bright silver coins. "Certainly, Mr. Mayberry," she said helpfully; "don't you?"

"I know it would be perjury and an obstruction of justice!" he shouted. His face was red.

"Unpleasant words, Mr. Mayberry. But then," she shrugged, "it's an unpleasant world sometimes, isn't it?"

Mayberry sank back in his chair. "All right," he finally said, "I've got to think this over."

"I wouldn't spend too much time on it," Ann-Charlotte comforted him.

"The whole state, most of the country, is talking about the case," Mayberry said unhappily. "It's hard to lock away the suspicion of murder." He looked directly at Reese. "It'll be at your heels for the rest of your life, yapping and snarling."

"I know." Reese's words were as tired as his features. He seemed old.

Lillith turned from Mayberry to stare at him and there was anxiety, almost fear, in her eyes. "Oh, no!" She seemed to be pleading. "It couldn't, could it, Reese?"

"I don't know. I'm afraid he's right."

Lillith wheeled to Mayberry. "But," she exclaimed passionately, "Reese couldn't have murdered Cary. It's impossible."

"You'd be surprised," Mayberry replied unflinchingly, "how many things are possible between men when a beautiful woman and several million dollars are involved." His sweeping glance included all of them. "I don't know whether I'm finished with this," he said soberly. "There's a lot of pressure on me." He regarded Ann-Charlotte. "I haven't any doubt but what you'd do just what you said. If I think I'm right, I'll go ahead and press for an indictment."

Ann-Charlotte laughed. "You can read about the crusades in history books."

The County Solicitor wasn't amused. "I'm a practical politician, not a crusader; but," his eyes grew hard, "I don't like the stench of murder. It bothers me." There was a momentary silence. "Good day," he added. "Thank you for coming down. I'll find you, Benton," he suggested gently, "if and when I want you."

"I'll be around." Reese held the door for Lillith and Ann-Charlotte. "Here or in Winton."

Outside, in the bright sunlight which suddenly seemed to beat upon them with the stark glare of a spotlight, they walked down the courthouse steps between rows of silently appraising men and women who had been drawn by the news that the County Solicitor had summoned the Whitfields and Reese Benton for questioning. The crowd stared hungrily into their faces, and their eyes were shot with envy, contempt, and vicious curiosity. As they descended the broad steps the ranks narrowed, until, near the bottom, it became necessary for Reese to elbow a lane, clearing a way for Lillith and Ann-Charlotte.

Near the car in a tight huddle were a dozen reporters. As the trio moved out of the crowd, three photographers backed away, frantically taking pictures. They had gone through the same maneuvers earlier, and Lillith couldn't help but wonder what they could possibly want with so many photographs. The reporters were alertly guarded in their approach.

"Will you give us a statement, Mrs. Whitfield?" "What was the subject of your interview with Mr. Mayberry?" "Is there to be a further investigation?" A young girl, crisp and efficient, pushed within a foot of Lillith. "Do you think your husband was murdered, Mrs. Whitfield?" She held her pencil poised above a sheaf of copy paper, blocking their way to the car.

Lillith bit nervously at her lip and then was ashamed of her uncertainty. "I think," she said and the group came to life with electric eagerness, "my husband died by his own hand. As far as I am concerned there need be no further investigation." She was not unaware of the fact that several of the newspapermen glanced with quick significance at each other. They don't believe me, she thought miserably. They'll never believe. In their own smart, sophisticated minds, they think Reese was my lover and killed Cary, and they try to say it without using those words. If they had only known Cary, they would understand. How can I tell them?

The three of them rode in the front seat, with Reese driving, the pleas from the reporters for something more they could print ringing in their ears. The county seat was a run of twenty-five or thirty miles from the lodge, and at the fork in the highway where they would have to turn off for Harlen Reese slowed down.

"We don't have to go back." He made the statement seem a question.

"Suits me," Ann-Charlotte agreed immediately, "but if you are looking for cover, you won't find it. Long ago I discovered city editors have more reporters than there are places to hide."

"But," there was subdued anguish in the cry, "what more can they possibly want? What is there to say?" Lillith was frightened by the prospect of a never-ending chase.

"I'm going to cut Lucy up into small pieces and feed her to the buzzards." Ann-Charlotte spoke with quiet fury. "Why did that stupid wench have to say she heard Reese threaten to kill Cary?"

Reese brought the car to a halt at the crossroads. "She didn't mean to cause trouble. The police probably scared the life out of her."

"Well, then, you were a fool to say it." Ann-Charlotte shook her head. "This family gets itself in the damnedest messes."

"I don't want to go back to the lodge," Lillith said abruptly. "I don't care where we go, but not there, now."

"The Hill?" Reese waited.

"I guess so," Lillith looked to him for approval. "We'll have to start from someplace."

"If it gets too tough, we can always toss Old Andy out in the yard and crawl in his crypt. Come creep into my crypt, Clorinda," Ann-Charlotte hummed softly to herself.

The return to Winton seemed interminable. None of them felt like talking, and Reese drove with thoughtful determination, trying to put the trip and the events of the past few days behind him. He marveled a little at Ann-Charlotte's indifference to what had happened, even though he knew her well enough to be certain she didn't care about Cary. Even so, he thought, she might display a surface regret.

The afternoon was lengthening into long patches of purple shadows by the time they reached Winton. Throughout the drive, save when they stopped for a brief roadside lunch, Lillith had remained silent. Although her hands were folded simply in her lap, Reese had the feeling she was reaching out to him, and when their arms touched he wanted to stop the car and take her in his arms. She had been a little surprised at Ann-Charlotte's threat to nail Mayberry's political hide to a convenient barn, and he had watched the warm gratitude flood her eyes at the challenge. Lil, he mused regretfully, hadn't quite grown up. Ann-Charlotte never did anything without a reason. She realized what he had known since Cary's body had been found. The end was written in capitals.

As he turned into The Hill's driveway, he thought with bitter certainty that nothing could crack the deep foundations of Old Andrew's citadel. Life beat furiously, and it strained, creaked, and complained but never gave way. The roots were strongly embedded, perpetuating themselves as they were destroyed; springing up and budding from catastrophe. Within Lillith, beside him at the moment, was the embryo of Cary's child as proof.

XXXI

W ITH his back resting against the rough trunk of an old tree Reese stood in the darkness, staring out and down over Winton's lights, and knew he was seeing the town from The Hill for the last time. Behind him the big house reared its ugly form, shadowed and mysteriously aloof; a setting on an unpeopled stage in an empty theater. It had no part with reality now but stood there waiting, perhaps, for a new set of characters to give it life.

Turning slightly, Reese looked up the slope past the squat sepulcher holding the dust of Old Andrew to the uneven roof line that tore a pattern out of the sky and wondered what ambitions possessed that almost forgotten Whitfield as he watched the house take shape. Within those somber walls man's dream of a dynasty might be spun and as easily lost. The house, though, could wait to fulfill its purpose. Time didn't press upon it, for Andrew had built too well with his hands. Only his loins had failed him.

Studying the house, noting the few scattered lights picking out oblongs in the living room and the bedrooms upstairs, Reese tried to imagine what the family would have been if Joe instead of Cassius had been its head. A strong hand had been needed, and the one Cassius had placed on the helm had been weak and uncertain. Suppose, he thought, Joe had been the father of Cary and Ann-Charlotte? Old Andrew would be sleeping better these nights.

From the shadows he could mark the winding driveway and tried to see himself as he had been on that day when he trudged its length; defiant and a little afraid, wondering, not about the future, but concerned only with the uncertain present. It was possible to understand so many things now; things which someone should have told him then. He, too, had failed; not Old Andrew, as had the others, but himself. Ann-Charlotte had flung the charge lightly. We get into the damnedest messes. They didn't get into them. They made them.

Tomorrow he would walk down from The Hill. He had no plans. It seemed better that way. Cary, who, step by step, had been baffling and frustrating, had managed, even in death, to snatch away the only

332

thing he ever really wanted. There was galling irony in this knowl-edge, for Cary hadn't been worth it.

He tried to think of all the splendid copybook words he had read and heard about the nobility of sacrifice, and they had an empty sound. A heel ground at his heart as he prepared to do what he knew must be done. He wondered if Cary had known; if, deep in his foggy mind, he had been able to see ahead this far? With a twisted smile he tossed away the notion. Cary had never been that smart.

He thought Lillith must understand what he was going to do but she fought against it, battening the truth down and pretending it wasn't there.

A twig snapped lightly and his head jerked up. Lillith stood just above him on the narrow, terraced ledge. Without speaking he walked over and stretched out his arms. She dropped into them and he held her while her face remained buried in the hollow of his shoulder.

"I missed you," the words were muffled, "and couldn't stand it any longer." There was something pathetically young in her attitude of confident submission.

"I had to come out for a little while by myself." He tilted her head, searching her face with eyes accustomed to the dark. "Later I would have come back."

"You are going away, aren't you?"

Reese kissed her with the foolish idea that this, somehow, would delay the decision. Tomorrow would come soon enough.

"I'll leave after you go." He tried to make the statement sound unimportant.

"But we've never had a chance, Reese. I don't want to go. You're my life. I can't imagine it without you now. What are you giving me to take away?"

He released her, clinging only to her hand. "Let's walk," he sug-gested.

Without purpose they strolled up and past the house, taking the path winding toward the lake. The night wrapped them in a dark cocoon where the things that must be said could be spoken.

"I'm giving you my life to take away." He whispered the words. "You know that. It's all I have, and a poor gift."

"But why, Reese? Why do we have to care?"

He had to smile. It was a trick she had, asking questions already answered.

"A million people could give you a reason." He spoke without emo-

333

tion. "A million people and Christopher Mayberry, who think I shot Cary." He halted in the path and turned her by the shoulders. "Even now he may be getting ready to ask for an indictment."

She faced him confidently. "But you didn't, Reese. I know and you know. We don't have to care what others say or believe."

"How do you know I didn't? There was time, opportunity, and motive. What makes you so confident?"

It was too dark to see her face clearly, but he knew there was a quick smile on her lips as she rejected the idea.

"Maybe," he added, "you shouldn't answer, because there might even come a time when you will wonder. Cary's child will wonder, also. Don't forget that. The years have a way of turning over and revealing old skeletons."

"But what of us?" She didn't attempt to hide the desperation. "Is there nothing left?"

His arms secured her and her hair was soft against his face. "Time," he said.

"But that isn't enough," she answered fiercely. "Do you think I can walk away from here and never see or think of you again?"

He turned her hand, palm up, and kissed it softly, folding her fingers over the spot. "Keep that for us."

"I won't." She snatched her hand away and rubbed it angrily against her dress as if to erase the commitment. "I'm not a child to be shunted off this way. I don't care what people say or think. It's you and I. Only the two of us count. It is your life and mine."

He touched her face with his fingertips. "That's why I am being careful with it."

Her impatience flickered and died, and she moved close to him, trying to hide. "Don't let me go, Reese. There isn't anything in the world I can't take if you are with me. Without you I'm lost."

His hands tightened. "You'll find your way," he said quietly, "and it won't be as lonely as you think. I'm going to kiss you good-by now."

XXXII

THE late afternoon sun dipped below the hazy, massed green of the distant stand of pine, and the hush of evening, when small sounds are magnified and the earth seems to be waiting for night, lay across the land.

From the edge of the porch where he sat smoking, his head resting against a narrow pillar, Reese fastened his eyes on the great orange disk shuttered by the branches. It moved with surprising speed; slicing its way down through the treetops, hurrying over the rim of the world as though late for an appointment. Lazily Reese scratched his scalp on the wood, rubbing against it with the quiet satisfaction of a cat. He wore a faded pair of blue jeans, a gray work shirt, unbuttoned halfway to his navel, and his feet were bare. All cropper, he thought with secret amusement, an' feelin' mighty comfortable.

Before him the yard was freshly raked bare of twigs and leaves. The porch was swept clean and the door no longer hung with loose dejection on rusty hinges. The house had a comfortable and weathered appearance; a little worn and weary, but essentially sound. In the rapidly gathering twilight it carried the rakish air of a jaunty derelict warming himself in the sun. Only the fields beyond the irrigation ditch still displayed evidence of neglect. They were stubble-filled, seared to a crisp yellow, unkempt and abandoned.

During the week he had been back at the cabin Reese kept busy with innumerable small tasks. He went about the odd jobs with a half-smile of derision, assuring himself that he wasn't being fooled. For a couple of dollars he could have hired a colored girl to come in and clean the place; but, somehow, it seemed fitting his own hands should be turned to the labor. Also, he needed something to do.

The house had been vacant for the past three weeks. Joseph, his tenant farmer, had finally admitted defeat and moved his brood into Winton proper, where he found steady work in a mill. For reasons which he never attempted to explain to himself Reese had kept the small farm and, when he left The Hill, sought it out as an old and sympathetic friend who could be counted upon not to ask unnecessary questions.

335

In return for the shelter he did small repair jobs; fitting a new board with inexpert hands, fixing a sagging step, stringing small curtains across the newly washed windows, or screwing hooks in the kitchen for a few pots and pans he bought. He worked long, from early morning until dusk, scrubbing and sweeping, and at night he was too tired to think much about anything. Without something to occupy his mind the days would have been unendurable.

From a paper read on the counter of a filling station lunchroom half a mile down the highway he learned that Lillith had left Winton. The reporter speculated on the fate of The Hill, and there was an editorial relating the past glories and magnificence of the Whitfield estate. It was even suggested that the place would be put up for public sale since, apparently, Cary Whitfield's widow had no intention of returning. Reese wondered what would become of the servants, and tried to imagine The Hill boarded up and silent. With concentrated and unsuccessful effort he attempted to shut Lillith from his mind, but she followed him throughout the day and shared the darkness of his room at night. There was no comfort in the knowledge that he and she had taken the only roads left to them, and he cried out in desperate loneliness, knowing there could be no reply.

He heard the approaching car long before he could see it, and followed its erratic course over the rutted, winding road behind the screening line of trees by the billowing cloud of dust. When it finally skidded to a stop in the lane before the porch, he didn't move but only watched with a curious mixture of irritation and admiration.

Ann-Charlotte, low in the driver's seat, looked at him over the door's edge for a moment without speaking. Finally, she tugged at a waved curl near her forehead with exaggerated respect.

"Servant, Squire." The greeting was properly humble, but her lips twitched with the effort of hiding a smile. When he made no reply she opened the door and swung out of the seat. Walking across the small yard she settled herself on the porch, copying his indolent position against a post. They stared at each other.

"I thought you had left." Reese spoke without meaning to and looked at her through partly closed eyes.

"So did I." She seemed to find something vaguely amusing in this admission. "Then I started thinking, which is always a bad thing for me to do, and came back to give it another pitch. I don't know why," she said apologetically, "it took me so long to figure out where you had to be. It couldn't have been anyplace else, could it?"

"I wasn't hiding." He flung the statement as a challenge. When she made no reply he reached for a cigarette in his shirt pocket, started to put it into his mouth, and then tossed it to her lap. "Here."

"Thank you." She nodded at the bare feet and fringed jeans. "Going to a masquerade?"

They smoked, finding no immediate use for words. Ann-Charlotte seemed to be satisfied to wait until he was ready to talk. The sun was down, leaving a bruised color in the west to mark its passing. A crimson, bluish afterglow touched the cabin's silvery gray boards and was reflected over the porch.

"You should have kept going." He spoke abruptly.

She glanced up. Her eyes were clear, steady, and without mockery. "I don't think so, Just Reese. I pulled off on a lot of detours, but they all led back here. I guess we always must have known they would."

"You won't like it here." He made the statement disinterestedly.

"Neither will you. That's what I'm counting on." She was being matter-of-fact but not impatient. "I can wait a little longer if necessary."

Reese studied the cigarette between his fingers, twisting his hand to deflect the smoke. "You're getting out of character, aren't you?" He asked the question without meeting her gaze.

For a moment he thought she hadn't heard. When she did speak, her voice was husky but controlled.

"Not with you. I never have been. That's why I am so sure it's right."

"I wonder." He almost sighed the question.

"You won't stay here, Reese. I know and you know that. Somewhere there is still a lot of the little boy about you, the sort of thing that makes a youngster sit on his own back fence and thumb his nose at the world. There isn't much fun in the game when no one pays attention."

He grinned with slow appreciation. "You're still pretty fresh, aren't you?"

She leaned forward, arms crossed in her lap. "There was never a chance for you, Reese. Not from the day you walked away from here and came to The Hill. I don't know when I learned that; maybe, just now." There was no laughter in her voice. "Between us we've managed to louse up our lives. We're a couple of no-good bastards, made for trouble."

337

"So," his voice was level, "you think we ought to pool it; double trouble?"

With the toe of her slipper she ground the cigarette butt into the lower step. "There are," she suggested, "one or two advantages in the idea."

"You being one of them."

Her tongue flicked on the inside of her cheek and her eyes danced. "I come under the head of an emolument."

He smiled then and drew himself up. She made no move until he extended his hands and then she took them, rising to her feet with elastic eagerness. Their bodies touched briefly and she moved into him, her face lifted.

"Now, Reese," she said. "Don't wait or think or wonder. There isn't time. This is our last chance."

He bent to kiss her and she was crying.